ABOUT PETER S. BEAGLE

"...One of my favorite writers."
MADELEINE L'ENGLE, AUTHOR OF *A Wrinkle in Time* &
A Swiftly Tilting Planet

"Peter S. Beagle illuminates with his own particular magic....
For years a loving readership has consulted him as an expert on
those hearts' reasons that reason does not know."
URSULA K. LE GUIN, AUTHOR OF *A Wizard of Earthsea* &
The Left Hand of Darkness

"...the only contemporary to remind one of Tolkien..."
Booklist

"Peter S. Beagle is (in no particular order) a wonderful writer, a
fine human being, and a bandit prince out to steal readers' hearts."
TAD WILLIAMS, AUTHOR OF *The Dragonbone Chair* &
Tailchaser's Song

"It's a fully rounded region, this other world of Peter Beagle's
imagination...an originality...that is wholly his own."
Kirkus

"[Beagle] has been compared, not unreasonably, with Lewis Carroll
and J.R.R. Tolkien, but he stands squarely...and triumphantly on
his own feet."
Saturday Review

"Not only does Peter Beagle make his fantasy worlds come vividly,
beautifully alive; he does it for the people who enter them."
POUL ANDERSON, AUTHOR OF *The High Crusade*

The Line Between

Peter S. Beagle

TACHYON PUBLICATIONS SAN FRANCISCO

Cover design by Ann Monn
Book design & composition by John D. Berry
The text typeface is Aldus nova, with Whitney display type

Tachyon Publications
1459 18th Street #139
San Francisco, CA 94107
(415) 285-5615
www.tachyonpublications.com

Edited by: Jacob Weisman

Trade paperback ISBN 10: 1-892391-36-8
Trade paperback ISBN 13: 978-1-892391-36-0

Limited hardcover ISBN 10: 1-892391-43-0
Limited hardcover ISBN 13: 978-1-892391-43-8

Printed in the United States of America
by Maple-Vail Manufacturing Group

First Edition: 2006

9 8 7 6 5 4 3 2 1

CONTENTS

Introduction

xi

Gordon, the Self-Made Cat

3

Two Hearts

13

Four Fables:

The Fable of the Moth

49

The Fable of the Tyrannosaurus Rex

50

The Fable of the Ostrich

53

The Fable of the Octopus

58

El Regalo

63

Quarry

99

Salt Wine

135

Mr. Sigerson

165

A Dance for Emilia

193

.

FOR PEGGY CARLISLE AND RICO JONES,

with love and faith.

Introduction

WHEN MY CHILDREN were still small enough to be suckered (that's the two youngest, not their older sister; she was *never* that small), I could keep them occupied in the car for some while by telling them that if they turned their heads fast enough they could look in their own ears. (What, you never bought yourself a single blessed moment of sanity by risking *your* children's cervical vertebrae, eyesight, digestion, or emotional well-being? — *Hypocrite lecteur, — mon semblable, — mon frère!* I want to see a note from your mother.)

In a very real sense, that's what I've been doing all my life — trying to turn my head in time to glimpse that creature, that color, that melody, that metamorphosis, that human situation to be found living just around the farthest corner of my vision. Ever since I was a small, shy, overweight boy — a boy who could most often be found curled up under the stairs of his Bronx apartment building, telling himself stories — I've been used to *almost* hearing voices, *almost* catching sight of Donne's "things invisible to see." Indeed, my favorite among my own novels, *The Innkeeper's Song*, had its birth on an island off Seattle, with me well-snuggled into the sweet spot between sleep and waking, when a rough, sour growl announced itself in my head, saying distinctly, "My name is Karsh. I am not a bad man."

There it is: that invisible boundary between conscious and not, between reality and fantasy, between here (whatever "here" is) and there (whatever "there" might be), between the seen and the seen's true nature. A line neither one thing nor ever quite the other, but now and eternally between.

As a writer, *the line between* is where I have always lived. It is my personal tightrope of choice, the one I most naturally walk, clutching only a small and somewhat silly-looking parasol of logic for a counterbalance. At times this precarious high-wire act exhausts and exasperates me, to the point where I feel that I'd give almost anything to step off the line, once and for all, and settle down to stories that, whatever their matter or milieu, don't always insist on *balancing* so. But this is what I do. Clearly. In life and art I have never been able to laugh without being intensely aware of tears, or to shine a light on horror without also illuminating beauty. So it goes still for everything I write.

I'm on the books as a fantasist, a genre writer, and I'd go on being considered one even if I wrote nothing but naturalistic novels and gritty urban-realist tales from here on in. Fair enough, I suppose; anyway, one of the few really nice things about growing old is that a whole lot of stuff simply stops mattering — categories among them. But fantasy to me means far more than a stock preindustrial landscape populated with figures out of Scottish ballads, French fairytales, and Germanic sagas of dungeons and dragons. Not that there's anything *wrong* with that. I've employed these beloved old standbys as often as most, and undoubtedly will again. You will find a few of them in this very book, approached from my own skewed angle. But that's not what I'm talking about here.

Fantasy to me has always been a certain mindset, a way of looking around. In speaking publicly on the subject, I often use as an example the classic films that Val Lewton produced (usually on a budget of approximately $1.98) for RKO in the 1940s. *Cat People, I Walked with a Zombie, Isle of the Dead, The Leopard Man, The Seventh Victim....* What keeps these sixty-year-old movies alive and fascinating today is not the special effects that Lewton couldn't afford anyway, but the trademark sense he creates that things invisible to viewer and characters alike are happening just off-camera. There are no demons in Lewton's work, no brain-eating Caribbean zombies (never mind that one's title; it's really *Jane Eyre* in Haiti), and no vampires — only the *possibility* of a vampire, which is infinitely scarier than red contact lenses and fake fangs. These movies remain categorized under *Horror* in the video store; but if there was one thing Val Lewton knew, it was that it is the shadow that terrifies, not the monster it hides. The monster is an actor in a monster suit. The shadow is always real.

Of the stories in this collection, "A Dance for Emilia" perhaps best exemplifies my notion of fantasy, which is especially appropriate since it is also by far the most autobiographical. Do I really believe that a lost life-long friend might return to the world in the body of his own aging cat? That doesn't matter — if I need to believe it I can manage the trick for any given ten minutes, as I do with belief in most things, including electricity, the Zone diet, and the laws of thermodynamics. What's important to me here, as a writer, is that I've grounded the single fantastic element of the tale in the most realistic atmosphere I could manage. Narrator Jake's life is like that of any stage actor I've ever known; semi-ghostly Sam's world is the world in which his real-life original lived and moved and ultimately died. Possessed cat or no, mystery or no, magic or no, the rent still has to be paid.

My favorite review of my work, of all that have been published in newspapers and magazines over forty-five years, has to be one by, of all people, the cartoonist Gahan Wilson. I can't quote the review precisely (at present it's packed away, along with ninety-nine percent of my belongings, in two storage units in Davis), but in paraphrase it credits me for avoiding tales of kings, High Elves, enchanted swords and assorted Armageddons, in favor of dealing with low-class types. My heroes and heroines, Wilson observes, are mostly peasants; my wizards are mostly out there in the rain, trying to light a fire, never mind summoning a genie. They live in the daily middle of their ordinary muddled lives, they are as complicated as we ourselves are complicated; they are *real*, and the more bizarre and unlikely the circumstance, the realer they become. I'm very proud of that.

I did write a "mainstream" novel once, very long ago, during the year I spent at Stanford University on the writing fellowship that first brought me to California. It's about a young American musician's romantic adventures in Paris; and if you wonder why it was never published, just remember that its author had all too recently been a young American writer having romantic adventures in Paris, and hadn't yet learned that *write what you know* is a gentle form of encouragement, not an act of law. There are no wizards or warriors in this novel; not a single shapeshifter or ancient goddess. There is nothing obviously fantastic in it at all (except for the mostly flattering picture of its protagonist, who looked and sounded, and — more to the point — acted as I wish I had). Yet despite this, the book is a fantasy to me, every bit as much a fairytale as *The Last Unicorn*, because of what its own shadows conceal. Hieronymus Bosch may have painted portraits of local burghers or churchmen, as well as *The Garden of Earthly Delights*, but he's still Bosch, and his monsters are visible in his subjects' eyes — they plainly see the demons and half-beasts smiling hungrily over Bosch's shoulder. Just so in this unpublished early book of mine. Even though I was consciously trying to be as realistic as possible, in every page the unreal, the uncanny, the magical all grin their own toothy grins from behind *papier-mâché* masks. A tweak or two, a shift of emphasis: that's all it would take for them to drop the masks and dance across the line.

As I've said, I never consciously chose this way of telling stories — barring some moment of negotiation under that Bronx stairway which I have since forgotten, it seems rather to have chosen me. It's a mixed blessing to be chosen, whether by a deity or a style, or by a way of seeing. But it's who I am, and it's what I do. These *between* stories are the ones I have to tell. I hope they find you well, and that you enjoy them.

Peter S. Beagle
Oakland, California
2006

THE LINE BETWEEN

Gordon, the Self-Made Cat

The first draft of "Gordon, the Self-Made Cat" was written more than forty years ago, when I was living on nine wild acres in the hills north of Santa Cruz, California, with my young family. We had an unguessable number of cats in those days, if you count not only the indoor and outdoor residents, but also the visitors who treated our peeling red shack as a sort of bed-and-breakfast establishment. What we definitely *didn't* have was a mouse problem (gophers were another matter). I made up the valiant Gordon to amuse the children, sent his story off to an animation company that had requested ideas for a feature film, shrugged at their almost immediate rejection, then buried the piece in my battered filing cabinet and completely forgot about it. It didn't surface again until 2001, when some friends stumbled across it while helping me move.

I'm currently working on expanding it, adding new characters and more adventures, for eventual book publication. I've always loved *Charlotte's Web* and *Stuart Little*; the longer version of *Gordon* will be my own small nod in that very challenging direction.

ONCE UPON A TIME to a family of house mice there was born a son named Gordon. He looked very much like his father and mother and all his brothers and sisters, who were gray and had bright, twitchy, black eyes, but what went on inside Gordon was very different from what went on inside the rest of his family. He was forever asking why everything had to be the way it was, and never satisfied with the answer. Why did mice eat cheese? Why did they live in the dark and only go out when it was dark? Where did mice come from, anyway? *What were people?* Why did people smell so funny? Suppose mice were big and people were tiny? Suppose mice could fly? Most mice don't ask many questions, but Gordon never stopped.

One evening, when Gordon was only a few weeks old, his next-to-eldest sister was sent out to see if anything interesting had been left open in the pantry. She never returned. Gordon's father shrugged sadly and spread his front paws, and said, "The cat."

"What's a cat?" Gordon asked.

His mother and father looked at one another and sighed. "They have to know sometime," his father said. "Better he learns it at home than on the streets."

His mother sniffled a little and said, "But he's so young," and his father answered, "Cats don't care." So they told Gordon about cats right then, expecting him to start crying and saying that there weren't any such things. It's a hard idea to get used to. But Gordon only asked, "Why do cats eat mice?"

"I guess we taste very good," his father said.

Gordon said, "But cats don't have to eat mice. They get plenty of other food that probably tastes as good. Why should anybody eat anybody if he doesn't have to?"

"Gordon," said his father. "Listen to me. There are two kinds of creatures in the world. There are animals that hunt, and animals that are hunted. We mice just happen to be the kind of animal that gets hunted, and it doesn't really matter if the cat *is* hungry or not. It's the way life is. It's really a great honor to be the hunted, if you just look at it the right way."

"Phooey on that," said Gordon. "Where do I go to learn to be a cat?"

They thought he was joking, but as soon as Gordon was old enough to go places by himself, he packed a clean shirt and some peanut butter, and started off for cat school. "I love you very much," he said to his parents before he left, "but this business of being hunted for the rest of my life just because I happened to be born a mouse is not for me." And off he went, all by himself.

All cats go to school, you know, whether you ever see them going or not. Dogs don't, but cats always have and always will. There are a great many cat schools, so Gordon found one easily enough, and he walked bravely up the front steps and knocked at the door. He said that he wanted to speak to the Principal.

He almost expected to be eaten right there, but the cats — students and teachers alike — were so astonished that they let him pass through, and one of the teachers took him to the Principal's office. Gordon could feel the cats looking at him, and hear the sounds their noses made as they smelled how good he was, but he held on tight to the suitcase with his shirt and the peanut butter, and he never looked back.

The Principal was a fat old tiger cat who chewed on his tail all the time he was talking to Gordon. "You must be out of your mind," he said when Gordon told him he wanted to be a cat. "I'd smack you up this minute, but it's bad luck to eat crazies. Get out of here! The day mice go to cat school...."

"Why not?" said Gordon. "Is it in writing? Where does it say that I can't go to school here if I want?"

Well, of course there's nothing in the rules of cat schools that says mice can't enroll. Nobody ever thought of putting it in.

The Principal folded his paws and said, "Gordon, look at it this way — "

"You look at it *my* way," said Gordon. "I want to be a cat, and I bet I'd make a better one than the dopey-looking animals I've seen in this school. Most of them look as if they wouldn't even make good mice! So let's make a deal. You let me come to school here and study for one term, and if at the end of that time I'm not doing better than any cat in the school — if even one cat has better grades than I have — then you can eat me and that'll be the end of it. Is that fair?"

No cat can resist a challenge like that. But before agreeing, the Principal insisted on one small change: at the end of the term, if Gordon didn't have the very best marks in the school, then the privilege of eating him would go to the cat that did.

"Ought to encourage some of those louts to work harder," the Principal said to himself, as Gordon left his office. "He's crazy, but he's right — most of them wouldn't even make good mice. I almost hope he does it."

So Gordon went to cat school. Every day he sat at his special little desk, surrounded by a hundred kittens and half-grown cats who would have liked nothing better than to leap on him and play games with him for a while before they gobbled him. He learned how to wash himself, and what to do to keep his claws sharp, and how to watch everything in the room while pretending to be asleep. There was a class on Dealing With Dogs, and another on Getting Down From Trees, which is much harder than climbing up, and also a particularly scholarly seminar on the various meanings of "Bad Kitty!" Gordon's personal favorite was the Visions class, which had to do with the enchanting things all cats can see that no one else ever does — the great, gliding ancestors, and faraway castles, and mysterious forests full of monsters to chase. The Professor of Visions told his colleagues that he had never had such a brilliant student. "It would be a crime to eat such a mouse!" he proclaimed everywhere. "An absolute, shameful, yummy crime."

The class in Mouse-Hunting was a bit awkward at first, because usually the teacher asks one of the students to be the mouse, and in Gordon's case the Principal felt that would be too risky. But Gordon insisted on being chased like everyone else, and not only was he never caught (well, *almost* never; there was one blue Persian who could turn on a dime), but when he took his own turn at chasing, he proved to be a natural expert. In fact his instant mastery of the Flying Pounce caused his teacher and the entire class to sit up and applaud. Gordon took three bows and an encore.

There was also a class where the cats learned the necessities of getting along with people: how to lie in laps, how to keep from scratching furniture even when you feel you have to, what to do when children pick you up, and how to ask for food or affection in such a sweet manner that people call other people to look at you. These classes always made Gordon a little sad. He didn't suppose that he would ever be a real "people" cat, for who would want to hold a mouse on his lap, or scratch it behind the ears while it purred? Still, he paid strict attention in People Class, as he did in all the others, for all the cats knew that whoever did best in school that term would be the one who ate him, and they worked harder than they ever had in their lives. The Principal said that they were becoming the best students in the school's history, and he talked openly about making this a regular thing, one mouse to a term.

When all the marks were in, and all the grades added up, two students led the rankings: Gordon and the blue Persian. Their scores weren't even a whisker's thickness apart. In the really important classes, like Running And Pouncing, Climbing, Stalking, and Waiting For The Prey To Forget You're Still There; and in matters of feline manners such as Washing, Tail Etiquette, The Elegant Yawn, Sleeping In Undignified Positions, and Making Sure You Get Enough Food Without Looking Greedy (101 *and* 102) — in all of these Gordon and the blue Persian were first, and the rest nowhere. Besides that, both could meow in five different dialects: Persian, Abyssinian, Siamese, Burmese (which almost no cat who isn't Burmese ever learns), and basic tiger.

But there can only be one Top Cat to a term; no ties allowed. In order to decide the matter once and for all between them, the Principal announced that Gordon and the blue Persian would have to face one another in a competitive mouse roundup.

The Persian and Gordon got along quite well, all things considered, so they shook paws — carefully — and the Persian purred, "No hard feelings."

"None at all," Gordon answered. "If anyone here got to eat me, I'd much rather it was you."

"Very sporting of you," the Persian said. "I hope so too."

"But it won't happen," Gordon said.

The blue Persian never had a chance. Once he and Gordon were set on their marks in a populous mouse neighborhood, Gordon ambushed and outsmarted and cornered all but a handful of the very quickest mice, and did it in a style so smooth, so effortlessly elegant — so *catlike* — that the Persian finally threw up his paws and surrendered. In front of the entire faculty and student body of the cat school, he announced, "I yield to Gordon. He's a better cat than I am, and I'm not ashamed to admit it. If all mice were like him, we cats would be vegetarians." (Persians are *very* dramatic.)

The cheering was so wild and thunderous that no one objected in the least when Gordon freed all the mice he had captured. Cats can appreciate a grand gesture, and everyone had already had lunch.

Gordon had won his bet, and, like the blue Persian, the Principal was cat enough to accept it graciously. He scheduled a celebration, which the whole school attended, and at the end of the party he announced that Gordon was now to be considered as much a cat as any student in the school, if not more so. He gave Gordon a little card to show that he was a cat in good standing, and all the students cheered, and Gordon made another speech that began, "Fellow cats...." As he spoke, he wished very much that his parents could be there to see what he had accomplished, and just how different things could be if you just asked questions and weren't afraid of new ideas.

Being acknowledged the best cat in the school didn't make Gordon let up in his studies. Instead, he worked even harder, and did so well that he graduated with the special degree of *felis maximus*, which is Latin for *some cat!* He stayed on at the school to teach a seminar in Evasive Maneuvers, which proved very popular, and a course in the Standing Jump (for a bird that comes flying over when you weren't looking).

The story of his new life spread everywhere among all mice, and grew very quickly into a myth more terrifying than any cat could have been. They whispered of "Gordon the Terrible," "Gordon, the Self-Made Cat," and, simply, "The Unspeakable," and told midnight tales of a gigantic mouse who lashed his tail and sprang at them with his razor claws out and his savage yellow eyes blazing; a mouse without pity who hunted them out in their deepest hiding places, walking without a sound. They believed unquestioningly that he ate mice like gingersnaps, and laughingly handed over to his cat friends those he was too full to devour. There was even a dreadful legend that Gordon had eaten his own family, and that he frequently took kittens from the school on field trips in order to teach them personally the secret mouse ways that no mere cat could ever have known.

These stories made Gordon deeply unhappy when he heard them, because he believed with absolute conviction that what he had achieved was for the good of all mice everywhere. Whether he trapped a lone mouse or cornered a dozen trembling in an attic or behind a refrigerator, he would say the same thing to them: "Look at me. *Look at me!* I am a mouse like you — nothing more, nothing less — and yet I walk with cats every day, and I am not eaten! I am respected, I am admired, I am even powerful among cats — and every one of you could be like me! Do not believe that we mice are born only to be hunted, humiliated, tormented, and finally gobbled up. It is not true! Instead of huddling in the shadows, in constant lifelong terror, pitiful little balls of fur, we too can be sleek, fierce hunters, fearing nothing and no one. Run now and spread the word! You must spread the word!"

Saying that, he would step back and let the mice scatter, hoping each time that they would finally understand what he was trying to show them. But it simply never happened. The mice always scurried away, convinced that they had escaped only by great good fortune, and myths and legends of the terrible Self-Made Cat were all that spread among them, growing ever more horrifying, ever more chilling. It didn't matter that not one mouse had ever actually seen Gordon doing any of the frightful things he was supposed to have done. That's the way it is with legends.

Now it happened that Gordon was walking down the street one day, on his way to a faculty meeting, padding along like a leopard, twitching his tail like a lion, and making the eager little noises in his throat that a tiger makes when he smells food. Quite suddenly an enormous shadow fell across his path, so big that he looked up to see if he were going through a tunnel. What he saw was a dog. What he actually saw was a leg, for this dog was huge, too big for even a full-grown cat to have understood his real size without looking twice. The dog rumbled, "Oh, goody! I love mice. Lots of phosphorus in mice. Yummy."

Gordon crouched, tail lashing, and lifted the fur along his spine. "Watch it, dog," he said warningly. "Don't mess with me, I'm telling you."

"Oh, how cute," the dog said. "He's playing he's a cat. I'm a cat too. Meow."

"I *am* a cat!" Gordon arched his back until it ached, hissing and spitting and growling in his throat, all more or less at the same time. "I *am!* You want to see my card? Look, right here."

"A crazy," the dog said wonderingly. "They say it's bad luck to eat a crazy. Good thing I'm not superstitious."

Having given the proper First Warning, exactly as he'd been taught, Gordon moved quickly to the Second — the lightning-swift slash of the right paw across the nose. Gordon had to leap straight up to reach the dog's big wet nose, but even with that handicap, he executed the Second Warning in superb style.

Instead of yelping and retreating in a properly humbled state, however, the dog only sneezed.

This, Gordon thought, is the difference between theory and practice.

But there was a reason that Gordon's seminar in Evasive Maneuvers was always so well attended. With astonishing daring, he went directly from the Second Warning right into the Fourth Avoidance, which involves a double feint — head looking *this* way, tail jerking *that* way — followed by a quick, threatening charge directly at the attacker, and *then* a leap to the side, which, done correctly, leaves one perfectly poised either for escape or the Flying Pounce, depending on the situation.

But the big dog had no idea that a classic Evasive Maneuver had just been performed upon him, leaving him looking like an idiot. He was used to looking like an idiot. He gave a delighted bounce, wuffed, "*Tag* — you're it!" and went straight for Gordon, who responded by going up a tree with the polished grace that always left his students too breathless to cheer. He found a comfortable branch and rested there, thinking ruefully that a real cat wouldn't have been so proud of being a cat as to waste time arguing about it.

The dog sat down too, grinning. "Be a bird now," he called to Gordon. "Let's see you be a bird and fly away."

Normally, Gordon could easily have stayed up in the tree longer than the dog felt like waiting below, but he was tired and rather thirsty, not to mention annoyed at the thought of being late for the faculty meeting. Something had to be done. But what?

He was bravely considering an original plan of leaping straight down at the dog, when three young mice happened along. They had been out shopping for their mother.

They were really very young, and as they had never seen Gordon the Terrible — though they had heard about him since they were blind babies — they didn't know who it was in the tree. All they saw was a fellow mouse in danger, and, being at the age when they didn't know any better than to do things like that, they carefully put down their packages and began luring the dog away from the tree. First one mouse would rush in at him and make the dog chase him a little way, and then another would come scampering from somewhere else, so that the dog would leave off chasing the first mouse and go after him.

The dog, who was actually quite good-natured, and not very hungry, had a fine time running after them all. He followed them farther and farther away from the tree, and had probably forgotten all about Gordon by the time the Unspeakable was able to spring down from the tree and vanish into the bushes.

Gordon would have waited to thank the three mice, but they had disappeared, along with the dog. Anxious not to miss his meeting, he dashed back to the school, slowing down before he got there to catch his breath and smooth his whiskers. "It could happen to anyone," he told himself. "There's nothing to be ashamed of." Yet there was something fundamentally troubling to Gordon about having run away. Feeling uncertain for the first time since he had marched up the front steps, he washed himself all over and stalked on into the school, outwardly calm and proud, the best cat anyone there would ever see, Gordon the Terrible, the Unspeakable — yes, the Self-Made Cat.

But another cat — the Assistant Professor of Tailchasing, in fact — had seen the whole incident, and had already interrupted the faculty meeting with the shocking tale.

The Principal tried to brush the news aside. "When it's time to climb a tree, you climb a tree," he said. "Any cat knows that." (He had become quite fond of Gordon, in his way.)

It wasn't enough. The Assistant Professor of Tailchasing (a chocolate-point Siamese who dreamed of one day heading the school himself) led the opposition. As the Assistant Professor saw it, Gordon was plainly a fraud, a pretender, a cat in card only, so friendly with his fellow mice that they had rushed to help him when he was in danger. In light of that, who could say what Gordon's *real* plans might be? Why had he come to the school in the first place? What if more like him followed? What if the mice were plotting to attack the cat school, all cat schools?

This thought rattled everyone at the table. With a mouse like Gordon in their midst, a mouse who knew far more about being a cat than the cats themselves, was any feline safe?

Just that quickly, fear replaced reason. Within minutes everyone but the Principal forgot how much they had liked and admired Gordon. Admitting him to the school had been a catastrophic mistake, one that must be set right without a moment's delay!

The Principal groaned and covered his eyes and sent for Gordon. He was almost crying as he took Gordon's cat card away.

Gordon protested like mad, of course. He spoke of Will and Choice, and Freedom, and the transforming power of Questioning Assumptions. But the Principal said sadly, "We just can't trust you, Gordon. Go away now, before I eat you myself. I always wondered what you'd taste like." Then he put his head down on his desk and really did begin to cry.

So Gordon packed his clean shirt and his leftover peanut butter and left the cat school. All the cats formed a double line to let him pass, their faces turned away, and nobody said a word. The Assistant Professor of Tailchasing was poised to pounce at the very last, but the Principal stepped on his tail.

Nobody ever heard of Gordon again. There were stories that he'd gone right on being a cat, even without his card; and there were other tales that said he had been driven out of the country by the mice themselves. But only the Principal knew for sure, because only the Principal had heard the words that Gordon was muttering to himself as he walked away from the cat school with his head held high.

"Woof," Gordon was murmuring thoughtfully. "Woof. Bow-wow. Shouldn't be too hard."

Two Hearts

Friends, family, and fans have all asked me, over the years, to write a sequel to *The Last Unicorn*. To each in turn I have responded with some variant of the following: "It can't be done. *The Last Unicorn* is a one-shot, meant from the beginning as a kind of spoof/tribute to the classic European fairytale, an homage to such beloved influences of mine as James Stephens, Lord Dunsany, T. H. White and James Thurber. Writing it was a nightmarish, seemingly endless labor, and when it was done I vowed never to attempt such a balancing act again. So thank you for asking, but no."

It wasn't a hard vow to keep: there were other books I wanted to write, and I have always had a real horror of repeating myself. Besides, like everyone else (and quite against my own personal wishes), I grew older. *The Last Unicorn* is a young man's work, and I am not quite him anymore in so many different ways.

Yet here I am, writing an introduction for a sequel to *The Last Unicorn*.

I blame Connor Cochran entirely for the existence of "Two Hearts." He proposed it as a bonus gift for the first 3,000 buyers of the audiobook of *The Last Unicorn*, and wheedled me into going along by assuring me that I needn't bring back a single one of the original cast — only the world of the novel, nothing more. So, of course, I presented him with four of the major characters, and references to a couple of others, and had an astonishingly fine time doing it. The trouble now, of course, is that I can't abandon Sooz, my young narrator. I'm going to have to bring her back and see where she wants to go...which will be, as I already know, into the real full-novel sequel to *The Last Unicorn*. Which I never wanted to write. *Bozhe moy*, as my Russian uncles used to say. *Heaven help me....*

MY BROTHER WILFRID keeps saying it's not fair that it should all have happened to me. Me being a girl, and a baby, and too stupid to lace up my own sandals properly. But *I* think it's fair. I think everything happened exactly the way it should have done. Except for the sad parts, and maybe those too.

I'm Sooz, and I am nine years old. Ten next month, on the anniversary of the day the griffin came. Wilfrid says it was because of me, that the griffin heard that the ugliest baby in the world had just been born, and it was going to eat me, but I was *too* ugly, even for a griffin. So it nested

13

in the Midwood (we call it that, but its real name is the Midnight Wood, because of the darkness under the trees), and stayed to eat our sheep and our goats. Griffins do that if they like a place.

But it didn't ever eat children, not until this year.

I only saw it once — I mean, once *before* — rising up above the trees one night, like a second moon. Only there wasn't a moon, then. There was nothing in the whole world but the griffin, golden feathers all blazing on its lion's body and eagle's wings, with its great front claws like teeth, and that monstrous beak that looked so huge for its head.... Wilfrid says I screamed for three days, but he's lying, and I *didn't* hide in the root cellar like he says either, I slept in the barn those two nights, with our dog Malka. Because I knew Malka wouldn't let anything get me.

I mean my parents wouldn't have, either, not if they could have stopped it. It's just that Malka is the biggest, fiercest dog in the whole village, and she's not afraid of anything. And after the griffin took Jehane, the blacksmith's little girl, you couldn't help seeing how frightened my father was, running back and forth with the other men, trying to organize some sort of patrol, so people could always tell when the griffin was coming. I know he was frightened for me and my mother, and doing everything he could to protect us, but it didn't make me feel any safer, and Malka did.

But nobody knew what to do, anyway. Not my father, nobody. It was bad enough when the griffin was only taking the sheep, because almost everyone here sells wool or cheese or sheepskin things to make a living. But once it took Jehane, early last spring, that changed everything. We sent messengers to the king — three of them — and each time the king sent someone back to us with them. The first time, it was one knight, all by himself. His name was Douros, and he gave me an apple. He rode away into the Midwood, singing, to look for the griffin, and we never saw him again.

The second time — after the griffin took Louli, the boy who worked for the miller — the king sent five knights together. One of them did come back, but he died before he could tell anyone what happened.

The third time an entire squadron came. That's what my father said, anyway. I don't know how many soldiers there are in a squadron, but it was a lot, and they were all over the village for two days, pitching their tents everywhere, stabling their horses in every barn, and boasting in the tavern how they'd soon take care of that griffin for us poor peasants. They had musicians playing when they marched into the Midwood — I remember that, and I remember when the music stopped, and the sounds we heard afterward.

After that, the village didn't send to the king anymore. We didn't want more of his men to die, and besides they weren't any help. So from then on all the children were hurried indoors when the sun went down, and the griffin woke from its day's rest to hunt again. We couldn't play together, or run errands or watch the flocks for our parents, or even sleep near open windows, for fear of the griffin. There was nothing for me to do but read books I already knew by heart, and complain to my mother and father, who were too tired from watching after Wilfrid and me to bother with us. They were guarding the other children too, turn and turn about with the other families — *and* our sheep, *and* our goats — so they were always tired, as well as frightened, and we were all angry with each other most of the time. It was the same for everybody.

And then the griffin took Felicitas.

Felicitas couldn't talk, but she was my best friend, always, since we were little. I always understood what she wanted to say, and she understood me, better than anyone, and we played in a special way that I won't ever play with anyone else. Her family thought she was a waste of food, because no boy would marry a dumb girl, so they let her eat with us most of the time. Wilfrid used to make fun of the whispery quack that was the one sound she could make, but I hit him with a rock, and after that he didn't do it anymore.

I didn't see it happen, but I still see it in my head. She *knew* not to go out, but she was always just so happy coming to us in the evening. And nobody at her house would have noticed her being gone. None of them ever noticed Felicitas.

The day I learned Felicitas was gone, that was the day I set off to see the king myself.

Well, the same *night*, actually — because there wasn't any chance of getting away from my house or the village in daylight. I don't know what I'd have done, really, except that my Uncle Ambrose was carting a load of sheepskins to market in Hagsgate, and you have to start long before sunup to be there by the time the market opens. Uncle Ambrose is my best uncle, but I knew I couldn't ask him to take me to the king — he'd have gone straight to my mother instead, and told her to give me sulphur and molasses and put me to bed with a mustard plaster. He gives his *horse* sulphur and molasses, even.

So I went to bed early that night, and I waited until everyone was asleep. I wanted to leave a note on my pillow, but I kept writing things and then tearing the notes up and throwing them in the fireplace, and I was afraid of somebody waking, or Uncle Ambrose leaving without me. Finally I just wrote, *I will come home soon.* I didn't take any clothes with me, or anything else, except a bit of cheese, because I thought the king must live somewhere near Hagsgate, which is the only big town I've ever seen. My mother and father were snoring in their room, but Wilfrid had fallen asleep right in front of the hearth, and they always leave him there when he does. If you rouse him to go to his own bed, he comes up fighting and crying. I don't know why.

I stood and looked down at him for the longest time. Wilfrid doesn't look nearly so mean when he's sleeping. My mother had banked the coals to make sure there'd be a fire for tomorrow's bread, and my father's moleskin trews were hanging there to dry, because he'd had to wade into the stockpond that afternoon to rescue a lamb. I moved them a little bit, so they wouldn't burn. I wound the clock — Wilfrid's supposed to do that every night, but he always forgets — and I thought how they'd all be hearing it ticking in the morning while they were looking everywhere for me, too frightened to eat any breakfast, and I turned to go back to my room.

But then I turned around again, and I climbed out of the kitchen window, because our front door squeaks so. I was afraid that Malka might wake in the barn and right away know I was up to something, because I can't ever fool Malka, only she didn't, and then I held my breath almost the whole way as I ran to Uncle Ambrose's house and scrambled right into his cart with the sheepskins. It was a cold night, but under that pile of sheepskins it was hot and nasty-smelling, and there wasn't anything to do but lie still and wait for Uncle Ambrose. So I mostly thought about Felicitas, to keep from feeling so bad about leaving home and everyone. That was bad enough — I never really *lost* anybody close before, not *forever* — but anyway it was different.

I don't know when Uncle Ambrose finally came, because I dozed off in the cart, and didn't wake until there was this jolt and a rattle and the sort of floppy grumble a horse makes when *he's* been waked up and doesn't like it — and we were off for Hagsgate. The half-moon was setting early, but I could see the village bumping by, not looking silvery in the light, but small and dull, no color to anything. And all the same I almost began to cry, because it already seemed so far away, though we hadn't even passed the stockpond yet, and I felt as though I'd never see it again. I would have climbed back out of the cart right then, if I hadn't known better.

Because the griffin was still up and hunting. I couldn't see it, of course, under the sheepskins (and I had my eyes shut, anyway), but its wings made a sound like a lot of knives being sharpened all together, and sometimes it gave a cry that was dreadful because it was so soft and gentle, and even a little sad and *scared*, as though it were imitating the sound Felicitas might have made when it took her. I burrowed deep down as I could, and tried to sleep again, but I couldn't.

Which was just as well, because I didn't want to ride all the way into Hagsgate, where Uncle Ambrose was bound to find me when he unloaded his sheepskins in the marketplace. So when I didn't hear the griffin anymore (they won't hunt far from their nests, if they don't have to), I put my head out over the tailboard of the cart and watched the stars going out, one by one, as the sky grew lighter. The dawn breeze came up as the moon went down.

When the cart stopped jouncing and shaking so much, I knew we must have turned onto the King's Highway, and when I could hear cows munching and talking softly to each other, I dropped into the road. I stood there for a little, brushing off lint and wool bits, and watching Uncle Ambrose's cart rolling on away from me. I hadn't ever been this far from home by myself. Or so lonely. The breeze brushed dry grass against my ankles, and I didn't have any idea which way to go.

I didn't even know the king's name — I'd never heard anyone call him anything but *the king*. I knew he didn't live in Hagsgate, but in a big castle somewhere nearby, only nearby's one thing when you're riding in a cart and different when you're walking. And I kept thinking about my family waking up and looking for me, and the cows' grazing sounds made me hungry, and I'd eaten all my cheese in the cart. I wished I had a penny with me — not to buy anything with, but only to toss up and let it tell me if I should turn left or right. I tried it with flat stones, but I never could find them after they came down. Finally I started off going left, not for any reason, but only because I have a little silver ring on my left hand that my mother gave me. There was a sort of path that way too, and I thought maybe I could walk around Hagsgate and then I'd think about what to do after that. I'm a good walker. I can walk anywhere, if you give me time.

Only it's easier on a real road. The path gave out after awhile, and I had to push my way through trees growing too close together, and then through so many brambly vines that my hair was full of stickers and my arms were all stinging and bleeding. I was tired and sweating, and almost crying — *almost* — and whenever I sat down to rest bugs and things kept crawling over me. Then I heard running water nearby, and that made me thirsty right away, so I tried to get down to the sound. I had to crawl most of the way, scratching my knees and elbows up something awful.

It wasn't much of a stream — in some places the water came up barely above my ankles — but I was so glad to see it I practically hugged and kissed it, flopping down with my face buried in it, the way I do with Malka's smelly old fur. And I drank until I couldn't hold any more, and then I sat on a stone and let the tiny fish tickle my nice cold feet, and felt the sun on my shoulders, and I didn't think about griffins or kings or my family or anything.

I only looked up when I heard the horses whickering a little way upstream. They were playing with the water, the way horses do, blowing bubbles like children. Plain old livery-stable horses, one brownish, one grayish. The gray's rider was out of the saddle, peering at the horse's left forefoot. I couldn't get a good look — they both had on plain cloaks, dark green, and trews so worn you couldn't make out the color — so I didn't know that one was a woman until I heard her voice. A nice voice, low, like Silky Joan, the lady my mother won't ever let me ask about, but with something rough in it too, as though she could scream like a hawk if she wanted to. She was saying, "There's no stone I can see. Maybe a thorn?"

The other rider, the one on the brown horse, answered her, "Or a bruise. Let me see."

That voice was lighter and younger-sounding than the woman's voice, but I already knew he was a man, because he was so tall. He got down off the brown horse and the woman moved aside to let him pick up her horse's foot. Before he did that, he put his hands on the horse's head, one on each side, and he said something to it that I couldn't quite hear. *And the horse said something back.* Not like a neigh, or a whinny, or any of the sounds horses make, but like one person talking to another. I can't say it any better than that. The tall man bent down then, and he took hold of the foot and looked at it for a long time, and the horse didn't move or switch its tail or anything.

"A stone splinter," the man said after a while. "It's very small, but it's worked itself deep into the hoof, and there's an ulcer brewing. I can't think why I didn't notice it straightaway."

"Well," the woman said. She touched his shoulder. "You can't notice everything."

The tall man seemed angry with himself, the way my father gets when he's forgotten to close the pasture gate properly, and our neighbor's black ram gets in and fights with our poor old Brimstone. He said, "I can. I'm supposed to." Then he turned his back to the horse and bent over that forefoot, the way our blacksmith does, and he went to work on it.

I couldn't see what he was doing, not exactly. He didn't have any picks or pries, like the blacksmith, and all I'm sure of is that I *think* he was singing to the horse. But I'm not sure it was proper singing. It sounded more like the little made-up rhymes that really small children chant to themselves when they're playing in the dirt, all alone. No tune, just up and down, *dee-dah, dee-dah, dee*...boring even for a horse, I'd have thought. He kept doing it for a long time, still bending with that hoof in his hand. All at once he stopped singing and stood up, holding something that glinted in the sun the way the stream did, and he showed it to the horse, first thing. "There," he said, "there, that's what it was. It's all right now."

He tossed the thing away and picked up the hoof again, not singing, only touching it very lightly with one finger, brushing across it again and again. Then he set the foot down, and the horse stamped once, hard, and whinnied, and the tall man turned to the woman and said, "We ought to camp here for the night, all the same. They're both weary, and my back hurts."

The woman laughed. A deep, sweet, slow sound, it was. I'd never heard a laugh like that. She said, "The greatest wizard walking the world, and your back hurts? Heal it as you healed mine, the time the tree fell on me. That took you all of five minutes, I believe."

"Longer than that," the man answered her. "You were delirious, you wouldn't remember." He touched her hair, which was thick and pretty, even though it was mostly gray. "You know how I am about that," he said. "I still like being mortal too much to use magic on myself. It spoils it somehow — it dulls the feeling. I've told you before."

The woman said *"Mmphh,"* the way I've heard my mother say it a thousand times. "Well, *I've* been mortal all my life, and some days...."

She didn't finish what she was saying, and the tall man smiled, the way you could tell he was teasing her. "Some days, what?"

"Nothing," the woman said, "nothing, nothing." She sounded irritable for a moment, but she put her hands on the man's arms, and she said in a different voice, "Some days — some early mornings — when the wind smells of blossoms I'll never see, and there are fawns playing in the misty orchards, and you're yawning and mumbling and scratching your head, and growling that we'll see rain before nightfall, and probably hail as well...on such mornings I wish with all my heart that we could both live forever, and I think you were a great fool to give it up." She laughed again, but it sounded shaky now, a little. She said, "Then I remember things I'd rather not remember, so then my stomach acts up, and all sorts of other things start *twingeing* me — never mind what they are, or where they hurt, whether it's my body or my head, or my heart. And then I think, *no, I suppose not, maybe not."* The tall man put his arms around her, and for a moment she rested her head on his chest. I couldn't hear what she said after that.

I didn't think I'd made any noise, but the man raised his voice a little, not looking at me, not lifting his head, and he said, "Child, there's food here." First I couldn't move, I was so frightened. He *couldn't* have seen me through the brush and all the alder trees. And then I started remembering how hungry I was, and I started toward them without knowing I was doing it. I actually looked down at my feet and watched them moving like somebody else's feet, as though they were the hungry ones, only they had to have me take them to the food. The man and the woman stood very still and waited for me.

Close to, the woman looked younger than her voice, and the tall man looked older. No, that isn't it, that's not what I mean. She wasn't young at all, but the gray hair made her face younger, and she held herself really straight, like the lady who comes when people in our village are having babies. She holds her face all stiff too, that one, and I don't like her much. This woman's face wasn't beautiful, I suppose, but it was a face you'd want to snuggle up to on a cold night. That's the best I know how to say it.

The man...one minute he looked younger than my father, and the next

he'd be looking older than anybody I ever saw, older than people are supposed to *be*, maybe. He didn't have any gray hair himself, but he did have
a lot of lines, but that's not what I'm talking about either. It was the eyes.
His eyes were green, green, *green*, not like grass, not like emeralds — I
saw an emerald once, a gypsy woman showed me — and not anything
like apples or limes or such stuff. Maybe like the ocean, except I've never
seen the ocean, so I don't know. If you go deep enough into the woods
(not the Midwood, of course not, but any other sort of woods), sooner or
later you'll always come to a place where even the *shadows* are green, and
that's the way his eyes were. I was afraid of his eyes at first.

The woman gave me a peach and watched me bite into it, too hungry to thank her. She asked me, "Girl, what are you doing here? Are you
lost?"

"No, I'm not," I mumbled with my mouth full. "I just don't know
where I am, that's different." They both laughed, but it wasn't a mean,
making-fun laugh. I told them, "My name's Sooz, and I have to see the
king. He lives somewhere right nearby, doesn't he?"

They looked at each other. I couldn't tell what they were thinking, but
the tall man raised his eyebrows, and the woman shook her head a bit,
slowly. They looked at each other for a long time, until the woman said,
"Well, not nearby, but not so very far, either. We were bound on our way
to visit him ourselves."

"Good," I said. "Oh, *good*." I was trying to sound as grown-up as they
were, but it was hard, because I was so happy to find out that they could
take me to the king. I said, "I'll go along with you, then."

The woman was against it before I got the first words out. She said to
the tall man, "No, we couldn't. We don't know how things are." She looked
sad about it, but she looked firm, too. She said, "Girl, it's not you worries
me. The king is a good man, and an old friend, but it has been a long time,
and kings change. Even more than other people, kings change."

"I have to see him," I said. "You go on, then. I'm not going home until
I see him." I finished the peach, and the man handed me a chunk of dried
fish and smiled at the woman as I tore into it. He said quietly to her, "It
seems to me that you and I both remember asking to be taken along on a
quest. I can't speak for you, but I begged."

But the woman wouldn't let up. "We could be bringing her into great
peril. You can't take the chance, it isn't right!"

He began to answer her, but I interrupted — my mother would have slapped me halfway across the kitchen. I shouted at them, "I'm *coming* from great peril. There's a griffin nested in the Midwood, and he's eaten Jehane and Louli and — and my Felicitas —" and then I *did* start weeping, and I didn't care. I just stood there and shook and wailed, and dropped the dried fish. I tried to pick it up, still crying so hard I couldn't see it, but the woman stopped me and gave me her scarf to dry my eyes and blow my nose. It smelled nice.

"Child," the tall man kept saying, "child, don't take on so, we didn't know about the griffin." The woman was holding me against her side, smoothing my hair and glaring at him as though it was his fault that I was howling like that. She said, "Of course we'll take you with us, girl dear — there, never mind, of course we will. That's a fearful matter, a griffin, but the king will know what to do about it. The king eats griffins for breakfast snacks — spreads them on toast with orange marmalade and gobbles them up, I promise you." And so on, being silly, but making me feel better, while the man went on pleading with me not to cry. I finally stopped when he pulled a big red handkerchief out of his pocket, twisted and knotted it into a bird-shape, and made it fly away. Uncle Ambrose does tricks with coins and shells, but he can't do anything like that.

His name was Schmendrick, which I still think is the funniest name I've heard in my life. The woman's name was Molly Grue. We didn't leave right away, because of the horses, but made camp where we were instead. I was waiting for the man, Schmendrick, to do it by magic, but he only built a fire, set out their blankets, and drew water from the stream like anyone else, while she hobbled the horses and put them to graze. I gathered firewood.

The woman, Molly, told me that the king's name was Lir, and that they had known him when he was a very young man, before he became king. "He is a true hero," she said, "a dragonslayer, a giantkiller, a rescuer of maidens, a solver of impossible riddles. He may be the greatest hero of all, because he's a good man as well. They aren't always."

"But you didn't want me to meet him," I said. "Why was that?"

Molly sighed. We were sitting under a tree, watching the sun go down, and she was brushing things out of my hair. She said, "He's old now. Schmendrick has trouble with time — I'll tell you why one day, it's a long story — and he doesn't understand that Lir may no longer be the man he was. It could be a sad reunion." She started braiding my hair around my head, so it wouldn't get in the way. "I've had an unhappy feeling about this journey from the beginning, Sooz. But *he* took a notion that Lir needed us, so here we are. You can't argue with him when he gets like that."

"A good wife isn't supposed to argue with her husband," I said. "My mother says you wait until he goes out, or he's asleep, and then you do what you want."

Molly laughed, that rich, funny sound of hers, like a kind of deep gurgle. "Sooz, I've only known you a few hours, but I'd bet every penny I've got right now — aye, and all of Schmendrick's too — that you'll be arguing on your wedding night with whomever you marry. Anyway, Schmendrick and I aren't married. We're together, that's all. We've been together quite a long while."

"Oh," I said. I didn't know any people who were together like that, not the way she said it. "Well, you *look* married. You sort of do."

Molly's face didn't change, but she put an arm around my shoulders and hugged me close for a moment. She whispered in my ear, "I wouldn't marry him if he were the last man in the world. He eats wild radishes in bed. *Crunch, crunch, crunch,* all night — *crunch, crunch, crunch.*" I giggled, and the tall man looked over at us from where he was washing a pan in the stream. The last of the sunlight was on him, and those green eyes were bright as new leaves. One of them winked at me, and I *felt* it, the way you feel a tiny breeze on your skin when it's hot. Then he went back to scrubbing the pan.

"Will it take us long to reach the king?" I asked her. "You said he didn't live too far, and I'm scared the griffin will eat somebody else while I'm gone. I need to be home."

Molly finished with my hair and gave it a gentle tug in back to bring my head up and make me look straight into her eyes. They were as gray as Schmendrick's were green, and I already knew that they turned darker or lighter gray depending on her mood. "What do you expect to happen when you meet King Lir, Sooz?" she asked me right back. "What did you have in mind when you set off to find him?"

I was surprised. "Well, I'm going to get him to come back to my village with me. All those knights he keeps sending aren't doing any good at all, so he'll just have to take care of that griffin himself. He's the king. It's his job."

"Yes," Molly said, but she said it so softly I could barely hear her. She patted my arm once, lightly, and then she got up and walked away to sit by herself near the fire. She made it look as though she was banking the fire, but she wasn't really.

We started out early the next morning. Molly had me in front of her on her horse for a time, but by and by Schmendrick took me up on his, to spare the other one's sore foot. He was more comfortable to lean against than I'd expected — bony in some places, nice and springy in others. He didn't talk much, but he sang a lot as we went along, sometimes in languages I couldn't make out a word of, sometimes making up silly songs to make me laugh, like this one:

> *Soozli, Soozli,*
> *speaking loozli,*
> *you disturb my oozli-goozli.*
> *Soozli, Soozli,*
> *would you choozli*
> *to become my squoozli-squoozli?*

He didn't do anything magic, except maybe once, when a crow kept diving at the horse — out of meanness; that's all, there wasn't a nest anywhere — making the poor thing dance and shy and skitter until I almost fell off. Schmendrick finally turned in the saddle and *looked* at it, and the next minute a hawk came swooping out of nowhere and chased that crow screaming into a thornbush where the hawk couldn't follow. I guess that was magic.

It was actually pretty country we were passing through, once we got onto the proper road. Trees, meadows, little soft valleys, hillsides covered with wildflowers I didn't know. You could see they got a lot more rain here than we do where I live. It's a good thing sheep don't need grazing, the way cows do. They'll go where the goats go, and goats will go anywhere. We're like that in my village, we have to be. But I liked this land better.

Schmendrick told me it hadn't always been like that. "Before Lir, this was all barren desert where nothing grew — *nothing*, Sooz. It was said that the country was under a curse, and in a way it was, but I'll tell you about that another time." People *always* say that when you're a child, and

I hate it. "But Lir changed everything. The land was so glad to see him that it began blooming and blossoming the moment he became king, and it has done so ever since. Except poor Hagsgate, but that's another story too." His voice got slower and deeper when he talked about Hagsgate, as though he weren't talking to me.

I twisted my neck around to look up at him. "Do you think King Lir will come back with me and kill that griffin? I think Molly thinks he won't, because he's so old." I hadn't known I was worried about that until I actually said it.

"Why, of course he will, girl." Schmendrick winked at me again. "He never could resist the plea of a maiden in distress, the more difficult and dangerous the deed, the better. If he did not spur to your village's aid himself at the first call, it was surely because he was engaged on some other heroic venture. I'm as certain as I can be that as soon as you make your request — remember to curtsey properly — he'll snatch up his great sword and spear, whisk you up to his saddlebow, and be off after your griffin with the road smoking behind him. Young or old, that's always been his way." He rumpled my hair in the back. "Molly overworries. That's *her* way. We are who we are."

"What's a curtsey?" I asked him. I know now, because Molly showed me, but I didn't then. He didn't laugh, except with his eyes, then gestured for me to face forward again as he went back to singing.

> *Soozli, Soozli,*
> *you amuse me,*
> *right down to my solesli-shoesli.*
> *Soozli, Soozli,*
> *I bring newsli —*
> *we could wed next stewsli-Tuesli.*

I learned that the king had lived in a castle on a cliff by the sea when he was young, less than a day's journey from Hagsgate, but it fell down — Schmendrick wouldn't tell me how — so he built a new one somewhere else. I was sorry about that, because I've never seen the sea, and I've always wanted to, and I still haven't. But I'd never seen a castle, either, so there was that. I leaned back against his chest and fell asleep.

They'd been traveling slowly, taking time to let Molly's horse heal, but once its hoof was all right we galloped most of the rest of the way. Those horses of theirs didn't look magic or special, but they could run for hours without getting tired, and when I helped to rub them down and curry them, they were hardly sweating. They slept on their sides, like people, not standing up, the way our horses do.

Even so, it took us three full days to reach King Lir. Molly said he had bad memories of the castle that fell down, so that was why this one was as far from the sea as he could make it, and as different from the old one. It was on a hill, so the king could see anyone coming along the road, but there wasn't a moat, and there weren't any guards in armor, and there was only one banner on the walls. It was blue, with a picture of a white unicorn on it. Nothing else.

I was disappointed. I tried not to show it, but Molly saw. "You wanted a fortress," she said to me gently. "You were expecting dark stone towers, flags and cannons and knights, trumpeters blowing from the battlements. I'm sorry. It being your first castle, and all."

"No, it's a *pretty* castle," I said. And it *was* pretty, sitting peacefully on its hilltop in the sunlight, surrounded by all those wildflowers. There was a marketplace, I could see now, and there were huts like ours snugged up against the castle walls, so that the people could come inside for protection, if they needed to. I said, "Just looking at it, you can see that the king is a nice man."

Molly was looking at me with her head a little bit to one side. She said, "He is a hero, Sooz. Remember that, whatever else you see, whatever you think. Lir is a hero."

"Well, I know *that*," I said. "I'm sure he'll help me. I am."

But I wasn't. The moment I saw that nice, friendly castle, I wasn't a bit sure.

We didn't have any trouble getting in. The gate simply opened when Schmendrick knocked once, and he and Molly and I walked in through the market, where people were selling all kinds of fruits and vegetables, pots and pans and clothing and so on, the way they do in our village. They all called to us to come over to their barrows and buy things, but nobody tried to stop us going into the castle. There were two men at the two great doors, and they did ask us our names and why we wanted to see King Lir. The moment Schmendrick told them his name, they stepped back quickly and let us by, so I began to think that maybe he actually was a great magician, even if I never saw him do anything but little tricks and little songs. The men didn't offer to take him to the king, and he didn't ask.

Molly was right. I *was* expecting the castle to be all cold and shadowy, with queens looking sideways at us, and big men clanking by in armor. But the halls we followed Schmendrick through were full of sunlight from long, high windows, and the people we saw mostly nodded and smiled at us. We passed a stone stair curling up out of sight, and I was sure that the king must live at the top, but Schmendrick never looked at it. He led us straight through the great hall — they had a fireplace big enough to roast three cows! — and on past the kitchens and the scullery and the laundry, to a room under another stair. *That* was dark. You wouldn't have found it unless you knew where to look. Schmendrick didn't knock at that door, and he didn't say anything magic to make it open. He just stood outside and waited, and by and by it rattled open, and we went in.

The king was in there. All by himself, the king was in there.

He was sitting on an ordinary wooden chair, not a throne. It was a really small room, the same size as my mother's weaving room, so maybe that's why he looked so big. He was as tall as Schmendrick, but he seemed so much *wider*. I was ready for him to have a long beard, spreading out all across his chest, but he only had a short one, like my father, except white. He wore a red and gold mantle, and there was a real golden crown on his white head, not much bigger than the wreaths we put on our champion rams at the end of the year. He had a kind face, with a big old nose, and big blue eyes, like a little boy. But his eyes were so tired and heavy, I didn't know how he kept them open. Sometimes he didn't. There was nobody else in the little room, and he peered at the three of us as though he knew he knew us, but not *why*. He tried to smile.

Schmendrick said very gently, "Majesty, it is Schmendrick and Molly, Molly Grue." The king blinked at him.

"Molly with the cat," Molly whispered. "You remember the cat, Lir."

"Yes," the king said. It seemed to take him forever to speak that one word. "The cat, yes, of course." But he didn't say anything after that, and we stood there and stood there, and the king kept smiling at something I couldn't see.

Schmendrick said to Molly, "*She* used to forget herself like that." His voice had changed, the same way it changed when he was talking about the way the land used to be. He said, "And then you would always remind her that she was a unicorn."

And the king changed too then. All at once his eyes were clear and shining with feeling, like Molly's eyes, and he *saw* us for the first time. He said softly, "Oh, my friends!" and he stood up and came to us and put his arms around Schmendrick and Molly. And I saw that he had been a hero, and that he was still a hero, and I began to think it might be all right, after all. Maybe it was really going to be all right.

"And who may this princess be?" he asked, looking straight at me. He had the proper voice for a king, deep and strong, but not frightening, not mean. I tried to tell him my name, but I couldn't make a sound, so he actually knelt on one knee in front of me, and he took my hand. He said, "I have often been of some use to princesses in distress. Command me."

"I'm not a princess, I'm Sooz," I said, "and I'm from a village you wouldn't even know, and there's a griffin eating the children." It all tumbled out like that, in one breath, but he didn't laugh or look at me any differently. What he did was ask me the name of my village, and I told him, and he said, "But indeed I know it, madam. I have been there. And now I will have the pleasure of returning."

Over his shoulder I saw Schmendrick and Molly staring at each other. Schmendrick was about to say something, but then they both turned toward the door, because a small dark woman, about my mother's age, only dressed in tunic, trews and boots like Molly, had just come in. She said in a small, worried voice, "I am so truly sorry that I was not here to greet His Majesty's old companions. No need to tell me your illustrious names — my own is Lisene, and I am the king's royal secretary, translator, and protector." She took King Lir's arm, very politely and carefully, and began moving him back to his chair.

Schmendrick seemed to take a minute getting his own breath back. He said, "I have never known my old friend Lir to need any of those services. Especially a protector."

Lisene was busy with the king and didn't look at Schmendrick as she answered him. "How long has it been since you saw him last?" Schmendrick didn't answer. Lisene's voice was quiet still, but not so nervous. "Time sets its claw in us all, my lord, sooner or later. We are none of us that which we were." King Lir sat down obediently on his chair and closed his eyes.

I could tell that Schmendrick was angry, and growing angrier as he stood there, but he didn't show it. My father gets angry like that, which is how I knew. He said, "His Majesty has agreed to return to this young person's village with her, in order to rid her people of a marauding griffin. We will start out tomorrow."

Lisene swung around on us so fast that I was sure she was going to start shouting and giving everybody orders. But she didn't do anything like that. You could never have told that she was the least bit annoyed or alarmed. All she said was, "I am afraid that will not be possible, my lord. The king is in no fit condition for such a journey, nor certainly for such a deed."

"The king thinks rather differently." Schmendrick was talking through clenched teeth now.

"Does he, then?" Lisene pointed at King Lir, and I saw that he had fallen asleep in his chair. His head was drooping — I was afraid his crown was going to fall off — and his mouth hung open. Lisene said, "You came seeking the peerless warrior you remember, and you have found a spent, senile old man. Believe me, I understand your distress, but you must see —"

Schmendrick cut her off. I never understood what people meant when they talked about someone's eyes actually flashing, but at least green eyes can do it. He looked even taller than he was, and when he pointed a finger at Lisene I honestly expected the small woman to catch fire or maybe melt away. Schmendrick's voice was especially frightening because it was so quiet. He said, "Hear me now. I am Schmendrick the Magician, and I see my old friend Lir, as I have always seen him, wise and powerful and good, beloved of a unicorn."

And with that word, for a second time, the king woke up. He blinked once, then gripped the arms of the chair and pushed himself to his feet. He didn't look at us, but at Lisene, and he said, "I will go with them. It is my task and my gift. You will see to it that I am made ready."

Lisene said, "Majesty, no! Majesty, I beg you!"

King Lir reached out and took Lisene's head between his big hands, and I saw that there was love between them. He said, "It is what I am for. You know that as well as *he* does. See to it, Lisene, and keep all well for me while I am gone."

Lisene looked so sad, so *lost*, that I didn't know what to think, about her or King Lir or anything. I didn't realize that I had moved back against Molly Grue until I felt her hand in my hair. She didn't say anything, but it was nice smelling her there. Lisene said, very quietly, "I will see to it."

She turned around then and started for the door with her head lowered. I think she wanted to pass us by without looking at us at all, but she couldn't do it. Right at the door, her head came up and she stared at Schmendrick so hard that I pushed into Molly's skirt so I couldn't see her eyes. I heard her say, as though she could barely make the words come out, "His death be on your head, magician." I think she was crying, only not, the way grown people do.

And I heard Schmendrick's answer, and his voice was so cold I wouldn't have recognized it if I didn't know. "He has died before. Better that death — better this, better *any* death — than the one he was dying in that chair. If the griffin kills him, it will yet have saved his life." I heard the door close.

I asked Molly, speaking as low as I could, "What did he mean, about the king having died?" But she put me to one side, and she went to King Lir and knelt in front of him, reaching up to take one of his hands between hers. She said, "Lord...Majesty...friend...dear friend — remember. Oh, please, please *remember.*"

The old man was swaying on his feet, but he put his other hand on Molly's head and he mumbled, "Child, Sooz — is that your pretty name, Sooz? — of course I will come to your village. The griffin was never hatched that dares harm King Lir's people." He sat down hard in the chair again, but he held onto her hand tightly. He looked at her, with his blue eyes wide and his mouth trembling a little. He said, "But you must remind me, little one. When I...when I lose myself — when I lose *her* — you must remind me that I am still searching, still waiting...that I have never forgotten her, never turned from all she taught me. I sit in this place...I *sit*...because a king has to sit, you see...but in my mind, in my poor mind, I am always away with *her*...."

I didn't have any idea what he was talking about. I do now.

He fell asleep again then, holding Molly's hand. She sat with him for a long time, resting her head on his knee. Schmendrick went off to make sure Lisene was doing what she was supposed to do, getting everything ready for the king's departure. There was a lot of clattering and shouting already, enough so you'd have thought a war was starting, but nobody came in to see King Lir or speak to him, wish him luck or anything. It was almost as though he wasn't really there.

Me, I tried to write a letter home, with pictures of the king and the castle, but I fell asleep like him, and I slept the rest of that day and all night too. I woke up in a bed I couldn't remember getting into, with Schmendrick looking down at me, saying, "Up, child, on your feet. You started all this uproar — it's time for you to see it through. The king is coming to slay your griffin."

I was out of bed before he'd finished speaking. I said, "Now? Are we going right now?"

Schmendrick shrugged his shoulders. "By noon, anyway, if I can finally get Lisene and the rest of them to understand that they are *not* coming. Lisene wants to bring fifty men-at-arms, a dozen wagonloads of supplies, a regiment of runners to send messages back and forth, and every wretched physician in the kingdom." He sighed and spread his hands. "I may have to turn the lot of them to stone if we are to be off today."

I thought he was probably joking, but I already knew that you couldn't be sure with Schmendrick. He said, "If Lir comes with a train of followers, there will be no Lir. Do you understand me, Sooz?" I shook my head. Schmendrick said, "It is my fault. If I had made sure to visit here more often, there were things I could have done to restore the Lir Molly and I once knew. My fault, my thoughtlessness."

I remembered Molly telling me, "Schmendrick has trouble with time." I still didn't know what she meant, nor this either. I said, "It's just the way old people get. We have old men in our village who talk like him. One woman, too, Mam Jennet. She always cries when it rains."

Schmendrick clenched his fist and pounded it against his leg. "King Lir is *not* mad, girl, nor is he senile, as Lisene called him. He is *Lir*, Lir still, I promise you that. It is only here, in this castle, surrounded by good, loyal people who love him — who will love him to death, if they are allowed — that he sinks into...into the condition you have seen." He didn't say anything more for a moment; then he stooped a little to peer closely at me. "Did you notice the change in him when I spoke of unicorns?"

"Unicorn," I answered. "One unicorn who loved him. I noticed."

Schmendrick kept looking at me in a new way, as though we'd never met before. He said, "Your pardon, Sooz. I keep taking you for a child. Yes. One unicorn. He has not seen her since he became king, but he is what he is because of her. And when I speak that word, when Molly or I say her name — which I have not done yet — then he is recalled to himself." He paused for a moment, and then added, very softly, "As we had so often to do for her, so long ago."

"I didn't know unicorns had names," I said. "I didn't know they ever loved people."

"They don't. Only this one." He turned and walked away swiftly, saying over his shoulder, "Her name was Amalthea. Go find Molly, she'll see you fed."

The room I'd slept in wasn't big, not for something in a castle. Catania, the headwoman of our village, has a bedroom nearly as large, which I know because I play with her daughter Sophia. But the sheets I'd been under were embroidered with a crown, and engraved on the headboard was a picture of the blue banner with the white unicorn. I had slept the night in King Lir's own bed while he dozed in an old wooden chair.

I didn't wait to have breakfast with Molly, but ran straight to the little room where I had last seen the king. He was there, but so changed that I froze in the doorway, trying to get my breath. Three men were bustling around him like tailors, dressing him in his armor: all the padding underneath, first, and then the different pieces for the arms and legs and shoulders. I don't know any of the names. The men hadn't put his helmet on him, so his head stuck out at the top, white-haired and big-nosed and blue-eyed, but he didn't look silly like that. He looked like a giant.

When he saw me, he smiled, and it was a warm, happy smile, but it was a little frightening too, almost a little terrible, like the time I saw the griffin burning in the black sky. It was a hero's smile. I'd never seen one before. He called to me, "Little one, come and buckle on my sword, if you would. It would be an honor for me."

The men had to show me how you do it. The swordbelt, all by itself, was so heavy it kept slipping through my fingers, and I did need help with the buckle. But I put the sword into its sheath alone, although I needed both hands to lift it. When it slid home it made a sound like a great door slamming shut. King Lir touched my face with one of his cold iron gloves and said, "Thank you, little one. The next time that blade is drawn, it will be to free your village. You have my word."

Schmendrick came in then, took one look, and just shook his head. He said, "This is the most ridiculous...It is four days' ride — perhaps five

— with the weather turning hot enough to broil a lobster on an iceberg. There's no need for armor until he faces the griffin." You could see how stupid he felt they all were, but King Lir smiled at him the same way he'd smiled at me, and Schmendrick stopped talking.

King Lir said, "Old friend, I go forth as I mean to return. It is my way."

Schmendrick looked like a little boy himself for a moment. All he could say was, "Your business. Don't blame me, that's all. At *least* leave the helmet off."

He was about to turn away and stalk out of the room, but Molly came up behind him and said, "Oh, Majesty — Lir — how grand! How beautiful you are!" She sounded the way my Aunt Zerelda sounds when she's carrying on about my brother Wilfrid. He could mess his pants and jump in a hog pen, and Aunt Zerelda would still think he was the best, smartest boy in the whole world. But Molly was different. She brushed those tailors, or whatever they were, straight aside, and she stood on tiptoe to smooth King Lir's white hair, and I heard her whisper, "I wish *she* could see you."

King Lir looked at her for a long time without saying anything. Schmendrick stood there, off to the side, and he didn't say anything either, but they were together, the three of them. I wish that Felicitas and I could have been together like that when we got old. Could have had time. Then King Lir looked at *me*, and he said, "The child is waiting." And that's how we set off for home. The king, Schmendrick, Molly, and me.

To the last minute, poor old Lisene kept trying to get King Lir to take some knights or soldiers with him. She actually followed us on foot when we left, calling, "Highness — Majesty — if you will have none else, take me! Take me!" At that the king stopped and turned and went back to her. He got down off his horse and embraced Lisene, and I don't know what they said to each other, but Lisene didn't follow anymore after that.

I rode with the king most of the time, sitting up in front of him on his skittery black mare. I wasn't sure I could trust her not to bite me, or to kick me when I wasn't looking, but King Lir told me, "It is only peaceful times that make her nervous, be assured of that. When dragons charge her, belching death — for the fumes are more dangerous than the flames, little one — when your griffin swoops down at her, you will see her at her best." I still didn't like her much, but I did like the king. He didn't sing to me, the way Schmendrick had, but he told me stories, and they weren't fables or fairytales. These were real, true stories, and he knew they were true because they had all happened to him! I never heard stories like those, and I never will again. I know that for certain.

He told me more things to keep in mind if you have to fight a dragon, and he told me how he learned that ogres aren't always as stupid as they look, and why you should never swim in a mountain pool when the snows are melting, and how you can *sometimes* make friends with a troll. He talked about his father's castle, where he grew up, and about how he met Schmendrick and Molly there, and even about Molly's cat, which he said was a little thing with a funny crooked ear. But when I asked him why the castle fell down, he wouldn't exactly say, no more than Schmendrick would. His voice became very quiet and faraway. "I forget things, you know, little one," he said. "I try to hold on, but I do forget."

Well, I knew *that*. He kept calling Molly Sooz, and he never called me anything but *little one*, and Schmendrick kept having to remind him where we were bound and why. That was always at night, though. He was usually fine during the daytime. And when he did turn confused again, and wander off (not just in his mind, either — I found him in the woods one night, talking to a tree as though it was his father), all you had to do was mention a white unicorn named Amalthea, and he'd come to himself almost right away. Generally it was Schmendrick who did that, but I brought him back that time, holding my hand and telling me how you can recognize a pooka, and why you need to. But I could never get him to say a word about the unicorn.

Autumn comes early where I live. The days were still hot, and the king never would take his armor off, except to sleep, not even his helmet with the big blue plume on top, but at night I burrowed in between Molly and Schmendrick for warmth, and you could hear the stags belling everywhere all the time, crazy with the season. One of them actually charged King Lir's horse while I was riding with him, and Schmendrick was about to do something magic to the stag, the same way he'd done with the crow. But the king laughed and rode straight at him, right *into* those horns. I screamed, but the black mare never hesitated, and the stag turned at the last moment and ambled out of sight in the brush. He was wagging his tail in circles, the way goats do, and looking as puzzled and dreamy as King Lir himself.

I was proud, once I got over being frightened. But both Schmendrick and Molly scolded him, and he kept apologizing to me for the rest of the day for having put me in danger, as Molly had once said he would. "I forgot you were with me, little one, and for that I will always ask your pardon." Then he smiled at me with that beautiful, terrible hero's smile I'd seen before, and he said, "But oh, little one, the remembering!" And that night he didn't wander away and get himself lost. Instead he sat happily by the fire with us and sang a whole long song about the adventures of an outlaw called Captain Cully. I'd never heard of him, but it's a really good song.

We reached my village late on the afternoon of the fourth day, and Schmendrick made us stop together before we rode in. He said, directly to me, "Sooz, if you tell them that this is the king himself, there will be nothing but noise and joy and celebration, and nobody will get any rest with all that carrying-on. It would be best for you to tell them that we have brought King Lir's greatest knight with us, and that he needs a night to purify himself in prayer and meditation before he deals with your griffin." He took hold of my chin and made me look into his green, green eyes, and he said, "Girl, you have to trust me. I always know what I'm doing — that's my trouble. Tell your people what I've said." And Molly touched me and looked at me without saying anything, so I knew it was all right.

I left them camped on the outskirts of the village, and walked home by myself. Malka met me first. She smelled me before I even reached Simon and Elsie's tavern, and she came running and crashed into my legs and knocked me over, and then pinned me down with her paws on my shoulders, and kept licking my face until I had to nip her nose to make her let me up and run to the house with me. My father was out with the flock, but my mother and Wilfrid were there, and they grabbed me and nearly strangled me, and they cried over me — rotten, stupid Wilfrid too! — because everyone had been so certain that I'd been taken and eaten by the griffin. After that, once she got done crying, my mother spanked me for running off in Uncle Ambrose's cart without telling anyone, and when my father came in, he spanked me all over again. But I didn't mind.

I told them I'd seen King Lir in person, and been in his castle, and I said what Schmendrick had told me to say, but nobody was much cheered by it. My father just sat down and grunted, "Oh, aye — another great warrior for our comfort and the griffin's dessert. Your bloody king won't ever come here his bloody self, you can be sure of that." My mother reproached him for talking like that in front of Wilfrid and me, but he went on, "Maybe he cared about places like this, people like us once, but he's old now, and old kings only care who's going to be king after them. You can't tell me anything different."

I wanted more than anything to tell him that King Lir *was* here, less than half a mile from our doorstep, but I didn't, and not only because Schmendrick had told me not to. I wasn't sure what the king might look like, white-haired and shaky and not here all the time, to people like my father. I wasn't sure what he looked like to me, for that matter. He was a lovely, dignified old man who told wonderful stories, but when I tried to imagine him riding alone into the Midwood to do battle with a griffin, a griffin that had already eaten his best knights...to be honest, I couldn't do it. Now that I'd actually brought him all the way home with me, as I'd set out to do, I was suddenly afraid that I'd drawn him to his death. And I knew I wouldn't ever forgive myself if that happened.

I wanted so much to see them that night, Schmendrick and Molly and the king. I wanted to sleep out there on the ground with them, and listen to their talk, and then maybe I'd not worry so much about the morning. But of course there wasn't a chance of that. My family would hardly let me out of their sight to wash my face. Wilfrid kept following me around, asking endless questions about the castle, and my father took me to Catania, who had me tell the whole story over again, and agreed with him that whomever the king had sent this time wasn't likely to be any more use than the others had been. And my mother kept feeding me and scolding me and hugging me, all more or less at the same time. And then, in the night, we heard the griffin, making that soft, lonely, horrible sound it makes when it's hunting. So I didn't get very much sleep, between one thing and another.

But at sunrise, after I'd helped Wilfrid milk the goats, they let me run out to the camp, as long as Malka came with me, which was practically like having my mother along. Molly was already helping King Lir into his armor, and Schmendrick was burying the remains of last night's dinner, as though they were starting one more ordinary day on their journey to somewhere. They greeted me, and Schmendrick thanked me for doing as he'd asked, so that the king could have a restful night before he —

I didn't let him finish. I didn't know I was going to do it, I swear, but I ran up to King Lir, and I threw my arms around him, and I said, "Don't go! I changed my mind, don't go!" Just like Lisene.

King Lir looked down at me. He seemed as tall as a tree right then, and he patted my head very gently with his iron glove. He said, "Little one, I have a griffin to slay. It is my job."

Which was what I'd said myself, though it seemed like years ago, and that made it so much worse. I said a second time, "I changed my mind! Somebody else can fight the griffin, you don't have to! You go home! You go home *now* and live your life, and be the king, and everything...." I was babbling and sniffling, and generally being a baby, I know that. I'm glad Wilfrid didn't see me.

King Lir kept petting me with one hand and trying to put me aside with the other, but I wouldn't let go. I think I was actually trying to pull his sword out of its sheath, to take it away from him. He said, "No, no, little one, you don't understand. There are some monsters that only a king can kill. I have always known that — I should never, never have sent those poor men to die in my place. No one else in all the land can do this for you and your village. Most truly now, it is my job." And he kissed my hand, the way he must have kissed the hands of so many queens. He kissed my hand too, just like theirs.

Molly came up then and took me away from him. She held me close, and she stroked my hair, and she told me, "Child, Sooz, there's no turning back for him now, or for you either. It was your fate to bring this last cause to him, and his fate to take it up, and neither of you could have done differently, being who you are. And now you must be as brave as he is, and see it all play out." She caught herself there, and changed it. "Rather, you must wait to learn how it has played out, because you are certainly not coming into that forest with us."

"I'm coming," I said. "You can't stop me. Nobody can." I wasn't sniffling or anything anymore. I said it like that, that's all.

Molly held me at arm's length, and she shook me a little bit. She said, "Sooz, if you can tell me that your parents have given their permission, then you may come. Have they done so?"

I didn't answer her. She shook me again, gentler this time, saying, "Oh, that was wicked of me, forgive me, my dear friend. I knew the day we met that you could never learn to lie." Then she took both of my hands between hers, and she said, "Lead us to the Midwood, if you will, Sooz, and we will say our farewells there. Will you do that for us? For me?"

I nodded, but I still didn't speak. I couldn't, my throat was hurting so much. Molly squeezed my hands and said, "Thank you." Schmendrick came up and made some kind of sign to her with his eyes, or his eyebrows, because she said, "Yes, I know," although he hadn't said a thing. So she went to King Lir with him, and I was alone, trying to stop shaking. I managed it, after a while.

The Midwood isn't far. They wouldn't really have needed my help to find it. You can see the beginning of it from the roof of Ellis the baker's house, which is the tallest one on that side of the village. It's always dark, even from a distance, even if you're not actually in it. I don't know if that's because they're oak trees (we have all sorts of tales and sayings about oaken woods, and the creatures that live there) or maybe because of some enchantment, or because of the griffin. Maybe it was different before the griffin came. Uncle Ambrose says it's been a bad place all his life, but my father says no, he and his friends used to hunt there, and he actually picnicked there once or twice with my mother, when they were young.

King Lir rode in front, looking grand and almost young, with his head up and the blue plume on his helmet floating above him, more like a banner than a feather. I was going to ride with Molly, but the king leaned from his saddle as I started past, and swooped me up before him, saying, "You shall guide and company me, little one, until we reach the forest." I was proud of that, but I was frightened too, because he was so happy, and I knew he was going to his death, trying to make up for all those knights he'd sent to fight the griffin. I didn't try to warn him. He wouldn't have heard me, and I knew that too. Me and poor old Lisene.

He told me all about griffins as we rode. He said, "If you should ever have dealings with a griffin, little one, you must remember that they are not like dragons. A dragon is simply a dragon — make yourself small when it dives down at you, but hold your ground and strike at the underbelly, and you've won the day. But a griffin, now...a griffin is two highly dissimilar creatures, eagle and lion, fused together by some god with a god's sense of humor. And so there is an eagle's heart beating in the beast, and a lion's heart as well, and you must pierce them both to have any hope of surviving the battle." He was as cheerful as he could be about it all, holding me safe on the saddle, and saying over and over, the way old people do, "Two hearts, never forget that — many people do. Eagle heart, lion heart — eagle heart, lion heart. *Never* forget, little one."

We passed a lot of people I knew, out with their sheep and goats, and they all waved to me, and called, and made jokes, and so on. They cheered for King Lir, but they didn't bow to him, or take off their caps, because nobody recognized him, nobody knew. He seemed delighted about that, which most kings probably wouldn't be. But he's the only king I've met, so I can't say.

The Midwood seemed to be reaching out for us before we were anywhere near it, long fingery shadows stretching across the empty fields, and the leaves flickering and blinking, though there wasn't any wind. A forest is usually really noisy, day and night, if you stand still and listen to the birds and the insects and the streams and such, but the Midwood is always silent, silent. That reaches out too, the silence.

We halted a stone's throw from the forest, and King Lir said to me, "We part here, little one," and set me down on the ground as carefully as though he was putting a bird back in its nest. He said to Schmendrick, "I know better than to try to keep you and Sooz from following —" he kept on calling Molly by my name, every time, I don't know why — "but I enjoin you, in the name of great Nikos himself, and in the name of our long and precious friendship...." He stopped there, and he didn't say anything more for such a while that I was afraid he was back to forgetting who he was and why he was there, the way he had been. But then he went on, clear and ringing as one of those mad stags, "I charge you in *her* name, in the name of the Lady Amalthea, not to assist me in any way from the moment we pass the very first tree, but to leave me altogether to what is mine to do. Is that understood between us, dear ones of my heart?"

Schmendrick hated it. You didn't have to be magic to see that. It was so plain, even to me, that he had been planning to take over the battle as soon as they were actually facing the griffin. But King Lir was looking right at him with those young blue eyes, and with a little bit of a smile on his face, and Schmendrick simply didn't know what to do. There wasn't anything he *could* do, so he finally nodded and mumbled, "If that is Your Majesty's wish." The king couldn't hear him at all the first time, so he made him say it again.

And then, of course, everybody had to say goodbye to me, since I wasn't allowed to go any further with them. Molly said she knew we'd see each other again, and Schmendrick told me that I had the makings of a real warrior queen, only he was certain I was too smart to be one. And King Lir...King Lir said to me, very quietly, so nobody else could hear, "Little one, if I had married and had a daughter, I would have asked no more than that she should be as brave and kind and loyal as you. Remember that, as I will remember you to my last day."

Which was all nice, and I wished my mother and father could have heard what all these grown people were saying about me. But then they turned and rode on into the Midwood, the three of them, and only Molly looked back at me. And I think *that* was to make sure I wasn't following, because I was supposed just to go home and wait to find out if my friends were alive or dead, and if the griffin was going to be eating any more children. It was all over.

And maybe I would have gone home and let it be all over, if it hadn't been for Malka.

She should have been with the sheep and not with me, of course — that's her job, the same way King Lir was doing his job, going to meet the griffin. But Malka thinks I'm a sheep too, the most stupid, aggravating sheep she ever had to guard, forever wandering away into some kind of danger. All the way to the Midwood she had trotted quietly alongside the king's horse, but now that we were alone again she came rushing up and bounced all over me, barking like thunder and knocking me down, hard, the way she does whenever I'm not where she wants me to be. I always brace myself when I see her coming, but it never helps.

What she does then, before I'm on my feet, is take the hem of my smock in her jaws and start tugging me in the direction she thinks I should go. But this time...this time she suddenly got up, as though she'd forgotten all about me, and she stared past me at the Midwood with all the white showing in her eyes and a low sound coming out of her that I don't think she knew she could make. The next moment, she was gone, racing into the forest with foam flying from her mouth and her big ragged ears flat back. I called, but she couldn't have heard me, baying and barking the way she was.

Well, I didn't have any choice. King Lir and Schmendrick and Molly all had a choice, going after the Midwood griffin, but Malka was my dog, and she didn't know what she was facing, and I *couldn't* let her face it by herself. So there wasn't anything else for me to do. I took an enormous long breath and looked around me, and then I walked into the forest after her.

Actually, I ran, as long as I could, and then I walked until I could run again, and then I ran some more. There aren't any paths into the Midwood, because nobody goes there, so it wasn't hard to see where three horses had pushed through the undergrowth, and then a dog's tracks on top of the hoofprints. It was very quiet with no wind, not one bird calling, no sound but my own panting. I couldn't even hear Malka anymore. I was hoping that maybe they'd come on the griffin while it was asleep, and King Lir had already killed it in its nest. I didn't think so, though. He'd probably have decided it wasn't honorable to attack a sleeping griffin, and wakened it up for a fair fight. I hadn't known him very long, but I knew what he'd do.

Then, a little way ahead of me, the whole forest exploded.

It was too much noise for me to sort it out in my head. There was Malka absolutely *howling*, and birds bursting up everywhere out of the brush, and Schmendrick or the king or someone was shouting, only I couldn't make out any of the words. And underneath it all was something that wasn't loud at all, a sound somewhere between a growl and that terrible soft call, like a frightened child. Then — just as I broke into the clearing — the rattle and scrape of knives, only much louder this time, as the griffin shot straight up with the sun on its wings. Its cold golden eyes *bit* into mine, and its beak was open so wide you could see down and down the blazing red gullet. It filled the sky.

And King Lir, astride his black mare, filled the clearing. He was as huge as the griffin, and his sword was the size of a boar spear, and he shook it at the griffin, daring it to light down and fight him on the ground. But the griffin was staying out of range, circling overhead to get a good look at these strange new people. Malka was utterly off her head, screaming and hurling herself into the air again and again, snapping at the griffin's lion feet and eagle claws, but coming down each time without so much as an iron feather between her teeth. I lunged and caught her in the air, trying to drag her away before the griffin turned on her, but she fought me, scratching my face with her own dull dog claws, until I had to let her go. The last time she leaped, the griffin suddenly stooped and caught her full on her side with one huge wing, so hard that she couldn't get a sound out, no more than I could. She flew all the way across the clearing, slammed into a tree, fell to the ground, and after that she didn't move.

Molly told me later that that was when King Lir struck for the griffin's lion heart. I didn't see it. I was flying across the clearing myself, throwing myself over Malka, in case the griffin came after her again, and I didn't see anything except her staring eyes and the blood on her side. But I did hear the griffin's roar when it happened, and when I could turn my head, I saw the blood splashing along *its* side, and the back legs squinching up against its belly, the way you do when you're really hurting. King Lir shouted like a boy. He threw that great sword as high as the griffin, and snatched it back again, and then he charged toward the griffin as it wobbled lower and lower, with its crippled lion half dragging it out of the air. It landed with a saggy thump, just like Malka, and there was a moment when I was absolutely sure it was dead. I remember I was thinking, very far away, *this is good, I'm glad, I'm sure I'm glad.*

But Schmendrick was screaming at the king, "Two hearts! *Two hearts!*" until his voice split with it, and Molly was on me, trying to drag me away from the griffin, and *I* was hanging onto Malka — she'd gotten so *heavy* — and I don't know what else was happening right then, because all I was seeing and thinking about was Malka. And all I was feeling was her heart not beating under mine.

She guarded my cradle when I was born. I cut my teeth on her poor ears, and she never made one sound. My mother says so.

King Lir wasn't seeing or hearing any of us. There was nothing in the world for him but the griffin, which was flopping and struggling lopsidedly in the middle of the clearing. I couldn't help feeling sorry for it, even then, even after it had killed Malka and my friends, and all the sheep and goats too, and I don't know how many else. And King Lir must have felt the same way, because he got down from his black mare and went straight up to the griffin, and he spoke to it, lowering his sword until the tip was on the ground. He said, "You were a noble and terrible adversary — surely the last such I will ever confront. We have accomplished what we were born to do, the two of us. I thank you for your death."

And on that last word, the griffin had him.

It was the eagle, lunging up at him, dragging the lion half along, the way I'd been dragging Malka's dead weight. King Lir stepped back, swinging the sword fast enough to take off the griffin's head, but it was faster than he was. That dreadful beak caught him at the waist, shearing through his armor the way an axe would smash through piecrust, and he doubled over without a sound that I heard, looking like wetwash on the line. There was blood, and worse, and I couldn't have said if he was dead or alive. I thought the griffin was going to bite him in two.

I shook loose from Molly. She was calling to Schmendrick to *do* something, but of course he couldn't, and she knew it, because he'd promised King Lir that he wouldn't interfere by magic, whatever happened. But I wasn't a magician, and I hadn't promised anything to anybody. I told Malka I'd be right back.

The griffin didn't see me coming. It was bending its head down over King Lir, hiding him with its wings. The lion part trailing along so limply in the dust made it more fearful to see, though I can't say why, and it was making a sort of cooing, purring sound all the time. I had a big rock in my left hand, and a dead branch in my right, and I was bawling something, but I don't remember what. You can scare wolves away from the flock sometimes if you run at them like that, determined.

I can throw things hard with either hand — Wilfrid found *that* out when I was still small — and the griffin looked up fast when the rock hit it on the side of its neck. It didn't like that, but it was too busy with King Lir to bother with me. I didn't think for a minute that my branch was going to be any use on even a half-dead griffin, but I threw it as far as I could, so that the griffin would look away for a moment, and as soon as it did I made a little run and a big sprawling dive for the hilt of the king's sword, which was sticking out under him where he'd fallen. I knew I could lift it because of having buckled it on him when we set out together.

But I couldn't get it free. He was too heavy, like Malka. But I wouldn't give up or let go. I kept pulling and pulling on that sword, and I didn't feel Molly pulling at *me* again, and I didn't notice the griffin starting to scrabble toward me over King Lir's body. I did hear Schmendrick, sounding a long way off, and I thought he was singing one of the nonsense songs he'd made up for me, only why would he be doing something like that just now? Then I did finally look up, to push my sweaty hair off my face, just before the griffin grabbed me up in one of its claws, yanking me away from Molly to throw me down on top of King Lir. His armor was so cold against my cheek, it was as though the armor had died with him.

The griffin looked into my eyes. That was the worst of all, worse than the pain where the claw had me, worse than not seeing my parents and stupid Wilfrid anymore, worse than knowing that I hadn't been able to save either the king or Malka. Griffins can't talk (dragons do, but only to heroes, King Lir told me), but those golden eyes were saying into my eyes, "Yes, I will die soon, but you are all dead now, all of you, and I will pick your bones before the ravens have mine. And your folk will remember what I was, and what I did to them, when there is no one left in your vile, pitiful anthill who remembers your name. So I have won." And I knew it was true.

Then there wasn't anything but that beak and that burning gullet opening over me.

Then there was.

I thought it was a cloud. I was so dazed and terrified that I really thought it was a white cloud, only traveling so low and so fast that it smashed the griffin off King Lir and away from me, and sent me tumbling into Molly's arms at the same time. She held me tightly, practically smothering me, and it wasn't until I wriggled my head free that I saw what had come to us. I can see it still, in my mind. I see it right now.

They don't look *anything* like horses. I don't know where people got that notion. Four legs and a tail, yes, but the hooves are split, like a deer's hooves, or a goat's, and the head is smaller and more — *pointy* — than a horse's head. And the whole body is different from a horse, it's like saying a snowflake looks like a cow. The horn looks too long and heavy for the body, you can't imagine how a neck that delicate can hold up a horn that size. But it can.

Schmendrick was on his knees, with his eyes closed and his lips moving, as though he was still singing. Molly kept whispering, "Amalthea... Amalthea..." not to me, not to anybody. The unicorn was facing the griffin across the king's body. Its front feet were skittering and dancing a little, but its back legs were setting themselves to charge, the way rams do. Only rams put their heads down, while the unicorn held its head high, so that the horn caught the sunlight and glowed like a seashell. It gave a cry that made me want to dive back into Molly's skirt and cover my ears, it was so raw and so...*hurt*. Then its head did go down.

Dying or not, the griffin put up a furious fight. It came hopping to meet the unicorn, but then it was out of the way at the last minute, with its bloody beak snapping at the unicorn's legs as it flashed by. But each time that happened, the unicorn would turn instantly, much quicker than a horse could have turned, and come charging back before the griffin could get itself braced again. It wasn't a bit fair, but I didn't feel sorry for the griffin anymore.

The last time, the unicorn slashed sideways with its horn, using it like a club, and knocked the griffin clean off its feet. But it was up before the unicorn could turn, and it actually leaped into the air, dead lion half and all, just high enough to come down on the unicorn's back, raking with its eagle claws and trying to bite through the unicorn's neck, the way it did with King Lir. I screamed then, I couldn't help it, but the unicorn reared up until I thought it was going to go over backwards, and it flung the griffin to the ground, whirled and drove its horn straight through the iron feathers to the eagle heart. It trampled the body for a good while after, but it didn't need to.

Schmendrick and Molly ran to King Lir. They didn't look at the griffin, or even pay very much attention to the unicorn. I wanted to go to Malka, but I followed them to where he lay. I'd seen what the griffin had done to him, closer than they had, and I didn't see how he could still be alive. But he was, just barely. He opened his eyes when we kneeled beside him, and he smiled so sweetly at us all, and he said, "Lisene? Lisene, I should have a bath, shouldn't I?"

I didn't cry. Molly didn't cry. Schmendrick did. He said, "No, Majesty. No, you do not need bathing, truly."

King Lir looked puzzled. "But I smell bad, Lisene. I think I must have wet myself." He reached for my hand and held it so hard. "Little one," he said. "Little one, I know you. Do not be ashamed of me because I am old."

I squeezed his hand back, as hard as I could. "Hello, Your Majesty," I said. "Hello." I didn't know what else to say.

Then his face was suddenly young and happy and wonderful, and he was gazing far past me, reaching toward something with his eyes. I felt a breath on my shoulder, and I turned my head and saw the unicorn. It was bleeding from a lot of deep scratches and bites, especially around its neck, but all you could see in its dark eyes was King Lir. I moved aside so it could get to him, but when I turned back, the king was gone. I'm nine, almost ten. I know when people are gone.

The unicorn stood over King Lir's body for a long time. I went off after a while to sit beside Malka, and Molly came and sat with me. But Schmendrick stayed kneeling by King Lir, and he was talking to the unicorn. I couldn't hear what he was saying, but I could tell from his face that he was asking for something, a favor. My mother says she can always tell before I open my mouth. The unicorn wasn't answering, of course — they can't talk either, I'm almost sure — but Schmendrick kept at it until the unicorn turned its head and looked at him. Then he stopped, and he stood up and walked away by himself. The unicorn stayed where she was.

Molly was saying how brave Malka had been, and telling me that she'd never known another dog who attacked a griffin. She asked if Malka had ever had pups, and I said, yes, but none of them was Malka. It was very strange. She was trying hard to make me feel better, and I was trying to comfort her because she couldn't. But all the while I felt so cold, almost as far away from everything as Malka had gone. I closed her eyes, the way you do with people, and I sat there and I stroked her side, over and over.

I didn't notice the unicorn. Molly must have, but she didn't say anything. I went on petting Malka, and I didn't look up until the horn came slanting over my shoulder. Close to, you could see blood drying in the shining spirals, but I wasn't afraid. I wasn't anything. Then the horn touched Malka, very lightly, right where I was stroking her, and Malka opened her eyes.

It took her a while to understand that she was alive. It took me longer. She ran her tongue out first, panting and panting, looking so *thirsty*. We could hear a stream trickling somewhere close, and Molly went and found it, and brought water back in her cupped hands. Malka lapped it all up, and then she tried to stand and fell down, like a puppy. But she kept trying, and at last she was properly on her feet, and she tried to lick my face, but she missed it the first few times. I only started crying when she finally managed it.

When she saw the unicorn, she did a funny thing. She stared at it for a moment, and then she bowed or curtseyed, in a dog way, stretching out her front legs and putting her head down on the ground between them. The unicorn nosed at her, very gently, so as not to knock her over again. It looked at me for the first time...or maybe I really looked at *it* for the first time, past the horn and the hooves and the magical whiteness, all the way into those endless eyes. And what they did, somehow, the unicorn's eyes, was to free me from the griffin's eyes. Because the awfulness of what I'd seen there didn't go away when the griffin died, not even when Malka came alive again. But the unicorn had all the world in her eyes, all the world I'm never going to see, but it doesn't matter, because now I *have* seen it, and it's beautiful, and I was in there too. And when I think of Jehane, and Louli, and my Felicitas who could only talk with her eyes, just like the unicorn, I'll think of them, and not the griffin. That's how it was when the unicorn and I looked at each other.

I didn't see if the unicorn said goodbye to Molly and Schmendrick, and I didn't see when it went away. I didn't want to. I did hear Schmendrick saying, "A dog. I nearly kill myself singing her to Lir, calling her as no other has *ever* called a unicorn — and she brings back, not him, but the dog. And here I'd always thought she had no sense of humor."

But Molly said, "She loved him too. That's why she let him go. Keep your voice down." I was going to tell her it didn't matter, that I knew Schmendrick was saying that because he was so sad, but she came over and petted Malka with me, and I didn't have to. She said, "We will escort you and Malka home now, as befits two great ladies. Then we will take the king home too."

"And I'll never see you again," I said. "No more than I'll see him."

Molly asked me, "How old are you, Sooz?"

"Nine," I said. "Almost ten. You know that."

"You can whistle?" I nodded. Molly looked around quickly, as though she were going to steal something. She bent close to me, and she whispered, "I will give you a present, Sooz, but you are not to open it until the day when you turn seventeen. On that day you must walk out away from your village, walk out all alone into some quiet place that is special to you, and you must whistle like this." And she whistled a little ripple of music for me to whistle back to her, repeating and repeating it until she was satisfied that I had it exactly. "Don't whistle it anymore," she told me. "Don't whistle it aloud again, not once, until your seventeenth birthday, but keep whistling it inside you. Do you understand the difference, Sooz?"

"I'm not a baby," I said. "I understand. What will happen when I do whistle it?"

Molly smiled at me. She said, "Someone will come to you. Maybe the greatest magician in the world, maybe only an old lady with a soft spot for valiant, impudent children." She cupped my cheek in her hand. "And just maybe even a unicorn. Because beautiful things will always want to see you again, Sooz, and be listening for you. Take an old lady's word for it. Someone will come."

They put King Lir on his own horse, and I rode with Schmendrick, and they came all the way home with me, right to the door, to tell my mother and father that the griffin was dead, and that I had helped, and you should have seen Wilfrid's face when they said *that!* Then they both hugged me, and Molly said in my ear, "Remember — not till you're seventeen!" and they rode away, taking the king back to his castle to be buried among his own folk. And I had a cup of cold milk and went out with Malka and my father to pen the flock for the night.

So that's what happened to me. I practice the music Molly taught me in my head, all the time, I even dream it some nights, but I don't ever whistle it aloud. I talk to Malka about our adventure, because I have to talk to *someone*. And I promise her that when the time comes she'll be there with me, in the special place I've already picked out. She'll be an old dog lady then, of course, but it doesn't matter. Someone will come to us both.

I hope it's them, those two. A unicorn is very nice, but they're my friends. I want to feel Molly holding me again, and hear the stories she didn't have time to tell me, and I want to hear Schmendrick singing that silly song:

> *Soozli, Soozli,*
> *speaking loozli,*
> *you disturb my oozli-goozli.*
> *Soozli, Soozli,*
> *would you choozli*
> *to become my squoozli-squoozli...?*

I can wait.

Four Fables

My father introduced me early on to George Ade's *Fables in Slang*; later, I discovered James Thurber's two books of *Fables for Our Time* on my own, and quite loved them.

"The Fable of the Moth" was first published in the 1960s, in Al Young's legendary little magazine *Love*, and owes something to Don Marquis' tales of archy and mehitabel. The other three fables in this set were written specifically for this collection. They tend to suggest a dark — even cynical — view of the human condition, but then it has always seemed to me that fables and fabulists mostly do that. Aesop was lynched, after all, according to Herodotus.

The Fable of the Moth

ONCE THERE WAS a young moth who did not believe that the proper end for all mothkind was a zish and a frizzle. Whenever he saw a friend or a cousin or a total stranger rushing to a rendezvous with a menorah or a Coleman stove, he could feel a bit of his heart blacken and crumble. One evening, he called all the moths of the world together and preached to them. "Consider the sweetness of the world," he cried passionately. "Consider the moon, consider wet grass, consider company. Consider glove linings, camel's hair coats, fur stoles, feather boas, consider the heartbreaking, lost-innocence flavor of cashmere. Life is good, and love is all that matters. Why will we seek death, why do we truly hunger for nothing but the hateful hug of the candle, the bitter kiss of the filament? Accidents of the universe we may be, but we are beautiful accidents and we must not live as though we were ugly. The flame is a cheat, and love is the only."

All the other moths wept. They pressed around him by the billions, calling him a saint and vowing to change their lives. "What the world needs now is love," they cried as one bug. But then the lights began to come on all over the world, for it was nearing dinnertime. Fires were kindled, gas rings burned blue, electric coils glowed red, floodlights and searchlights and flashlights and porch lights blinked and creaked and blazed their mystery. And as one bug, as though nothing had been said, every moth at that historic assembly flew off on their nightly quest for cremation. The air sang with their eagerness.

"Come back! Come back!" called the poor moth, feeling his whole heart sizzle up this time. "What have I been telling you? I said that this was no way to live, that you must keep yourselves for love — and you knew the truth when you heard it. Why do you continue to embrace death when you know the truth?"

An old gypsy moth, her beauty ruined by a lifetime of singeing herself against nothing but arc lights at night games, paused by him for a moment. "Sonny, we couldn't agree with you more," she said. "Love is all that matters, and all that other stuff is as shadow. But there's just something about a good fire."

MORAL: *Everybody knows better. That's the problem, not the answer.*

The Fable of the Tyrannosaurus Rex

ONCE UPON A VERY LONG AGO, in a hot and steamy jungle, on an Earth that was mostly hot and steamy jungle, there lived a youngish *Tyrannosaurus Rex*. (Actually, we should probably refer to her as a *Tyrannosaurus Regina*, since she was a female, but never mind.) Not quite fully grown, she measured almost forty feet from nose to tail tip, weighed more than six tons, and had teeth the size of bananas. Although no intellectual, she was of a generally good-humored disposition, accepting with equanimity the fact that being as huge as she was meant that she was always hungry, except in her sleep. This, fortunately, she had been constructed to deal with.

Thanks to her size this Tyrannosaurus was, without a doubt, the queen of her late-Cretaceous world, which, in addition to great predators like herself, included the pack-hunting *Velociraptor*, the three-horned *Triceratops*, the *Iguanodon*, with its horse/duck face, and the long-necked, whiptailed *Alamosaurus*. But the world was populated also by assorted smaller animals — *much* smaller, most of them — distinguished from one another, as far as she was concerned, largely by their degree of quickness and crunchiness, and the amount of fur that was likely to get caught between her fangs. In fact, she rarely bothered to pursue them, since it generally cost her more in effort than the caloric intake was worth. She did eat them now and then, as we snap up potato chips or M&Ms, but never considered them anything like a real meal, or even so much as *hors d'oeuvres*. It was just a reflex, something to do.

One afternoon, however, almost absent-mindedly, she pinned a tiny creature to earth under her left foot. It saved itself from being crushed only by wriggling frantically into the space between two of her toes, while simultaneously avoiding the rending claws in which they ended. As the Tyrannosaurus bent her head daintily to snatch it up, she heard a minuscule cry, "Wait! Wait! I have a very important message for you!"

The Tyrannosaurus — an innocent in many ways — had never had a personal message in her life, and the notion was an exciting one. Her forearms were small and weak, compared to her immense hind legs, but she was able to grip the nondescript little animal and lift him fifteen feet up, where she held him nose to nose, his beady red-brown eyes meeting her huge yellow ones with their long slit pupils. "Be quick," she advised him, "for I am hungry, and where there's one of you, there's usually a whole lot, like zucchini. What was the message you wanted to give me?"

The creature, if somewhat slow of action, atoned for this failing by thinking far faster than any dinosaur. "A large asteroid is about to crash into the Earth," it chirped brightly back at the Tyrannosaurus. "So if you happen to be nursing any unacted desires, now would be the time. To act them out, I mean," it added, realizing that the Tyrannosaurus was blinking in puzzlement at him. "It'll happen next Thursday."

"Asteroid," the Tyrannosaurus pondered. "What is an asteroid?" Before the little creature she held could answer, she asked, "Come to think of it, what's Thursday?"

"An asteroid is a rock," the animal informed her. "A big rock up in the sky, drifting through space. This one is about half the size of that mountain on the horizon, the one visible over the trees, and it's heading straight for us, and nothing can stop it. You and most other life on Earth are doomed."

"My goodness," said the Tyrannosaurus. "I'm certainly glad you told me about this." After a thoughtful moment, she inquired, "What does it all mean?"

"For you and most of your kind, absolute annihilation," the animal piped cheerfully. "For mine — evolution."

"I'm not very good with big words," the Tyrannosaurus said apologetically. "If you could...."

"You'll all be gone," the little creature said. "When the asteroid crashes into the Earth, it will raise a vast cloud of dust and debris that will circle the planet for years, cutting off all sunlight. You dinosaurs won't be able to survive the drastic change in the climate — you'll mostly vanish within a couple of generations. Then — just as when the fall of great trees makes room at last for the small ones struggling in their shadow — then we mammals will take our rightful place in the returning sun." Observing what it took to be a stricken expression on the Tyrannosaurus's yard-wide face, it added, "I'm really sorry. I just thought you should know."

"And your sort," the Tyrannosaurus ventured, "you will...evolute?"

"*Evolve*," the creature corrected her. "That means to change over time into something quite different in size or shape, or in your very nature, from what you were originally. My friend Max, for instance — smaller than I am right now — Max is going to evolve into a horse, if you'll believe it. And Louise, who came out of the sea with the rest of us, in the beginning — Louise is planning to go back there and become a whale. A blue whale, I think she said. It'll take millions of years, of course, but she's never in a hurry, Louise. And me —" here it preened itself as grandly as anyone possibly can in the grasp of a Tyrannosaurus Rex, fifteen feet in the air. "Me, I'm a sort of shrew or something right now, but I'm on my way to being a mammal with just two legs that will write books and fight wars, and won't believe in evolution. How cool is that?"

"And me?" the Tyrannosaurus asked, rather wistfully. "Everything will be changing — everyone will be turning into something else. Don't my relatives and I get to evolve at all?"

"You won't. But there's a bigger picture," the shrew reassured her. "It will take a good while, but some of your kind are going to fly, my dear. Those of your descendants who survive will find their scales turning gradually to feathers; their mighty jaws will in time become a highly adaptable beak, and they'll learn to build nests and sing songs. And hunt bugs."

"Well," said the Tyrannosaurus. "I can't say I follow all of this, but I guess it's better than being anni...annihil...what you said. But where does this Thursday come into it? What exactly *is* a Thursday?"

"Thursday —" began the shrew, but found itself at a disadvantage in trying to explain the arbitrary concept of days, weeks, months and years to a beast who understood nothing beyond sunrise and sunset, light and dark, sun and moon. He said finally, "Thursday will happen three sleeps from now."

"Oh, *three* sleeps!" the Tyrannosaurus cried in great relief. "You should have said — I thought it was *two!* Well, there's plenty of time, then," and she promptly gulped down the shrew in one bite.

Savory, she thought. Nice crunch, too. But then again, there's that hair. They'd be better without the hair.

Turning away, she caught the scent of a nearby triceratops on the wind, and was about to start in that new and tempting direction when she was hit squarely on the back of the neck by the asteroid, blazing from its descent through the atmosphere. As advertised, its impact killed her and wiped out most of the dinosaurs in a very short while, at least by geological standards. The shrew had simply miscalculated the asteroid's arrival time — which is hardly a surprise, as he didn't really have a good grasp on Thursdays, either.

MORAL: *Gemini, Virgo, Aries or Taurus,*
   knowing our future tends to bore us,
   just like that poor Tyrannosaurus.

The Fable of the Ostrich

ONCE UPON A TIME, in a remote corner of Africa, there was a young ostrich who refused to put his head in the sand at the slightest sign of danger. He strolled around unafraid, even when lions were near, cheerfully mocking his parents, his relations, and all his friends, every one of whom believed absolutely that their only safety lay in blind immobility. "It makes you invisible, foolish boy!" his father was forever shouting at him in vain. "You can't see the lion — the lion can't see you! What part of Q.E.D. don't you understand?"

"But the lion *always* sees us!" the ostrich would retort, equally exasperated. "What do you think happened to Uncle Julius? Cousin Hilda?

Cousin Wilbraham? What good did hiding their stupid heads do them?"

"Oh," his father said. "Them. Well." He looked slightly embarrassed, which is hard for an ostrich. "Yes," he said. "Well, it's obvious, they moved. You mustn't *move*, not so much as a tail feather, that's half of it right there. *Head out of sight and hold still*, it's foolproof. Do you think your mother and I would still be here if it weren't foolproof?"

"The only thing foolproof," the young ostrich replied disdainfully, "is the fact that we can outrun lions — if we see them in time, which we can't do with our heads in the sand. That, and the fact that we can kick a lion into another time zone — which we also can't do —"

"Enough!" His father swatted at him with a wing, but missed. "We are ostriches, not eagles, and we have a heritage to maintain. Head out of sight and hold still — that's our legacy to you, and one day you'll thank me for it. Go away now. You're upsetting your mother."

So the young ostrich went away, angry and unconvinced. He attempted to enlist others to his cause, but not one disciple joined him in challenging this first and deepest-rooted of ostrich traditions. "You may very well be right," his friends told him, "we wouldn't be a bit surprised to see you vindicated one day. But right now there's a big, hungry-looking lion prowling over there, and if you'll excuse us...."

And they would hurry off to shove their heads deep into the coolest, softest patch of sand they could find, leaving their feathered rumps to cope with the consequences. Which suited lions well enough, on the whole, but deeply distressed the young ostrich. He continued doing everything he could to persuade other birds to change their behavior, but consistently met with such failure that he was cast down into utter despair.

It was then that he went to the Eldest Lion.

The pilgrimage across the wide savannas was a hard and perilous one, taking the young ostrich several days, even on his powerful naked legs. He would never have dared such a thing, of course, if the Eldest Lion had not long since grown toothless, mangy and cripplingly arthritic. His heavy claws were blunt and useless, more of his once-black mane fell out every time he shook his head, and he survived entirely on the loyalty of two lionesses who hunted for him, and who snarled away all challengers to his feeble rule. But he was known for a wisdom most lions rarely live long enough to achieve, and the young ostrich felt that his counsel was worth the risk of approaching him in his den. Being very young, he also felt quick enough on his feet to take the chance.

Standing within a conversational distance of the Eldest Lion's lair, he called to him politely, until the great, shaggy — and distinctly smelly — beast shambled to the cave entrance to demand, "What does my lunch want of me? I must ask you, of your kindness, lunch, to come just a little closer. My hearing is not what it was — alas, what is? A little closer, only."

The young ostrich replied courteously, without taking a further step, "I thank you for the invitation, mightiest of lords, but I am only a humble and rather unsightly fowl, unworthy even to set foot on your royal shadow. Sir, Eldest, I have come a far journey to ask you a single simple question, after which I promise to retire to the midden-heap my folk call home and presume no more upon your grace." His mother had always placed much stress on the importance of manners.

The Eldest Lion squinted at him through cataract-fogged eyes, mumbling to himself. "Talks nicely, for a lunch. Nobody speaks properly anymore." Raising his deep, ragged voice, he inquired, "I will grant your request, civilized lunch. What wisdom will you have of me?"

For a moment the words he had come such a distance to say stuck in the young ostrich's throat (it is not true that ostriches can swallow and digest anything); but then they came tumbling out of him in one frantic burst. "Can you lions see us when we bury our heads in the sand? Are we really invisible? Because I don't think we are."

It seemed to the young ostrich that the Eldest Lion — most likely due to senility — had not understood the question at all. He blinked and sneezed and snorted, and the ostrich thought he even drooled, just a trifle. Only after some time did the ostrich realize that the Eldest Lion was, after his fashion, laughing.

"Invisible?" the ancient feline rumbled. "*Invisible?* Your stupidity is a legend among my people. We tell each other ostrich jokes as we sprawl in the sun after a kill, drowsily blowing away the feathers. Even the tiniest cub — even an ancestor like myself, half-blind and three-quarters dead — even we marvel at the existence of a creature so idiotic as to believe that hiding its head could keep it safe. We regard you as the gods' gift to our own idiots, the ones who can't learn to hunt anything else, and would surely starve but for you."

His laughter turned into a fusillade of spluttering coughs, and the young ostrich began to move cautiously away, because a lion's cough does not always signify illness, no matter how old he is. But the Eldest Lion called him back, grunting, "Wait a bit, my good lunch, I enjoy chatting with you. It's certainly a change from trying to make conversation with people whose jaws are occupied chewing my food for me. If you have other questions for me — though I dare not hope that a second could possibly be as foolish as that first — then, by all means, ask away." He lay down heavily, with his paws crossed in front of him, so as to appear less threatening.

"I have only one further question, great lord," the young ostrich ventured, "but I ask it with all my heart. If you were an ostrich —" here he had to pause for a time, because the Eldest Lion had gone into an even more tumultuous coughing spasm, waving him silent until he could control himself. "Tell me, if you were an ostrich, how would *you* conceal yourself from such as yourself? Lions, leopards, packs of hyenas and wild dogs...what would be *your* tactic?" He held his breath, waiting for the answer.

"It is extremely difficult for me to conceive of such an eventuality," the Eldest Lion replied grandly, "but one thing seems obvious, even to someone at the very top of the food chain. To bury your head while continuing to expose your entire body strikes me as the height of absurdity — "

"Exactly what I've been telling them and telling them!" the young ostrich broke in excitedly.

The Eldest Lion gave him a look no less imperious and menacing for being rheumy. "I ate the last person who interrupted me," he remarked to the air.

The ostrich apologized humbly, and the Eldest Lion continued, "As I was saying, the truly creative approach would be to reverse the policy, to keep the *body* hidden, leaving only the head visible — and thus, I might add, much better able to survey the situation." He paused for a moment, and then added thoughtfully, "I will confide to you, naïve lunch, that we lions are not nearly as crafty as you plainly suppose. We are creatures of habit, of routine, as indeed are most animals. Faced with an ostrich head sticking out of the sand, any lion would blink, shake his own head, and seek a meal somewhere else. I can assure you of this."

"Bury the *body*, *not* the head! Yes...yes...oh, *yes!*" The young ostrich was actually dancing with delight, which is a rare thing to see, and even the Eldest Lion's wise, weary, wicked eyes widened at the sight. "*Thank you, sir — sir, thank you! What a wonder, imagine — you, a lion, have changed the course of ostrich history!*" About to race off, he hesitated briefly, saying, "Sir, I would gladly let you devour me, out of gratitude for this revelation, but then there would be no one to carry the word back to my people, and that would be unforgivable of me. I trust you understand my dilemma?"

"Yes, yes, oh, *yes*," the Eldest Lion replied in grumbling mimicry. "Go away now. I see my lionesses coming home, bringing me a much tastier meal than gristly shanks and dusty feathers. Go away, silly lunch."

The two lionesses were indeed returning, and the young ostrich evaded their interest, not by burying any part of himself in the sand or elsewhere, but by taking to his heels and striding away at his best speed. He ran nearly all the way home, so excited and exalted he was by the inspiration he carried. Nor did he stop to rest, once he arrived, but immediately began spreading the words of wisdom that he had received from the Eldest Lion. "The *body*, not the head! All these generations, and we've been doing it all wrong! It's the *body* we bury, not the head!" He became an evangel of the new strategy, traveling tirelessly to proclaim his message to any and every ostrich who would listen. "It's the *body*, not the head!"

Some time afterward, one of the Eldest Lion's lionesses, who had been away visiting family, reported noticing a number of ostriches who, upon sighting her, promptly dug themselves down into the sand until only their heads, perched atop mounds of earth, remained visible, gazing down at her out of round, solemn eyes. "You've never seen anything like it," she told him. "They looked like fuzzy cabbages with beaks."

The Eldest Lion stared at her, wide-eyed as one of the ostriches. "They bought it?" he growled in disbelief. "Oh, you're kidding. They really... with their heads *really* sticking up? All of them?"

"Every one that *I* saw," the lioness replied. "I never laughed so much in my life."

"They bought it," the Eldest Lion repeated dazedly. "Well, I certainly hope you ate a couple at least, to teach them...well, to teach them *something*." He was seriously confused.

But the lioness shook her head. "I told you, I was laughing too hard even to *think* about eating." The Eldest Lion retired to the darkest corner of his cave and lay down. He said nothing further then, but the two lionesses heard him muttering in the night, over and over, "Who knew? Who knew?"

And from that day to this, unique to that region of Africa, all ostriches respond to peril by burying themselves instantly, leaving only their heads in view. No trick works every time; but considering that predators are almost invariably reduced to helpless, hysterical laughter at the ridiculous sight — lions have a tendency to ruptures, leopards to actual heart attacks — the record of survival is truly remarkable.

MORAL: *Stupidity always wins, as long as it's stupid enough.*

The Fable of the Octopus

ONCE, DEEP DOWN under the sea, down with the starfish and the sting rays and the conger eels, there lived an octopus who wanted to see God.

Octopi are among the most intelligent creatures in the sea, and shyly thoughtful as well, and this particular octopus spent a great deal of time in profound pondering and wondering. Often, curled on the deck of the sunken ship where he laired, he would allow perfectly edible prey to swim or scuttle by, while he silently questioned the *here* and the *now*, the *if* and the *then*, and — most especially — the *may* and the *might* and the *why*. Even among his family and friends, such rumination was considered somewhat excessive, but it was his way, and it suited him. He planned eventually to write a book of some sort, employing his own ink for the purpose. It was to be called *Concerns of a Cephalopod,* or possibly *Mollusc Meditations.*

Being as reflective as he was, the octopus had never envisioned God in his own image. He had met a number of his legendary giant cousins, and found them vulgar, insensitive sorts, totally — and perhaps understandably — preoccupied with nourishing their vast bodies; utterly uninterested in speculation or abstract thought. As for his many natural predators — the hammerhead and tiger shark, the barracuda, the orca, the sea lion, the moray eel — he dismissed them all in turn as equally shallow, equally lacking in the least suggestion of the celestial, however competent they might be at winkling his kind out of their rocky lairs and devouring them. The octopus was no romantic, but it seemed to him that God must of necessity have a deeper appreciation than this of the eternal mystery of everything, and surely other interests besides mating and lunch. The orca offered to debate the point with him, from a safe distance, before an invited audience, but the octopus was also not a fool.

For a while he did consider the possibility that the wandering albatross might conceivably be God. This was an easy notion for an octopus to entertain, since he glimpsed the albatross only when he occasionally slithered ashore in the twilight, to hunt the small crabs that scurried over the sand at that hour. He would look up then — difficult for an octopus — and sometimes catch sight of the great white wings, still as the clouds through which they slanted down the darkening sky. "So alone," he would think then. "So splendid, and so alone. What other words would suit the nature of divinity?"

But even the beauty and majesty of the albatross could never quite satisfy the octopus's spiritual hunger. It seemed to him that something else was essential to fulfilling his vision of God, and yet he had no word, no image, for what it should be. In time this came to trouble him to the point where he hardly ate or slept, but only brooded in his shipwreck den, concerning himself with no other question. His eight muscular arms themselves took sides in the matter, for each had its own opinion, and they often quarreled and wrestled with each other, which he hardly noticed. When anxious relatives came to visit, he most often hid from them, changing color to match wood or stone or shadow, as octopi will do. They were strangers to him; he no longer recognized any of them anymore.

Then, as suddenly as he himself might once have pounced out of darkness to seize a flatfish or a whelk, a grand new thought took hold of him. What if the old fisherman — the white-bearded one who sometimes rowed out to poke around his ship with a rusty trident when low tide exposed its barnacled hull and splintered masts — what if *he* might perhaps be God? He was poorly clad, beyond doubt, and permanently dirty, but there was a certain dignity about him all the same, and a bright imagination in his salt-reddened eyes that even the orca's eyes somehow lacked. More, he moved as easily on the waters as on land, both by day and night, seemingly not bound to prescribed sleeping and feeding hours like all other creatures. What if, after all the octopus's weary time of searching and wondering, God should have been searching for *him?*

Like every sea creature, the octopus knew that any human being holding any sharp object is a danger to everyone within reach, never to be trusted with body or soul. Nevertheless, he was helpless before his own curiosity; and the next time the fisherman came prowling out with the dawn tide, the octopus could not keep from climbing warily from the ship's keel...to the rudder...then to the broken, dangling taffrail, and clinging there to watch the old man prying and scraping under the hull, filling the rough-sewn waterproof bag at his belt with muddy mussels and the occasional long-necked clam. He was muddy to the waist himself, and smelled bad, but he hummed and grunted cheerfully as he toiled, and the octopus stared at him in great awe.

At last it became impossible for the octopus to hold his yearning at bay any longer. Taking his courage in all eight arms, he crawled all the way up onto the deck, fully exposed to the astonished gaze of the old fisherman. Haltingly, but clearly, he asked aloud, "Are you God?"

The fisherman's expression changed very slowly, passing from hard, patient resignation through dawning disbelief on the way to a kind of worn radiance. "No, my friend," he responded finally. "I am not God, no more than you. But I think you and I are equally part of God as we stand here," and he swept his arm wide to take in all the slow, dark shiver of the sea as it breathed under the blue and silver morning. "Surely we two are not merely surrounded by this divine splendor — we both belong to it, we are *of* it, now and for always. How else should it be?"

"The sea," the octopus said slowly. "The sea..."

"And the land," said the fisherman. "And the sky. And the firelights glittering beyond the sky. All things taken together form the whole, including things like an octopus and an old man, who play their tiny parts and wonder."

"My thoughts and questions were too small...I have lived in God all my life, and never known. Is this truly what you tell me?"

"Just so," the old man beamed. "Just so."

The octopus was speechless with joy. He stretched forth a tentative tentacle, and the fisherman took firm hold of it in his own rough hand. As they stood together, both of them equally enraptured by their newfound accord, the octopus asked shyly, "Do you suppose that God is aware that we are here, within It — part of It?"

"I have no idea," the fisherman replied placidly. "What matters is that *we* know."

There was a rough *thump* as the boat tilted suddenly starboard and nose down, its gentle rocking halted. The sea lowered, falling away from the boat in a great rush, exposing faded paint and barnacles to the air. Shifting gravel and rock clawed at the hull and rudder. The octopus, automatically exerting his suckers against the deck, was unmoved, but the fisherman went tumbling, and above and below and around them the world itself seemed to open a great mouth and draw breath ever more steadily toward the west.

"And that?" the octopus inquired. He pointed with a second tentacle toward the naked expanse of ocean floor over which the tide had withdrawn almost to the horizon — surest sign of an approaching tsunami. "Is that also part of God, like us?"

"I am afraid so," replied the old fisherman, braced now against the slanting rail. "Along with typhoons, stinging jellyfish, my wife's parents and really bad oysters. In such a case, I regard it as no sin to head for the high ground. The shore is far, true, but I was fast on my feet as a young man and this life has kept me fit. I will live, and buy another boat, and fish again."

"I wish you well," said the octopus, "but I am afraid my own options are somewhat more constrained. For escape I require the freedom of the deep sea, which is now entirely out of reach. No. God's great shrug will be here soon enough. I will watch it come, and when it arrives I will give it both our greetings."

"You'll be killed," said the fisherman.

The octopus was hardly equipped to smile, but the fisherman could hear one in his voice all the same. "I shall still be with God."

"That particular form of deep metaphysical appreciation will come to you soon enough without the help of fatalism or fifty-foot waves," said the fisherman, pulling the half-filled canvas bag from his belt. "Besides, *our* conversation has just begun."

Quick as the eels he was so good at catching, the fisherman slid over the rail and dropped to the exposed seabed. Once there he knelt down and pulled the open canvas bag back and forth through the silty, cross-cut shallows, losing his catch, but harvesting a full crop of seawater.

"Well? Are you coming?" the fisherman shouted up to the octopus. He held out the brimming bag exactly like the promise it was. "Time and tide, my many-armed friend. Time and tide!"

In the years that followed — and these were many, for the fisherman and the octopus did survive the tsunami, *just* — these two unlikely philosophers spent a great deal of time together. The fisherman found in the octopus a companion who shared all his interests, including Schopenhauer, Kierkegaard (whom the octopus found "a trifle nervous"), current events both above and below the water, and favorite kinds of fish. The octopus, in turn, learned more than he had ever imagined learning about the worlds of space and thought, and in time he even wrote his book. After suffering rejections from all the major publishing houses, it finally caught the attention of an editor at a Midwestern university press. That worthy, favoring the poetic over the literal, tacked *Eight Arms to Hold You* above the manuscript's original title — *Octopoidal Observations* — advertised the book as allegory, and watched it enjoy two and a half years on the New Age bestseller lists. Every three months he dutifully sent a royalty check and a forwarded packet of fan letters to a certain coastal post office box; and if the checks were never cashed, well, what business was it of his? Authors were eccentric — no one knew *that* better than he, as he said often.

The octopus's book found no underwater readership, of course, since in the ocean, just as on land, reviewers tend to be sharks. But the one-sidedness and anonymity of his fame never troubled him. When not visiting the fisherman, he was content to nibble on passing hermit crabs and drowse among the rocks in a favorite tide pool (his own sunken hulk having been smashed to as many flinders as the fisherman's old boat), thinking deeply, storing up questions and debating points to spring on his patient and honorable friend.

And he never asked if anyone or anything was God, not ever again. He didn't have to.

MORAL: *The best answer to any question? It's always a surprise.*

El Regalo

Sometimes a story interests me too much, for one reason or another, simply to let it go: I need to know what happens later. This doesn't happen often, and when it does I hate it, but there you are.

And so it is with this one. I *need* to know what comes next for Angie and Marvyn (not to mention *El Viejo*). That's why somewhere up ahead there will be a full novel detailing the further adventures of these two Korean-American siblings. I plan on giving it the title which inspired this story in the first place: *My Stupid Brother Marvyn the Witch*.

"YOU CAN'T KILL HIM," Mr. Luke said. "Your mother wouldn't like it." After some consideration, he added, "I'd be rather annoyed myself."

"But wait," Angie said, in the dramatic tones of a television commercial for some miraculous mop. "There's more. I didn't tell you about the brandied cupcakes —"

"Yes, you did."

"And about him telling Jennifer Williams what I got her for her birthday, and she pitched a fit, because she had two of them already — "

"He meant well," her father said cautiously. "I'm pretty sure."

"And then when he finked to Mom about me and Orlando Cruz, and we weren't doing *anything* — "

"Nevertheless. No killing."

Angie brushed sweaty mouse-brown hair off her forehead and regrouped. "Can I at least maim him a little? Trust me, he's earned it."

"I don't doubt you," Mr. Luke agreed. "But you're twelve, and Marvyn's eight. Eight and a half. You're bigger than he is, so beating him up isn't fair. When you're...oh, say, twenty, and he's sixteen and a half — okay, you can try it then. Not until."

Angie's wordless grunt might or might not have been assent. She started out of the room, but her father called her back, holding out his right hand. "Pinky-swear, kid." Angie eyed him warily, but hooked her little finger around his without hesitation, which was a mistake. "You did that much too easily," her father said, frowning. "Swear by Buffy."

"What? You can't swear by a television show!"

"Where is that written? Repeat after me — 'I swear by *Buffy the Vampire Slayer* — '"

"You really *don't* trust me!"

"'I swear by *Buffy the Vampire Slayer* that I will keep my hands off my baby brother —'"

"My baby brother, the monster! He's gotten worse since he started sticking that y in his name —"

"'— and I will stop calling him Ex-Lax —'"

"Come on, I only do that when he makes me really mad —"

"'— until he shall have attained the age of sixteen years and six months, after which time —'"

"After which time I get to pound him into marmalade. Deal. I can wait." She grinned; then turned self-conscious, making a performance of pulling down her upper lip to cover the shiny new braces. At the door, she looked over her shoulder and said lightly, "You are way too smart to be a father."

From behind his book, Mr. Luke answered, "I've often thought so myself."

Angie spent the rest of the evening in her room, doing homework on the phone with Melissa Feldman, her best friend. Finished, feeling virtuously entitled to some low-fat chocolate reward, she wandered down the hall toward the kitchen, passing her brother's room on the way. Looking in — not because of any special interest, but because Marvyn invariably hung around her own doorway, gazing in aimless fascination at whatever she was doing, until shooed away — she saw him on the floor, playing with Milady, the gray, ancient family cat. Nothing unusual about that: Marvyn and Milady had been an item since he was old enough to realize that the cat wasn't something to eat. What halted Angie as though she had walked into a wall was that they were playing Monopoly, and that Milady appeared to be winning.

Angie leaned in the doorway, entranced and alarmed at the same time. Marvyn had to throw the dice for both Milady and himself, and the old cat was too riddled with arthritis to handle the pastel Monopoly money easily. But she waited her turn, and moved her piece — she had the silver top hat — very carefully, as though considering possible options. And she already had a hotel on Park Place.

Marvyn jumped up and slammed the door as soon as he noticed his sister watching the game, and Angie went on to liberate a larger-than-planned remnant of sorbet. Somewhere near the bottom of the container she finally managed to stuff what she'd just glimpsed deep in the part of her mind she called her "forgettery." As she'd once said to her friend Melissa, "There's such a thing as too much information, and it is not going to get me. I am never going to know more than I want to know about stuff. Look at the President."

For the next week or so Marvyn made a point of staying out of Angie's way, which was all by itself enough to put her mildly on edge. If she knew one thing about her brother, it was that the time to worry was when you didn't see him. All the same, on the surface things were peaceful enough, and continued so until the evening when Marvyn went dancing with the garbage.

The next day being pickup day, Mrs. Luke had handed him two big green plastic bags of trash for the rolling bins down the driveway. Marvyn had made enough of a fuss about the task that Angie stayed by the open front window to make sure that he didn't simply drop the bags in the grass, and vanish into one of his mysterious hideouts. Mrs. Luke was back in the living room with the news on, but Angie was still at the window when Marvyn looked around quickly, mumbled a few words she couldn't catch, and then did a thing with his left hand, so fast she saw no more than a blurry twitch. And the two garbage bags went dancing.

Angie's buckling knees dropped her to the couch under the window, though she never noticed it. Marvyn let go of the bags altogether, and they rocked alongside him — backwards, forwards, sideways, in perfect timing, with perfect steps, turning with him as though he were the star and they his backup singers. To Angie's astonishment, he was snapping his fingers and moonwalking, as she had never imagined he could do — and the bags were pushing out green arms and legs as the three of them danced down the driveway. When they reached the cans, Marvyn's partners promptly went limp and were nothing but plastic garbage bags again. Marvyn plopped them in, dusted his hands, and turned to walk back to the house.

When he saw Angie watching, neither of them spoke. Angie beckoned. They met at the door and stared at each other. Angie said only, "My room."

Marvyn dragged in behind her, looking everywhere and nowhere at once, and definitely not at his sister. Angie sat down on the bed and studied him: chubby and messy-looking, with an unmanageable sprawl of rusty-brown hair and an eyepatch meant to tame a wandering left eye. She said, "Talk to me."

"About what?" Marvyn had a deep, foggy voice for eight and a half — Mr. Luke always insisted that it had changed before Marvyn was born. "I didn't break your CD case."

"Yes, you did," Angie said. "But forget that. Let's talk about garbage bags. Let's talk about Monopoly."

Marvyn was utterly businesslike about lies: in a crisis he always told the truth, until he thought of something better. He said, "I'm warning you right now, you won't believe me."

"I never do. Make it a good one."

"Okay," Marvyn said. "I'm a witch."

When Angie could speak, she said the first thing that came into her head, which embarrassed her forever after. "You can't be a witch. You're a wizard, or a warlock or something." Like we're having a sane conversation, she thought.

Marvyn shook his head so hard that his eyepatch almost came loose. "Uh-uh! That's all books and movies and stuff. You're a man witch or you're a woman witch, that's it. I'm a man witch."

"You'll be a dead witch if you don't quit shitting me," Angie told him. But her brother knew he had her, and he grinned like a pirate (at home he often tied a bandanna around his head, and he was constantly after Mrs. Luke to buy him a parrot). He said, "You can ask Lidia. She was the one who knew."

Lidia del Carmen de Madero y Gomez had been the Lukes' housekeeper since well before Angie's birth. She was from Ciego de Avila in Cuba, and claimed to have changed Fidel Castro's diapers as a girl working for his family. For all her years — no one seemed to know her age; certainly not the Lukes — Lidia's eyes remained as clear as a child's, and Angie had on occasion nearly wept with envy of her beautiful wrinkled deep-dark skin. For her part, Lidia got on well with Angie, spoke Spanish with her mother, and was teaching Mr. Luke to cook Cuban food. But

Marvyn had been hers since his infancy, beyond question or interference. They went to Spanish-language movies on Saturdays, and shopped together in the Bowen Street *barrio*.

"The one who knew," Angie said. "Knew what? Is Lidia a witch too?"

Marvyn's look suggested that he was wondering where their parents had actually found their daughter. "No, of course she's not a witch. She's a *santera*."

Angie stared. She knew as much about *Santería* as anyone growing up in a big city with a growing population of Africans and South Americans — which wasn't much. Newspaper articles and television specials had informed her that *santeros* sacrificed chickens and goats and did...things with the blood. She tried to imagine Marvyn with a chicken, doing things, and couldn't. Not even Marvyn.

"So Lidia got you into it?" she finally asked. "Now you're a *santero* too?"

"Nah, I'm a witch, I told you." Marvyn's disgusted impatience was approaching critical mass.

Angie said, "Wicca? You're into the Goddess thing? There's a girl in my home room, Devlin Margulies, and she's a Wiccan, and that's all she talks about. Sabbats and esbats, and drawing down the moon, and the rest of it. She's got skin like a cheese-grater."

Marvyn blinked at her. "What's a Wiccan?" He sprawled suddenly on her bed, grabbing Milady as she hobbled in and pooting loudly on her furry stomach. "I already knew I could sort of mess with things — you remember the rubber duck, and that time at the baseball game?" Angie remembered. Especially the rubber duck. "Anyway, Lidia took me to meet this real old lady, in the farmers' market, she's even older than her, her name's Yemaya, something like that, she smokes this funny little pipe all the time. Anyway, she took hold of me, my face, and she looked in my eyes, and then she closed her eyes, and she just sat like that for so long!" He giggled. "I thought she'd fallen asleep, and I started to pull away, but Lidia wouldn't let me. So she sat like that, and she sat, and then she opened her eyes and she told me I was a witch, a *brujo*. And Lidia bought me a two-scoop ice-cream cone. Coffee and chocolate, with M&Ms."

"You won't have a tooth in your head by the time you're fifteen." Angie didn't know what to say, what questions to ask. "So that's it? The old lady, she gives you witch lessons or something?"

"Nah — I told you, she's a big *santera*, that's different. I only saw her that one time. She kept telling Lidia that I had *el regalo* — I think that means the gift, she said that a lot — and I should keep practicing. Like you with the clarinet."

Angie winced. Her hands were small and stubby-fingered, and music slipped through them like rain. Her parents, sympathizing, had offered to cancel the clarinet lessons, but Angie refused. As she confessed to her friend Melissa, she had no skill at accepting defeat.

Now she asked, "So how do you practice? Boogieing with garbage bags?"

Marvyn shook his head. "That's getting old — so's playing board games with Milady. I was thinking maybe I could make the dishes wash themselves, like in *Beauty and the Beast*. I bet I could do that."

"You could enchant my homework," Angie suggested. "My algebra, for starters."

Her brother snorted. "Hey, I'm just a kid, I've got my limits! I mean, your homework?"

"Right," Angie said. "Right. Look, what about laying a major spell on Tim Hubley, the next time he's over here with Melissa? Like making his feet go flat so he can't play basketball — that's the only reason she likes him, anyway. Or —" her voice became slower and more hesitant "— what about getting Jake Petrakis to fall madly, wildly, totally in love with me? That'd be...funny."

Marvyn was occupied with Milady. "Girl stuff, who cares about all that? I want to be so good at soccer everybody'll want to be on my team — I want fat Josh Wilson to have patches over both eyes, so he'll leave me alone. I want Mom to order thin-crust pepperoni pizza every night, and I want Dad to —"

"No spells on Mom and Dad, not ever!" Angie was on her feet, leaning menacingly over him. "You got that, Ex-Lax? You mess with them even once, believe me, you'd better be one hella witch to keep me from strangling you. Understood?"

Marvyn nodded. Angie said, "Okay, I tell you what. How about practicing on Aunt Caroline when she comes next weekend?"

Marvyn's pudgy pirate face lit up at the suggestion. Aunt Caroline was their mother's older sister, celebrated in the Luke family for knowing everything about everything. A pleasant, perfectly decent person, her perpetual air of placid expertise would have turned a saint into a serial killer. Name a country, and Aunt Caroline had spent enough time there to know more about the place than a native; bring up a newspaper story, and without fail Aunt Caroline could tell you something about it that hadn't been in the paper; catch a cold, and Aunt Caroline could recite the maiden name of the top medical researcher in rhinoviruses' mother. (Mr. Luke said often that Aunt Caroline's motto was, "Say something, and I'll bet you're wrong.")

"Nothing dangerous," Angie commanded, "nothing scary. And nothing embarrassing or anything."

Marvyn looked sulky. "It's not going to be any fun that way."

"If it's too gross, they'll know you did it," his sister pointed out. "I would." Marvyn, who loved secrets and hidden identities, yielded.

During the week before Aunt Caroline's arrival, Marvyn kept so quietly to himself that Mrs. Luke worried about his health. Angie kept as close an eye on him as possible, but couldn't be at all sure what he might be planning — no more than he, she suspected. Once she caught him changing the TV channels without the remote; and once, left alone in the kitchen to peel potatoes and carrots for a stew, he had the peeler do it while he read the Sunday funnies. The apparent smallness of his ambitions relieved Angie's vague unease, lulling her into complacency about the big family dinner that was traditional on the first night of a visit from Aunt Caroline.

Aunt Caroline was, among other things, the sort of woman incapable of going anywhere without attempting to buy it. Her own house was jammed to the attic with sightseer souvenirs from all over the world: children's toys from Slovenia, sculptures from Afghanistan, napkin rings from Kenya shaped like lions and giraffes, legions of brass bangles, boxes and statues of gods from India, and so many Russian *matryoshka* dolls fitting inside each other that she gave them away as stocking-stuffers every Christmas. She never came to the table at the Lukes without bringing some new acquisition for approval; so dinner with Aunt Caroline, in Mr. Luke's words, was always Show and Tell time.

Her most recent hegira had brought her back to West Africa for the third or fourth time, and provided her with the most evil-looking doll Angie had ever seen. Standing beside Aunt Caroline's plate, it was about two feet high, with bat ears, too many fingers, and eyes like bright green marbles streaked with scarlet threads. Aunt Caroline explained rapturously that it was a fertility doll unique to a single Benin tribe, which Angie found impossible to credit. "No way!" she announced loudly. "Not for one minute am I even thinking about having babies with that thing staring at me! It doesn't even look pregnant, the way they do. No way in the world!"

Aunt Caroline had already had two of Mr. Luke's margaritas, and was working on a third. She replied with some heat that not all fertility figures came equipped with cannonball breasts, globular bellies and callipygous rumps — "Some of them are remarkably slender, even by Western standards!" Aunt Caroline herself, by anyone's standards, was built along the general lines of a chopstick.

Angie was drawing breath for a response when she heard her father say behind her, "Well, Jesus Harrison Christ," and then her mother's soft gasp, "Caroline." But Aunt Caroline was busy explaining to her niece that she knew absolutely nothing about fertility. Mrs. Luke said, considerably louder, "Caroline, shut up, your doll!"

Aunt Caroline said, "What, what?" and then turned, along with Angie. They both screamed.

The doll was growing all the things Aunt Caroline had been insisting it didn't need to qualify as a fertility figure. It was carved from ebony, or from something even harder, but it was pushing out breasts and belly and hips much as Marvyn's two garbage bags had suddenly developed arms and legs. Even its expression had changed, from hungry slyness to a downright silly grin, as though it were about to kiss someone, anyone. It took a few shaky steps forward on the table and put its foot in the salsa.

Then the babies started coming.

They came pattering down on the dinner table, fast and hard, like wooden rain, one after another, after another, after another...perfect little copies, miniatures, of the madly smiling doll-thing, plopping out of it — *just like Milady used to drop kittens in my lap*, Angie thought absurdly. One of them fell into her plate, and one bounced into the soup, and a couple rolled into Mr. Luke's lap, making him knock his chair over trying to get out of the way. Mrs. Luke was trying to grab them all up at once, which wasn't possible, and Aunt Caroline sat where she was and shrieked. And the doll kept grinning and having babies.

Marvyn was standing against the wall, looking both as terrified as

Aunt Caroline and as stupidly pleased as the doll-thing. Angie caught his eye and made a fierce signal, *enough, quit, turn it off*, but either her brother was having too good a time, or else had no idea how to undo whatever spell he had raised. One of the miniatures hit her in the head, and she had a vision of her whole family being drowned in wooden doll-babies, everyone gurgling and reaching up pathetically toward the surface before they all went under for the third time. Another baby caromed off the soup tureen into her left ear, one sharp ebony fingertip drawing blood.

It stopped, finally — Angie never learned how Marvyn regained control — and things almost quieted down, except for Aunt Caroline. The fertility doll got the look of glazed joy off its face and went back to being a skinny, ugly, duty-free airport souvenir, while the doll-babies seemed to melt away exactly as though they had been made of ice instead of wood. Angie was quick enough to see one of them actually dissolving into nothingness directly in front of Aunt Caroline, who at this point stopped screaming and began hiccoughing and beating the table with her palms. Mr. Luke pounded her on the back, and Angie volunteered to practice her Heimlich maneuver, but was overruled. Aunt Caroline went to bed early.

Later, in Marvyn's room, he kept his own bed between himself and Angie, indignantly demanding, "What? You said not scary — what's scary about a doll having babies? I thought it was cute."

"Cute," Angie said. "Uh-huh." She was wondering, in a distant sort of way, how much prison time she might get if she actually murdered her brother. *Ten years? Five, with good behavior and a lot of psychiatrists? I could manage it.* "And what did I tell you about not embarrassing Aunt Caroline?"

"How did I embarrass her?" Marvyn's visible eye was wide with outraged innocence. "She shouldn't drink so much, that's her problem. She embarrassed me."

"They're going to figure it out, you know," Angie warned him. "Maybe not Aunt Caroline, but Mom for sure. She's a witch herself that way. Your cover is blown, buddy."

But to her own astonishment, not a word was ever said about the episode, the next day or any other — not by her observant mother, not by her dryly perceptive father, nor even by Aunt Caroline, who might reasonably have been expected at least to comment at breakfast. A baffled Angie remarked to Milady, drowsing on her pillow, "I guess if a thing's weird enough, somehow nobody saw it." This explanation didn't satisfy her, not by a long shot, but lacking anything better she was stuck with it. The old cat blinked in squeezy-eyed agreement, wriggled herself into a more comfortable position, and fell asleep still purring.

Angie kept Marvyn more closely under her eye after that than she had done since he was quite small, and first showing a penchant for playing in traffic. Whether this observation was the cause or not, he did remain more or less on his best behavior, barring the time he turned the air in the bicycle tires of a boy who had stolen his superhero comic book to cement. There was also the affair of the enchanted soccer ball, which kept rolling back to him as though it couldn't bear to be with anyone else. And Angie learned to be extremely careful when making herself a sandwich, because if she lost track of her brother for too long, the sandwich was liable to acquire an extra ingredient. Paprika was one, tabasco another; and Scotch Bonnet peppers were a special favorite. But there were others less hot and even more objectionable. As she snarled to a sympathetic Melissa Feldman, who had two brothers of her own, "They ought to be able to jail kids just for being eight and a half."

Then there was the matter of Marvyn's attitude toward Angie's attitude about Jake Petrakis.

Jake Petrakis was a year ahead of Angie at school. He was half-Greek and half-Irish, and his blue eyes and thick poppy-colored hair contrasted so richly with his olive skin that she had not been able to look directly at him since the fourth grade. He was on the swim team, and he was the president of the Chess Club, and he went with Ashleigh Sutton, queen of the junior class, rechristened "Ghastly Ashleigh" by the loyal Melissa. But he spoke kindly and cheerfully to Angie without fail, always saying *Hey, Angie,* and *How's it going, Angie?* and *See you in the fall, Angie, have a good summer.* She clutched such things to herself, every one of them, and at the same time could not bear them.

Marvyn was as merciless as a mosquito when it came to Jake Petrakis. He made swooning, kissing noises whenever he spied Angie looking at Jake's picture in her yearbook, and drove her wild by holding invented conversations between them, just loudly enough for her to hear. His increasing ability at witchcraft meant that scented, decorated, and misspelled love notes were likely to flutter down onto her bed at any moment, as were long-stemmed roses, imitation jewelry (Marvyn had limited experience and poor taste), and small, smudgy photos of Jake and Ashleigh together. Mr. Luke had to invoke Angie's oath more than once, and to sweeten it with a promise of a new bicycle if Marvyn made it through the year undamaged. Angie held out for a mountain bike, and her father sighed. "That was always a myth, about the gypsies stealing children," he said, rather wistfully. "It was surely the other way around. Deal."

Yet there were intermittent peaceful moments between Marvyn and Angie, several occurring in Marvyn's room. It was a far tidier place than Angie's room, for all the clothes on the floor and battered board game boxes sticking out from under the bed. Marvyn had mounted *National Geographic* foldout maps all around the walls, lining them up so perfectly that the creases were invisible; and on one special wall were prints and photos of a lot of people with strange staring eyes. Angie recognized Rasputin, and knew a few of the other names — Aleister Crowley, for one, and a man in Renaissance dress called Dr. John Dee. There were two women, as well: the young witch Willow, from *Buffy the Vampire Slayer*, and a daguerreotype of a black woman wearing a kind of turban folded into points. No Harry Potter, however. Marvyn had never taken to Harry Potter.

There was also, one day after school, a very young kitten wobbling among the books littering Marvyn's bed. A surprised Angie picked it up and held it over her face, feeling its purring between her hands. It was a dark, dusty gray, rather like Milady — indeed, Angie had never seen another cat of that exact color. She nuzzled its tummy happily, asking it, "Who are you, huh? Who could you ever be?"

Marvyn was feeding his angelfish, and didn't look up. He said, "She's Milady."

Angie dropped the kitten on the bed. Marvyn said, "I mean, she's Milady when she was young. I went back and got her."

When he did turn around, he was grinning the maddening pirate grin Angie could never stand, savoring her shock. It took her a minute to find words, and more time to make them come out. She said, "You went back. You went back in time?"

"It was easy," Marvyn said. "Forward's *hard* — I don't think I could ever get really forward. Maybe Dr. Dee could do it." He picked up the kitten and handed her back to his sister. It was Milady, down to the crooked left ear and the funny short tail with the darker bit on the end. He said,

"She was hurting all the time, she was so old. I thought, if she could — you know — start over, before she got the arthritis...."

He didn't finish. Angie said slowly, "So where's Milady? The other one? I mean, if you brought this one...I mean, how can they be in the same world?"

"They can't," Marvyn said. "The old Milady's gone."

Angie's throat closed up. Her eyes filled, and so did her nose, and she had to blow it before she could speak again. Looking at the kitten, she knew it was Milady, and made herself think about how good it would be to have her once again bouncing around the house, no longer limping grotesquely and meowing with the pain. But she had loved the old cat all her life, and never known her as a kitten, and when the new Milady started to climb into her lap, Angie pushed her away.

"All right," she said to Marvyn. "All right. How did you get...back, or whatever?"

Marvyn shrugged and went back to his fish. "No big deal. You just have to concentrate the right way."

Angie bounced a plastic Wiffle ball off the back of his neck, and he turned around, annoyed. "Leave me alone! Okay, you want to know — there's a spell, words you have to say over and over and over, until you're sick of them, and there's herbs in it too. You have to light them, and hang over them, and you shut your eyes and keep breathing them in and saying the words —"

"I knew I'd been smelling something weird in your room lately. I thought you were sneaking takeout curry to bed with you again."

"And then you open your eyes, and there you are," Marvyn said. "I told you, no big deal."

"There you are where? How do you know where you'll come out? When you'll come out? Click your heels together three times and say there's no place like home?"

"No, dork, you just *know*." And that was all Angie could get out of him — not, as she came to realize, because he wouldn't tell her, but because he couldn't. Witch or no witch, he was still a small boy, with almost no real idea of what he was doing. He was winging it all, playing it all by ear.

Arguing with Marvyn always gave her a headache, and her history homework — the rise of the English merchant class — was starting to look good in comparison. She went back to her own bedroom and read two

whole chapters, and when the kitten Milady came stumbling and squeak-
ing in, Angie let her sleep on the desk. "What the hell," she told it, "it's
not your fault."

That evening, when Mr. and Mrs. Luke got home, Angie told them that
Milady had died peacefully of illness and old age while they were at work,
and was now buried in the back garden. (Marvyn had wanted to make
it a horrible hit-and-run accident, complete with a black SUV and half-
glimpsed license plate starting with the letter Q, but Angie vetoed this.)
Marvyn's contribution to her solemn explanation was to explain that he
had seen the new kitten in a petshop window, "and she just looked so
much like Milady, and I used my whole allowance, and I'll take care of
her, I promise!" Their mother, not being a true cat person, accepted the
story easily enough, but Angie was never sure about Mr. Luke. She found
him too often sitting with the kitten on his lap, the two of them staring
solemnly at each other.

But she saw very little evidence of Marvyn fooling any further with
time. Nor, for that matter, was he showing the interest she would have
expected in turning himself into the world's best second-grade soccer
player, ratcheting up his test scores high enough to be in college by the
age of eleven, or simply getting even with people (since Marvyn forgot nothing and had a hit list going back to day-care). She could almost
always tell when he'd been making his bed by magic, or making the window plants grow too fast, but he seemed content to remain on that level.
Angie let it go.

Once she did catch him crawling on the ceiling, like Spider-Man, but
she yelled at him and he fell on the bed and threw up. And there was,
of course, the time — two times, actually — when, with Mrs. Luke away,
Marvyn organized all the shoes in her closet into a chorus line, and had
them tapping and kicking together like the Rockettes. It was fun for
Angie to watch, but she made him stop because they were her mother's shoes. What if her clothes joined in? The notion was more than she
wanted to deal with.

As it was, there was already plenty to deal with just then. Besides her
schoolwork, there was band practice, and Melissa's problems with her
boyfriend; not to mention the endless hours spent at the dentist, correct-
ing a slight overbite. Melissa insisted that it made her look sexy, but the
suggestion had the wrong effect on Angie's mother. In any case, as far as

Angie could see, all Marvyn was doing was playing with a new box of toys, like an elaborate electric train layout, or a top-of-the-line Erector set. She was even able to imagine him getting bored with magic itself after a while. Marvyn had a low threshold for boredom.

Angie was in the orchestra, as well as the band, because of a chronic shortage of woodwinds, but she liked the marching band better. You were out of doors, performing at parades and football games, part of the joyful noise, and it was always more exciting than standing up in a dark, hushed auditorium playing for people you could hardly see. "Besides," as she confided to her mother, "in marching band nobody really notices how you sound. They just want you to keep in step."

On a bright spring afternoon, rehearsing "The Washington Post March" with the full band, Angie's clarinet abruptly went mad. No "licorice stick" now, but a stick of rapturous dynamite, it took off on flights of rowdy improvisation, doing outrageous somersaults, backflips, and cartwheels with the melody — things that Angie knew she could never have conceived of, even if her skill had been equal to the inspiration. Her bandmates, up and down the line, were turning to stare at her, and she wanted urgently to wail, "Hey, I'm not the one, it's my stupid brother, you know I can't play like that." But the music kept spilling out, excessive, absurd, unstoppable — unlike the march, which finally lurched to a disorderly halt. Angie had never been so embarrassed in her life.

Mr. Bishow, the bandmaster, came bumbling through the milling musicians to tell her, "Angie, that was fantastic — that was dazzling! I never knew you had such spirit, such freedom, such wit in your music!" He patted her — hugged her even, quickly and cautiously — then stepped back almost immediately and said, "Don't ever do it again."

"Like I'd have a choice," Angie mumbled, but Mr. Bishow was already shepherding the band back into formation for "Semper Fidelis" *and* "High Society," which Angie fumbled her way through as always, two bars behind the rest of the woodwinds. She was slouching disconsolately off the field when Jake Petrakis, his dark-gold hair still glinting damply from swimming practice, ran over to her to say, "Hey, Angie, cool," then punched her on the shoulder, as he would have done another boy, and dashed off again to meet one of his relay-team partners. And Angie went on home, and waited for Marvyn behind the door of his room.

She seized him by the hair the moment he walked in, and he squalled, "All right, let go, all right! I thought you'd like it!"

"Like it?" Angie shook him, hard. "*Like* it? You evil little ogre, you almost got me kicked out of the band! What else are you lining up for me that you think I'll *like?*"

"Nothing, I swear!" But he was giggling even while she was shaking him. "Okay, I was going to make you so beautiful, even Mom and Dad wouldn't recognize you, but I quit on that. Too much work." Angie grabbed for his hair again, but Marvyn ducked. "So what I thought, maybe I really could get Jake what's-his-face to go crazy about you. There's all kinds of spells and things for that —"

"Don't you dare," Angie said. She repeated the warning calmly and quietly. "Don't. You. Dare."

Marvyn was still giggling. "Nah, I didn't think you'd go for it. Would have been fun, though." Suddenly he was all earnestness, staring up at his sister out of one visible eye, strangely serious, even with his nose running. He said, "It is fun, Angie. It's the most fun I've ever had."

"Yeah, I'll bet," she said grimly. "Just leave me out of it from now on, if you've got any plans for the third grade." She stalked into the kitchen, looking for apple juice.

Marvyn tagged after her, chattering nervously about school, soccer games, the Milady-kitten's rapid growth, and a possible romance in his angelfish tank. "I'm sorry about the band thing, I won't do it again. I just thought it'd be nice if you could play really well, just one time. Did you like the music part, anyway?"

Angie did not trust herself to answer him. She was reaching for the apple juice bottle when the top flew off by itself, bouncing straight up at her face. As she flinched back, a glass came skidding down the counter toward her. She grabbed it before it crashed into the refrigerator, then turned and screamed at Marvyn, "Damn it, Ex-Lax, you quit that! You're going to hurt somebody, trying to do every damn thing by magic!"

"You said the D-word twice!" Marvyn shouted back at her. "I'm telling Mom!" But he made no move to leave the kitchen, and after a moment a small, grubby tear came sliding down from under the eyepatch. "I'm not using magic for everything! I just use it for the boring stuff, mostly. Like the garbage, and vacuuming up, and like putting my clothes away.

And Milady's litter box, when it's my turn. That kind of stuff, okay?"

Angie studied him, marveling as always at his capacity for looking heartwrenchingly innocent. She said, "No point to it when I'm cleaning her box, right? Never mind — just stay out of my way, I've got a French midterm tomorrow." She poured the apple juice, put it back, snatched a raisin cookie and headed for her room. But she paused in the doorway, for no reason she could ever name, except perhaps the way Marvyn had moved to follow her and then stopped himself. "What? Wipe your nose, it's gross. What's the matter now?"

"Nothing," Marvyn mumbled. He wiped his nose on his sleeve, which didn't help. He said, "Only I get scared, Angie. It's scary, doing the stuff I can do."

"What scary? Scary how? A minute ago it was more fun than you've ever had in your life."

"It is!" He moved closer, strangely hesitant: neither witch, nor pirate nor seraph, but an anxious, burdened small boy. "Only sometimes it's like too much fun. Sometimes, right in the middle, I think maybe I should stop, but I can't. Like one time, I was by myself, and I was just fooling around...and I sort of made this *thing*, which was really interesting, only it came out funny and then I couldn't unmake it for the longest time, and I was scared Mom and Dad would come home —"

Angie, grimly weighing her past French grades in her mind, reached back for another raisin cookie. "I told you before, you're going to get yourself into real trouble doing crazy stuff like that. Just quit, before something happens by magic that you can't fix by magic. You want advice, I just gave you advice. See you around."

Marvyn wandered forlornly after her to the door of her room. When she turned to close it, he mumbled, "I wish I were as old as you. So I'd know what to do."

"Ha," Angie said, and shut the door.

Whereupon, heedless of French irregular verbs, she sat down at her desk and began writing a letter to Jake Petrakis.

Neither then nor even much later was Angie ever able to explain to anyone why she had written that letter at precisely that time. Because he had slapped her shoulder and told her she — or at least her music — was cool? Because she had seen him, that same afternoon, totally tangled up with Ghastly Ashleigh in a shadowy corner of the library stacks? Because of Marvyn's relentless teasing? Or simply because she was twelve years old, and it was time for her to write such a letter to someone? Whatever the cause, she wrote what she wrote, and then she folded it up and put it away in her desk drawer.

Then she took it out, and put it back in, and then she finally put it into her backpack. And there the letter stayed for nearly three months, well past midterms, finals, and football, until the fateful Friday night when Angie was out with Melissa, walking and window-shopping in downtown Avicenna, placidly drifting in and out of every coffeeshop along Parnell Street. She told Melissa about the letter then, and Melissa promptly went into a fit of the giggles, which turned into hiccups and required another cappuccino to pacify them. When she could speak coherently, she said, "You ought to send it to him. You've got to send it to him."

Angie was outraged, at first. "No way! I wrote it for me, not for a test or a class, and damn sure not for Jake Petrakis. What kind of a dipshit do you think I am?"

Melissa grinned at her out of mocking green eyes. "The kind of dipshit who's got that letter in your backpack right now, and I bet it's in an envelope with an address and a stamp on it."

"It doesn't have a stamp! And the envelope's just to protect it! I just like having it with me, that's all —"

"And the address?"

"Just for practice, okay? But I didn't sign it, and there's no return address, so that shows you!"

"Right." Melissa nodded. "Right. That definitely shows me."

"Drop it," Angie told her, and Melissa dropped it then. But it was a Friday night, and both of them were allowed to stay out late, as long as they were together, and Avicenna has a lot of coffeeshops. Enough lattes and cappuccinos, with double shots of espresso, brought them to a state of cheerfully jittery abandon in which everything in the world was supremely, ridiculously funny. Melissa never left the subject of Angie's letter alone for very long — "Come on, what's the worst that could happen? Him reading it and maybe figuring out you wrote it? Listen, the really worst thing would be you being an old, old lady still wishing you'd told Jake Petrakis how you felt when you were young. And now he's married, and he's a grandfather, and probably dead, for all you know —"

"Quit it!" But Angie was giggling almost as much as Melissa now, and somehow they were walking down quiet Lovisi Street, past the gas station and the boarded-up health-food store, to find the darkened Petrakis house and tiptoe up the steps to the porch. Facing the front door, Angie dithered for a moment, but Melissa said, "An old lady, in a home, for God's sake, and he'll never know," and Angie took a quick breath and pushed the letter under the door. They ran all the way back to Parnell Street, laughing so wildly that they could barely breathe....

...and Angie woke up in the morning whispering *omigod, omigod, omigod,* over and over, even before she was fully awake. She lay in bed for a good hour, praying silently and desperately that the night before had been some crazy, awful dream, and that when she dug into her backpack the letter would still be there. But she knew dreadfully better, and she never bothered to look for it on her frantic way to the telephone. Melissa said soothingly, "Well, at least you didn't sign the thing. There's that, anyway."

"I sort of lied about that," Angie said. Her friend did not answer. Angie said, "Please, you have to come with me. Please."

"Get over there," Melissa said finally. "Go, now — I'll meet you."

Living closer, Angie reached the Petrakis house first, but had no intention of ringing the bell until Melissa got there. She was pacing back and forth on the porch, cursing herself, banging her fists against her legs, and wondering whether she could go to live with her father's sister Peggy in Grand Rapids, when the woman next door called over to tell her that the Petrakises were all out of town at a family gathering. "Left yesterday afternoon. Asked me to keep an eye on the place, cause they won't be back till sometime Sunday night. That's how come I'm kind of watching out." She smiled warningly at Angie before she went back indoors.

The very large dog standing behind her stayed outside. He looked about the size of a Winnebago, and plainly had already made up his mind about Angie. She said, "Nice doggie," and he growled. When she tried out "Hey, sweet thing," which was what her father said to all animals, the dog showed his front teeth, and the hair stood up around his shoulders, and he lay down to keep an eye on things himself. Angie said sadly, "I'm usually really good with dogs."

When Melissa arrived, she said, "Well, you shoved it under the door, so it can't be that far inside. Maybe if we got something like a stick or a wire clotheshanger to hook it back with." But whenever they looked toward the neighboring house, they saw a curtain swaying, and finally they walked away, trying to decide what else to do. But there was nothing; and after a while Angie's throat was too swollen with not crying for her to talk without pain. She walked Melissa back to the bus stop, and they hugged goodbye as though they might never meet again.

Melissa said, "You know, my mother says nothing's ever as bad as you thought it was going to be. I mean, it can't be, because nothing beats all the horrible stuff you can imagine. So maybe...you know..." but she broke down before she could finish. She hugged Angie again and went home.

Alone in her own house, Angie sat quite still in the kitchen and went on not crying. Her entire face hurt with it, and her eyes felt unbearably heavy. Her mind was not moving at all, and she was vaguely grateful for that. She sat there until Marvyn walked in from playing basketball with his friends. Shorter than everyone else, he generally got stepped on a lot, and always came home scraped and bruised. Angie had rather expected him to try making himself taller, or able to jump higher, but he hadn't done anything of the sort so far. He looked at her now, bounced and shot an invisible basketball, and asked quietly, "What's the matter?"

It may have been the unexpected froggy gentleness of his voice, or simply the sudden fact of his having asked the question at all. Whatever the reason, Angie abruptly burst into furious tears, the rage directed entirely at herself, both for writing the letter to Jake Petrakis in the first place, and for crying about it now. She gestured to Marvyn to go away, but — amazing her further — he stood stolidly waiting for her to grow quiet. When at last she did, he repeated the question. "Angie. What's wrong?"

Angie told him. She was about to add a disclaimer — "You laugh even once, Ex-Lax —" when she realized that it wouldn't be necessary. Marvyn was scratching his head, scrunching up his brow until the eye-patch danced; then abruptly jamming both hands in his pockets and tilting his head back: the poster boy for careless insouciance. He said, almost absently, "I could get it back."

"Oh, right." Angie did not even look up. "Right."

"I could so!" Marvyn was instantly his normal self again: so much for casualness and dispassion. "There's all kinds of things I could do."

Angie dampened a paper towel and tried to do something with her hot, tear-streaked face. "Name two."

"Okay, I will! You remember which mailbox you put it in?"

"Under the door," Angie mumbled. "I put it under the door."

Marvyn snickered then. "*Aww*, like a Valentine." Angie hadn't the energy to hit him, but she made a grab at him anyway, for appearance's sake. "Well, I could make it walk right back out the door, that's one way. Or I bet I could just open the door, if nobody's home. Easiest trick in the world, for us witches."

"They're gone till Sunday night," Angie said. "But there's this lady next door, she's watching the place like a hawk. And even when she's not, she's got this immense dog. I don't care if you're the hottest witch in the world, you do not want to mess with this werewolf."

Marvyn, who — as Angie knew — was wary of big dogs, went back to scratching his head. "Too easy, anyway. No fun, forget it." He sat down next to her, completely absorbed in the problem. "How about I...no, that's kid stuff, anybody could do it. But there's a spell...I could make the letter self-destruct, right there in the house, like in that old TV show. It'd just be a little fluffy pile of ashes — they'd vacuum it up and never know. How about that?" Before Angie could express an opinion, he was already shaking his head. "Still too easy. A baby spell, for beginners. I hate those."

"Easy is good," Angie told him earnestly. "I like easy. And you *are* a beginner."

Marvyn was immediately outraged, his normal bass-baritone rumble going up to a wounded squeak. "I am not! No way in the world I'm a beginner!" He was up and stamping his feet, as he had not done since he was two. "I tell you what — just for that, I'm going to get your letter back for you, but I'm not going to tell you how. You'll see, that's all. You just wait and see."

He was stalking away toward his room when Angie called after him, with the first glimmer both of hope and of humor that she had felt in approximately a century, "All right, you're a big bad witch king. What do you want?"

Marvyn turned and stared, uncomprehending.

Angie said, "Nothing for nothing, that's my bro. So let's hear it — what's your price for saving my life?"

If Marvyn's voice had gone up any higher, only bats could have heard it. "I'm rescuing you, and you think I want something for it? Julius Christmas!" which was the only swearword he was ever allowed to get away with. "You don't have anything I want, anyway. Except maybe...."

He let the thought hang in space, uncompleted. Angie said, "Except maybe what?"

Marvyn swung on the doorframe one-handed, grinning his pirate grin at her. "I hate you calling me Ex-Lax. You know I hate it, and you keep doing it."

"Okay, I won't do it anymore, ever again. I promise."

"Mmm. Not good enough." The grin had grown distinctly evil. "I think you ought to call me O Mighty One for two weeks."

"What?" Now Angie was on her feet, misery briefly forgotten. "Give it up, Ex-Lax — two weeks? No chance!" They glared at each other in silence for a long moment before she finally said, "A week. Don't push it. One week, no more. And not in front of people!"

"Ten days." Marvyn folded his arms. "Starting right now." Angie went on glowering. Marvyn said, "You want that letter?"

"Yes."

Marvyn waited.

"Yes, O Mighty One." Triumphant, Marvyn held out his hand and Angie slapped it. She said, "When?"

"Tonight. No, tomorrow — going to the movies with Sunil and his family tonight. Tomorrow." He wandered off, and Angie took her first deep breath in what felt like a year and a half. She wished she could tell Melissa that things were going to be all right, but she didn't dare; so she spent the day trying to appear normal — just the usual Angie, aimlessly content on a Saturday afternoon. When Marvyn came home from the movies, he spent the rest of the evening reading *Hellboy* comics in his room, with the Milady-kitten on his stomach. He was still doing it when Angie gave up peeking in at him and went to bed.

But he was gone on Sunday morning. Angie knew it the moment she woke up.

She had no idea where he could be, or why. She had rather expected him to work whatever spell he settled on in his bedroom, under the stern gaze of his wizard mentors. But he wasn't there, and he didn't come to breakfast. Angie told their mother that they'd been up late watching television together, and that she should probably let Marvyn sleep in. And when Mrs. Luke grew worried after breakfast, Angie went to his room herself, returning with word that Marvyn was working intensely on a project for his art class, and wasn't feeling sociable. Normally she would never have gotten away with it, but her parents were on their way to brunch and a concert, leaving her with the usual instructions to feed and water the cat, use the twenty on the cabinet for something moderately healthy, and to check on Marvyn "now and then," which actually meant frequently. ("The day we don't tell you that," Mr. Luke said once, when she objected to the regular duty, "will be the very day the kid steals a kayak and heads for Tahiti." Angie found it hard to argue the point.)

Alone in the empty house — more alone than she felt she had ever been — Angie turned constantly in circles, wandering from room to room with no least notion of what to do. As the hours passed and her brother failed to return, she found herself calling out to him aloud. "Marvyn? Marvyn, I swear, if you're doing this to drive me crazy...O Mighty One, where are you? You get back here, never mind the damn letter, just get back!" She stopped doing this after a time, because the cracks and tremors in her voice embarrassed her, and made her even more afraid.

Strangely, she seemed to feel him in the house all that time. She kept whirling to look over her shoulder, thinking that he might be sneaking up on her to scare her, a favorite game since his infancy. But he was never there.

Somewhere around noon the doorbell rang, and Angie tripped over herself scrambling to answer it, even though she had no hope — almost no hope — of its being Marvyn. But it was Lidia at the door — Angie had forgotten that she usually came to clean on Sunday afternoons. She stood there, old and smiling, and Angie hugged her wildly and wailed, "Lidia, Lidia, *socorro*, help me, *ayúdame*, Lidia." She had learned Spanish from the housekeeper when she was too little to know she was learning it.

Lidia put her hands on Angie's shoulders. She put her back a little and looked into her face, saying, "*Chuchi, dime qué pasa contigo?*" She had called Angie *Chuchi* since childhood, never explaining the origin or meaning of the word.

"It's Marvyn," Angie whispered. "It's Marvyn." She started to explain about the letter, and Marvyn's promise, but Lidia only nodded and asked no questions. She said firmly, "*El Viejo puede ayudar.*"

Too frantic to pay attention to gender, Angie took her to mean Yemaya, the old woman in the farmer's market who had told Marvyn that he was a *brujo*. She said, "You mean *la santera*," but Lidia shook her head hard. "No, no, *El Viejo.* You go out there, you ask to see *El Viejo. Solamente El Viejo. Los otros no pueden ayudarte.*"

The others can't help you. Only the old man. Angie asked where she could find *El Viejo,* and Lidia directed her to a *Santería* shop on Bowen Street. She drew a crude map, made sure Angie had money with her, kissed her on the cheek and made a blessing sign on her forehead. *"Cuidado, Chuchi,"* she said with a kind of cheerful solemnity, and Angie was out and running for the Gonzales Avenue bus, the same one she took to school. This time she stayed on a good deal farther.

The shop had no sign, and no street number, and it was so small that Angie kept walking past it for some while. Her attention was finally caught by the objects in the one dim window, and on the shelves to right and left. There was an astonishing variety of incense, and of candles encased in glass with pictures of black saints, as well as boxes marked Fast Money Ritual Kit, and bottles of Elegua Floor Wash, whose label read "Keeps Trouble From Crossing Your Threshold." When Angie entered, the musky scent of the place made her feel dizzy and heavy and out of herself, as she always felt when she had a cold coming on. She heard a rooster crowing, somewhere in back.

She didn't see the old woman until her chair creaked slightly, because she was sitting in a corner, halfway hidden by long hanging garments like church choir robes, but with symbols and patterns on them that Angie had never seen before. The woman was very old, much older even than Lidia, and she had an absurdly small pipe in her toothless mouth. Angie said, "Yemaya?" The old woman looked at her with eyes like dead planets.

Angie's Spanish dried up completely, followed almost immediately by her English. She said, "My brother...my little brother...I'm supposed to ask for *El Viejo.* The old one, *viejo santero?* Lidia said." She ran out of words in either language at that point. A puff of smoke crawled from the little pipe, but the old woman made no other response.

Then, behind her, she heard a curtain being pulled aside. A hoarse, slow voice said, *"Quieres El Viejo?* Me."

Angie turned and saw him, coming toward her out of a long hallway whose end she could not see. He moved deliberately, and it seemed to take him forever to reach her, as though he were returning from another world. He was black, dressed all in black, and he wore dark glasses, even in the dark, tiny shop. His hair was so white that it hurt her eyes when she stared. He said, "Your brother."

"Yes," Angie said. "Yes. He's doing magic for me — he's getting something I need — and I don't know where he is, but I know he's in trouble, and I want him back!" She did not cry or break down — Marvyn would never be able to say that she cried over him — but it was a near thing.

El Viejo pushed the dark glasses up on his forehead, and Angie saw that he was younger than she had first thought — certainly younger than Lidia — and that there were thick white half-circles under his eyes. She never knew whether they were somehow natural, or the result of heavy makeup; what she did see was that they made his eyes look bigger and brighter — all pupil, nothing more. They should have made him look at least slightly comical, like a reverse-image raccoon, but they didn't.

"I know you brother," *El Viejo* said. Angie fought to hold herself still as he came closer, smiling at her with the tips of his teeth. "A *brujito* — little, little witch, we know. Mama and me, we been watching." He nodded toward the old woman in the chair, who hadn't moved an inch or said a word since Angie's arrival. Angie smelled a damp, musty aroma, like potatoes going bad.

"Tell me where he is. Lidia said you could help." Close to, she could see blue highlights in *El Viejo*'s skin, and a kind of V-shaped scar on each cheek. He was wearing a narrow black tie, which she had not noticed at first; for some reason, the vision of him tying it in the morning, in front of a mirror, was more chilling to her than anything else about him. He grinned fully at her now, showing teeth that she had expected to be yellow and stinking, but which were all white and square and a little too large. He said, "*Tu hermano está perdido*. Lost in Thursday."

"Thursday?" It took her a dazed moment to comprehend, and longer to get the words out. "Oh, God, he went back! Like with Milady — he went back to before I...when the letter was still in my backpack. The little showoff — he said forward was hard, coming forward — he wanted to show me he could do it. And he got stuck. Idiot, idiot, idiot!" *El Viejo* chuckled softly, nodding, saying nothing.

"You have to go find him, get him out of there, right now — I've got money." She began digging frantically in her coat pockets.

"No, no money." *El Viejo* waved her offering aside, studying her out of eyes the color of almost-ripened plums. The white markings under them looked real; the eyes didn't. He said, "I take you. We find you brother together."

Angie's legs were trembling so much that they hurt. She wanted to assent, but it was simply not possible. "No. I can't. I can't. You go back there and get him."

El Viejo laughed then: an enormous, astonishing Santa Claus *ho-ho-HO*, so rich and reassuring that it made Angie smile even as he was snatching her up and stuffing her under one arm. By the time she had recovered from her bewilderment enough to start kicking and fighting, he was walking away with her down the long hall he had come out of a moment before. Angie screamed until her voice splintered in her throat, but she could not hear herself: from the moment *El Viejo* stepped back into the darkness of the hallway, all sound had ended. She could hear neither his footsteps nor his laughter — though she could feel him laughing against her — and certainly not her own panicky racket. They could be in outer space. They could be anywhere.

Dazed and disoriented as she was, the hallway seemed to go soundlessly on and on, until wherever they truly were, it could never have been the tiny *Santería* shop she had entered only — when? — minutes before. It was a cold place, smelling like an old basement; and for all its darkness, Angie had a sense of things happening far too fast on all sides, just out of range of her smothered vision. She could distinguish none of them clearly, but there was a sparkle to them all the same.

And then she was in Marvyn's room.

And it was unquestionably Marvyn's room: there were the bearded and beaded occultists on the walls; there were the flannel winter sheets that he slept on all year because they had pictures of the New York Mets ballplayers; there was the complete set of *Star Trek* action figures that Angie had given him at Christmas, posed just so on his bookcase. And there, sitting on the edge of his bed, was Marvyn, looking lonelier than anyone Angie had ever seen in her life.

He didn't move or look up until *El Viejo* abruptly dumped her down in front of him and stood back, grinning like a beartrap. Then he jumped to his feet, burst into tears and started frenziedly climbing her, snuffling, "Angie, Angie, Angie," all the way up. Angie held him, trying somehow to preserve her neck and hair and back all at once, while mumbling, "It's all right, it's okay, I'm here. It's okay, Marvyn."

Behind her, *El Viejo* chuckled, "Crybaby witch — little, little *brujito* crybaby." Angie hefted her blubbering baby brother like a shopping bag, holding him on her hip as she had done when he was little, and turned to face the old man. She said, "Thank you. You can take us home now."

El Viejo smiled — not a grin this time, but a long, slow shutmouth smile like a paper cut. He said, "Maybe we let *him* do it, yes?" and then he turned and walked away and was gone, as though he had simply slipped between the molecules of the air. Angie stood with Marvyn in her arms, trying to peel him off like a Band-Aid, while he clung to her with his chin digging hard into the top of her head. She finally managed to dump him down on the bed and stood over him, demanding, "What happened? What were you thinking?" Marvyn was still crying too hard to answer her. Angie said, "You just had to do it this way, didn't you? No silly little beginner spells — you're playing with the big guys now, right, O Mighty One? So what happened? How come you couldn't get back?"

"I don't know!" Marvyn's face was red and puffy with tears, and the tears kept coming while Angie tried to straighten his eyepatch. It was impossible for him to get much out without breaking down again, but he kept wailing, "I don't know what went wrong! I did everything you're supposed to, but I couldn't make it work! I don't know...maybe I forgot...." He could not finish.

"Herbs," Angie said, as gently and calmly as she could. "You left your magic herbs back —" she had been going to say "back home," but she stopped, because they *were* back home, sitting on Marvyn's bed in Marvyn's room, and the confusion was too much for her to deal with just then. She said, "Just tell me. You left the stupid herbs."

Marvyn shook his head until the tears flew, protesting, "No, I didn't, I didn't — look!" He pointed to a handful of grubby dried weeds scattered on the bed — Lidia would have thrown them out in a minute. Marvyn gulped and wiped his nose and tried to stop crying. He said, "They're really hard to find, maybe they're not fresh anymore, I don't know — they've always looked like that. But now they don't work," and he was wailing afresh. Angie told him that Dr. John Dee and Willow would both have been ashamed of him, but it didn't help.

But she also sat with him and put her arm around him, and smoothed his messy hair, and said, "Come on, let's think this out. Maybe it's the herbs losing their juice, maybe it's something else. You did everything the way you did the other time, with Milady?"

"I thought I did." Marvyn's voice was small and shy, not his usual deep croak. "But I don't know anymore, Angie — the more I think about it, the more I don't know. It's all messed up, I can't remember anything now."

"Okay," Angie said. "Okay. So how about we just run through it all again? We'll do it together. You try everything you do remember about — you know — moving around in time, and I'll copy you. I'll do whatever you say."

Marvyn wiped his nose again and nodded. They sat down cross-legged on the floor, and Marvyn produced the grimy book of paper matches that he always carried with him, in case of firecrackers. Following his directions Angie placed all the crumbly herbs into Milady's dish, and her brother lit them. Or tried to: they didn't blaze up, but smoked and smoldered and smelled like old dust, setting both Angie and Marvyn sneezing almost immediately. Angie coughed and asked, "Did that happen the other time?" Marvyn did not answer.

There was a moment when she thought the charm might actually be going to work. The room around them grew blurry — slightly blurry, granted — and Angie heard indistinct faraway sounds that might have been themselves hurtling forward to sheltering Sunday. But when the fumes of Marvyn's herbs cleared away, they were still sitting in Thursday — they both knew it without saying a word. Angie said, "Okay, so much for that. What about all that special concentration you were telling me about? You think maybe your mind wandered? You pronounce any spells the wrong way? Think, Marvyn!"

"I am thinking! I told you forward was hard!" Marvyn looked ready to start crying again, but he didn't. He said slowly, "Something's wrong, but it's not me. I don't think it's me. Something's *pushing*...." He brightened suddenly. "Maybe we should hold hands or something. Because of there being two of us this time. We could try that."

So they tried the spell that way, and then they tried working it inside a pentagram they made with masking tape on the floor, as Angie had seen such things done on *Buffy the Vampire Slayer*, even though Marvyn said that didn't really mean anything, and they tried the herbs again, in a special order that Marvyn thought he remembered. They even tried it with Angie saying the spell, after Marvyn had coached her, just on the chance that his voice itself might have been throwing off the pitch or the pronunciation. Nothing helped.

Marvyn gave up before Angie did. Suddenly, while she was trying the spell over herself, one more time — some of the words seemed to heat up in her mouth as she spoke them — he collapsed into a wretched ball of desolation on the floor, moaning over and over, "We're finished, it's finished, we'll never get out of Thursday!" Angie understood that he was only a terrified little boy, but she was frightened too, and it would have relieved her to slap him and scream at him. Instead, she tried as best she could to reassure him, saying, "He'll come back for us. He has to."

Her brother sat up, knuckles to his eyes. "No, he doesn't have to! Don't you understand? He knows I'm a witch like him, and he's just going to leave me here, out of his way. I'm sorry, Angie, I'm really sorry!" Angie had almost never heard that word from Marvyn, and never twice in the same sentence.

"Later for all that," she said. "I was just wondering — do you think we could get Mom and Dad's attention when they get home? You think they'd realize what's happened to us?"

Marvyn shook his head. "You haven't seen me all the time I've been gone. I saw you, and I screamed and hollered and everything, but you never knew. They won't either. We're not really in our house — we're just here. We'll always be here."

Angie meant to laugh confidently, to give them both courage, but it came out more of a hiccupy snort. "Oh, no. No way. There is no way I'm spending the rest of my life trapped in your stupid bedroom. We're going to try this useless mess one more time, and then...then I'll do something else." Marvyn seemed about to ask her what else she could try, but he checked himself, which was good.

They attempted the spell more than one more time. They tried it in every style they could think of except standing on their heads and reciting the words backward, and they might just as well have done that, for all the effect it had. Whether Marvyn's herbs had truly lost all potency, or whether Marvyn had simply forgotten some vital phrase, they could not even recapture the fragile awareness of something almost happening that they had both felt on the first trial. Again and again they opened their eyes to last Thursday.

"Okay," Angie said at last. She stood up, to stretch cramped legs, and began to wander around the room, twisting a couple of the useless herbs between her fingers. "Okay," she said again, coming to a halt midway between the bedroom door and the window, facing Marvyn's small bureau. A leg of his red Dr. Seuss pajamas was hanging out of one of the drawers.

"Okay," she said a third time. "Let's go home."

Marvyn had fallen into a kind of fetal position, sitting up but with his arms tight around his knees and his head down hard on them. He did not look up at her words. Angie raised her voice. "Let's go, Marvyn. That hallway — tunnel-thing, whatever it is — it comes out right about where I'm standing. That's where *El Viejo* brought me, and that's the way he left when he...left. That's the way back to Sunday."

"It doesn't matter," Marvyn whimpered. "*El Viejo*...he's him! He's *him!*"

Angie promptly lost what little remained of her patience. She stalked over to Marvyn and shook him to his feet, dragging him to a spot in the air as though she were pointing out a painting in a gallery. "And you're Marvyn Luke, and you're the big bad new witch in town! You said it yourself — if you weren't, he'd never have bothered sticking you away here. Not even nine, and you can eat his lunch, and he knows it! Straighten your patch and take us home, bro." She nudged him playfully. "Oh, forgive me — I meant to say, O Mighty One."

"You don't have to call me that anymore." Marvyn's legs could barely hold him up, and he sagged against her, a dead weight of despair. "I can't, Angie. I can't get us home. I'm sorry...."

The good thing — and Angie knew it then — would have been to turn and comfort him: to take his cold, wet face between her hands and tell him that all would yet be well, that they would soon be eating popcorn with far too much butter on it in his real room in their real house. But she was near her own limit, and pretending calm courage for his sake was prodding her, in spite of herself, closer to the edge. Without looking at Marvyn, she snapped, "Well, I'm not about to die in last Thursday! I'm walking out of here the same way he did, and you can come with me or not, that's up to you. But I'll tell you one thing, Ex-Lax — I won't be looking back."

And she stepped forward, walking briskly toward the dangling Dr. Seuss pajamas...

...and into a thick, sweet-smelling grayness that instantly filled her eyes and mouth, her nose and her ears, disorienting her so completely that she flailed her arms madly, all sense of direction lost, with no idea of which way she might be headed; drowning in syrup like a trapped bee or butterfly. Once she thought she heard Marvyn's voice, and called out for him — "I'm here, I'm here!" But she did not hear him again.

Then, between one lunge for air and another, the grayness was gone, leaving not so much as a dampness on her skin, nor even a sickly after-taste of sugar in her mouth. She was back in the time-tunnel, as she had come to think of it, recognizing the uniquely dank odor: a little like the ashes of a long-dead fire, and a little like what she imagined moonlight might smell like, if it had a smell. The image was an ironic one, for she could see no more than she had when *El Viejo* was lugging her the other way under his arm. She could not even distinguish the ground under her feet; she knew only that it felt more like slippery stone than anything else, and she was careful to keep her footing as she plodded steadily for-ward.

The darkness was absolute — strange solace, in a way, since she could imagine Marvyn walking close behind her, even though he never answered her, no matter how often or how frantically she called his name. She moved along slowly, forcing her way through the clinging murk, vaguely conscious, as before, of a distant, flickering sense of sound and motion on every side of her. If there were walls to the time-tunnel, she could not touch them; if it had a roof, no air currents betrayed it; if there were any living creature in it besides herself, she felt no sign. And if time actually passed there, Angie could never have said. She moved along, her eyes closed, her mind empty, except for the formless fear that she was not moving at all, but merely raising and setting down her feet in the same place, endlessly. She wondered if she was hungry.

Not until she opened her eyes in a different darkness to the crowing of a rooster and a familiar heavy aroma did she realize that she was walking down the hallway leading from the *Santería* shop to...wherever she had really been — and where Marvyn still must be, for he plainly had not fol-lowed her. She promptly turned and started back toward last Thursday, but halted at the deep, slightly grating chuckle behind her. She did not turn again, but stood very still.

El Viejo walked a slow full circle around her before he faced her, grin-ning down at her like the man in the moon. The dark glasses were off, and the twin scars on his cheeks were blazing up as though they had been slashed into him a moment before. He said, "I know. Before even I see you, I know."

Angie hit him in the stomach as hard as she could. It was like punching a frozen slab of beef, and she gasped in pain, instantly certain that she had broken her hand. But she hit him again, and again, screaming at the top of her voice, "Bring my brother back! If you don't bring him right back here, right now, I'll kill you! I will!"

El Viejo caught her hands, surprisingly gently, still laughing to himself. "Little girl, listen, listen now. *Niñita*, nobody else — nobody — ever do what you do. You understand? Nobody but me ever walk that road back from where I leave you, understand?" The big white half-circles under his eyes were stretching and curling like live things.

Angie pulled away from him with all her strength, as she had hit him. She said, "No. That's Marvyn. Marvyn's the witch, the *brujo* — don't go telling people it's me. Marvyn's the one with the power."

"Him?" Angie had never heard such monumental scorn packed into one syllable. *El Viejo* said, "Your brother nothing, nobody, we no bother with him. Forget him — you the one got the *regalo*, you just don't know." The big white teeth filled her vision; she saw nothing else. "I show you — me, *El Viejo*. I show you what you are."

It was beyond praise, beyond flattery. For all her dread and dislike of *El Viejo*, to have someone of his wicked wisdom tell her that she was like him in some awful, splendid way made Angie shiver in her heart. She wanted to turn away more than she had ever wanted anything — even Jake Petrakis — but the long walk home to Sunday was easier than breaking the clench of the white-haired man's malevolent presence would have been. Having often felt (and almost as often dismissed the notion) that Marvyn was special in the family by virtue of being the baby, and a boy — and now a potent witch — she let herself revel in the thought that the real gift was hers, not his, and that if she chose she had only to stretch out her hand to have her command settle home in it. It was at once the most frightening and the most purely, completely gratifying feeling she had ever known.

But it was not tempting. Angie knew the difference.

"Forget it," she said. "Forget it, buster. You've got nothing to show me."

El Viejo did not answer her. The old, old eyes that were all pupil continued slipping over her like hands, and Angie went on glaring back with the brown eyes she despaired of because they could never be as deep-set and deep green as her mother's eyes. They stood so — for how long, she never knew — until *El Viejo* turned and opened his mouth as though to speak to the silent old lady whose own stone eyes seemed not to have blinked since Angie had first entered the *Santería* shop, a childhood ago. Whatever he meant to say, he never got the words out, because Marvyn came back then.

He came down the dark hall from a long way off, as *El Viejo* had done the first time she saw him — as she herself had trudged forever, only moments ago. But Marvyn had come a further journey: Angie could see that beyond doubt in the way he stumbled along, looking like a shadow casting a person. He was struggling to carry something in his arms, but she could not make out what it was. As long as she watched him approaching, he seemed hardly to draw any nearer.

Whatever he held looked too heavy for a small boy: it threatened constantly to slip from his hands, and he kept shifting it from one shoulder to the other, and back again. Before Angie could see it clearly, *El Viejo* screamed, and she knew on the instant that she would never hear a more terrible sound in her life. He might have been being skinned alive, or having his soul torn out of his body — she never even tried to tell herself what it was like, because there were no words. Nor did she tell anyone that she fell down at the sound, fell flat down on her hands and knees, and rocked and whimpered until the scream stopped. It went on for a long time.

When it finally stopped, *El Viejo* was gone, and Marvyn was standing beside her with a baby in his arms. It was black and immediately endearing, with big, bright, strikingly watchful eyes. Angie looked into them once, and looked quickly away.

Marvyn looked worn and exhausted. His eyepatch was gone, and the left eye that Angie had not seen for months was as bloodshot as though he had just come off a three-day drunk — though she noticed that it was not wandering at all. He said in a small, dazed voice, "I had to go back a really long way, Angie. Really long."

Angie wanted to hold him, but she was afraid of the baby. Marvyn looked toward the old woman in the corner and sighed; then hitched up his burden one more time and clumped over to her. He said, "Ma'am, I think this is yours?" Adults always commented on Marvyn's excellent manners.

The old woman moved then, for the first time. She moved like a wave,

Angie thought: a wave seen from a cliff or an airplane, crawling along so slowly that it seemed impossible for it ever to break, ever to reach the shore. But the sea was in that motion, all of it caught up in that one wave; and when she set down her pipe, took the baby from Marvyn and smiled, that was the wave too. She looked down at the baby, and said one word, which Angie did not catch. Then Angie had her brother by the arm, and they were out of the shop. Marvyn never looked back, but Angie did, in time to see the old woman baring blue gums in soundless laughter.

All the way home in a taxi, Angie prayed silently that her parents hadn't returned yet. Lidia was waiting, and together they whisked Marvyn into bed without any serious protest. Lidia washed his face with a rough cloth, and then slapped him and shouted at him in Spanish — Angie learned a few words she couldn't wait to use — and then she kissed him and left, and Angie brought him a pitcher of orange juice and a whole plate of gingersnaps, and sat on the bed and said, "What happened?"

Marvyn was already working on the cookies as though he hadn't eaten in days — which, in a sense, was quite true. He asked, with his mouth full, "What's *malcriado* mean?"

"What? Oh. Like badly raised, badly brought up — troublemaking kid. About the only thing Lidia didn't call you. Why?"

"Well, that's what that lady called...him. The baby."

"Right," Angie said. "Leave me a couple of those, and tell me how he got to be a baby. You did like with Milady?"

"Uh-huh. Only I had to go way, way, way back, like I told you." Marvyn's voice took on the faraway sound it had had in the *Santería* shop. "Angie, he's so old."

Angie said nothing. Marvyn said in a whisper, "I couldn't follow you, Angie. I was scared."

"Forget it," she answered. She had meant to be soothing, but the words burst out of her. "If you just hadn't had to show off, if you'd gotten that letter back some simple, ordinary way —" Her entire chest froze solid at the word. "The letter! We forgot all about my stupid letter!" She leaned forward and snatched the plate of cookies away from Marvyn. "Did you forget? You forgot, didn't you?" She was shaking as had not happened even when *El Viejo* had hold of her. "Oh, God, after all that!"

But Marvyn was smiling for the first time in a very long while. "Calm down, be cool — I've got it here." He dug her letter to Jake Petrakis —

more than a little grimy by now — out of his back pocket and held it out to Angie. "There. Don't say I never did nuttin' for you." It was a favorite phrase of his, gleaned from a television show, and most often employed when he had fed Milady, washed his breakfast dish, or folded his clothes. "Take it, open it up," he said now. "Make sure it's the right one."

"I don't need to," Angie protested irritably. "It's my letter — believe me, I know it when I see it." But she opened the envelope anyway and with-drew a single folded sheet of paper, which she glanced at...then *stared* at, in absolute disbelief.

She handed the sheet to Marvyn. It was empty on both sides.

"Well, you did your job all right," she said, mildly enough, to her stunned, slack-jawed brother. "No question about that. I'm just trying to figure out why we had to go through this whole incredible hooha for a blank sheet of paper."

Marvyn actually shrank away from her in the bed.

"I didn't do it, Angie! I swear!" Marvyn scrambled to his feet, stand-ing up on the bed with his hands raised, as though to ward her off in case she attacked him. "I just grabbed it out of your backpack — I never even looked at it."

"And what, I wrote the whole thing in grapefruit juice, so nobody could read it unless you held it over a lamp or something? Come on, it doesn't matter now. Get your feet off your damn pillow and sit down."

Marvyn obeyed warily, crouching rather than sitting next to her on the edge of the bed. They were silent together for a little while before he said, "You did that. With the letter. You wanted it not written so much, it just *wasn't.* That's what happened."

"Oh, right," she said. "Me being the dynamite witch around here. I told you, it doesn't matter."

"It matters." She had grown so unused to seeing a two-eyed Marvyn that his expression seemed more than doubly earnest to her just then. He said, quite quietly, "You are the dynamite witch, Angie. He was after you, not me."

This time she did not answer him. Marvyn said, "I was the bait. I do garbage bags and clarinets — okay, and I make ugly dolls walk around. What's he care about that? But he knew you'd come after me, so he held me there — back there in Thursday — until he could grab you. Only he didn't figure you could walk all the way home on your own, without any spells or anything. I know that's how it happened, Angie! That's how I know you're the real witch."

"No," she said, raising her voice now. "No, I was just pissed-off, that's different. Never underestimate the power of a pissed-off woman, O Mighty One. But you...you went all the way back, on *your* own, and you grabbed *him*. You're going to be *way* stronger and better than he is, and he knows it. He just figured he'd get rid of the competition early on, while he had the chance. Not a generous guy, *El Viejo*."

Marvyn's chubby face turned gray. "But I'm *not* like him! I don't want to be like him!" Both eyes suddenly filled with tears, and he clung to his sister as he had not done since his return. "It was horrible, Angie, it was so horrible. You were gone, and I was all alone, and I didn't know what to do, only I had to do *something*. And I remembered Milady, and I figured if he wasn't letting me come forward I'd go the other way, and I was so scared and mad I just walked and walked and walked in the dark, until I...." He was crying so hard that Angie could hardly make the words out. "I don't want to be a witch anymore, Angie, I don't *want* to! And I don't want *you* being a witch either...."

Angie held him and rocked him, as she had loved doing when he was three or four years old, and the cookies got scattered all over the bed. "It's all right," she told him, with one ear listening for their parents' car pulling into the garage. "*Shh, shh*, it's all right, it's over, we're safe, it's okay, *shh*. It's okay, we're not going to be witches, neither one of us." She laid him down and pulled the covers back over him. "You go to sleep now."

Marvyn looked up at her, and then at the wizards' wall beyond her shoulder. "I might take some of those down," he mumbled. "Maybe put some soccer players up for a while. The Brazilian team's really good." He was just beginning to doze off in her arms, when suddenly he sat up again and said, "Angie? The baby?"

"What about the baby? I thought he made a beautiful baby, *El Viejo*. Mad as hell, but lovable."

"It was bigger when we left," Marvyn said. Angie stared at him. "I looked back at it in that lady's lap, and it was already bigger than when I was carrying it. He's starting over, Angie, like Milady."

"Better him than me," Angie said. "I hope he gets a kid brother this time, he's got it coming." She heard the car, and then the sound of a key in the lock. She said, "Go to sleep, don't worry about it. After what we've been through, we can handle anything. The two of us. And without witchcraft. Whichever one of us it is — no witch stuff."

Marvyn smiled drowsily. "Unless we really, *really* need it." Angie held out her hand and they slapped palms in formal agreement. She looked down at her fingers and said, "*Ick!* Blow your *nose!*"

But Marvyn was asleep.

Quarry

This story was born of my inability to stay away from the world I created as the back-drop for my personal favorite among my novels, *The Innkeeper's Song*. The immediate provocation came during a phone conversation, when the party of the second part asked me just how two of the characters from that novel — the wandering mercenary Soukyan and his shapeshifting fox companion — ever met. I had absolutely no idea, so I wrote "Quarry" to find out.

I NEVER WENT BACK to my room that night. I knew I had an hour at most before they would have guards on the door. What was on my back, at my belt, and in my pockets was all I took — that, and all the *tilgit* the cook could scrape together and cram into my pouch. We had been friends since the day I arrived at *that place*, a scrawny, stubborn child, ready to die rather than ever admit my terror and my pain. "So," she said, as I burst into her kitchen. "Running you came to me, twenty years gone, blood all over you, and running you leave. Tell me nothing, just drink this." I have no idea what was in that bottle she fetched from under her skirts and made me empty on the spot, but it kept me warm on my way all that night, and the *tilgit* — disgusting dried marshweed as it is — lasted me three days.

Looking back, I shiver to think how little I understood, not only the peril I was in, but the true extent of the power I fled. I did know better than to make for Sumildene, where a stranger stands out like a sailor in a convent; but if I had had the brains of a bedbug, I'd never have tried to cut through the marshes toward the Queen's Road. In the first place, that grand highway is laced with toll bridges, manned by toll collectors, every four or five miles; in the second, the Queen's Road is so well-banked and pruned and well-maintained that should you be caught out there by day-light, there's no cover, nowhere to run — no rutted smuggler's alley to duck into, not so much as a proper tree to climb. But I didn't know that then, among other things.

What I did understand, beyond doubt, was that they could not afford to let me leave. I do not say *escape*, because they would never have thought of it in such a way. To their minds, they had offered me their greatest honor, never before granted one so young, and I had not only rejected it, but lied in their clever, clever faces, accepting so humbly, falteringly telling them again and again of my bewildered gratitude, unworthy peasant that I was. And even then I did know that they were not deceived for a single moment, and they knew I knew, and blessed me, one after the other, to let me know. I dream that twilight chamber still — the tall chairs, the cold stone table, the tiny green *tintan* birds murmuring themselves to sleep in the vines outside the window, those smiling, wise, gentle eyes on me — and each time I wake between sweated sheets, my mouth wrenched with pleas for my life. Old as I am, and still.

If I were to leave, and it became known that I had done so, and without any retribution, others would go too, in time. Not very many — there were as yet only a few who shared my disquiet and my growing suspicions — but even one unpunished deserter was more than they could afford to tolerate.

I had no doubt at all that they would grieve my death. They were not unkind people, for monsters.

The cook hid me in the scullery, covering me with aprons and dishrags. It was not yet full dark when I left, but she felt it risky for me to wait longer. When we said farewell, she shoved one of her paring knives into my belt, gave me a swift, light buffet on the ear, said, "So. On your way then," pushed me out of a hidden half-door into the dusk, and slapped it shut behind me. I felt lonelier in that moment, blinking around me with the crickets chirping and the breeze turning chill, and that great house filling half the evening sky, than I ever have again.

As I say, I made straight for the marshes, not only meaning to strike the Queen's Road, but confident that the boggy ground would hide my footprints. It might indeed have concealed them from the eyes of ordinary trackers, but not from those who were after me within another hour. I knew little of them, the Hunters, though over twenty years I had occasionally heard this whisper or that behind this or that slightly trembling hand. Just once, not long after I came to *that place*, I was sent to the woods to gather kindling, and there I did glimpse two small brown-clad persons in a tree. They must have seen me, but they moved neither foot nor finger, nor turned their heads, but kept sitting there like a pair of dull brown birds, half-curled, half-crouched, gazing back toward the great house, waiting for something, waiting for someone. I never saw them again, nor any like them; not until they came for me.

Not those two, of course — or maybe they were the same ones; it is hard to be sure of any Hunter's age or face or identity. For all I know, they do not truly exist most of the time, but bide in their nowhere until *that place* summons them into being to pursue some runaway like me. What I do know, better than most, is that they never give up. You have to kill them.

I had killed once before — in my ignorance, I supposed the cook was the only one who knew — but I had no skill in it, and no weapon with me but the cook's little knife: nothing to daunt those who now followed. I knew the small start I had was meaningless, and I went plunging through the marshes, increasingly indifferent to how much noise I made, or to the animals and undergrowth I disturbed. Strong I was, yes, and swift enough, but also brainless with panic and hamstrung by inexperience. A child could have tracked me, let alone a Hunter.

That I was not taken that first night had nothing to do with any craft or wiliness of mine. What happened was that I slipped on a straggling *tilgit* frond (wild, the stuff is as slimy-slick as any snail-road), took a shattering tumble down a slope I never saw, and finished by cracking my head open against a mossy, jagged rock. Amazingly, I did not lose consciousness then, but managed to crawl off into a sort of shallow half-burrow at the base of the hill. There I scraped every bit of rotting vegetation within reach over myself, having a dazed notion of smothering my scent. I vaguely recall packing handfuls of leaves and spiderwebs against my bleeding wound, and making some sort of effort to cover the betraying stains, before I fainted away.

I woke in the late afternoon of the next day, frantically hungry, but so weak and sick that I could not manage so much as a mouthful of the *tilgit*. The bleeding had stopped — though I dared not remove my ragged, mushy poultice for another full day — and after a time I was able to stand up and stay on my feet, just barely. I lurched from my earthen shroud and stood for some while, lightheaded yet, but steadily more lucid, sniffing and staring for any sign of my shadows. Not that I was in the best shape to spy them out — giddy as I was, they could likely have walked straight up to me and disemboweled me with their empty hands, as they can do. But they were nowhere to be seen or sensed.

I drank from a mucky trickle I found slipping by under the leaves, then grubbed my way back into my poor nest again and slept until nightfall. For all my panicky blundering, I knew by the stars that I was headed in the general direction of the Queen's Road, which I continued to believe meant sanctuary and the start of my new and blessedly ordinary life among ordinary folk.

I covered more distance than I expected that night, for all my lingering faintness and my new prudence, trying now to make as little noise as possible, and leave as little trace of my passage. I met no one, and when I went to ground at dawn in a riverbank cave — some *sheknath*'s winter lair, by the smell of it — there was still no more indication of anyone trailing me than there had been since I began my flight. But I was not fool enough to suppose myself clear of pursuit, not quite. I merely hoped, which was just as bad.

The Queen's Road was further away than I had supposed: for all the terrible and tempting knowledge that I and others like me acquired in *that place*, practical geography was unheard of. I kept moving, trailing after the hard stars through the marshes as intently as the Hunters were surely trailing me. More than once, the bog sucked both shoes off my feet, taking them down so deeply that I would waste a good half-hour fishing for them; again and again, a sudden screen of burly *jukli* vines or some sticky nameless creepers barred my passage, so I must either lower my head and bull on through, or else blunder somehow around the obstacle and pray not to lose the way, which I most often did.

Nearing dawn of the fourth day, I heard the rumble of cartwheels, like a faraway storm, and the piercing squawk, unmistakable, of their *pashidi* drivers' clan-whistles along with them, and realized that I was nearing the Queen's Road.

If the Hunters were following as closely as I feared, was this to be the end of the game — were they poised to cut me down as I raced wildly, recklessly, toward imaginary safety? Did they expect me to abandon all caution and charge forward into daylight and the open, whooping with joy and triumph? They had excellent reason to do so, as idiotic a tar-

get as I must have made for them a dozen times over. But even idiots —
even terrified young idiots — may learn one or two things in four days of
being pursued through a quagmire by silent, invisible hounds. I waited
that day out under a leech-bush: few trackers will ever investigate one of
those closely; and if you lie *very* still, there is a fairish chance that the ser-
rated, brittle-seeming leaves will not come seeking your blood. At moon-
set I started on.

Just as the ground began to feel somewhat more solid, just as the first
lights of the Queen's Road began to glimmer through the thinning vegetation...there they were, there they were, both of them, each standing away
at an angle, making me the third point of a murderous triangle. They simply *appeared* — can you understand? — assembling themselves out of the
marsh dawn: weaponless both, their arms hanging at their sides, loose
and unthreatening. One was smiling; one was not — there was no other
way to tell them apart. In the dimness, I saw laughter in their eyes, and a
weariness such as even I have never imagined, and death.

They let me by. They turned their backs to me and let me pass, fading
so completely into the gray sunrise that I was almost willing to believe
them visions, savage mirages born of my own fear and exhaustion. But
with that combination came a weary understanding of my own. They
were playing with me, taking pleasure in allowing me to run loose for
a bit, but letting me know that whenever they tired of the game I was
theirs, in the dark marshes or on the wide white highway, and not a thing
I could do about it. At my age, I am entitled to forget what I forget — terror and triumph alike, grief and the wildest joy alike — and so I have, and
well rid of every one of them I am. But that instant, that particular rec-
ognition, remains indelible. Some memories do come to live with you for
good and all, like wives or husbands.

I went forward. There was nothing else to do. The marshes fell away
around me, rapidly giving place to nondescript country, half-ragged, halfway domesticated to give a sort of shoulder to the road. Farmers were
already opening their fruit and vegetable stands along that border; mer-
chants' boys from towns further along were bawling their employers'
wares to the carters and wagoners; and as I stumbled up, a *shukri*-trainer
passed in front of me, holding his arms out, like a scarecrow, for folk to
see his sharp-toothed pets scurrying up and down his body, and more
of them pouring from each pocket as he strode along. Ragged, scabbed

and filthy as I was, not one traveler turned his head as I slipped onto the Queen's Road.

On the one hand, I blessed their unconcern; on the other, that same indifference told me clearly that none of them would raise a finger if they saw me taken, snatched back before their eyes to *that place* and whatever doom might await me there. Only the collectors at their tollgates might be at all likely to mourn the fate of a potential contributor — and I had nothing for them anyway, which was going to be another problem in a couple of miles. But right then was problem enough for me: friendless on a strange road, utterly vulnerable, utterly without resources, flying — well, trudging — from the only home I had known since the age of nine, and from the small, satisfied assassins it had sent after me. And out of *tilgit* as well.

The Queen's Road runs straight all the way from Bitava to Fors na' Shachim, but in those days there was a curious sort of elbow: unleveled, anciently furrowed, a last untamed remnant of the original wagon-road, beginning just before the first tollgate I was to reach. I could see it from a good distance, and made up my mind to dodge away onto it — without any notion of where the path might come out, but with some mad fancy of at once eluding both the killers and the collectors. Sometimes, in those nights when the dreams and memories I cannot always tell apart anymore keep me awake, I try to imagine what my life would have been if I had actually carried my plan through. Different, most likely. Shorter, surely.

Even this early, the road was steadily growing more crowded with traffic, wheeled and afoot, slowing my pace to that of my closest neighbor — which, in this case, happened to be a bullock-cart loaded higher than my head with *jejebhai* manure. Absolutely the only thing the creatures are good for; we had a pair on the farm where I was a boy — if I ever was, if any of that ever happened. Ignoring the smell, I kept as close to the cart as I could, hoping that it would hide me from the toll-collectors' sight when I struck off onto that odd little bend. My legs were tensing for the first swift, desperate stride, when I heard the voice at my ear, saying only one word, "*No.*"

A slightly muffled voice, but distinctive — there was a sharpness to it, and a hint of a strange cold amusement, all in a single word. I whirled, saw nothing but the manure cart, determined that I had misheard a driver's grunt, or even a wheel-squeak, and set myself a second time to make my move.

Once again the voice, more insistent now, almost a bark: "*No,* fool!"

It was not the driver; he never looked at me. I was being addressed — commanded — by the manure pile.

It shifted slightly as I gaped, and I saw the eyes then. They were gray and very bright, with a suggestion of pale yellow far under the grayness. All I could make out of the face in which they were set was a thick white mustache below and brows nearly as heavy above. The man — for it was a human face, I was practically sure — was burrowed as deeply into the *jejebhai* dung as though he were lolling under the most luxurious of quilts and bolsters on a winter's night. He beckoned me to join him.

I stopped where I was, letting the cart jolt past me. The sharp voice from the manure was clearer this time, and that much more annoyed with me. "Boy, if you have any visions of a life beyond the next five minutes, you will do as I tell you. *Now.*" The last word was no louder than the others, but it brought me scrambling into that cartload of muck faster than ever I have since lunged into a warm bed, with a woman waiting. The man made room for me with a low, harsh chuckle.

"Lie still, so," he told me. "Lie still, make no smallest row, and we will pass the gate like royalty. And those who follow will watch you pass, and never take your scent. Thank me later —" I had opened my mouth to speak, but he put a rough palm over it, shaking his white head. "Down, down," he whispered, and to my disgust he pushed himself even further into the manure pile, all but vanishing into the darkness and the stench. And I did the same.

He saved my life, in every likelihood, for we left that gate and half a dozen like it behind as we continued our malodorous excursion, while the driver, all unwitting, paid our toll each time. Only with the last barrier safely past did we slide from the cart, tumble to the roadside and such cover as there was, and rise to face each other in daylight. We reeked beyond the telling of it — in honesty, almost beyond the smelling of it, so inured to the odor had our nostrils become. We stank beyond anything but laughter, and that was what we did then, grimacing and howling and falling down on the dry grass, pointing helplessly at each other and going off again into great, ridiculous whoops of mirth and relief, until we wore ourselves out and could barely breathe, let alone laugh. The old man's laughter was as shrill and cold as the mating cries of *shukris*, but it was laughter even so.

He was old indeed, now I saw him in daylight, even under a crust of filth and all that still stuck to the filth — straw, twigs, dead spiders, bullock-hair. His own hair and brows were as white as his mustache, and the gray eyes streaked with rheum; yet his cheeks were absurdly pink, like a young girl's cheeks, and he carried himself as straight as any young man. Young as I was myself, and unwise as I was, when I first looked into his eyes, I already knew far better than to trust him. And nonetheless, knowing, I wanted to. He can do that.

"I think we bathe," he said to me. "Before anything else, I do think we bathe."

"I think so too," I said. "Yes." He jerked his white head, and we walked away from the Queen's Road, off back into the wild woods.

"I am Soukyan," I offered, but to that he made no response. He clearly knew the country, for he led me directly to a fast-flowing stream, and then to a pool lower down, where the water gathered and swirled. We cleaned ourselves there, though it took us a long time, so mucky we were; and afterward, naked-new as raw carrots, we lay in the sun and talked for a while. I told truth, for the most part, leaving out only some minor details of *that place* — things I had good reason not to think about just then — and he...ah, well, what he told me of his life, of how he came to hail me from that dungheap, was such a stew of lies and the odd honesty that I've never studied out the right of it yet, no more than I have ever learned his own name. The truth is not in him, and I would be dearly disappointed if it should show its poor face now. He was there — leave it at that. He was there at the particular moment when I needed a friend, however fraudulent. It has happened so since.

"So," he said at last, stretching himself in the sun. "And what's to be done with you now?" — for all the world as though he had all the disposing of me and my future. "If you fancy that your followers have forsaken you, merely because we once stank our way past them, I'd greatly enjoy to have the writing of your will. They will run behind you until you die — they will never return to their masters without you, or whatever's left of you. On that you have my word."

"I know that well enough," said I, trying my best to appear as knowledgeable as he. "But perhaps I am not to be taken so easily." The old man snorted with as much contempt as I have ever heard in a single exhalation of breath, and rolled to his feet, deceptively, alarmingly graceful. He crouched naked on his haunches, facing me, studying me, smiling with pointed teeth.

"Without me, you die," he said, quite quietly. "You know it and I know it. Say it back to me." I only stared, and he snapped, "*Say it back.* Without me?"

And I said it, because I knew it was true. "Without you, I would be dead." The old man nodded approvingly. The yellow glint was stronger in the gray eyes.

"Now," he said. "I have my own purposes, my own small annoyance to manage. I could deal with it myself, as I've done many a time — never think otherwise — but it suits me to share roads with you for a little. It suits me." He was studying me as closely as I have ever been considered, even by those at *that place*, and I could not guess what he saw. "It suits me," he said for a third time. "We may yet prove of some use to each other."

"We may, or we may not," I said, more than a bit sharply, for I was annoyed at the condescension in his glance. "I may seem a gormless boy to you, but I know this country, and I know how to handle myself." The first claim was a lie; of the second, all I can say is that I believed it then. I went on, probably more belligerent for my fear: "Indeed, I may well owe you my life, and I will repay you as I can, my word on it. But as to whether we should ally ourselves...sir, I hope only to put the width of the world between myself and those who seek me — I have no plans beyond that. Of what your own plans, your own desires may be, you will have to inform me, for I have no notion at all."

He seemed to approve my boldness; at any rate, he laughed that short, yapping laugh of his and said, "For the moment, my plans run with yours. We're dried enough — dress yourself, so, and we'll be off and gone while our little friends are still puzzling over how we could have slipped their grasp. They'll riddle it out quickly enough, but we'll have the heels of them a while yet." And I could not help finding comfort in noticing that "your followers" had now become "our little friends."

So we ourselves were allies of a sort, united by common interests, whatever they were. Having no goal, nor any vision of a life beyond flight, I had no real choice but to go where he led, since on my own the only question would have been whether I should be caught before I stumbled into a swamp and got eaten by a *lourijakh*. For all his age, he marched along with an air of absolute serenity, no matter if we were beating our way through some near-impenetrable thornwood or crossing high barrens in the deepest night. Wherever he was bound — which was only one of the things he did not share with me — we encountered few other travelers on our way to it. An old lone wizard making his *lamisetha*; a couple of deserters from someone's army, who wanted to sell us their uniforms; a little band of prospectors, too busy quarreling over the exact location of a legendary hidden *drast* mine to pay overmuch attention to us. I think there was a water witch as well, but at this reach it is hard to be entirely sure.

By now I would not have trusted my woodcraft for half a minute, but it was obvious from our first day together that my new friend had enough of that for the pair of us. Every night, before we slept — turn and turn about, always one on watch — and every morning, before anything at all, he prowled the area in a wide, constantly shifting radius, clearly going by his nose as much as his sight and hearing. Most of the time he was out of my view, but on occasion I would hear a kind of whuffling snort, usually followed by a low, disdainful grunt. In his own time he'd come trotting jauntily up from the brushy hollow or the dry ravine, shaking his dusty white hair in the moonlight, to say, "Two weeks, near enough, and not up with us yet? Not taking advantage of my years and your inexperience to pounce on us in the dark hours and pull us apart like a couple of boiled chickens? Indeed, I begin to lose respect for our legendary entourage — as stupid as the rest, they are, after all." And what he meant by *the rest*, I could not imagine then.

Respect the Hunters or no, he never slackened our pace, nor ever grew careless in covering our tracks. We were angling eastward, into the first folds of the Skagats — the Burnt Hills, your people call them, I believe. At the time I had no name at all for them, nor for any other feature of this new landscape. For all the teachings I had absorbed at *that place*, for all the sly secret knowledge that was the true foundation of the great house, for all the wicked wisdom that I would shed even today, if I could, as a snake scours itself free of its skin against a stone…nevertheless, then I knew next to nothing of the actual world in which that knowledge moved. We were deliberately kept quite ignorant, you see, in certain ways.

He ridiculed me constantly about that. I see him still, cross-legged across the night's fire from me, jabbing out with a longnailed forefinger, demanding, "And you mean to sit there and tell me that you've never heard of the Mildasi people, or the Achali? You know the lineage, the lovers, and the true fate of every queen who ever ruled in Fors — you know the deep cause of the Fishermen's Rebellion, and what really came of it — you know the entire history of the Old Arrangement, which cannot be written — but you have absolutely no inkling where Byrnarik Bay's to be found, nor the Northern Barrens, nor can you so much as guess at the course of the Susathi. Well, you've had such an education as never was, that's all I can say. And it's worthless to us, all of it worthless, nothing but a waste of head-space, taking up room that could have been better occupied if you'd been taught to read track, steal a horse or shoot a bow. *Worthless.*"

"I can shoot a bow," I told him once. "My father taught me."

"Oh, indeed? I must remember to stand behind you when you loose off." There was a deal more of that as we journeyed on. I found it tedious most often, and sometimes hurtful; but there was a benefit, too, because he began taking it on himself to instruct me in the nature and fabric of this new world — and this new life, as well — as though I were visiting from the most foreign of far-off lands. Which, in ways even he could not have known, I was.

One thing I did understand from the first day was that he was plainly a fugitive himself, no whit different from me, for all his conceit. Why else would he have been hiding in a dung-cart, eager to commandeer the company of such a bumpkin as I? Kindly concern for my survival in a dangerous world might be part of it, but he was hardly combing our backtrail every night on my behalf. I knew that much from the way he slept — when he slept — most often on his back, his arms and legs curled close and scrabbling in the air, running and running behind his closed eyes, just as a hound will do. I knew it from the way he would cry out, not in any tongue I knew, but in strange yelps and whimpers and near-growls that seemed sometimes to border on language, so close to real words that I was sure I almost caught them, and that if he only kept on a bit longer, or if I dared bend a bit closer, I'd understand who — or what — was pursuing him through his dreams. Once he woke, and saw me there, studying him; and though his entire body tensed like a crossbow, he never moved.

The gray eyes had gone full yellow, the pupils slitted almost to invisibility. They held me until he closed them again, and I crept away to my blanket. In the morning, he made no mention of my spying on his sleep, but I never imagined that he had forgotten.

So young I was then, all that way back, and so much I knew, and he was quite right — none of it was to prove the smallest use in the world I entered on our journey. That nameless, tireless, endlessly scornful old man showed me the way to prepare and cook *aidallah*, which looks like a dungball itself, is more nourishing than *tilgit* and tastes far better, and which is poisonous if you don't strip every last bit of the inner rind. He taught me to carry my silly little knife out of sight in a secret place; he taught me how to sense a *sheknath*'s presence a good mile before winding it, and — when we were sneaking through green, steamy Taritaja country — how to avoid the mantraps those cannibal folk set for travelers. (I was on my way over the lip of two of them before he snatched me back, dancing with scorn, laughing his yap-laugh and informing me that no one would ever eat *my* brain to gain wisdom.) And, in spite of all my efforts, I cannot imagine forgetting my first introduction to the sandslugs of the Oriskany plains. There isn't a wound they can't clean out, nor an infection they can't digest; but it is not a comfortable process, and I prefer not to speak of it any further. Nevertheless, more than once I have come a very long way to find them again.

But cunning and knowing as that old man was, even he could detect no sign of the Hunters from the moment when we joined fortunes on the Queen's Road. Today I'd have the wit to be frightened more every day by their absence; but then I was for once too interested in puzzling out the cause of my companion's night terrors, and the identity of his pursuers to be much concerned with my own. And on the twentieth twilight that we shared, dropping down from the Skagats into high desert country, I finally caught sight of it for a single instant: the cause.

It stalked out of a light evening haze on long bird legs — three of them. The third appeared to be more tail than leg — the creature leaned back on it briefly, regarding us — but it definitely had long toes or claws of its own. As for the head and upper body, I had only a dazed impression of something approaching the human, and more fearsome for that. In another moment, it was gone, soundless for all its size; and the old man was up out of a doze, teeth bared, crouching to launch himself in any direction. When he turned to me, I'd no idea whether I should have seen what I had, or whether it would be wisest to feign distraction. But he never gave me the chance to choose.

I cannot say that I actually saw the change. I never do, not really. Never any more than a sort of sway in the air — you could not even call it a ripple — and there he is: there, like that first time: red-brown mask, the body a deeper red, throat and chest and tail-tip white-gold, bright yellow eyes seeing me — *me*, lost young Soukyan, always the same — seeing me truly and terribly, all the way down. Always. The fox.

One wild glare before he sprang away into the mist, and I did not see him again for a day and another night. Nor the great bird-legged thing either, though I sat up both nights, expecting its return. It was plainly seeking him, not me — whatever it might be, it was no Hunter — but what if it saw me as his partner, his henchman, as liable as he for whatever wrong it might be avenging? And what if I *had* become a shapeshifter's partner, unaware? Not all alliances are written, or spoken, or signed. Oh, I had no trouble staying awake those two nights. I thought it quite likely that I might never sleep again.

Or eat again, either, come to that. As I have told you, I never went back to my room at *that place*, which meant leaving my bow there. I wished now that I had chanced fetching it: not only because I had killed a man with that bow when I was barely tall enough to aim and draw, but because without it, on my own, I was bound to go very hungry indeed. I stayed close to our camp — what point in wandering off into unknown country in search of a half-mad, half-sinister old man? — and merely waited, making do with such scraps and stores as we had, drinking from a nearby waterhole, little more than a muddy footprint. Once, in that second night, something large and silent crossed the moon; but when I challenged it there was no response, and nothing to see. I sat down again and threw more wood on my fire.

He came back in human form, almost out of nowhere, but not quite — I never saw that change, either, but I did see, far behind him, coming around a thicket beyond the waterhole, the two sets of footprints, man and animal, and the exact place where one supplanted the other. Plainly, he did not care whether I saw it or not. He sat down across from me, as always, took a quick glance at our depleted larder, and said irritably, "You ate every last one of the *sushal* eggs. Greedy."

"Yes. I did." Formal, careful, both of us, just as though we had never shared a dung-cart. We stared at each other in silence for some while, and then I asked him, most politely, "What are you?"

"What I need to be," he answered. "Now this, now that, as necessary. As are we all."

I was surprised by my own sudden fury at his blandly philosophical air. "We do not *all* turn into foxes," I said. "We do not *all* abandon our friends —" I remember that I hesitated over the word, but then came out with it strongly — "leaving them to face monsters alone. Nor do we *all* lie to them from sunup to sundown, as you have done to me. I have no use for you, and we have no future together. Come tomorrow, I go alone."

"Well, now, that would be an extremely foolish mistake, and most probably fatal as well." He was as calmly judicial as any human could have been, but he was *not* human, *not* human. He said, "Consider — did I not keep you from your enemies, when they were as close on your heels as your own dirty skin? Have I not counseled you well during this journey you and I have made together? That *monster*, as you call it, did you no harm — nor even properly frighted you, am I right? Say honestly." I had no fitting answer, though I opened my mouth half a dozen times, while he sat there and smiled at me. "So. Now. Sit still, and I will tell you everything you wish to know."

Which, of course, he did not.

This is what he did tell me:

"What you saw — that was no monster, but something far worse. That was a Goro." He waited only a moment for me to show that I knew the name; quite rightly not expecting this, he went on. "The Goro are the bravest, fiercest folk who walk the earth. To be killed by a Goro is considered a great honor, for they deign to slay only the bravest and fiercest of their enemies — merely to make an enemy of a Goro is an honor as well. However short-lived."

"Which is what you have done," I said, when he paused. He looked not at all guilty or ashamed, but distinctly embarrassed.

"You could say that, I suppose," he replied. "In a way. It was a mistake — I made a serious mistake, and I'm not too proud to admit it, even to you." I had never heard him sound as he did then: half-defiant, yet very nearly mumbling, like a child caught out in a lie. He said, "I stole a Goro's dream."

I looked at him. I did not laugh — I don't recall that I said anything — but he sneered at me anyway. His eyes were entirely gray now, narrow with disdain, and somewhat more angled than I had noticed before. "Mock me, then — why should you not? Your notion of dreams will have them all gossamer, all insubstantial film and gauze and wispy vapors. I tell you now that the dream of a Goro is as real and solid as your imbecile self, and each one takes solid form in our world, no matter if we recognize it or not for what it is. Understand me, fool!" He had grown notably heated, and there was a long silence between us before he spoke again.

"Understand me. Your life may well depend on it." For just that moment, the eyes were almost pleading. "It happened that I was among the Goro some time ago, traveling in...that *shape* you have seen." In all the time that we have known each other, he has never spoken the word *fox*, not to me. He said, "A Goro's dream, once dreamed, will manifest itself to us as it chooses — a grassblade or a jewel, a weed or a log of wood, who knows why? In my case...in my case — pure chance, mind you — it turned out to be a shiny stone. The *shape* likes shiny things." His voice trailed away, again a guilty child's voice.

"So you took it," I said. "Blame the shape, if you like — no matter to me — but it was you did the stealing. I may be only a fool, but I can follow you that far."

"It is not so simple!" he began angrily, but he caught himself then, and went on more calmly. "Well, well, your morality's no matter to me either. What should matter to you is that a stolen dream cries out to its begetter. No Goro will ever rest until his dream is safe home again, and the thief gathered to his ancestors in very small pieces. Most often, some of the pieces are lacking." He smiled at me.

"A grassblade?" I demanded. "A stone — a stick of wood? To pursue and kill for a discarded stick, no use to anyone? You neglected to mention that your brave, fierce Goro are also quite mad."

The old man sighed, a long and elaborately despairing sigh. "They are no more mad than yourself — a good deal less so, more than likely. And a Goro's dream is of considerable use — to a Goro, no one else. They keep them all, can you follow *that*? A Goro will hoard every physical manifestation of every dream he dreams in his life, even if at the end it seems only to amount to a heap of dead twigs and dried flower petals. Because he is bound to present the whole unsightly clutter to his gods, when he goes to them. And if even one is missing — one single feather, candle-end, teacup, seashell fragment — then the Goro will suffer bitterly after death. So they believe, and they take poorly to having it named nonsense. Which I am very nearly sure it is."

When he was not railing directly at me, his arrogance trickled away swiftly, leaving him plainly uneasy, shapeshifter or no. I found this rather shamefully enjoyable. I said, "So. This one wants his shiny stone back, and it has called him all this way on your trail. It does seem to me —"

"That I might simply return it to him? Apologies — some small token gift, perhaps — and no harm done?" This time his short laugh sounded like a branch snapping in a storm. "Indeed, nothing would suit me better. It is only a useless pebble, as you say — the *shape* lost all interest in it long ago. Unfortunately, for such an offense against a Goro — such a sin, if you like — vengeance is required." Speaking those words silenced him again for a long moment: his eyes flicked constantly past and beyond me, and his whole body had grown so taut that I half-expected him to turn back into a fox as we sat together. For the first time in our acquaintance, I pitied him.

"Vengeance is required," he repeated presently. "It is a true sacrament among the Goro, much more than a matter of settling tribal scores. Something to do with evening all things out, restoring the proper balance of the world. Smoothing the rumples, you might say. Very philosophical, the Goro, when they have a moment." He was doing his best to appear composed, you see, though he must have known I knew better. He does that.

"All as may be," I said. "What's clear to me is that we now have two different sets of assassins to deal with, each lot unstoppable —"

"The Goro are *not* assassins," he interrupted me. "They are a civilized and honorable people, according to their lights." He was genuinely indignant.

"Splendid," I said. "Then by all means, you must stay where you are and allow yourself to be honorably slaughtered, so as to right the balance of things. For myself, I'll give them a run, in any case," and I was on my feet and groping for my belongings. Wonderful, what weeks of flight can do for a naturally mild temper.

He rose with me, nodding warningly, if such a thing can be. "Aye, we'd best be moving. I can't speak for your lot, but the day's coming on hot, and our Goro will sleep out the worst of it, if I know them at all. Pack and follow."

That brusquely — *pack and follow*. And so I did, for there was no more choice in the matter than there ever had been. The old man set a fierce pace that day, not only demanding greater speed from me than ever, but also doubling back, zigzagging like a hare with a *shukri* one jump behind; then inexplicably going to ground for half an hour at a time, absolutely motionless and silent until we abruptly started on again, with no more explanation than before. During those stretches he often slipped out of sight, each time hissing me to stillness, and I knew that he would take the fox-shape (or would it take him? which was real?) to scout back along the way we had come. But whether we were a trifle safer, or whether death was a little closer on our heels, I could never be sure. He never once said.

The country continued high desert, simmering with mirages, but there were moments in the ever-colder nights when I could smell fresh water; or perhaps I felt its presence in the water composing my own body. The old man did finally reveal that in less than a week, at our current rate, we should strike the Nai, the greatest river in this part of the country, which actually begins in the Skagats. There are always boats, he assured me — scows and barges and little schooners, going up and down with dried fish for this settlement, nails and harness for that one, a full load of lumber for the new town building back of the old port. Paying passengers were quite common on the Nai, as well as the non-paying sort — and here he winked elaborately at me, looking enough like the grandfather I still think I almost remember that I had to look away for a moment. Increasingly, as the years pass, I prefer the fox-shape.

"Not that this will lose our Goro friend," he said, "not for a moment. They're seagoing people — a river is a city street to the Goro. But they dislike rivers, exactly as a countryman dislikes the city, and the further they are from the sea, the more tense and uneasy they become. Now the Nai will take us all the way to Druchank, which is a hellpit, unless it has changed greatly since I was last there. But from Druchank it's a long, long journey to the smell of salt, yet no more than two days to..."

And here he stopped. It was not a pause for breath or memory, not an instant's halt to find words — no interruption, but an end, as though he had never intended to say more. He only looked at me, not with his usual mockery, nor with any expression that I could read. But he clearly would not speak again until I did, and I had a strong sense that I did not want to ask what I had to ask, and get an answer. I said, at last, "Two days to where?"

"To the place of our stand." The voice had no laughter in it, but no fear either. "To the place where we turn and meet them all. Yours and mine."

It was long ago, that moment. I am reasonably certain that I did not say anything bold or heroic in answer, as I can be fairly sure that I did not shame myself. Beyond that...beyond that, I can only recall a sense that all the skin of my face had suddenly grown too tight for my head. The rest is stories. *He* might remember exactly how it was, but he lies.

I do recollect his response to whatever I finally said. "Yes, it *will* come to that, and we will not be able to avoid facing them. I thought we might, but I always look circumstance in the eye." (And would try to steal both eyes, and then charge poor blind circumstance for his time, but never mind.) He said, "Your Hunters and my Goro —" no more sharing of shadows, apparently — "there's no shaking them, none of them. I would know if there were a way." I didn't doubt that. "The best we can do is to choose the ground on which we make our stand, and I have long since chosen the Mihanachakali." I blinked at him. That I remember, blinking so stupidly, nothing to say.

The Mihanachakali was deep delta once — rich, bountiful farmland, until the Nai changed course, over a century ago. The word means *black river valley* — I suppose because the Nai used to carry so much sweet silt to the region when it flooded every year or two. You wouldn't know that now, nor could I believe it at the time, trudging away from Druchank (which was just as foul a hole as he remembered, and remains so), into country grown so parched, so entirely dried out, that the soil had forgotten how to hold even the little mist that the river provided now and again. We met no one, but every turn in the road brought us past one more abandoned house, one more ruin of a shed or a byre; eventually the road became one more desiccated furrow crumbling away to the flat, pale horizon. The desert had never been anything but what it was; this waste was far wilder, far lonelier, because of the ghosts. Because of the ghosts that I could feel, even if I couldn't see them — the people who had lived here, tried to live here, who had dug in and hung on as long as they could while the earth itself turned ghost under their feet, under their splintery wooden ploughs and spades. I hated it as instinctively and deeply and sadly as I have ever hated a place on earth, but the old man tramped on without ever looking back for me. And as I stumbled after him over the cold, wrinkled land, he talked constantly to himself, so that I could not help but overhear.

"Near, near — they never move, once they...twice before, twice, and then that other time...listen for it, smell it out, find it, find it, so close...no mistake, it cannot have moved, I *will* not be mistaken, listen for it, reach for it, find it, find it, *find it!*" He crouched lower and lower as we plodded on, until he might as well have taken the fox-form, so increasingly taut, elongated and pointed had his shadow become. To me during those two days crossing the Mihanachakali, he spoke not at all.

Then, nearing sundown on the second day, he abruptly broke off the long mumbled conversation with himself. Between one stride and the next, he froze in place, one foot poised off the ground, exactly as I have seen a stalking fox do when the chosen kill suddenly raises its head and sniffs the air. "Here," he said quietly, and it seemed not so much a word but a single breath that had chosen shape on its own, like a Goro's dream. "Here," he said again. "Here it was. I remembered. I *knew*."

We had halted in what appeared to me to be the exact middle of any-where. River off *that* way, give or take; a few shriveled hills lumping up *that* way; no-color evening sky baking above...I could never have imag-ined surroundings less suitable for a gallant last stand. It wouldn't have taken a Goro and two Hunters to pick us off as we stood there with the sunset at our backs: two small, weary figures, weaponless, exposed to attack on all sides, our only possible shelter a burned-out farmhouse, nothing but four walls, a caved-in roof, a crumbling chimney, and what looked to be a root cellar. A shepherd with a sling could have potted us like sparrows.

"I knew," he repeated, looking much more like his former superior self. "Not whether it would *be* here, but that it would be *here*." It made no sense, and I told him so, and the yap-laugh sounded more elated than I had yet heard it. "Think for once, idiot! No, no — *don't* think, forget about thinking! Try remembering, try to remember something, anything you didn't learn at that bloody asylum of yours. Something your mother told you about such places — something the old people used to say, something children would whisper in their beds to frighten each other. Something even a fool just might already know — remember! Remember?"

And I did. I remembered half-finished stories of houses that were not quite...that were not there all the time...rumors, quickly hushed by parents, of house-things blooming now and then from haunted soil, springing up like mushrooms in moonlight...I remembered an uncle's absently-mumbled account of a friend, journeying, who took advantage of what appeared to be a shepherd's mountain hut and was not seen again — no more than the hut itself — and someone else's tale of bachelor cousins who settled into an empty cottage no one seemed to want, lived there comfortably enough for some years, and then...I did remember.

"Those are fables," I said. "Legends, nothing more. If you mean *that* over there, I see nothing but a gutted hovel that was most likely greatly improved by a proper fire. Let it appear, let it vanish — either way, we are both going to die. Of course, I may once again have missed something."

He could not have been more delighted. "Excellent. I must tell you, I might have felt a trifle anxious if you had actually grasped my plan." The pale yellow glow was rising in his eyes. "The true nature of that house is not important, and in any case would take too long to explain to an oaf. What matters is that if once our pursuers pass its door, they will not ever emerge again — therefore, we two must become bait and deadfall together, luring them on to disaster." Everything obviously depended on our pursuers running us to this earth at the same time; if they fell upon each other in their lust to slaughter us, so much the better, but he was plainly not counting on this. "Once we've cozened them into that corner," and he gestured toward the thing that looked so like a ruinous farm-house, "why, then, our troubles are over, and no burying to plague us, either." He kicked disdainfully at the stone-hard soil, and the laugh was far more fox than human.

I said, as calmly and carefully as I could, "This is not going to work. There are too many unknowns, too many possibilities. What if they do *not* arrive together? What if, instead of clashing, they cooperate to hunt us down? Much too likely that we will be the ones trapped in your — your *corner* — with no way out, helpless and doomed. This is absurd."

Oh, but he was furious then! Totally enraged, how he stamped back and forth, glaring at me, even his mustache crouched to spring, every white hair abristle. If he had been in the fox-shape — well, who knows? — perhaps he might indeed have leaped at my throat. "Ignorant, ignorant! *Unknowns, possibilities* — you know nothing, you are *fit* for nothing but my bidding." He stamped a few more times, and then turned to stalk away toward the farmhouse...toward the thing that looked like a farmhouse. When I made to follow, he waved me back without turning his head. "Stay!" he ordered, as you command a dog. "Keep watch, call when they come in sight. You can do that much."

"And what then?" I shouted after him, as angry as he by now. "Have you any further instructions for the help? When I call to you, what then?"

Still walking, still not looking back, he answered, "Then you run, imbecile! Toward the house — *toward*, but not *into!* Do try to remember that." On the last words, he vanished into the shadow of the farmhouse. And I...why, I took up my ridiculous guard, stolidly patrolling the dead fields in the twilight, just as though I understood what I was to expect, and exactly what I would do when it turned up. The wind was turning steadily colder, and I kept tripping on the ruts and tussocks I paced, even falling on my face once. I am almost certain that he could not have seen me.

In an hour, or two hours, the half-moon rose: the shape of a broken button, the color of a knife. I am grateful for it still; without it, I would surely never have seen the pair of them flitting across the dark toward me from different directions, dodging my glance, constantly dropping flat themselves, taking advantage of every dimness, every little swell of ground. The sight of them froze me, froze the tongue in my mouth. I could no more have cried out warning than I could have flown up to that moon by flapping my arms. They knew it, too. I could see their smiles slicing through the moonlight.

I was not altogether without defenses. They had taught us somewhat of *kuj'mai* — the north-coast style — in *that place*, and I was confident that I could take passable care of myself in most situations. But not here, not in this situation, not for a minute, not against those two. My mind wanted to run away, and my body wanted to wet and befoul itself. Somehow I did neither, no more than I made a sound.

The worst moment — my stomach remembers it exactly, if my mind blurs details — was when I suddenly realized that I had lost sight of them, moon or no. Then panic took me entirely, and I turned and fled toward the farmhouse-thing, as instructed, my eyes clenched almost shut, fully expecting to be effortlessly overtaken at any moment, as a *sheknath* drags down its victim from behind. They would be laughing — were laughing already, I knew it, even if I couldn't hear them. I could feel their laughter pulling me down.

When the first hand clutched at my neck, I did turn to fight them. I like to remember that. I did shriek in terror — yes, I admit that without shame — but only once; then I whirled in that grasp, as I had been taught, and struck out with right hand and left foot, in proper *kuj'mai* style, aiming at once to shatter a kidney and paralyze a breathing center. I connected with neither, but found myself dangling in the air, screaming defiance into a face like no face I knew. It had a lizard's scales, almost purple in color, the round black eyes of some predatory bird — but glaring with a savage philosophy that never burdened the brain of any bird — a nose somewhere between a snout and a beak, and a long narrow muzzle fringed with a great many small, shy fangs. The Goro.

"*Where is he?*" it demanded in the Common Tongue. Its voice was higher than I had imagined, sounding as though it had scales on it as well, and it spoke with a peculiar near-lisp which would likely have been funny if I had not been hearing it with a set of three-inch talons very nearly meeting in my throat. The Goro said again, almost whispering, "Where is he? You have exactly three *daks* to tell me."

What measure of time a *dak* might be, I cannot tell you to this day, but it still sounds short. What I can say is that all that kept me from betraying the old man on the instant was the fact that I could barely make a sound, once I had heard that voice and the hissing, murderous wisdom in that voice. I managed to croak out, "Sir, I do not know, honestly" — I did say *sir*, I am sure of that anyway — but the Goro only gripped me the tighter, until I felt my tongue and eyes and even my teeth about to explode from my head. It wanted the shapeshifter's life, not mine; but to the wrath in that clench, what difference. In another moment I would be just as dead as if it had been I who stole a dream. The pure injustice of it would have made me weep, if I could have.

Then the Hunters hit him (or her, I never knew), one from either side. The Goro was so intent on strangling information out of me that it never sensed or saw them until they were upon it. It uttered a kind of soft, wheezing roar, hurled me away into a dry ditch, and turned on them, slashing out with claws at one, striking at the other's throat, all fangs bared to the yellow gums. But they were quicker: they spun away like dancers, lashing back with their weaponless hands — and, amazingly, hurting the creature. Its own attacks drew blood from exposed flesh, but theirs brought grunts of surprised pain from deep in the Goro's belly; and after that first skirmish it halted abruptly, standing quite still to take their measure properly. Still struggling for each breath, I found myself absurdly sympathetic. It knew nothing of Hunters, after all, while I knew a little.

But then again, they had plainly never encountered such an opponent. They seemed no more eager to charge a second time than it was to come at them. One took a few cautious steps forward, pausing immediately when the Goro growled. The Hunter's tone was blithe and merry, as I had always been told their voices were. "We have no dispute with you, friend," and he pointed one deadly forefinger at me as I cowered behind the creature who had so nearly killed me a moment before. The Hunter said, "We seek *him.*"

"Do you so?" Those three slow words, in the Goro's voice, would have made me reconsider the path to paradise. The reply was implicit before the Goro spoke again. "He is mine. I need what he knows."

"Ah, but so do we, you see." The Hunter might have been lightly debating some dainty point of poetry or religion with a fine lady, such as drifted smokily now and then through the chill halls of *that place.* He continued, "What *we* need will come back to where it belongs. He will...stay here."

"Ah," said the Goro in turn, and the little sigh, coming from such a great creature, seemed oddly gentle, even wistful. The Goro said, "I also have no wish to kill you. You should go away now."

"We cannot." The other Hunter spoke for the first time, sounding almost apologetic. "There it is, unfortunately."

I had at that point climbed halfway out of the ditch, moving as cautiously and — I hoped — as inconspicuously as I possibly could, when the Goro turned and saw me. It uttered that same chilling wheeze, feinted a charge, which sent me diving back down to bang my head on stony mud, and then wheeled faster than anything that big should have been able to move, swinging its clawed tail to knock the nearer Hunter a good twenty feet away. He regained his feet swiftly enough, but he was obviously stunned, and only stood shaking his head as the Goro came at him again. The second Hunter leaped on its back, chopping and jabbing at it with those hands that could break bones and lay open flesh, but the Goro paid no more heed than if the Hunter had been pelting it with flowers.

It simply shook him off and struck his dazed partner so hard — this time with a paw — that I heard his neck snap from where I stood. It does not, by the way, sound like a dry twig, as some say. Not at all.

I scrambled all the way out of the ditch on my second try, and poised low on the edge, ready to bolt this way or that, according to what the Goro did next. Vaguely I recalled that the old man had ordered me to run for the house once I had gained the attention of all parties; but, what with the situation having altered, I thought that perhaps I might not move much for some while — possibly a year, or even two. The surviving Hunter, mortally bound to avenge his comrade, let out a howl of purest grief and fury and sprang wildly at the Goro — who, amazingly, backed away so fast that the Hunter literally fell short, and very nearly sprawled at the Goro's feet, still crying vengeance. The Goro could have killed him simply by stepping on him, or with a quick slash of its tail, but it did no such thing. Rather, it backed further, allowing him to rise without any hindrance, and the two of them faced each other under the half-moon, the Hunter crouched and panting, the Goro studying him thoughtfully out of lidless black eyes.

The Hunter said, his voice still lightly amused, "I am not afraid of you. We have killed —" he caught himself then, and for a single moment, a splinter of a moment, I saw real, rending pain in his own pitiless eyes — "*I* have killed a score greater than you, and each time walked away unscathed. You will not live to say the same."

"Perhaps not," said the Goro, and nothing more than that. It continued to stand where it was, motionless as a long-legged *gantiya* waiting in the marshes for a minnow, while the Hunter, just as immobile, seemed to vibrate with bursting, famished energy. I began to ease away from the ditch, one slow-sliding foot at a time, freezing for what seemed hours between steps and wishing desperately now for the moon to sink or cloud over. There came no sound or signal from the farmhouse-thing; for all I knew, the old man had taken full advantage of the Goro's distraction to abandon me to its mercy, and that of my own pursuer. Neither of them had yet paid any further heed to me, but each waited with a terrible patience for the other's eyes to make the first move. At the last, the eyes are all you have.

Gradually gaining an idiotic confidence in my chances of slipping off unnoticed, I forgot completely how I had earlier tripped in a rut and sprawled on my face, until I did it again. I made no sound, for all my certainty that I had broken my nose, but they heard me. The Hunter gave a sudden short laugh, far more terrifying than the Goro's strange, strangled roar, and came bounding at me, flying over those same furrows like a dolphin taking the sunset waves. I was paralyzed — I have no memory of reacting, until I found myself on my back, curled into a half-ball, as a *shukri* brought to bay will do, biting and clawing madly at an assailant too vast for the malodorous little beast even to conceive of. The Hunter was over me like nightfall: still perfectly efficient, for all his fury, contemptuously ignoring my flailing attempts at both attack and defense, while seeking the one place for the one blow he would ever need to strike. He found it.

He found it perhaps half a second after I found the cook's paring knife in the place where the old man had scornfully insisted that I carry it. Thought was not involved — the frantic, scrabbling thing at the end of my arm clutched the worn wooden handle and lunged blindly upward, slanting the blade along the Hunter's rib cage, which turned it like a melting candle. I felt the warm, slow trickle — *ah, they could bleed, then!* — but the Hunter's face never changed; if anything, he smiled with a kind of taunting triumph. *Yes, I can bleed, but that will not help you. Nothing will help you.* Nevertheless, he missed his strike, and I somehow rolled away, momentarily out of range and still, still alive.

The Hunter's hands were open, empty, hanging at his sides. The brown tunic was dark under his left arm, but he never stopped smiling. He said clearly, "There is no hope. No hope for you, no escape. You must know that."

"Yes," I said. "Yes, I know." And I did know, utterly, beyond any delusion. I said, "Come ahead, then."

To do myself some justice, he moved in rather more deliberately this time, as though I might have given him something to consider. I caught a moment's glimpse of the Goro standing off a little way, apparently waiting for us to destroy each other, as the old man had hoped it and the Hunters would do. The Hunter eased toward me, sideways-on, giving my paring knife the smallest target possible, which was certainly a compliment of a sort. I feinted a couple of times, left and right, as I had seen it done. He laughed, saying, "Good — very good. Really." A curious way to hear one's death sentence spoken.

Suddenly I had had enough of being quarry: the one pursued, the one hunted down, dragged down, the one helplessly watching his derisive executioner approach, himself unable to stir hand or foot. Without anything resembling a strategy, let alone a hope, I flung myself at the Hunter like a stone tumbling downhill. He stepped nimbly aside, but surprise slowed him just a trifle, and I hurtled into him, bringing us down together for a second time, and jarring the wind out of his laughter.

For a moment I was actually on top, clutching at the Hunter's throat with one hand, brandishing my little knife over him with the other. Then he smiled teasingly at me, like a father pretending to let a child pin him at wrestling, and he took the knife away from me and snapped it between his fingers. His face and clothes were splotched with blood now, but he seemed no whit weaker as he shrugged me aside and kneeled on my arms. He said kindly, "You gave us a better run than we expected. I will be quick."

Then he made a mistake.

Under the chuckling benignity, contempt, always, for every living soul but Hunters. Under the gracious amusement, contempt, utter sneering contempt. They cannot help it, it is what they are, and it is their only weakness. He tossed the broken handle of the paring knife — with its one remaining jag of blade — lightly into my face, and raised a hand for the killing blow. When he did that, his body weight shifted — only the least bit, but his right knee shifted with it, and slipped in a smear of blood. My half-numb left arm pulled free.

There was no stabbing possible with that fraction of a knife — literally no point to it, as you might say. I thought only to *mark* him, to make him know that he had *not* killed a pitiful child, but a man grown. One last time I slashed feebly at his smiling face, but he turned his head slightly, and I missed my target completely, raking the side of his neck. I remember my disappointment — *well, failed at that, too, my last act in this world.* I remember.

It was no dribble this time, no ooze, but a fierce leap like a living animal over my hand — even Hunters have an artery there — followed immediately by a lover's triumphant blurt of breath into my face. The Hunter's eyes widened, and he started to say something, and he died in my arms.

I might have lain there for a little while — I don't know. It cannot have been long, because the body was abruptly snatched off mine and flung back and away, like a snug blanket on a winter's morning, when your mother wants you out feeding the *jejebhais*. The Goro hauled me to my feet.

"*Him*," it said, and nothing more. It made no menacing gesture, uttered no horrifying threat; none of that was necessary. Now here is where the foolishness comes in. I had every hysterical intention of crying, "Lord, lord, please, do not slay me, and I will lead you straight to where he hides, only spare my wretched life." I meant to, I find no disgrace in telling you this, especially since what I actually heard myself say — quite politely, as I recall — was, "You will have to kill me, sir." For that miserable, lying, insulting, shapeshifting old man, I did that, and he jeered at me for it, later on. Ah, well, we begin as we are meant to continue, I suppose.

The Goro regarded me out of those eyes that could neither blink (though I saw a sort of pinkish membrane flick across them from time to time) nor reveal the slightest feeling. It said, "That would serve no useful purpose. You will take me to him."

As I have said, it raised no deadly paw, showed no more teeth than the long muzzle normally showed. But I *felt* the command, and the implacable will behind the command — I *felt* the Goro in my mind and my belly, and to disobey was not possible. Not possible...I can tell you nothing more. Except, perhaps, that I was young. Today, withered relic that I am become, I might yet perhaps hold that will at bay. It was not possible then.

"Yes," I said. "Yes." The Goro came up to me, moving with a curious shuffling grace, if one can say that, wrapping that tail around its haunches as daintily as a lace shawl. It gripped me between neck and shoulder and turned me. I said nothing further, but started slowly toward the farmhouse that was not a farmhouse — or perhaps it was? What did I know of anything's reality anymore? My ribs were so badly bruised that I could not draw a full breath, and there was something wrong with the arm that had killed the Hunter. The half-moon was setting now, silvering the shadows and filling the hard ruts with shivering, deceiving light, and it was cold, and I was a child in a man's body, wishing I were safe back in *that place*.

Nearing the farmhouse, the Goro halted, tightening its clutch on my shoulder. Weary and bewildered as I was — no, more than bewildered, half-mad, surely — I studied the house, *looked* at it for the first time, and could not imagine anyone ever having taken it for anybody's home. The dark waiting beyond the sagging door sprang out to greet us with a stench far beyond stench: not the smell that anciently abandoned places have, of wood rotted into black slush, blankets moldering on the skeleton of a bed, but of an unhuman awareness having nothing to do with our notions of life or shelter, or even ordinary fear. The thing's camouflage — how long in evolving? how can it have begun to pass itself off as something belonging to this world? — might serve well enough from a distance, on a dark night, but surely close to…? Then I glanced back at the Goro.

The Goro had forgotten me completely, though its paw remembered. Its eyes continued to tell me nothing, but it was staring at the farmhouse-thing with an intensity that would have been rapture in a human expression. It lisped, much more to itself than to me, "He is in there. I have run him to earth at last."

"No," I said, once more to my own astonishment. "No. It is a trap. Believe me."

"I honor your loyalty," the Goro said. It bent its awful head and made a curious gesture with its free paw which I have never seen again, and which may have meant blessing, or merely a compliment. I try not to think about it. It said, "But you cannot know him as I do. He is here because what he stole from me is here. Because his honor demands that he face me to keep it, as mine demands that he pay the price of a stolen dream. We understand each other, we two."

"Nonsense," I said. I felt oddly lightheaded, and even bold, in the midst of my leg-caving, bladder-squeezing terror. "He has no honor, and he cares nothing for your dream, or for anything but his continual false-hearted existence. And that is no house, but a horror from somewhere more alien to you than you are to me. Please — I am trying to save *you*, not him. Believe me, please."

The Goro looked at me. I have no more idea now than I did then of what it can have been thinking, nor of what it made of my warning. Did it take me seriously and begin silently altering its plans? Had it assumed from the first that, as some sort of partner of its old enemy, nothing I said must ever be trusted for a moment? All I know is what happened — which is that out of the side of my eye I saw the fox burst from the shadows that the farmhouse was real enough to cast in this world, under this moon, and come racing straight toward the Goro and me. In the moonlight, he shone red as the Hunter's blood.

He halted halfway, cocking his head to one side and grinning to show the small stone held in his jaws. I did not notice it immediately: it was barely more than a pebble, less bright than the sharp teeth that gripped it, or the mocking yellow eyes above it. The Goro's crystallized dream, the cause of the unending flight and pursuit that had called to me from a wagonload of manure. The fox tilted his head back, tossed the stone up at the sinking moon, and caught it again.

And the Goro went mad. Nothing I had seen of its raging power, even when it was battling the two Hunters, could possibly have prepared me for what I saw in the next moment. The eyes, the lidless eyes that I had thought could never express any emotion...I was in a midnight fire at sea once, off Cape Dylee, when the waves themselves seemed alight to the horizon, all leaping and dancing with an air of blazing delight at our doom. The Goro's eyes were like that as it lunged forward, not shambling at all now, but charging like a rock-*targ*, full-speed with the second stride. It was making a sound that it had not made before: if an avalanche had breath, if an entire forest were to fall at once, you might hear something —*something*— like what I heard then. Not a roar, not a bellow, not a howl — no word in any language I know will suit that sound. Flesh never made that sound; it came through the Goro out of the tortured earth, and that is all there is to that. That is what I believe.

The fox wheeled and raced away, his red brush joyously, insultingly high, and the Goro went after him. I stumbled forward, shouting, "*No!*" but I might as well have been crying out to a forest or an avalanche. Distraught, battered, uncertain of anything at all, it may be that I was deceived, but it seemed to me that the shadow of the farmhouse-thing reared up as they neared it, spreading out to shapelessness and *reaching*... I knew the fox well enough to anticipate his swerving away at the last possible minute, but I miscalculated, and so did he. The shadow's long, long arms cut off his escape on three sides, taking him in mid-leap, as a frog laps a fly out of the air. I thought I heard him utter a single small puppyish yelp, not like a fox at all.

The Goro went straight in after him, never trying to elude the shadow's grasp — I doubt it saw anything but the little dull pebble in the fox's jaws. It vanished as instantly and completely as he had, without a sound.

Telling you this tale, I notice that I am constantly pausing to marvel at my own stupidity. Each time I offer the same defense: I was young, I was inexperienced, I had been reared in a stranger place than any scoffer can possibly have known...all of it true, and none of it resembling an explanation for what I did next. Which was to plunge my naked hands into the devouring shadow, fumbling to rescue *anything* from its grip — the fox, the Goro, some poor creature consumed before we three ever came within its notice, within range of its desire. Today I can only say that I pitied the Goro, and that the old man — the fox, as you will — was my guide, occasionally my mentor, and somehow nearly my friend, may the gods pity *me*. Have to do, won't it?

Where was I? Yes, I remember — groping blindly in the shadow on the chance of dragging one or the other of them back into the moonlight of this world. My arms vanished to the wrists, the forearms, past the elbows, into...into the flame of the stars? Into the eternal, unimaginable cold of the gulfs between them? I do not know to this day; for that, you must study my scarred old flesh and form your own opinion. What I know is that my hands closed on something they could not feel, and in turn I hauled them back, though I could not connect them, even in my mind, with a human body, mine or anyone else's. I screamed all the time, of course, but the pain had nothing to do with me — it was far too terrible, too *grand*, to belong to one person alone. I felt almost guilty keeping it for myself.

The shadow fought me. Whatever I had seized between my burning, frozen hands — and I could not tell whether it was as small a thing as the fox or as great as the Goro — the shadow wanted it back, and very nearly took it from me. And why I did not, *would* not, allow that to happen, I cannot put into words for you. I think it was the hands' decision, surely not my own. They were the ones who suffered, they were the ones entitled to choose — *yes, no, hang on, let go*...I was standing far — oh, very far indeed — to one side, looking on.

Did I pull what I held free by means of my pure heart and failing strength, or did the shadow finally give in, for its own reasons? I know what I believe, but none of that matters. What does matter is that when my hands came back to me, they held the fox between them. A seemingly lifeless fox, certainly; a fox without a breath or a heartbeat that I could detect; a fox beyond bedraggled, looking half his normal size, with most of his fur gone, the rest staring limply, and his proud brush as naked as a rat's tail. Indeed, the only indication that he still lived was the fact that he was unconsciously trying to shapeshift in my hands. The shiver of the air around him, the sudden slight smudging of his outline...I jumped back, as I had not recoiled from the house-thing's shadow, letting him fall to the ground.

He landed without the least thump, so insubstantial he was. The transformation simply faded and failed; though whether that means that the fox-shape is his natural form and the other nothing but a garment he was too weak to assume, I have never known. The moon was down, and with the approach of false dawn, the shadow was retreating, the house-thing itself withering absurdly, like an overripe vegetable, its sides slumping inwards while its insides — or whatever they might have been — seemed to ooze palely into the rising day, out to where the shadow had lain in wait for prey. Only for a moment...then the whole creature collapsed and vanished before my eyes, and the one trace of its passage was a dusty hole in the ground. A small hole, the sort of hole that remains when you have pulled a plant up by its roots. Or think you have.

There was no sign of the Goro. When I looked back at the fox, he was actually shaking himself and trying to get to his feet. It took him some while, for his legs kept splaying out from under him, and even when he managed to balance more or less firmly on all four of them, his yellow eyes were obviously not seeing me, nor much else. Once the fox-shape was finally under control, he promptly abandoned it for that of the old man, who looked just as much of a disaster, if not even more so. The white mustache appeared to have been chewed nearly away; one burly white eyebrow was altogether gone, as were patches of the white mane, and the skin of his face and neck might have been through fire or frostbite. But he turned to stare toward the place where the house that was not a house had stood, and he grinned like a skull.

"Exactly as I planned it," he pronounced. "Rid of the lot of them, we are, for good and all, thanks to my foresight. I *knew* it was surely time for the beast to return to that spot, and I *knew* the Goro would care for nothing else, once it caught sight of me and that stone." Amazingly, he patted my shoulder with a still-shaky hand. "And you dealt with your little friends remarkably well — far better than I expected, truth be told. I may have misjudged you somewhat."

"As you misjudged the thing's reach," I said, and he had the grace to look discomfited. I said, "Before you thank me —" which he had shown no sign of doing — "you should know that I was simply trying to save whomever I could catch hold of. I would have been just as relieved to see the Goro standing where you are."

"Not for long," he replied with that supremely superior air that I have never seen matched in all these years. "The Goro consider needing any sort of assistance — let alone having to be *rescued* — to be dishonorable in its very nature. He'd have quickly removed a witness to his sin, likely enough." I suspected that to be a lie — which it is, for the most part — but said nothing, only watching as he gradually recovered his swagger, if not his mustache. It was fascinating to observe, rather like seeing a newborn butterfly's wings slowly plumping in the sun. He said then — oddly quietly, I remember — "You are much better off with me. Whatever you think of me."

When he said that, just for that moment, he looked like no crafty shapeshifter but such a senile clown as one sees in the wayside puppet plays where the young wife always runs off with a soldier. He studied my hands and arms, which by now were hurting so much that in a way they did not hurt at all, if you can understand that. "I know something that will help those," he said. "It will not help enough, but you will be glad of it."

Not yet true dawn, and I could feel how hot the day would be in that barren, utterly used-up land that is called the Mihanachakali. There was dust on my lips already, and sweat beginning to rise on my scalp. A few scrawny *rukshi* birds were beginning to circle high over the Hunters' bodies. I turned away and began to walk — inevitably back the way we had come, there being no other real road in any direction. The old man kept pace with me, pattering brightly at my side, cheerfully informing me, "The coast's what we want — salt water always straightens the mind and clears the spirit. We'll have to go back to Druchank — no help for that, alas — but three days further down the Nai —"

I halted then and stood facing him. "Listen to me," I said. "Listen closely. I am bound as far from Goros and Hunters, from foxes that are not foxes and houses that are not houses as a young fool can get. I want nothing to do with the lot of you, or with anything that is like you. There must be a human life I am fit to lead, and I will find it out, wherever it hides from me. I will find my life."

"Rather like our recent companions seeking after us," he murmured, and now he sounded like his old taunting self, but somehow subdued also. "Well, so. I will bid you good luck and goodbye in advance, then, for all that we do appear to be traveling the same road —"

"We are *not*," I said, loud enough to make my poor head ache and my battered ribs cringe. I began walking again, and he followed. I said, "Whichever road you take, land or water, I will go some other way. If I have to climb back into a manure wagon a second time, I will be shut of you."

"I have indeed misjudged you," he continued, as though I had never spoken. "There is promising stuff to you, and with time and tutelage you may blossom into adequacy yet. It will be interesting to observe."

"I will write you a letter," I said through my teeth. There would plainly be no ridding myself of him until Druchank, but I was determined not to speak further word with him again. And I did not, not until the second night, when we had made early camp close enough to Druchank to smell its foulness on a dank little breeze. Hungry and weary, I weakened enough to ask him abruptly, "That house — whatever it was — you called it *the beast*. It was alive, then? Some sort of animal?"

"Say *vegetable*, and you may hit nearer the mark," he answered me. "They come and go, those things — never many, but always where they grew before, and always in the exact guise they wore the last time. I have seen one that you would take for a grand, shady *keema* tree without any question, and another that looks like a sweet little dance pavilion in the woods that no one seems to remember building. I cannot say where they are from, nor what exactly becomes of their victims — only that it is a short blooming season, and if they take no prey they rot and die back before your eyes. As that one did." He yawned as the fox yawned, showing all his teeth, and added, "A pity, really. I have...made use of that one before."

"And you led me there," I said. "You told me nothing, and you led me there."

He shrugged cheerfully. "I tried to tell you — a little, anyway — but you did not care to hear. My fault?" I did not answer him. A breeze had come up, carrying with it the smell of the Nai — somewhat fresher than that of the town — and the bray of a boat horn.

"It had already taken the Goro," I said finally, "and still it died."

"Ah, well, a Goro's not to everybody's taste." He yawned again, and suddenly barked with laughter. "Probably gave the poor old thing a belly-ache—no wonder!" He literally fell over on his back at the thought, laughing, waving his arms and legs in the air, purely delighted at the image, and more so with himself for creating it. I watched him from where I lay, feeling a curious mixture of ironic admiration, genuine revulsion, and something uncomfortably like affection, which shocked me when I made myself name it to myself. As it occasionally does even now.

"I tried to stop the Goro," I said. "I told him that it was a trick, that you were deceiving him. I begged him not to fall into your trap."

The old man did not seem even slightly perturbed. "Didn't listen, did he? They never do. That's the nature of a Goro. Just as not wanting to know things is the nature of humans."

"And your nature?" I challenged him. "What is the nature of whatever you are?" He considered this for some time, still lying on his back with his arms folded on his chest in the formal manner of a corpse. But his eyes were wide open, and in the twilight they were more gray than fox-yellow just then.

"Deceptive," he offered at last. "That's fair enough — deceptive. Misleading, too, and altogether unreliable." But he seemed not quite satisfied with any of the words, and thought about it for a while longer. At last he said, "Illusory. Good as any, *illusory*. That will do."

I lay long awake that night, reflecting on all that I had passed through — and all that had passed through and over me — since I fled across another night from *that place*, with the Hunters behind me. Deceptive, misleading, illusory, even so he had done me no real ill, when you thought about it. Led me into peril, true, but preserved me from it more than once. And he had certainly taught me much that I needed to know, if I were to make my way forward to wherever I was making my way to in this world. I could have had worse counselors, and doubtless would yet, on my journey.

My hands and arms pained me still, but far less than they had, as I leaned to nudge him out of his usual twitchy fox-sleep. He had searched out a couple of fat-leaved weeds that morning, pounded them for a good hour, mixed the resulting mash with what I tried not to suspect was his own urine, and spread it from my palms to my shoulders, where it crusted cool and stiff. I had barely touched his own shoulder before his eyes opened, yellow as they always are when he first wakes. I wonder what his dreams would look like, if they were to take daylight substance, as a Goro's do.

"Three more days on the Nai brings us where?" I asked him.

Salt Wine

If my business manager and I hadn't been schlepping ourselves and a carload of books from the Bay Area to Las Vegas for a *Star Trek* convention, this story would not exist. It's a very long drive, and extremely boring, and the night sky was crackling with heat lightning, and we'd run out of Sondheim songs. For conversation's sake, we turned to discussing a possible title for this collection, and after a series of remarkably lame suggestions, the phrase *Salt Wine and Secrets* suddenly popped up like a slice of fresh toast. Evocative and curiously haunting, obviously it would only work if there were a story called "Salt Wine" in the book. And I hadn't a notion of what salt wine might be, nor what secrets it might engender. I said I'd think about it.

On the way home, a few days later, slogging through a pounding rainstorm, I announced that I just maybe had the beginning of a mini-hint of a story idea. "It's something about *merrows*, that's all I know."

I usually get one clue like that per story — the rest is strictly up for grabs. If the Muse is late for work, you start without her.

Looking back at "Salt Wine," I realize that almost every story I've ever written from a first-person point of view has been completely improvised according to the narrator's voice. It's a matter of trusting the source; of assuming that the storyteller knows what he or she is doing, even if I don't, and that the tale will structure itself and tell me when it's done. It's a form of possession, I suppose, but generally a benign one.

So here's Ben Hazeltine, stepping from wherever those voices that visit me live, to tell you a story. There's a secret in it.

ALL RIGHT, THEN. First off, this ain't a story about some seagoing candy-trews dandy Captain Jack, or whatever you want to call him, who falls in love with a mermaid and breaks his troth to a mortal woman to live with his fish-lady under the sea. None of that in this story, I can promise you; and our man's no captain, but a plain blue-eyed sailorman named Henry Lee, AB, who starts out good for nowt much but reefing a sail, holystoning a deck, taking a turn in the crow's-nest, talking his way out of a tight spot, and lending his weight to the turning of a capstan and his voice to the bellowing of a chanty. He drank some, and most often when he drank it ended with him going at it with one or another of his mates. Lost part of an ear that way off Panama, he did, and even got flogged once for pouring grog on the captain. But there was never no harm in Henry Lee, not in them days. Anybody remembers him'll tell you that.

Me name's Ben Hazeltine. I remember Henry Lee, and I'll tell you why.

I met Henry Lee when we was both green hands on the *Mary Brannum*, out of Cardiff, and we stayed messmates on and off, depending. Didn't always ship out together, nowt like that — just seemed to happen so. Any road, come one rainy spring, we was on the beach together, out of work. Too many hands, not enough ships — you get that, some seasons. Captains can take their pick those times, and Henry Lee and I weren't neither one anybody's first pick. Isle of Pines, just south of Cuba — devil of a place to be stranded, I'll tell you. Knew we'd land a berth sooner or later — always had before — only we'd no idea when, and both of us hungry enough to eat a seagull, but too weak to grab one. I'll tell you the God's truth, we'd gotten to where we was looking at bloody starfish and those Portygee man-o'-war jellies and wondering...well, there you are, that's how bad it were. I've been in worse spots, but not many.

Now back then, there was mermaids all over the place, like you don't see so much today. Partial to warm waters, they are — the Caribbean, Mediterranean, the Gulf Stream — but I've seen them off the Orkneys, and even off Greenland a time or two, that's a fact. What's *not* a fact is the singing. Combing their hair, yes; they're women, after all, and that's what women do, and how you going to comb your hair out underwater? But I never heard one mermaid sing, not once.

And they ain't all beautiful — stop a clock, some of them would.

Now, what you *didn't* see much of in the old times, and don't hardly be seeing at all these days, was mer*men*. Merrows, some folk call them. Ugly as fried sin, the lot: not a one but's got a runny red nose, nasty straggly hair — red too, mostly, I don't know why — stumpy green teeth sticking up and out every which way, skin like a crocodile's arse. You get a look at one of those, it don't take much to figure why your mermaid takes to hanging around sailors. Put me up against a merrow, happen even *I* start looking decent enough, by and by.

Any road, like I told you, Henry Lee and I was pretty well down to eating our boots — or we would have been if we'd had any. We was stumbling along the beach one morning, guts too empty to growl, looking for someone to beg or borrow from — or maybe just chew up on the spot, either way — when there's a sudden commotion out in the water, and someone screaming for help. Well, I knew it were a merrow straight-away, and so did Henry Lee — you can't ever mistake a merrow's creaky, squawky voice, once you've heard it — and when we ran to look, we saw he had a real reason to scream. Big hammerhead had him cornered against the reef, circling and circling him, the way they do when they're working up to a strike. No, I tell a lie, I misremember — it were a bull shark, not a hammerhead. Hammer, he swims in big packs, he'll stay out in the deep water, but your bull, they'll come right in close, right into the shallows. And they'll leave salmon or tuna to go after a merrow. Just how they are.

Now merrows are tough as they're unsightly, you don't never want to be disputing a fish or a female with a merrow. But to a bull shark, a mer-row's a nice bit of Cornish pasty. This one were flapping his arms at the bull, hitting out with his tail — worst thing he could have done; they'll go for the tail first thing, that's the good part. I says to Henry Lee, I says, "Look sharp, mate — might be *summat* over for us." Sharks is real slap-dash about their meals, and we was *hungry*.

But Henry Lee, he gives me just the one look, with his eyes all big and strange — and then rot me if he ain't off like a pistol shot, diving into the surf and heading straight for the reef and that screaming merrow. Ain't too many sailors can really swim, you know, but Henry Lee, he were a Devon man, and he used to say he swam before he could walk. He had a knife in his belt — won it playing euchre with a Malay pirate — and I could see it glinting between his teeth as he slipped through them waves like a dolphin, which is a shark's mortal enemy, you know. Butt 'em in the side, what they do, in the belly, knock 'em right out of the water. I've seen it done.

That bull shark never knew Henry Lee were coming till he were on its back, hanging on like a jockey and stabbing everywhere he could reach. Blood enough in the water, I couldn't hardly see anything — I could just hear that merrow, still screeching his ugly head off. Time I caught sight of Henry Lee again, he were halfway back to shore, grinning at me around that bloody knife, and a few fins already slicing in to finish off their mate, ta ever so. I practically dragged Henry Lee out of the water, 'acos of he were bleeding too — shark's hide'll take your own skin off, and his thighs looked like he'd been buggering a hedgehog.

"Barking mad," I told him. "Barking, roaring, *howling* mad! God's frig-ging *teeth*, you ought to be put somewhere you can't hurt yourself — aye, nor nobody else. What in frigging Jesus' frigging name *possessed* you, you louse-ridden get?"

See, it weren't that we was all such mates back then, me and Henry Lee, it were more that I thought I *knew* him — knew what he'd do when, and what he wouldn't; knew what I could trust him for, and what I'd better see to meself. There's times your life can depend on that kind of knowing — weren't for that, I wouldn't be here, telling this. I says it again, "What the Christ possessed you, Henry bleeding Lee?"

But he'd already got his back to me, looking out toward the reef, water still roiling with the sharks fighting for leftovers. "Where's that merrow gone?" he wanted to know. "He was just there — where's he got to?" He was set to swim right back out there, if I hadn't grabbed him again.

"Panama by now, if he's got the sense of a weevil," says I. "More sense than you, anyway. What kind of bloody idiot risks his life for a bloody merrow?"

"An idiot who knows how a merrow can reward you!" Henry Lee turned back around to face me, and I swear his blue eyes had gone black and wild as the sea off Halifax. "Didn't you never hear about that? You save a merrow's life, he's bound to give you all his treasure, all the plun-der he's ever gathered from shipwrecks, sea fights — everything he's got in his cave, it's the rule. He don't have no choice, it's the *rule!*"

I couldn't help it, I were laughing before he got halfway through. "Aye, Henry Lee," I says. "Aye, I've heard that story, and you know where I heard it? At me mam's tit, that's where, and at every tit since, and every mess where I ever put me feet under the table. Pull the other one, chum, that tale's got long white whiskers on it." Wouldn't laugh at him so today, but there you are. I were younger then.

Well, Henry Lee just gave me that look, one more time, and after that he didn't speak no more about merrows and treasures. But he were up all that night — we slept on the beach, y'see, and every time I roused, the fool were pacing the water's edge, this way and that, gaping out into the bloody black, plain waiting for that grateful merrow to show up with his arms full of gold and jewels and I don't know what, all for him, along of being saved from the sharks. *"Rule,"* thinks I. "Rule, me royal pink bum," and went back to sleep.

But there's treasure and there's treasure — depends how you look at it, I reckon. Very next day, Henry Lee found himself a berth aboard a whaler bound home for Boston and short a foremast hand. He tried to get me signed on too, but...well, I knew the captain, and the captain remembered me, so that were the end of that. You'd not believe the grudges some of them hold.

Me, I lucked onto a Spanish ship, a week or ten days later — she'd stopped to take on water, and I got talking with the cook, who needed another messboy. I've had better berths, but it got me to Málaga — and after that, one thing led to another, and I didn't see Henry Lee again for six or seven years, must have been, the way it happens with seamen. I thought about him often enough, riding that bull shark to rescue that merrow who were going to make him rich, and I asked after him any time I met an English hand, or a Yankee, but never a word could anyone tell me — not until I rounded a fruitstall in the marketplace at Velha Goa, and almost ran over him!

How *I* got there's no great matter — I were a cook meself by then, on a wallowing scow of an East Indiaman, and trying to get some greens and fresh fruit into the crew's hardtack diet, if just to sweeten the farts in the fo'c'sle. As for why I were running, with a box of mangoes in me arms... well, that don't figure in this story neither, so never you mind.

Henry Lee looked the same as I remembered him — still not shaving more than every three days, I'd warrant, still as blue-eyed an innocent as ever cracked a bos'un's head with a beer bottle. Only change in him I could see, he didn't look like a sailor no more. Hard to explain; he were dressing just the same as ever — singlet, blue canvas pants, same rope-sole shoes, even the very same dirty white cap he always wore — but *summat* was different about him. Might have been the way he walked — he'd lost that little roll we all have, walked like he'd not been to sea in his life. Aye, might have been that.

Well, he give a great whoop to see me, and he grabbed hold of me, mangoes and all, and dragged me off into a dark little Portygee tavern — smelled of dried fish and fried onions, I remember, and cloves under it all. They knew him there — landlord patted his back, kissed him on the cheek, brought us some kind of mulled ale, and left us alone. And Henry Lee sat there with his arms folded and grinned at me, not saying a word, until I finally told him he looked like a blasted old hen, squatting over one solitary egg, and it likely rotten at that. "Talk or be damned to you," I says. "The drink's not good enough to keep me from walking out of this fleapit."

Henry Lee burst out laughing then, and he grabbed both me hands across the table, saying, "Ah, it's just so grand to see you, old Ben, I don't know what to say first, I swear I don't."

"Tell about the money, mate," I says, and didn't he stare *then?* I says, "Your clothes are for shite, right enough, but you're walking like a man with money in every pocket — you talk like your mouth's full of money, and you're scared it'll all spill out if you open your lips too wide. Now, last time I saw you, you hadn't a farthing to bless yourself with, so let's talk about that, hey? That merrow turn up with his life savings, after all?" And *I* laughed, because I'd meant it as a joke. I did.

Henry Lee didn't laugh. He looked startled, and then he leaned so close I could see where he'd lost a side tooth and picked up a scar right by his left eyebrow — made him look younger, somehow, those things did along with that missing bit of ear — and he dropped his voice almost to a whisper, no matter there wasn't a soul near us. "No," says he, "no, Ben, he did better than that, a deal better than that. He taught me the making of salt wine."

Aye, that's how I looked at him — exactly the way you're eyeing me now. Like I'm barking mad, and Jesus and the saints wouldn't have me. And the way you mumbled, "*Salt wine?*" — I said it just the same as you, tucking me head down like that, getting me legs under me, in case things turned ugly. I did it true. But Henry Lee only sat back and grinned again. "You heard me, Ben," he says. "You heard me clear enough."

"Salt wine," I says, and different this time, slowly. "Salt wine...that'd be like pickled beer? Oysters in honey, that kind of thing, is it? How about bloody fried marmalade, then?" Takes me a bit of time to get properly worked up, mind, but foolery will do it. "Whale blubber curry," I says. "Boiled nor'easter."

For answer, Henry Lee reaches into those dirty canvas pants and comes up with a cheap pewter flask, two for sixpence in any chandlery. Doesn't say one word — just hands it to me, folds his hands on the table and waits. I take me time, study the flask — got a naked lady and a six-point buck on one side, and somebody in a flying chariot looks like it's caught fire on the other. I start to say how I don't drink much wine —

never did, not Spanish sherry, nor even port, nor none of that Frenchy slop — but Henry Lee flicks one finger to tell me I'm to shut me gob and taste. So that's what I did.

All right, this is the hard part to explain. Nor about merrows, nor neither the part about some bloody fool jumping on the back of a bull shark — the part about the wine. Because it *were* wine in that flask, and it *were* salty, and right there's where I run aground on a lee shore, trying to make you taste and see summat you never will, if your luck holds. *Salt wine* — not red nor neither white, but gray-green, like the deep sea, and smelling like the sea, filling your head with the sea, but wine all the same. *Salt wine....*

First swallow, I lost meself. I didn't think I were ever coming back.

Weren't nothing like being drunk. I've downed enough rum, enough brandy, dropped off to sleep in enough jolly company and wakened in enough stinking alleys behind enough shebeens to know the difference. This were more...this were like I'd fallen overboard from me, from meself, and not a single boat lowered to find me. But it didn't matter none, because *summat* were bearing me up, *summat* were surging under me, big and fast and wild, as it might have been a dolphin between me legs, tearing along through the sea — or the air, might be we were flying, I'd not have known — carrying somebody off to somewhere, and who it was I can't tell you now no more than I could have then. But it weren't me, I'll take me affydavy on that. I weren't there. I weren't anywhere or anybody, and just then that were just where I wanted to be.

Just then...Aye, you give me a choice just then, happen I might have chosen...But I'd just had that one swallow, after all, so in a bit there I were, me as ever was, back at that tavern table with Henry Lee, and him still grinning like a dog with two tails, and he says to me, "Well, Ben?"

When I can talk, I ask him, "You can make this swill yourself?" and when he nods, "Then I'd say your merrow earned his keep. Not half bad."

"Best *you* ever turned into piss," Henry says. I don't say nowt back, and after a bit, he leans forward, drops his voice way down again, and says, "It's our fortune, Ben. Yours and mine. I'm swearing on my mother's grave."

"If the dollymop's even got one," I says, because of course he don't know who his mam was, no more than I know mine. They just dropped us both and went their mortal ways, good luck to us all. I tell him, "Never mind the swearing, just lay out what you mean by *our fortune*. I didn't save no merrow — fact, I halfway tried to save *you* from trying to save him. He don't owe me nowt, and nor do you." And I'm on me feet and ready to scarper — just grab up those mangoes and walk. Ain't a living soul thinks I've got no pride, but I bloody do.

But Henry Lee's up with me, catching ahold of me arm like an octopus, and he's saying, "No, no, Ben, you don't understand. I need you, you have to help me, sit down and *listen*." And he pulls and pushes me back down, and leans right over me, so close I can see the scar as cuts into his hairline, where the third mate of the *Boston Annie* got him with a marlinspike, happened off the Azores. He says, "I can make it, the salt wine, but I need a partner to market it for me. I've got no head for business — I don't know the first thing about selling. You've got to ship it, travel with it, be my factor. Because I can't do this without you, d'you see, Ben?"

"No, I don't see a frigging thing," I says in his face. "I'm no more a factor than you're a bloody nun. What I am's a seacook, and it's past time I was back aboard me ship, so by your leave —"

Henry Lee's still gripping me arm so it *hurts*, and I can't pry his fingers loose. "Ben, *listen!*" he fair bellows again. "This is Goa, not the City of London — the Indians won't ever deal honestly with a Britisher who doesn't have an army behind him — why should they? — and the Portuguese bankers don't trust me any more than I'd trust a single one of them not to steal the spots off a leopard and come back later for the whiskers. There's a few British financiers, but *they* don't trust anyone who didn't go to Eton or Harrow. Now you're a lot more fly than you ever let on, I've always known that —"

"Too kind," I says, but he don't hear. He goes on, "You're the one who always knew when we were being cheated — by the captain, by the company, by the lady of the house, didn't matter. Any *souk* in the world, any marketplace, I always let you do the bargaining — *always*. You'd haggle forever over a penny, a peseta, a single anna — and you'd get your price every time. Remember? I surely remember."

"Ain't nothing like running a business," I tell him. "What you're talking about is responsibility, and I never been responsible for nowt but the job I were paid to do right. I like it that way, Henry Lee, it suits me. What you're talking about —"

"I'm talking about a *future*, Ben. Spend your whole life going from berth to berth, ship to ship — where are you at the end of it? Another rotting hulk, like all the rest, careened on the beach, and no tide ever coming again to float you off. I'm offering you the security of a decent roof over your head, good meals on your table, and a few teeth left in your mouth to chew them with." He lets go of me then, but his blue eyes don't. He says, "I'd outfit you, I'd pay your way, and I'd give you one-third of the profits — ah, hell, make it forty, forty percent, what do you say? It'll be worth it to me to sleep snug a'nights, knowing my old shipmate's minding the shop and putting the cat out. What do you say, Ben? Will you do it for me?"

I look at him for a good while, not saying nowt. I remember him one time, talking a drunken gang of Yankee sailors out of dropping us into New York harbor for British spies — wound up buying us drinks, they did, which bloody near killed us anyway. And Piraeus — God's teeth, Piraeus — when the fool put the comehither on the right woman at the wrong time, and there we was, locked in a cellar for two days and nights, while her husband and his mates went on and on, just upstairs, about how to slaughter us so we'd remember it. Henry Lee, he finally got them persuaded that I were carrying some sort of horrible disease, rot your cods off, you leave it long enough, make your nose fall into your soup. They pushed the cellar key under the door and was likely in Istanbul, time we got out of that house. Me, I didn't stop feeling me nose for another two days.

So I know what Henry Lee can do, talking, and I sniff all around his words, like a fox who smells the bait and knows the trap's there, somewhere, underneath. I keep telling him, over and over, "Henry Lee, I never been no better than you with figures — I'd likely run you bankrupt inside of a month." Never stops him — he just grins and answers back, "I'm bankrupt already, Ben. I'm not swimming in boodle, like you thought — I've gone and sunk all I own into a thousand cases of salt wine. Nothing more to lose, you see — there's no way you can make anything any the worse. So what do you say now?"

I don't answer, but I up with that naked-lady flask, and I take another swallow. This time I know what's coming, and I set meself for it, but the salt wine catches me up again, lifts me and tosses me like before, same as if I was a ship with me mainmast gone, and the waves doing what they like with me. No, it's not like before — I don't lose Ben Hazeltine, nor I don't forget who I am. What happens, I *find* summat. I find *everything*. I can't rightly stand up proper, 'acos I don't know which way up *is*, and I feel the eyes rocking in me head, and I'm dribbling wine like I've not done since I were a babby...but for a minute, two minutes — no more, I couldn't have stood no more — everything in the world makes sense to me. For one minute, I'm the flyest cove in the whole world.

Then it's gone — gone, thank God or Old Horny, either one — and I'm back to old ordinary, and Henry Lee's watching me, not a word, and when I can talk I say, "There's more. I know you, and I know there's more. You want me to come in with you, Henry Lee, you tell me the part you're not telling me. Now."

He don't answer straight off — just keeps looking at me out of those nursery-blue eyes. I decide I'd best help him on a bit, so I say, "Right, then, don't mind if we do talk about merrows. Last time I saw you, you was risking your life for the ugliest one of them ugly buggers, and him having to hand over every farthing he'd got sewn into his underwear, because that's the frigging rule, right? So when did that happen, hey? We never seen him again, far as *I* know."

"He found me," Henry Lee says. "Took him a while, but he caught up with me in Port of Spain. It's important to them, keeping their word, though you wouldn't think so." He keeps cracking his knuckles, the way he always used to do when he weren't sure the captain were swallowing his tale about why we was gone three days in Singapore. "I had it wrong," he says, "that rule thing. I expected he'd come with his whole fortune in his arms, but all the merrow has to bring you is the thing that's most precious to him in the world. The most precious thing in the world to that merrow I saved — I call him Gorblimey, that's as close as I can get to his name — the most precious thing to him was that recipe for salt wine. It's only some of them know how to make it, and they've never given it to a human before. I'm the only one."

Me head's still humming like a honey tree, only it's swarming with the ghosts of all the things I knew for two minutes. Henry Lee goes on, "He couldn't write it down for me — they can't read or write, of course, none of them, I'd never thought about that — so he made me learn it by heart. All that night, over and over, the two of us, me hiding in a lifeboat, him floating in the ship's shadow, over and over and *over*, till I couldn't have remembered my own name. He was so afraid I'd get it wrong."

"How would you know?" I can't help asking him. "Summat like that wine, how could you tell if it *were* wrong, or gone bad?"

Henry Lee bristles up at me, the way he'd have his ears flat back if he was a cat. "I make it exactly the way Gorblimey taught me — *exactly*. There's no chance of any mistake, Gorblimey himself wouldn't know whether I made it or he did. Get that right out of your headpiece, Ben, and just tell me if you'll help me. *Now*," he growls, mimicking me to the life. He'd land in the brig, anyway once every voyage, imitating the officers.

Now, I'm not blaming nobody, you may lay to that. I'm not even blaming the salt wine, although I could. What I done, I done out of me own chuckleheadedness, not because I was drunk, not because Henry Lee and me'd been shipmates. No, it were the money, and that's the God's truth — just the money. He were right, you can live on a seacook's pay, but that's all you *can* do. Can't retire, and maybe open a little seaside inn — can't marry, can't live nowhere but on a bloody ship...no, it's no life, not without the needful, and there's not many can afford to be too choosy how they come by it. I says, "Might do, Henry Lee. Forty percent. Might do. *Might*."

Henry Lee just lit up all at once, one big *wooosh*, like a Guy Fawkes bonfire. "Ah, Ben. Ah, Ben, I knew you'd turn up trumps, old growly truepenny Ben. You won't be sorry, my old mate," and he claps me on the shoulder, near enough knocking me over. "I promise you won't be sorry."

So I left that Indiaman tub looking for another cook, and I signed on right there as Henry Lee's factor — his partner, his first mate, his right hand, whatever you like to call it. Took us a hungry year or so to get our feet under us, being just the two, but the word spread faster than you might have supposed. Aye, that were the thing about that salt wine — there were them as took to it like a Froggie to snails, and another sort couldn't even abide the *look* of it in the bottle. I were with that lot, and likely for the same reason — not 'acos it were nasty, but 'acos it were too good, too *much*, more than a body could thole, like the Scots say. I never touched it again after that second swig, never once, not in all the years I peddled salt wine fast as Henry Lee could make it. Not for cheer, not for sorrow, not even for a wedding toast when Henry Lee married, which I'll get to by and by. Couldn't thole it, that's all, couldn't risk it no more. Third time might eat me up, third time might make me disappear. I stayed faithful to rum and mother's-ruin, and let the rest go, for once in me fool life.

Year and a half, we had buyers wherever ships could sail. London, Liverpool, Marseilles, Hamburg, Amsterdam, Buenos Aires, Athens, New York, Naples...we did best in seaports, always. I didn't travel everywhere the wine went; we hired folk in time, me and Henry Lee, and we even bought a ship of our own. Weren't no big ship, not so's you'd take notice, but big enough for what we put aboard her, which was the best captain and crew anyone could ask for. That were me doing — Henry Lee wanted to spend more on a fancier ship, but I told him it weren't how many sails that mattered, but the hands on the halyards. And he listened to me, which he mostly did...aye, you couldn't never call him stupid, poor sod. I'll say that, anyway.

Used to look out for that merrow, Henry Lee's Gorblimey, times I were keeping the wine company on its way. Not that I'd likely have known him from any other of the ones I'd see now and again, chasing the flying fish or swimming along with the porpoises — even nastier, they looked, in the middle of those creatures — but I'd ponder whiles if he knew what were passing above his head, and what he'd be thinking about it if he did. But Henry Lee never spoke word about merrows nor mermaids, none of all that, not if he could help it. Choused him, whiles, I did, telling him he were afeard Gorblimey'd twig how well we was getting on, and come for his own piece, any day now. That'd rouse him every time, and he'd snap at me like a moray, so I belayed that. Might could be I shouldn't have, but who's to say? Who's to say now?

He'd other matters on his mind by then, what with building himself a slap-up new house on the seafront north of Velha Goa. Palace and a half, it were, to me own lookout, with two floors and two verandas and *four* chimneys — four chimneys, in a country where you might be lighting a fire maybe twice a year. But Henry Lee told me, never mind: didn't the grandest place in that Devon town where he were born have four chimneys, and hadn't he always wanted to live just so in a house just like that one? Couldn't say nowt much to that, could I? Me that used to stare hours into the cat's-meat shop window back home, cause I got it in me head the butcher were me da? He weren't, by the by, but you see?

But I did speak a word or two when Henry Lee up and got wed. Local girl, Julia Caterina and about five other names I disremember, with a couple of *da*s in between, like the Portygee nobs do. Pretty enough, she were, with dark brown hair for two or three, brown eyes to crack your heart, and a smile to make a priest give up Lent. Aye, and though she started with nobbut *hello* and *goodbye* and *whiskey-soda* in English, didn't she tackle to it till she shamed me, who never mastered no more than a score of words in her tongue, and not one of them fit for her ears. Good-tempered with it, too — though she fought her parents bare-knuckle and toe to toe, like Figg or Mendoza, until they let her toss over the grandee they'd promised her to, all for the love of a common Jack Tar, that being what he still were in their sight, didn't matter how many Bank of England notes he could wave at them. "She's a lady," I says, "for all she's a Portygee, and you're no more a gentleman than that monkey in your mango tree. Money don't make such as us into gentlemen, Henry Lee. All it does, it makes us rich monkeys. You know that, same as me."

"I'm plain daft over her, Ben," says he, like I'd never spoke at all. "Can't eat, can't sleep, can't do a thing but dream about having her near me all the time. Nothing for it but the altar."

"Speaking of altars," says I, "you'll have to turn Papist, and there's not one of her lot'll ever believe you mean it, no more than I would. And never mind her family — what about her friends, what about that whole world she's been part of since the day she were born? You reckon to sweep her up and away from all that, or try to ease yourself into it and hope they won't twig what you are? Which is it to be, then, hey?"

"I don't know, Ben," says Henry Lee, real quiet. "I don't know anything anymore." He said me name, but he weren't talking to me — maybe to that monkey, maybe to the waves out beyond the seawall. "The one thing I've got a good hold on, when I'm with her, it's like coming home. First time I saw her, it came over me, I've been gone a long time, and now I'm home."

Well, you can't talk sense to nobody in a state like that, so I wished them luck and left them to it. Aye, and I even danced at the wedding, sweating like a hog in a new silk suit, Chinee silk, and kicking the bride's shins with every turn. Danced with the mother-in-law too, with her crying on me shoulder the while, how she'd lost her poor angel forever to this soulless brute of an English *merchant*, which no matter he'd converted, he weren't no real Catholic, nor never would be. I tried to get *her* shins, that one, but she were quick, I'll say that for her.

So there's Henry Lee and his pretty new missus, and him so happy staying home with her, hosting grand gatherings just for folk to look at her, he weren't no use for nowt else, save telling me how happy he were. Oh, he still brewed up the salt wine himself — wouldn't trust me nor no other with the makings — but for the rest of it, I were near enough running the business without him. Took in the orders, paid the accounts, kept the books, supervised the packing and the shipping, every case, every bloody bottle. Even bought us a second ship — found her and bargained for her, paid cash down, all on me own hook. Long way from the Isle of Pines, hey?

Like I say, I didn't make all the voyages. Weren't any degree necessary for me to make none on 'em, tell the truth — and besides I were getting on, and coming to like the land more than I ever thought I would. But I never could shake me taste for the Buenos Aires run. I knew some women there, and a few men too...aye, that's a fine town, Buenos. A man could settle in that town, and I were thinking about it then.

So we're three days from landfall, and I'm on deck near sunset, taking the air and keeping a lookout for albatrosses. No finer bird than an albatross, you can keep your eagles. A quiet, quiet evening — wide red sky streaked with a bit of green, fine weather tomorrow. You can hear the gulls' wings, and fish jumping now and then, and the creaking of the strakes, and sometimes even the barrels of salt wine shifting down in the hold. Then I hear footsteps behind me, and I turn and see the bos'un's mate coming up on deck. Can't think of his name right now — a short, wide man, looked like a wine barrel himself, but tough as old boots. Monkey Sucker, that's it, that's what they called him. Because he liked to drink his rum out of a cocoanut, you see. Never see no one doing that, these days.

He weren't looking too hearty, old Monkey Sucker. Red eyes and walking funny, for a start, like his legs didn't belong to him, but I put that down to him nipping at the bung down below. Now I already told you, I never again laid lip to that salt wine from that first day to this, but folk that liked it, why, they'd be waiting on the docks when we landed, ready to unload the cargo themselves right on the spot. And half the crew was the same way, run yourself blind barmy trying to keep them out of the casks. Well, we done the practical, Henry Lee and me: we rigged the hold to keep all but the one barrel under lock and key. That one we left out and easy tapped, and it'd usually last us there and back, wherever we was bound. But this Monkey Sucker...no, he weren't just drunk, I saw that on second glance. Not drunk. I wish it *had* been that, for he weren't a bad sort.

"Mr. Hazeltine," he says to me. "Well, Mr. Hazeltine." Kept on saying me name like we'd just met, and he were trying to get a right fix on it. His voice didn't sound proper, neither, but it kept cracking and bleating — like a boy's voice when it's changing, you know. And there were summat bad wrong with his nose and his mouth.

"Monk," I says back, "you best get your arse below decks before the captain claps eyes on you. You look worse than a poxy bumboy on Sunday morning." The light's going fast now, but I can make out that his face is all bad swole up and somehow *twisty*-like, and there's three lines like welts on both sides of his neck. He's got his arms wrapped around himself, holding himself *tight*, the way you'd think he were about to birth four thousand babies at one go, like some fish do it. And he keeps mumbling me name, over and over, but he's not looking at me, not once, he's looking at the rail on the starboard side. Aye, I should have twigged to that straightaway, I know. I didn't, that's all.

Suddenly he says, "Water." Clear as clear, no mistake about it. "Water," and he points over the side. Excited, bobbing on his toes, like a nipper at Brighton. Third time, "*Water*," and at least I were the first to bawl, "Man overboard!" there's that. In the midst of all the noise and garboil, with everyone tumbling on deck to heave to, and the captain yelling at everyone to lower a boat, with the bos'un crazy trying to lower *two*, 'acos he and Monkey Sucker was old mates...in the midst of it all, I saw Monkey Sucker in the sea. I *saw* him, understand? He weren't splashing around, waving and screaming for help, and he weren't treading water neither. No, he's trying to swim, calm as can be — only he's trying to swim like a fish, laying himself flat in the water and *wriggling* his legs together, same as if he had a tail, understand? Only he didn't have no tail, and he sank like that, straight down, straight down. They kept that boat out all night, but they never did find him.

We reported the death to the customs people in Buenos Aires, and I sent word to Henry Lee back in Goa. The captain and the mates kept asking the crew about why Monkey Sucker had done it, scragged himself that way — were it the drink got him? Were it over some dockside bint? Did he owe triple interest on some loan to Silas Barker or Icepick Neddie

Frey? Couldn't get no answer, not one, that made no sense to them, nor to me neither.

Heading home, every barrel gone, hold full of Argentine wheat for ballast, now it's me turn to chat up the crew, on night watch or in the mess. I go at it like a good 'un, but there's not a soul can tell me anything I don't know.

I were first ashore before dawn at Velha Goa — funny to think of that fine Mandovi River all silted up today, whole place left to the snakes and the kites — and if I didn't run all the way to Henry Lee's house, may I never piss again. Man at the door to let me in, another man to take me hat and offer me a glass. I didn't take it.

I bellow for Henry Lee, and here he comes, rushing downstairs in his shirtsleeves, one shoe off and one on. "Ben, what is it? What's happened? Is it the ship?" Because he never could get used to having two ships of his own — always expected one or t'other to sink or burn, or be taken by the Barbary pirates. I didn't say nowt, just grabbed him by the arm and hauled him off into the room he calls the library. Shut the door, turn around, look into his frighted blue eyes. "It ain't the ship, Henry Lee," I tell him. "It's the hands."

"The hands," he says. "I don't understand."

"And it ain't the hands," I say, "it's the buyers. And it ain't the buyers." I take a breath, wish God'd put a noggin of rum in me fist right now, but there ain't no God. "It's the wine."

Henry Lee shakes his head. He reaches for a bottle on the sideboard, pours himself a drink. Salt wine, it is — I knock it out of his hand, so it splashes on his fancy rug, and now I'm whispering, because if I shout everything comes apart. "It's the wine, Henry Lee. You know it, and now I know."

That about him knowing, that was a guess, and now I'm the one looking away, 'acos of I don't want to find out I'm right. And because it's hard to say the bloody words, either way. "The salt wine," I says. "It frigging well killed a man, this time out, and I'm betting it's done it before."

"No," Henry Lee says. "No, Ben, that's not possible." But I look straight back at him, and I know what he's fighting not to think.

"Maybe he didn't mean no harm, your Gorblimey," I go on. "Maybe he'd no notion what his old precious gift would do to human beings. Maybe it depends on how much of it you drink, or how often." So still in that fine house, I can hear his Julia Caterina turning in the bed upstairs, murmuring into her pillow. I say, "Old Monkey Sucker, he never could keep away from the cask in the hold, maybe that's why...why it happened. Maybe if you don't drink too much."

"No," Henry Lee answers me, and his voice is real quiet too. "That wouldn't make sense, Ben. I drink salt wine every day. A lot of it."

He's always got a flask of the creature somewhere about him, true enough, and you won't see him go too long without his drop. But there's no sign of any change, not in his face, nor in his skin, nor his teeth — and that last time Monkey Sucker said "water" I could see his teeth had got all sprawled out-like, couldn't hardly close his mouth. But Henry Lee just went on looking like Henry Lee, except a little bit grayer, a bit wearier, a bit more pulled-down, like, the way quitting the sea will do to you. No merrow borning there, not that I could see.

"Well, then," says I, "it's not the amount of wine. But it *is* the wine. Tell me that's not so, and I'll believe you, Henry Lee. I will."

Because I never knew him lie to me. Might take his time getting around to telling me some things, but he wouldn't never lie outright. But he just shook his head again, and looked down, and he heaved a sigh sounded more like a death rattle. Says, "It could be. It could be. I don't know, Ben."

"You know," I says. "How long?" He don't answer, don't say nowt for a while — he just turns and turns in a little tight circle, this way and that, like a bear at a baiting. Finally he goes on, mumbling now, like he'd as soon I didn't hear. "The Tagus, last year, that time I took Julia Caterina to Lisbon. A man on the riverbank, he just *tumbled*...I didn't get a really good look, I couldn't be sure what I was seeing, I swear, Ben." I can't make no sound. Henry Lee grabs me hands, wrings them between his until they hurt. "Ben, it's like you said, maybe Gorblimey didn't know himself —"

I pull me hands free, and for a minute I have to close me eyes, 'acos if I was on a ship I'd be seasick. I hear meself saying, "Maybe he didn't. But we do. We know now."

"No, we don't! It still mightn't be the wine — it could be any number of things." He takes a deep, deep breath, plunges on. "Even if — even if that's so, obviously it's *just a few, a very few*, not one in a thousand, if even...I mean, you don't see it happening everywhere, it's just — it's like the way some folk can't abide shellfish, the way cheese gripes your gut, Ben, every time. It's got to be so with the salt wine."

"Even one," I says. It catches in me throat and comes out a whisper, so I can't tell if he's heard. We stand there, looking at each other, like we're waiting to be introduced. Henry Lee reaches for me hand again, but I step away. Henry Lee starts to say *summat*, but then he don't. There's blood in me mouth, I can taste it.

"I done bad things, Henry Lee," I says at last. "I know where I'm going when I go, and none to blame but me. I know who's waiting for me there, too — some nights I see their faces all around the room, plain as I now see you. But in me life I never done nothing, *nothing*...I got to get out of your house, Henry Lee."

And I'm for the door, because I can't look at him no more. He calls after me — once, twice — and I think he's bound sure to try and drag me back, maybe to gull me into seeing things his way, maybe just not to be alone. But he don't, and I walk on home along the seafront, a deal slower than I came. And when I get there — it were a plain little house, nobbut the one servant, and him not living in, because I can't abide folk around me when I rise — when I got there, I drank meself to sleep with me whole stock of good Christian rum. And in the morning I went to see Henry Lee's lawyer — *our* lawyer — Portygee-Goan, he were, name of Andres Furtado, near enough — and I started working an old fool name of Ben Hazeltine loose from the salt wine business. It took me some while.

Cost me a few bob, too, I don't mind saying. We'd made an agreement long back, Henry Lee and me, that if ever I wanted to sell me forty per-cent, he'd have to buy me out, will-he, nil-he. But I didn't want no more of that salt wine money — couldn't swallow the notion, no more than I could have swallowed a single mouthful of the stuff ever again after that second time.

So by and by, all what you call the legalities was taken care of, and there was I, on the beach again, in a manner of speaking. But at least I'd saved a bit — wouldn't last forever, but leastways I could bide me time finding other work, and not before the mast, neither. Too old to climb the rigging, too used to proper dining to go back to cooking in burned pots and rusty pannikins in some Grand Banks trawler's galley — aye, and far too fast-set in me ways of doing things to be taking orders from no captain hadn't seen what I've seen in this world. "Best bide ashore awhile, Ben Hazeltine," I says to meself, "and see who might be needing what you yet can do. There'll be someone," I says, "as there always is," and I'd believe it, too, days on end. But I'd been used to a lot of things regular, not only me meals. Henry Lee, he were one of them, him and his bloody salt wine. Not that I'd have gone back working for the fool — over the side meself first, and I can't swim no better than poor old Monkey Sucker. But still.

So when Henry Lee's young wife shows up at me door, all by herself, no husband, no servants, just her parasol and a whole great snowy spill of lace down her front, I asked her in like she were me long-lost baby sister. We weren't close, didn't know each other much past the salon and the dining room, but she were pretty and sweet, and I liked her the best I could. Like I tried to tell Henry Lee, I don't belong in the same room with no lady. Even when it's me own room.

Any road, she comes in, and she sat down, and she says, "Mr. Ben, my husband, he miss you very much." Never knew a woman quicker off the mark and to the point than little Mrs. Julia Caterina Five-other-names Lee. I can still see her, sitting in me best company chair, with her little fan and her hands in her lap, and that bit of a smile that she could never quite hide. Henry Lee said it were a nervous thing with her mouth, and that she were shamed by it, but I don't know.

"We're old partners, him and me," I answers her. "We was sailors together when we was young. But I'm done working with him, no point in pretending otherwise. You're wasting your time, ma'am, I have to tell you. He shouldn't ought to have sent you here."

"Oh, he did not sent me," she says quickly. "I come — how is it? — on my ownsome? And no, I do not imagine you to come back for him, I would not ask you such a thing, not for him. But you...I think for you this would be good." I gawk at her, and she smiles a real smile now. She says, "You come to us alone — no friend, no woman, never. I think you are lonely."

Not in me life. Nobody in me *life* has ever spoke that word about me. Nobody. Not me, not nobody, never. I can't do nothing but sit there and gawp. She goes on, "He has not many friends either, my Enrique. You, me — maybe one of my brothers, maybe the *abogao*, the lawyer. Not so many, eh?" And she puts out her hands toward me, a little way. Not for me to take them — more like giving me summat. She says, "I do not know what he have done to make you angry. So bad?"

I can't talk — it ain't in me just then, looking at those hands, at her face. I nod, that's all.

No tears, no begging, no trying to talk me round. She just nods herself, and gets up, and I escort her out to where her coachman's waiting. Settling back inside, she holds out one hand, but this time it's formal, it's what nobby Portygee ladies do. I kissed her mother's hand at the wedding, so I've got the trick of it — more like a breath, it is, more like you're smelling a flower. For half a minute, less, we're looking straight into each other's eyes, and I see the sadness. Maybe for Henry Lee, maybe for me — I never did know. Maybe it weren't never there.

But afterwards I couldn't stop thinking about her. I don't mean *her*, not like that, wouldn't have occurred to me. I mean what she said, and the way she looked at me, and her coming to see me by herself, which you won't never see no Portygee lady doing, high nor low. And saying that thing about me being lonely — true or not ain't the point. It were her *saying* it, and how I felt to hear her. I plain wanted to hear her again, is all.

But I didn't. It would have meant seeing Henry Lee, and I weren't no way up to that. I talked to him in me head every time I saw one or t'other of our ships slipping slow out of the harbor in the morning sun, sails filling and the company pennant snapping atop the mizzenmast. And her hold full of poison. I had time enough on me hands to spend with sailors ashore, and shillings enough to buy another round of what's-your-fancy, and questions enough to keep them talking and me mind unsettled. Because most of them hadn't noticed nothing — no shipmates turning, no buyers swimming out to sea, no changelings whispering to them from the dark water. But there was always a couple, two or even three who'd seen *summat* they'd as soon not have seen, and who'd have to down more than a few jars of the best before they'd speak about it even to each other. Aye, I knew *that* feeling, none better.

They wasn't all off our ships, neither. Velha were still a fair-sized port then, not like it is now, and there was traders and packets and merchantmen in from everywhere, big and small. I were down the harbor pretty regular, any road, sniffing after work — shaming, me age, but there you are — and I talked with whoever'd stay for it, officers and foremast hands alike. Near as I could work it out, Henry Lee were right, in his way — however much of the salt wine were going down however many throats all over the world, couldn't be more than almost nobody affected beyond waking next day with a bad case of the whips and jingles. Like he'd said to me, just a few, a very few, and what difference to old Ben Hazeltine? No lookout of mine no more, I were clear out of that whole clamjamfry altogether, and nobody in the world could say I weren't. Not one single soul in the world.

Only I'd been in it, you see. Right up to me whiskers in it, year on year — grown old in it, I had. Call it regret, call it guilt, call it what you like, all I knew was I'd sleep on straw in the workhouse and live on slops and sermons before I'd knock on Henry Lee's door again. Even to have *her* look at me one more time, the way she looked in me house, in me best chair. I've made few promises in me life, and kept less, but I made that one then, made it to meself. Suppose you could call it a vow, like, if that suits you.

And I kept that one. It weren't easy, whiles, what with me not finding nobbut portering to do, or might be pushing a barrow for a day or two, but I held to that vow right up to the day when one of Henry Lee's men come to say his master were in greatest need of me — put it just like that, "greatest need" — and would I please come right away, *please.* Tell the truth, I mightn't have come for Henry Lee himself, but that servant, trying to be so calm and proper, with his eyes so frantic...Goanese Konkany, he were, name of Gopi.

I didn't run there, like I'd last done — didn't even ride in the carriage he'd sent for me. I walked, and I took me own time about it, too, and I thought on just what I'd say, and what he'd do when I said it, and what I'd do then. And before I knew, I were standing on the steps of that fine house, with no butler waiting but Henry Lee himself, with both hands out to drag me inside. "Ben," he keeps saying, "ah, Ben, Ben, Ben." Like Monkey Sucker again, saying *Mr. Hazeltine, Mr. Hazeltine*, over and over.

He looked old, Henry Lee did. Hair gone gray — face slumped in like he'd lost all his teeth at once — shoulders bent to break your heart, the way you'd think he'd been stooping in a Welsh coal mine all his life. And the blue eyes of him...I only seen such eyes one time before, on a donkey that knew it were dying, and just wanted it over with. All I could think to say were, "You shouldn't never have left the sea, Henry Lee — not never." But I didn't say it.

He turned away and started up that grand long stair up to the second floor and the bedrooms, with his footsteps sounding like clods falling on a coffin. And I followed after, wishing the stair'd never end, but keep us climbing on and on for always, never getting where we had to go, and I wished I'd never left the sea neither.

I smelled it while we was still on the stair. It ain't a *bad* smell, considering: it's cold and clean, like the wind off Newfoundland or when you're just entering the Kattegat, bound for Copenhagen. Aye...aye, you could say it's a fishy smell, too, if you care to, which I don't. I'd smelled it before that day, and I've smelled it since, but I don't never smell it without thinking about her, *Señora* Julia Caterina Five-names Lee, Missus Henry Lee. Without seeing her there in the big bed.

He'd drawn every curtain, so you had to stand blind and blinking for a few minutes, till your eyes got used to the dark. She were lying under a down quilt — me wedding gift to the bride, Hindoo lady up in Ponda sewed it for me — but just as we came in she shrugged it off, and you could see her bare as a babby to the waist. Henry Lee, he rushes forward to pull the quilt back up, but she turns her head to look up at him, and he stops where he stands. She makes a queer little sound — hear it outside your window at night, you'd think it were a cat wanting in.

"She can talk still," says Henry Lee, desperate-like, turning to me. "She was talking this morning." I stare into Julia Caterina's pretty brown eyes — huge now, and steady going all greeny-black — and I want to tell Henry Lee, oh, she'll talk all right, no fear. Mermaids *chatter*, believe me — talk both your lugs off, they will, you give them the chance. Mermaids gets lonely.

"She drank so *little*," Henry Lee keeps saying. "She didn't really like any wine, French or Portuguese, or...ours. She only drank it to be polite, when we had guests. Because it was our business, after all. She understood about business." I look down at the quilt where it's covering her lower parts, and I look back at Henry Lee, and he shakes his head. "No, not yet," he whispers. *No tail yet*, is what he meant — *she's still got legs* — but he couldn't say it, no more than me. Julia Caterina reaches up for him, and he sits by her on the bed and kisses both her hands. I can just see the half-circle outlines beginning just below her boobies, very faint against the pale skin. *Scales*....

"How long?" Henry Lee asks, looking down into her face, like he's asking her, not me.

"You'd know better than me," I tells him straight. "I only seen one poor sailor, maybe cooked halfway. And no women."

Henry Lee closes his eyes. "I never..." I can't hardly hear him. He says, "I never...only that one time on the river, in the dark. I never saw."

"Aye, made sure of that didn't you?" I says. "You'll know next time."

He does look at me then, and his mouth makes one silent word — *don't*. After a bit he gets so he can breathe out, "Aren't I being punished enough?"

"Not nearly," I says. But Julia Caterina makes that sound again, and all on a sudden I'm so rotten sorry for her and Henry Lee I can't barely speak words meself. Nowt to do but rest me hand on his shoulder, while he sits there by his wife, and her *turning* under his own hands. Time we leave that sea-smelling room, it's dark outside, same as in.

And I didn't stir out of that house for the next nineteen days. Seems longer to me betimes, remembering — shorter too, other times, short as loving a wall and a barmaid — but nineteen days it were, with all the curtains drawn, every servant long fled, bar Gopi, him who'd come for me. That one, he stayed right along, went on shopping and cooking and sweeping; and if the smell and the closed rooms and us whispering up and down the stair — aye, and the sounds Henry Lee made alone in the night — if it all ever frighted him, he never said. A good man.

Like I figured, she never lost speech. I'd hear them talking hours on end, her and Henry Lee — always in the Portygee, of course, so's I couldn't make out none of it, which was good. Weren't for me to know what Henry Lee was saying to his wife, and her changing into a mermaid along of him getting rich. He tried to tell me some of their talk, but I didn't want to hear it then, and I've forgot it all now — made bleeding sure of *that*. I already know enough as I shouldn't, ta ever so.

Nineteen days. Nineteen mornings rising with me head so full of that sea-smell — stronger every day — I couldn't hardly swallow nowt but maybe porridge, couldn't never drink nowt but water. Nineteen nights lying awake hour on hour in one of the servants' garrets — I put meself there, 'acos I don't dream in them little cubbies the way I do in big echoey rooms such as Henry Lee had for his guests. I don't like dreaming, to this day I don't, and I liked it less then. Never closed me eyes until I had to, in that dark house.

Seventeenth night...seventeenth night, I've just finally gotten to sleep when Henry Lee wakes me, shaking me like the house is afire. I come up fighting and cursing — can't help it, always been that way — and I welt him a rouser on the earhole, but he drags me out of the bed and bundles me down to their room with a blanket around me shoulders. I keep pulling away from him, 'acos I know what I'm going to see, but he won't let go. His blue eyes look like he's been crying blood.

He'd covered her with every damp towel and rag in the house, but she'd thrown them all off...and there it is, there, laying out on the sheets that Henry Lee changes with his own hands every day, and Gopi takes to the *dhobi-wallah* for washing. There it is.

Everything's gone. Legs, feet, belly, all of it, *everything*, gone as though there'd never been nothing below her waist but that tail, scales flickering and glittering like wet emeralds in the candlelight. Look at it one way, it's a wonderful thing, that tail. It's the longest part of a mermaid or a merrow, and even when it's not moving at all, like hers wasn't just then, I swear you can see it *breathing* by itself, if you stand still and look close. In and out, slow, only a little, but you can see. It's them and it's *not* them, and that's all I'm going to say.

Now and then she'd twitch it a bit, flip the finny end some — getting used to it, like, having a tail. Each time she did that, Henry Lee'd draw his breath sharp, but all he said to me as we stood by the bed, he said, "It's made her more beautiful, Ben, hasn't it?" And it had that. She'd always had a good face, Julia Caterina, but the change had shaped it over, same as it had shaped her body. There was a wildness mixed in with the old sweetness now — mermaids is animals, some ways — and it had turned her, *whetted* her, into summat didn't have no end to how beautiful it could be. I told you early on, they ain't all beautiful, but even the ugly ones...see now, people got ends, people got *limits* — mermaids don't. Mermaids got no limits, except the sea.

She said his name, and her voice were different too — higher, yes, but mainly *clearer*, like all the clouds had blown off it. If that voice called for you, even soft, you'd hear it a long way. Henry Lee picked her up in his arms and put his cheek against hers, and she held onto him, and that tail tried to hold him too, bumping hard against his legs. I thought to slip out of there unnoticed, me and me blanket, but then Henry Lee said, quiet-like, "We could...I suppose we could put her in the water tonight, couldn't we, Ben?"

Well, I turned round on that fast, telling him, "Not near!" I pointed at the three double lines on both sides of her neck, so faint they were, still barely visible in her skin. "The gill slits ain't opened yet — drop her in a bathtub, she'd likely drown. Happen they might never open, I don't know. I'm telling you straight, I never seen this — I don't *know!*"

She looked at me then, and she smiled a little, but it weren't her smile. I leaned closer, and she said in English, so softly Henry Lee didn't hear, "Unbind my hair."

They don't all have long golden hair, that's just nursery talk. I seen one off Porto Rico had a mane red as sunset clouds, and I seen a fair old lot with thick dark hair like Julia Caterina's. But I never touched none of them before. It weren't me place to touch her neither, and Henry Lee standing by, too, but I done it anyway, like it were the hair asking me to do it, and not her. First twitch, it all come right down over me hands, ripe and heavy and *hot* — hot like I'd spilled cooking oil on meself, the way it clings and keeps burning, and water makes it worse. Truth, for a minute I thought me hands *was* ablaze — seemed like I could *see* them burning like fireships through that black swirly tangle wouldn't let them go. I yelled out then — I ain't shamed none to admit it, I know what I felt — and I snatched me hands right back, and of course there weren't a mark on them. And I looked into her eyes, and they was green and gray and green again, like the salt wine, and she laughed. She knew I were frighted and hurting, and she laughed and laughed.

I thought there were nothing left of her then — all gone, the little Portygee woman who'd sat in me chair and said something nobody else never said to me before. But then the eyes was hers again, all wide with fear and love, and she reached out for Henry Lee like she really were drowning. Aye, that were the worst of it, some way, those last two days, 'acos of one minute she'd be hissing like a cat, did he try to touch her or pet her, flopping away from him, the way you'd have thought he were her worst enemy in the world. Next minute, curled small in his arms, trembling all over, weeping dry-eyed, the way mermaids do, and him singing low to her in Portygee, sounded like nursery rhymes. Never saw him blubbing himself, not one tear.

She didn't stay in the bed much no more, but managed to get around the room using her arms and her tail — practicing-like, you see. Wouldn't eat nothing, no matter Henry Lee cozened her with the freshest fish and crab, mussels just out of the sea. Sometimes at first she'd take a little water, but by and by she'd show her teeth and knock the cup out of his hand. Mermaids don't drink, no more nor fish do.

They don't sleep, neither — not what you'd call sleeping — so there'd be one of us always by her, him or me, for fear she'd do herself a mischief. We wasn't doing much sleeping then ourselves, by then, so often enough we'd find ourselves side by side, not talking, just watching her while she watched the sea through the window and the moon ripened in the trees. The one time we ever did talk about it, he said to me, "You were right, Ben. I haven't been punished nearly enough for what I've done."

"Some get punished too much," I says, "and some not at all. Don't seem to make much difference, near as I can tell."

Henry Lee shakes his head. "You got out the moment you knew we might have harmed even one person. I stayed on. I'll never be quits for this, Ben."

I don't have no answer, except to tell him about a thing I did long ago that I'm still being punished for meself. I'd never told nobody before, and I'm not about to tell you now. I just did it to maybe help Henry Lee a little, which it didn't. He patted me back and squeezed me shoulder a little bit, but he didn't say no more, and nor did I. We sat together and watched Julia Caterina in the moonlight.

Come that nineteenth night, the moon rose full to bursting, big and bright and yellow as day, with one or two red streaks, like an egg gone bad, laying down a wrinkly-gold path you could have walked on to the horizon...or swum down, as the case might be. Julia Caterina went wild at the sight, beating at the window the way you'd have thought she were a moth trying to get to the candle. It come to me, she'd waited for this moon the same way the turtles wait to come ashore and lay their eggs in the light — the way those tiny fish I disremember flood over the beaches at high tide, millions of them, got to get those eggs buried *fast*, before the next wave sweeps them back out to sea. Now it were like the moon were waiting for her, and she knew the way there.

"Not yet," Henry Lee says, desperate-like, "not yet — *they've* not..." He didn't finish, but I knew he were talking about the pale lines on her neck, darker every day, but still not opened into proper gill slits. But right as he spoke, right then, those same lines swelled and split and flared red, and that sudden, they was there, making her more a fish than the tail ever could, because now she didn't need the land at all, or the air. Aye, now she could stay under water all the time, if she wanted. She were ready for the sea, and she knew it, no more to say.

Henry Lee carried her in his arms all the way down from his grand house — *their* house until two nights ago — to the water's edge, nobody to see nowt, just a couple of fishing boats anchored offshore. A dugout canoe, too, which you still used to see in them days. She wriggled out of his arms there, turning in the air like a cat, and a little wave splashed up in her face as she landed, making her laugh and splash back with her tail. Henry Lee were drenched right off, top to toe, but you could see he didn't know. Julia Caterina — her as had been Julia Caterina — she swam round and round, rolling and diving and admiring all she could do in the water. There's nothing *fits* the sea like a mermaid — not fish, not seals, dolphins, whales, nothing. There in the moonlight, the sea looked happy to be with her.

I can't swim, like I told you — I just waded in a few steps to watch her playing so. All on a sudden — for all the world like she'd heard a call from somewhere — she did a kind of a swirling cartwheel, gave a couple of hard kicks with that tail, and like *that*, she's away, no goodbye, clear of the shore, leaving her own foxfire trail down the middle of that moonlight path. I thought she were gone then, gone forever, and I didn't waste no time in gawping, but turned to see to Henry Lee. He were standing up to his knees in the water, taking his shirt off.

"Henry Lee," I says. "Henry Lee, what the Christ you doing?" He don't even look over at me, but throws the shirt back toward the shore and starts unbuttoning his trews. Bought from the only bespoke gentlemen's tailor in Velha Goa, those pants, still cost you half what you'd pay in Lisbon. Henry Lee just drops them in the water. Goes to work getting rid of his smallclothes, kicking off his soaked shoes, while I'm yapping at him about catching cold, pneumonia. Henry Lee smiles at me. Still got most all his teeth, which even the Portygee nobs can't say they do, most of them. He says, "She'll be lonely out there."

I said summat, must have. I don't recall what it were. Standing there naked, Henry Lee says, "She'll need me, Ben."

"She's got all she needs," I says. "You can't go after her."

"I promised I'd make it up to her," he says. "What I did. But there's no way, Ben, there's no way."

He moves on past me, walking straight ahead, water rising steady. I stumble and scramble in front of him, afeared as I can be, but he's not getting by. "You can't make it up," I tells him. "Some things, you can't ever make up — you live with them, that's all. That's the best you can do." He's taller by a head, but I'm bigger, wider. He's not getting by.

Henry Lee stops walking out toward the deep. Confused-like, shaking his head some, starts to say me name...then he looks over me shoulder and his eyes go wide, with the moon in them. "She's there," he whispers, "she came back for me. There, right *there*." And he points, straining on his toes like a nipper sees the Dutch-biscuit man coming down the street.

I turn me head, just for an instant, just to see where he's pointing. *Summat* glimmers in the shadow of the dugout, diving in and out of the moonlight, and maybe it's a dolphin, and maybe it's Henry Lee's wife, turning for one last look at her poor husband who'd driven both of their lives on the rocks. Didn't know then, don't know now. All I'm sure of is, the next minute I'm sitting on me arse in water up to me chin, and Henry Lee's past me and swimming straight for that glimmer — long, raking Devonshire strokes, looking like he could go on forever if he had to. And bright as the night was, I lost sight of him — and her too, *it*, whatever it were — before he'd reached that boat. Bawled for him till me voice went — even tried to go after him in the dugout — but he were gone. They were gone.

His body floated in next afternoon. Gopi found it, sloshing about in the shallows.

Her family turned over every bit of ground around that house of Henry Lee's, looking for where he'd buried her. I'm dead sure they believe to this day that he killed Julia Caterina and then drowned himself, out of remorse or some such. They was polite as pie whenever we met, no matter they couldn't never stand one solitary thing about me — but after she disappeared only times I saw them was at a *feria*, where they'd always cut me dead. I didn't take it personal.

The will left stock and business to the family, but left both ships to me. I sold one of them for enough money to get meself to Buenos Aires, like I'd been wanting, and start up in the freighting trade, convoying everything from pianos to salt beef, rum to birdseed, tea to railroad ties...whatever you might want moved from *here* to *there*. Got two young partners do most of the real work these days, but I still go along with a shipment, times, just to play I'm still a foremast hand — plain Able-bodied Seaman, same as Henry Lee. The way it was when we didn't know what he died knowing. What I'll die knowing.

He left me the recipe for salt wine, too. I burned it. I'd wanted to buy up the stock and pour every bottle into the sea — giving it back to the merrows, you could say — but the family wouldn't sell, not to me. Heard they sold it to a German dealer, right after I left Goa, and he took it all home to Berlin with him. Couldn't say, meself.

I seen her a time or two since. Once off the Hebrides — leastways, I'm near about sure it was her — and once in the Bay of Biscay. That time she came right up to the ship, calling to me by name, quiet-like. She hung about most of the night, calling, but I never went to the rail, 'acos I couldn't think of nothing to say.

Mr. Sigerson

I'm very proud of this story — written for Michael Kurland's anthology *Sherlock Holmes: The Hidden Years* — because it's my first mystery tale, and so far the only one.

I love reading mysteries, all sorts, and envy their authors almost as much as I envy musicians. I'd give a great deal to have the special mindset that creates a good mystery plot, and then peoples it with characters whom the reader feels don't draw their existence only from the plot. I'm no Holmes expert (though I've known the stories from childhood, and read them all aloud to my children); but I felt I knew the man well enough to chance presenting him through the eyes of a narrator who not only doesn't worship his brilliance but doesn't particularly like him. As much as anything I've done recently, I truly enjoyed being that crotchety, sardonic concertmaster, who admires Sherlock Holmes solely for his musical gifts, and to hell with the rest of the performance.

MY NAME IS Floresh Takesti. I am concertmaster of the Greater Bornitz Municipal Orchestra in the town of St. Radomir, in the Duchy of Bornitz, in the country of Selmira. I state this only because, firstly, there is a centuries-old dispute between our ducal family and the neighboring principality of Gradja over boundaries, bribed surveyors, and exactly who some people think they are; and, secondly, because Bornitz, greater or lesser, is quite a small holding, and has very little that can honestly be said to be its own. Our national language is a kind of untidy Low German, cluttered further by Romanian irregular verbs; our history appears to be largely accidental, and our literature consists primarily of drinking songs (some of them quite energetic). Our farmers grow barley and turnips, and a peculiarly nasty green thing that we tell strangers is kale. Our currency is anything that does not crumble when bitten; our fare is depressingly Slovakian, and our native dress, in all candor, vaguely suggests Swiss bellringers costumed by gleefully maniacal Turks. However, our folk music, as I can testify better than most, is entirely indigenous, since no other people would ever claim it. We are the property of the Austro-Hungarian Empire, or else we belong to the Ottomans; opinions vary, and no one on either side seems really to be interested. As I say, I tell you all this so that you will be under no possible misapprehension concerning our significance in this great turbulence of Europe. We have none.

Even my own standing as concertmaster here poses a peculiar but legitimate question. Traditionally, as elsewhere, an orchestra's first violinist is named concertmaster, and serves the conductor as assistant and counselor, and, when necessary, as a sort of intermediary between him and the other musicians. We did have a conductor once, many years ago, but he left us following a particularly upsetting incident, involving a policeman and a goat — and the Town Council has never been able since to locate a suitable replacement. Consequently, for good or ill, I have been conductor *de facto* for some dozen years, and our orchestra seems none the worse for it, on the whole. Granted, we have always lacked the proper — shall I say *crispness*? — to do justice to the Baroque composers, and we generally know far better than to attempt Beethoven at all; but I will assert that we perform Liszt, Saint-Saëns, and some Mendelssohn quite passably, not to mention lighter works by assorted Strausses and even Rossini. And our Gilbert & Sullivan closing medley almost never fails to provoke a standing ovation, when our audience is sober enough to rise. We may not be the Vienna *Schauspielhaus*, but we do our best. We have our pride.

It was on a spring evening of 1894 that he appeared at my door: the tall, irritating man we knew as Herr Sigerson, the Norwegian. You tell me now that he had other names, which I can well believe — I can tell you in turn that I always suspected he was surely not Norwegian. Norwegians have *manners*, if they have no cuisine; no Norwegian I ever knew was remotely as arrogant, implicitly superior, and generally impossible as this "Sigerson" person. And no, before you ask, it would be almost impossible for me to explain exactly what made him so impossible. His voice? His carriage? His regard, that way of studying one as though one were a canal on Mars, or a bacterium hitherto unknown to mankind? Whatever the immediate cause, I disliked him on sight; and should I learn from you today that he was in reality a prince of your England, this would not change my opinion by a hair. Strengthen it, in fact, I should think.

Nevertheless. Nevertheless, he was, beyond any debate or cavil, a better violinist than I. His tone was richer, his attack at once smoother and yet more vivid; his phrasing far more adventurous than I would ever have dared — or could have brought off, had I dared. I can be as jealous, and even spiteful, as the next man, but I am not a fool. He deserved to sit in the first violinist's chair — my chair for nineteen years. It was merely justice, nothing more.

When he first came to my house — as I recall, he was literally just off the mail coach that sometimes picks up a passenger or two from the weekly Bucharest train — he asked my name, gave his own, and handed me a letter of introduction written by a former schoolmate of mine long since gone on to better things. The letter informed me that the bearer was "a first-rate musician, well-schooled and knowledgeable, who has elected, for personal reasons, to seek a situation with a small provincial orchestra, one preferably located as far off the conventional routes of trade and travel as possible. Naturally, old friend, I thought of you..."

Naturally. Sigerson — he gave no other name then — watched in silence from under dark, slightly arched brows as I perused the letter. He was a tall man, as I have said, appearing to be somewhere in his early forties, with a bold, high-bridged nose — a tenor's nose — in a lean face. I remember clearly a thin scar, looking to be fairly recent, cutting sharply across his prominent left cheekbone. The mouth was a near-twin to that scar, easily as taut and pale, and with no more humor that I could see. His eyes were a flat gray, without any hint of blue, as such eyes most often have, and he had a habit of closing them and pressing his right and left-hand fingertips against each other when he was at his most attentive. I found this particularly irksome, as I did his voice, which was slightly high and slightly strident, to my ear at least. Another might not have noticed it.

I must be honest and admit to you that if the dislike at our first encounter was immediate, it was also entirely on my side. I do not imagine that Herr Sigerson concerned himself in the least over my good opinion, nor that he was even momentarily offended by not having it. He accepted the insulting wage St. Radomir could offer him as indifferently as he accepted my awe — yes, also admitted — when, by way of audition, he performed the Chevalier St-Georges' horrendously difficult *Etude in A Major* at my kitchen table, following it with something appropriately diabolical by Paganini. I told him that there was an attic room available at the Widow Ridnak's for next to nothing, upon which he thanked me courteously enough and rose to leave without another word, only turning at the door when I spoke his name.

"Herr Sigerson? Do you suppose that you might one day reveal to me your personal reasons for burying your considerable gifts in this particular corner of nowhere? I ask, not out of vulgar inquisitiveness, but simply as one musician to another."

He smiled then — I can quite exactly count the times when I ever saw him do such a thing. It was a very odd entity, that smile of his: not without mirth (there was wit and irony in the man, if not what I would call humor), but just below the slow amusement of his lips I felt — rather than saw — a small scornful twist, almost a grimace of contempt. Your Herr Sigerson does not really like human beings very much, does he? Music, yes.

"Herr Takesti," he replied, graciously enough, "please understand that such reasons as I may have for my presence here need in no way trouble St. Radomir. I have no mission, no ill purpose — no purpose at all, in fact, but only a deep desire for tranquility, along with a rather sentimental curiosity concerning the truest wellsprings of music, which do not lie in Vienna or Paris, but in just such backwaters and in such underschooled orchestras as yours." I was deciding whether to rise indignantly to the defense of my town, even though his acid estimate was entirely accurate, when he went on, the smile slightly warmer now, "And, if you will permit me to say so, while I may have displaced the first violin —" for I had already so informed him; why delay the plainly unavoidable? "— the conductor will find me loyal and conscientious while I remain in St. Radomir." Whereupon he took his leave, and I stood in my doorway and watched his tall figure casting its gaunt shadow ahead of him as he made his way down the path to the dirt road that leads to the Widow Ridnak's farm. He carried a suitcase in one hand, his violin case in the other, and he was whistling a melody that sounded like Sarasate. Yes, I believe it *was* Sarasate.

I had mentioned a rehearsal that night, but neither asked nor expected him to attend, only a few hours off the train. I cannot even remember telling him how to find the local beerhall where we have always rehearsed; yet there he was, indifferently polite as ever, tuning up with the rest of the strings. I gave a short, awkward speech, introducing our new first violin to the orchestra (at my prompting, he offered the transparently false Christian name of Oscar), and adding that, from what I had heard at my kitchen table, we could only gain from his accession to my former chair. Most of them were plainly disgruntled by the announcement — a flute and a trombone even wept briefly — which I found flattering, I must confess. But I reassured them that I had every intention of continuing as their devoted guide and leader, and they did seem to take at least some solace from that pledge. No orchestra is ever one big, happy family, but we were all old comrades, which is decidedly better for the music. They would quickly adapt to the changed situation.

In fact, they adapted perhaps a trifle too quickly for my entire comfort. Within an hour they were exclaiming over Sigerson's tone and his rhythmic sense, praising his dynamics as they never had mine — no, this is *not* jealousy, simply a fact — and already beginning to chatter about the possibility of expanding our increasingly stale repertoire, of a single fresh and innovative voice changing the entire character of the orchestra. Sigerson was modest under their admiration, even diffident, waving all applause away; for myself, I spoke not at all, except to bring the rehearsal back into order when necessary. We dispersed full of visions — anyway, they did. I recall that a couple of the woodwinds were proposing the Mozart Violin Concerto, which was at least conceivable; and that same trombone even left whispering, "*Symphonie Fantastique*," which was simply silly. He had them thinking like that, you see, in one rehearsal, without trying.

And we did make changes. Of course we did. You exploit the talent you have available, and Sigerson's presence made it possible for me to consider attempting works a good bit more demanding than the Greater Bornitz Municipal Orchestra had performed in its entire career. No, I should have said, "existence." Other orchestras have *careers*. We are merely happy still to be here.

Berlioz, no. They cannot play what he wrote in Paris, London, Vienna — how then in St. Radomir? Beethoven, no, not even with an entire string section of Sigersons. But Handel... Haydn...Mozart...Telemann...yes, *yes*, the more I thought of it, there was never any real reason why we could not cope decently with such works; it was never anything but my foolish anxiety — and, to be fair to myself, our national inferiority complex, if we are even a nation at all. Who are we, in darkest Selmira, operetta Selmira, joke Selmira, comically backward Selmira, Selmira the laughingstock of bleakly backward Eastern Europe — or so we would be, if anyone knew exactly where we were — to imagine ourselves remotely capable of producing real music? Well, by God, we *were* going to imagine it, and if we made fools of ourselves in the attempt, what was new in that? At least we would be a different sort of fools than we had been. St. Radomir, Bornitz, Selmira...they would never have seen such fools.

That was the effect he had on us, your Mr. Sigerson, and whatever I think of him, for that I will always be grateful. True to his word, he made absolutely no effort to supplant my musical judgment with his own, or to subvert my leadership in any way. There were certainly those who sought him out for advice on everything from interpretation to fingering to modern bowing technique, but for all but the most technical matters he always referred them back to me. I think that this may have been less an issue of loyalty than of complete lack of interest in any sort of authority or influence — as I knew the man, that simply was not in him. He seemed primarily to wish to play music, and to be let alone. And which desire had priority, I could not have told you, then or now.

Very well. You were asking me about the incident which, in my undoubtedly perverse humor, I choose to remember as The Matter of the Uxorious Cellist. Sigerson and I were allies — ill-matched ones, undoubtedly, but allies nonetheless — in this unlikely affair, and if we had not been, who's to say how it might have come out? On the other hand, if we had left it entirely alone...well, judge for yourself. Judge for yourself.

The Greater Bornitz Municipal Orchestra has always been weak in the lower strings, for some reason — it is very nearly a tradition with us. That year we boasted, remarkably, four cellists, two of them rather wispy young women who peeped around their instruments with an anxious and diffident air. The third, however, was a burly Russo-Bulgarian named Volodya Andrichev: blue-eyed, blue-chinned, wild-haired, the approximate size of a church door (and I mean an Orthodox church here), possessed of — or by — an attack that should by rights have set fire to his score. He *ate* music, if you understand me; he approached all composition as consumption, from Liszt and Rossini, at which he was splendid, to Schumann, whom he invariably left in shreds, no matter how I attempted to minimize his presence, or to conceal it outright. Nevertheless, I honored his passion and vivacity; and besides, I liked the man. He had the snuffling, shambling charm of the black bears that still wander our oak forests as though not entirely sure what they are doing here, but content enough nonetheless. I quite miss him, as much time as it's been.

His wife, Lyudmilla Plaschka, had been one of our better woodwinds, but retired on the day of their wedding, that being considered the only proper behavior for a married woman in those times. She was of Bohemian extraction, I believe: a round, blonde little person, distinctly appealing to a particular taste. I remember her singing (alto) with her church choir, eyes closed, hands clasped at her breast — a godly picture of innocent rapture. Yet every now and then, in the middle of a Bach cantata or some Requiem Mass, I would see those wide blue eyes come open, very briefly, regarding the tenor section with the slightest pagan glint in their corners. Basses, too, but especially the tenors. Odd, the detail with which these things come back to you.

He adored her, that big, clumsy, surly Andrichev, even more than he loved his superb Fabregas cello, and much in the same manner, since he plainly felt that both of them were vastly too good for him. Absolute adoration — I haven't encountered much of that in my life, not the real thing, the heart never meant for show that can't help showing itself. It was a touching thing to see, but annoying as well on occasion: during rehearsal, or even performance, I could always tell when his mind was wandering off home to his fluffy golden goddess. Played the devil with his vibrato every time, I can tell you.

To do her justice — very reluctantly — she had the decency, or the plain good sense, to avoid involvements with any of her husband's colleagues. As I have implied, she preferred fellow singers to instrumentalists anyway; and as Andrichev could not abide any sort of vocal recital ("Better cats on a back fence," he used to roar, "better a field full of donkeys in heat"), her inclinations and his rarely came into direct conflict. Thus, if we should chance to be performing in, say, Krasnogor, whose distance necessitates an overnight stay, while she was making merry music at home with Vlad, the clownish basso, or it might be Ruska, that nasal, off-key lyric tenor (*there* was a vibrato you could have driven a *droshky* through)...well, whatever the rest of us knew or thought, we kept our mouths shut. We played our Smetana and our Gilbert & Sullivan medley, and we kept our mouths shut.

I don't know when Andrichev found out, nor how. I cannot even say how we all suddenly knew that he knew, for his shy, growling, but essentially kindly manner seemed not to change at all with the discovery. The music told us, I think — it became even fiercer, more passionate — angrier, in short, even during what were meant to be singing *legato* passages. I refuse to believe, even now, that any member of the Greater Bornitz Municipal Orchestra would have informed him. We were all fond of him, in our different ways; and in this part of the world we tend not to view the truth as an absolute, ultimate good, but as something better measured out in a judiciously controlled fashion. It could very well have been one of his wife's friends who betrayed her — even one of her playmates with a drink too many inside him. I don't suppose it matters now. I am not sure that I would want to know, now.

In any event, this part of the world offers certain traditional options in such a case. A deceived husband has the unquestioned right — the divine right, if you like — to beat his unfaithful wife as brutally as his pride demands, but he may not cut her nose or ears off, except perhaps in one barbarous southern province where we almost never perform. He may banish her back to her family — who will not, as a rule, be at all happy to see her — or, as one violist of my acquaintance did, allow her to stay in his home, but on such terms...Let it go. We may play their music, but we are not altogether a Western people.

But Andrichev did none of these things. I doubt seriously that he ever confronted Lyudmilla with her infidelity, and I know that he never sought out any of her lovers, all of whom he could have pounded until the dust flew, like carpets on a clothesline. More and more withdrawn, drinking as he never used to, he spent most of his time at practice and rehearsal, clearly taking shelter in Brahms and Tschaikovsky and Grieg, and increasingly reluctant to go home. On several occasions he wound up staying the night with one Grigori Progorny — our fourth cellist, a competent enough technician and the nearest he had to an intimate — or with me, or even sprawled across three chairs in that cold, empty beerhall, always clutching his cello fiercely against him as he must have been used to holding his wife. None of us ever expressed the least compassion or fellow-feeling for his misery. He would not have liked it.

Sigerson was perfectly aware of the situation — for all his air of being concerned solely with tone and tempo and accuracy of phrasing, I came to realize that he missed very little of what was going on around him — but he never commented on it; not until after a performance in the nearby town of Ilyagi. Our gradually expanding repertoire was winning us both ovations and new bookings, but I was troubled even so. Andrichev's playing that evening had been, while undeniably vigorous, totally out of balance and sympathy with the requirements of Schubert and Scriabin, and even the least critical among us could not have helped but notice. On our way home, bumping and lurching over cowpaths and forest trails in the two wagons we still travel in, Sigerson said quietly, "I think you may have to speak with Mr. Andrichev."

Most of the others were asleep, and I needed to confide in someone, even the chilly Mr. Sigerson. I said, "He suffers. He has no outlet for his suffering but the music. I do not know what to do, or what to say to him. And I will not discharge him."

Surprisingly, Sigerson smiled at me in the pitch darkness of the wagon. A shadowy, stiff smile, it was, but a smile nevertheless. "I never imagined that you would, Herr Takesti. I am saying only —" and here he hesitated for a moment "— I am saying that if you do *not* speak to him, something perhaps tragic is quite likely to happen. What you may say is not nearly as important as the fact that he knows you are concerned for him. You are rather a forbidding person, concertmaster."

"*I?*" I demanded. I was absolutely stunned. "*I* am forbidding? There is no one, *no one*, in this orchestra who cannot come to me — who *has* not come to me — under any circumstances to discuss anything at all at any time. You know this yourself, Herr Sigerson." Oh, how well I remember how furious I was. Forbidding, indeed — this from *him!*

The smile only widened; it even warmed slightly. "Herr Takesti, this is perfectly true, and I would never deny it. Anyone may come to you, and welcome — but you do not yourself go out to them. Do you understand the difference?" After another momentary pause, while I was still taking this in, he added, "We are more alike than you may think, Herr Takesti."

The appalling notion that there might be some small truth in what he said kept me quiet for a time. Finally I mumbled, "I will speak to him. But it will be no help. Believe me, I know."

"I believe you." Sigerson's voice was almost gentle — totally unnatural for that querulous rasp of his. "I have known men like Andrichev, in other places, and I fear that the music will not always be outlet enough for what is happening to him. That is all I have to say."

And so it was. He began humming tunelessly to himself, which was another annoying habit of his, and he was snoring away like the rest by the time our horses clumped to a stop in front of their stable. Everyone dispersed, grumbling sleepily, except Andrichev, who insisted on sleeping in the wagon, and grew quite excited about it. He would have frozen to death, of course, which may well have been what he wanted, and perhaps a mercy, but I could not allow it. Progorny eventually persuaded him to come home with him, where he drank mutely for the rest of the night, and slept on the floor all through the next day. But he was waiting for me at rehearsal that evening.

What are you expecting? I must ask you that at this point. Are you waiting for poor Herr Andrichev to kill his wife — to stab or shoot or strangle the equally pitiable Lyudmilla Plaschka — or for her to have him knocked on the head by one of her lovers and to run off with *that* poor fool to Prague or Sofia? My apologies, but none of that happened. *This* is what happened.

It begins with the cello: Andrichev's Fabregas, made in Lisbon in 1802, not by Joao, the old man, but by his second son Antonio, who was better. One thinks of a Fabregas as a violin or a guitar, but they made a handful of cellos too, and there are none better anywhere, and few as good; the rich, proud, tender sound is surely unmistakable in this world. And what in God's own name Volodya Andrichev was doing with a genuine Fabregas I have no more idea than you, to this day. Nor can I say why I never asked him how he came by such a thing — perhaps I feared that he might tell me. In any event, it was his, and he loved it second only to Lyudmilla Plaschka, as I have said. And that cello, at least, truly returned his love. You would have to have heard him, merely practicing scales in his little house on a winter morning, to understand.

So, then — the cello. Now, next — early that fall, Lyudmilla fell ill. Suddenly, importantly, desperately ill, according to Progorny; Andrichev himself said next to nothing about it to the rest of us, except that it was some sort of respiratory matter. Either that, or a crippling, excruciating intestinal ailment; at this remove, such details are hard to recall, though I am sure I would be able to provide them had I liked Lyudmilla better. As it was, I felt concern only — forgive an old man's unpleasant frankness — for Andrichev's concern for her, which seemed in a likely way to destroy his career. He could not concentrate at rehearsal; the instinctive sense of cadence, of pulse, that was his great strength, fell to ruin; his bowing went straight to hell, and his phrasing — always as impulsive as a fifteen-year-old in June — became utterly erratic, which, believe me, is the very kindest word I can think of. On top of all that, he would instantly abandon a runthrough — or, once, a performance! — because word had been brought to him that Lyudmilla's illness had taken some awful turn. I could have slaughtered him without a qualm, and slept soundly afterward; so you may well imagine what I thought of Lyudmilla Plaschka. Murderous fancies or not, of course I favored him. Not because he suffered more than she — who ever knows? — but because he was one of *us*. Like that — like *us*. It comes down to that, at the last.

He sold the cello. To his friend Progorny. No fuss, no sentimental self-indulgence — his wife needed extensive (and expensive) medical care, and that was the end of that. Any one of us would have done the same; what was all the to-do about? At least, the Fabregas would stay in the family, just to his left, every night, while he himself made cheerful do on a second-hand DeLuca found pawned in Gradja. There are worse cellos than DeLucas. I am not saying there aren't.

But the bloody thing threw off the balance of the strings completely. How am I to explain this to you, who declare yourself no musician? We have always been weak in the lower registers, as I have admitted: Andrichev and that instrument of his had become, in a real sense, our saviors, giving us depth, solidity, a taproot, a place to come home to. Conductor and concertmaster, I can tell you that none of the Greater Bornitz Municipal Orchestra — and in this I include Herr Sigerson himself — actually took their time from me. Oh, they looked toward me dutifully enough, but the corners of their eyes were focused on the cello section at all times. As well they should have been. Rhythm was never my strong suit, and I am not a fool — I have told you that as well.

But there are cellos and cellos, and the absence of the Fabregas made all the difference in the world to us. That poor pawnshop DeLuca meant well, and it held its pitch and played the notes asked of it as well as anyone could have asked. Anyone who wasn't used — no, *attuned* — to the soft roar of the Fabregas, as our entire orchestra was attuned to it. It wasn't a fair judgment, but how could it have been? The *sound* wasn't the same; and, finally, the sound is everything. Everything. All else — balance, tempo, interpretation — you can do something about, if you choose; but the *sound* is there or it isn't, and that bloody ancient Fabregas was our sound and our soul. Yes, I know it must strike you as absurd. I should hope so.

Progorny gave it his best — no one ever doubted that. It was touching, poignant, in a way: he seemed so earnestly to believe that the mere possession of that peerless instrument would make him — had already made him — a musician equal to such a responsibility. Indeed, to my ear, his timbre was notably improved, his rhythm somewhat firmer, his melodic line at once more shapely and more sensible. But what of it? However kindly one listened, it wasn't the *sound*. The cello did not feel for him what it felt for Andrichev, and everyone knew it, and that is the long and the short of it. Musical instruments have neither pity nor any notion of justice, as I have reason to know. Especially the strings.

Whatever Progorny had paid him for the cello, it could not have been anything near its real value. And Lyudmilla grew worse. Not that I ever visited her in her sickbed, you understand, but you may believe that I received daily — hourly — dispatches and bulletins from Andrichev. It very nearly broke my peevish, cynical old heart to see him so distraught, so frantically disorganized, constantly racing back and forth between the rehearsal hall, the doctor's office, and his own house, doing the best he could to attend simultaneously to the wellbeing of his wife and that of his music. For an artist, this is, of course, impossible. Work or loved ones, passions or responsibilities...when it comes down to that, as it always does, someone goes over the side. Right, wrong, it is how things are. It is how we are.

Yes, of course, when I look back now, it was remiss of me not to go to Lyudmilla at the first word of her illness. But I didn't *like* her, you see — what a sour old person I must seem to you, so easily to detest both her and your hero Mr. Sigerson — and I was not hypocrite enough, in those days, to look into those ingenuous blue eyes and say that I prayed for the light of health swiftly to return to them once more. Yes, I wanted her to recover, almost as much as I wanted her to leave her husband alone to do what he was meant to do — very well, what *I* needed him to do. Let her have her lovers, by all means; let her sing duets with them all until she burst her pouter-pigeon breast; but let *me* have my best cellist back in the heart of my string section — and let *him* have his beautiful Fabregas under his thick, grubby, peasant hands again. Where it belonged.

Mind you, I had no idea how I would ransom it back, and reimburse Progorny (sad usurper, cuckolded by his own instrument) the money that had gone so straight to Lyudmilla's physician. And kept going to him, apparently, for Lyudmilla's condition somehow never seemed to improve.

Andrichev was soon enough selling or pawning other belongings — books to bedding, old clothes to old flowerpots, a warped and stringless *bouzouki*, a cracked and chipped set of dishes — anything for which anyone would give him even a few more coins for his wife's care. Many of us bought worthless articles from him out of a pity which, not long before, he would have rejected out of hand. I wonder whether Sigerson still has that cracked leather traveling bag with the broken lock — I think the motheaten fur cloak is somewhere in my attic. I *think* so.

None of us ever saw Lyudmilla Plaschka at all anymore — the doctor, a Romanian named Nastase, kept her quarantined in all but name — but we read her worsening condition, and the wasteful uselessness of each new treatment, in Andrichev's face. He shrank before our eyes, that bear, that ox, call him what you like; he hollowed and hunched until there seemed to be nothing more to him than could be found inside his cello. Less, because the Fabregas, and even the DeLuca, made music of their emptiness, and Andrichev's sound — there it is again, always the *sound* — grew thinner, dryer, more distant, like the cry of a lone cricket in a desert. I still squirm with bitter shame to recall how hard it became for me to look at him, as though his despair were somehow my doing. My only defense is that we were all like that with him then, all except his comrade Progorny. And Sigerson, remote and secretive as ever, who, nevertheless, made a point of complimenting his playing after each performance. I should have done that, honesty be damned — I know I should have. Perhaps that is why the memory of that man still irritates me, even now.

Then, one late summer afternoon, with Sigerson's comment, "We are more alike than you may think, Herr Takesti," continuing to plague me, I determined to pay a call on Lyudmilla Plaschka myself. I even brought flowers, not out of sympathy, but because flowers (especially a damp, slightly wilted fistful) generally get you admitted everywhere. I must say, I do enjoy not lying to you.

Andrichev's house, which looked much as he had in the good days — disheveled but sturdy — was located in the general direction of the Widow Ridnak's farm, but set some eight miles back into the barley fields, where the dark hills hang over everything like thunderheads ripe with rain. I arrived just in time to see Dr. Nastase — a youngish, strongly built man, a bit of a dandy, with a marked Varna accent — escorting a tattered, odorous beggar off the property, announcing vigorously, "My man, I've told you before, we're not having your sort here. Shift yourself smartly, or I'll set the dogs on you!" A curious sort of threat, I remember thinking at the time, since the entire dog population of the place consisted only of Lyudmilla's fat, flop-eared spaniel, who could barely be coaxed to harass a cat, let alone a largish beggar. The man mumbled indistinct threats, but the doctor was implacable, shoving him through the gate, latching and locking it, and warning him, "No more of this, sir, do you understand me? Show your face here again, and you'll find the police taking an interest in your habits. Do you understand?" The beggar indicated that he did, and meandered off, swearing vague, foggy oaths, as Dr. Nastase turned to me, all welcoming smiles now.

"Herr Takesti, it must be? I am so happy and honored to meet you, I can hardly find the words. Frau Lyudmilla speaks *so* highly of you — and as for Herr Andrichev..." And here he literally kissed his fingertips, may I be struck dead by lightning this minute if I lie. The last person I saw do such a thing was a Bucharest chef praising his own veal cutlets.

"I came to see Frau Lyudmilla," I began, but the doctor anticipated me, cutting me off like a diseased appendix.

"Alas, *maestro*, I cannot permit sickroom visits at the present time. You must understand, her illness is of a kind that can so very, very easily be tipped over into —" here he shrugged delicately "— by the slightest disturbance, the least suggestion of disorder. With diseases of this nature, a physician walks a fine line — like a musician, if you will allow me — between caution and laxity, overprotectiveness and plain careless negligence. I choose to err on the side of vigilance, as I am sure you can appreciate."

There was a good deal more in this vein. I finally interrupted him myself, saying, "In other words, Frau Lyudmilla is to receive no visitors but her husband. And perhaps not even he?" Dr. Nastase blushed — very slightly, but he had the sort of glassy skin that renders all emotions lucid — and I knew what I knew. And so, I had no doubt, did Volodya Andrichev, and his business was his business, as always. I handed over my flowers, left an earnest message, and then left myself, hurrying through the fields to catch up with that beggar. There was something about his bleary yellowish eyes....

Oh, but he was positively furious! It remains the only time I ever saw him overtaken by any strong emotion, most particularly anger. "How did you *know?*" he kept demanding. "I must insist that you tell me — it is more important than you can imagine. How did you recognize me?"

I put him off as well as I could. "It is hard to say, Herr Sigerson. Just a guess, really — call it an old man's fancy, if you like. I could as easily have been wrong."

He shook his head impatiently. "No, no, that won't do at all. Herr Takesti, for a variety of reasons, which need not concern us, I have spent a great deal of time perfecting the arts of concealment. Camouflage lies not nearly so much in costumes, cosmetics — such as the drops in my eyes that make them appear rheumy and degenerate — but in the smallest knacks of stance, bearing, movement, the way one speaks or carries oneself. I can stride like a Russian prince, if I must, or shuffle as humbly as his ostler —" and he promptly demonstrated both gaits to me, there in the muddy barley fields. "Or whine like a drunken old beggar, so that that scoundrel of a doctor never took me for anything but what he saw. Yet *you...*" and here he simply shook his head, which told me quite clearly his opinion of my perceptiveness. "I must know, Herr Takesti."

"Well," I said. I took my time over it. "No matter what concoction you may put in your eyes, there is no way to disguise their arrogance, their air — no, their *knowledge* — of knowing more than other people. It's as well that you surely never came near Lyudmilla Plaschka, looking like that. That doctor may be a fool, but she is none." It was cruel of me, but I was unable to keep from adding, "And even a woodwind would have noticed those fingernails. Properly filthy, yes — but so perfectly trimmed and shaped? Perhaps not." It was definitely cruel, and I enjoyed it very much.

The head-shake was somewhat different this time. "You humble me, Herr Takesti," which I did not believe for a minute. Then the head came up with a positive flirt of triumph. "But I did indeed see our invalid Lyudmilla Plaschka. That much I can claim."

It was my turn to gape in chagrin. "You *did?* Did she see *you?*" He laughed outright, as well he should have: a short single cough. "She did, but only for a moment — not nearly long enough for my arrogant eyes to betray me. There is a cook, especially hired by Dr. Nastase to prepare nutritious messes for his declining patient. A kindly woman, she let me into the kitchen and prepared me a small but warming meal — decidedly unhealthy, bless her fat red hands. When her attention was else-where, I took the opportunity to explore that area of the house, and was making a number of interesting discoveries when Lyudmilla Plaschka came tripping brightly along the corridor — not wrapped in a nightgown, mind you, nor in a snug, padded bed-jacket, but dressed like any hearty country housewife on her way to requisition a snack between meals. She screamed quite rightly when she noticed me, and I was rather hurriedly removing myself from the premises when I ran into the good doctor." He made the laugh-sound again. "The rest, obviously, you know."

I was still back at the moment of the encounter. "Tripping? Brightly?"

"Frau Plaschka," Sigerson said quietly, "is no more ill than you or I." He paused, deliberately theatrical, savoring my astonishment, and went on, "It is plain that with her lover, Dr. Nastase, she has conceived a plan to milk Volodya Andrichev of every penny he has, to cure her of her non-existent affliction. Perhaps she will induce him to sell the house — if he has sold his cello for her sake, anything is possible. You would under-stand this better than I."

A sop to my own vanity, that last, but I paid it no heed. "I cannot believe that she...that *anyone* could do such a thing. I *will* not believe it."

Sigerson sighed and, curiously enough, the sound was not in the least contemptuous. "I envy you, Herr Takesti. I truly envy all those who can set limits to their observation, who can choose what they will believe. For me, this is not possible. I have no choice but to see what is before me. I have no choice." He meant it, too — I never doubted that — and yet I never doubted either that he would ever have chosen differently.

"But why?" I felt abysmally stupid merely asking the question. I knew why well enough, and still I had to say it. "Andrichev is the most devoted husband I have ever seen in my life. Lyudmilla Plaschka will never find anyone to love her as he does. Can she not see that?"

Sigerson did not reply, but only looked steadily at me. I think that was actually a compliment. I said slowly, "Yes. I know. Some people cannot bear to be loved so. I know that, Herr Sigerson."

We became allies in that moment; the nearest thing to friends we ever could have become. Sigerson still said nothing, watching me. I said, "This is unjust. This is worse than a crime. They must be stopped, and they should be punished. What shall we do?"

"Wait," Sigerson said, simply and quietly. "We wait on circumstance and proper evidence. If we two — and perhaps one or two others — set ourselves to watch over that precious pair at all times, there is little chance of their making the slightest move without our knowledge. A little patience, Herr Takesti, patience and vigilance." He touched my shoulder lightly with his fingertips, the only time I can recall even so small a gesture of intimacy from him. "We will have them. A sad triumph, I grant you, but we will have them yet. Patience, patience, concertmaster."

And so we did wait, well into the fall, and we did trap them, inevitably: not like Aphrodite and Ares, in a golden net of a celestial cuckold's designing, but in the tangled, sweated sheets of their own foolishness. Lyudmilla Plaschka and her doctor never once suspected that they were under constant observation, if not by Sigerson and myself, what time we could spare from music, then by a gaggle of grimy urchins, children of local transients. Sigerson said that he had often employed such unbuttoned, foul-mouthed waifs in a similar capacity in other situations. I never doubted him. These proved, not only punctual and loyal, but small fiends for detail. Dr. Nastase's preferred hour for visiting his mistress (married himself, there were certain constraints on his mobility); Frau Andrichev's regular bedtime routine, which involved a Belgian liqueur and a platter of marzipan; even Volodya's customary practice schedule, and the remarks that he grumbled to himself as he tuned his cello — they had it all, not merely the gestures and the words, but the expression with which the words were pronounced. They could have gathered evidence for the Recording Angel, those revolting brats.

"I have discovered the time and destination of their flight," Sigerson told me one morning when I relieved him as sentinel — as spy, rather; I dislike euphemism. He had gained entrance into the house on several occasions since the first, knowing the occupants' habits so well by now that he was never surprised again. "They are interesting conspirators — I discovered the trunks and valises stored in a vacant, crumbling outbuilding easily enough, but it took me longer than I had expected to find the two first-class railway tickets from Bucharest through to Naples, and the boat vouchers for New York City. Do you know where those were hidden?" I shook my head blankly. "At the very bottom of the woodpile, wrapped quite tidily in oilcloth. Obviously, our friends will be taking their leave within the next two or three weeks, before the nights turn cold enough for a fire to be necessary."

"Impressive logic," I said. Sigerson allowed himself one of his distant smiles. I asked, "What about the money they've swindled out of poor Andrichev? They'll have hidden it in some bank account, surely — in Italy, perhaps, or Switzerland, or even America. How will we ever recover it for him?"

If only Sigerson could have seen his own eyes at that moment, he might have understood what I meant by the impossibility of masking their natural lofty expression. "I think we need have no concern on that score," he replied. "Those two are hardly the sort to trust such liquid assets to a bank, and I would venture that Lyudmilla Plaschka knows men too well ever to allow her spoils out of her sight. No, the money will be where she can quickly put her hands on it at any moment. I would expect to find it in her bedroom, most probably in a small leather traveling case under the far window. Though, to be candid —" here he rubbed his nose meditatively "— there are one or two other possible locations, unfortunately beyond my angle of vision. We shall learn the truth soon."

We learned it a bit sooner than either of us expected; not from our unwashed sentries, but from the owner of the livery stable from which we always hired our traveling wagons. He and I were haggling amiably enough over feed costs for our customary autumn tour of the provinces, when he mentioned that his good humor arose from a recent arrangement personally to deliver two passengers to the Bucharest railway station in his one *calèche*, behind his best team. It took remarkably few Serbian dinars to buy the names of his new clients from him, along with the time — eleven o'clock, tomorrow night! — and only a few more to get him to agree to take us with him when he went to collect them. Treachery is, I fear, the Selmiri national sport. It requires fewer people than football, and no uniforms at all.

I wanted to bring the whole matter before the police at this point, but Sigerson assured me that there would be no need for this. "From what I have seen of the St. Radomir constabulary, they are even more thickwitted than those of —" did he stumble momentarily? "— the gendarmes of Oslo, which I never thought possible. Trust me, our quarry will not slip the net now." He did preen himself slightly then. "Should Dr. Nastase offer physical resistance, I happen to be a practitioner of the ancient art of *baritsu* — and you should be well able to cope with any skirmish with Frau Andrichev." I honestly *think* that was not meant as condescension, though with Sigerson it was hard to tell. A month of surveillance had made it clear to us both that Lyudmilla Plaschka, when not on her death-bed, was certainly a spirited woman.

A full rehearsal was scheduled for the following night; I elected to cancel it entirely, rather than abridge it, musicians being easily distressed by interruptions in routine. There were some questions, some grumbling, but nothing I could not fob off with partial explanations. Sigerson and I were at the livery stable by ten o'clock, and it was still some minutes before eleven when the *calèche* drew up before the Andrichev house and the coachman blew his horn to announce our arrival.

The luggage was already on the threshold, as was an impatient Lyudmilla Plaschka, clad in sensible gray traveling skirt and shirtwaist, cleverly choosing no hat but a peasant's rough shawl, to hide her hair and shadow her features. She had, however, been unable to resist wearing what must have been her best traveling cloak, furred richly enough for a Siberian winter; it must have cost Volodya Andrichev six months' pay. She looked as eager as a child bound for a birthday party, but I truly felt my heart harden, watching her.

I stepped down from the *calèche* on the near side, Sigerson on the other, as Dr. Nastase came through the door. He was dressed even more nattily than usual, from his shoes — which even I could recognize as London-made — to his lambswool Russian-style hat. When he saw us — and the coachman on his box, leaning forward as though waiting like any theatregoer for the curtain to rise — he arched his eyebrows, but only said mildly, "I understood that this was to be a private carriage."

"And so it is indeed," Sigerson answered him, his own voice light and amused. "But the destination may not be entirely to your liking, Doctor." He came around the coach, moving very deliberately, as though trying not to startle a wild animal. He went on, "I am advised that the cuisine of the St. Radomir jail is considered —" he paused to ponder the *mot juste* "— questionable."

Dr. Nastase blinked at him, showing neither guilt nor fear, but only the beginning of irritation. "I do not understand you." Lyudmilla Plaschka put him aside, smoothly enough, but quite firmly, and came forward to demand, "Just what is your business here? We have no time for you." To the coachman she snapped, "The price we agreed on does not include other passengers. Take up our baggage and let them walk home."

The coachman spat tobacco juice and stayed where he was. Sigerson said, speaking pointedly to her and ignoring the doctor, "Madam, you know why we are here. The hospice is closed; the masquerade is over. You would be well-advised to accompany us peaceably to the police station."

I have known people whose consciences were almost unnaturally clean look guiltier than they. Lyudmilla Plaschka faltered, "Police station? Are you the police? But what have we done?"

My confidence wavered somewhat itself at those words — she might have been a schoolgirl wrongfully accused of cribbing the answers to an examination — but Sigerson remained perfectly self-assured. "You are accused of defrauding your husband of a large sum of money by feigning chronic, incurable illness, and of attempting further to flee the country with your ill-gotten gains and your lover. Whatever you have to say to this charge, you may say to the authorities." And he stepped up to take her arm, for all the world as though he were an authority himself.

Dr. Nastase rallied then, indignantly striking Sigerson's hand away before it had ever closed on Lyudmilla Plaschka's elbow. "You will not touch her!" he barked. "It is true that we have long been planning to elope, to begin our new life together in a warmer, more open land —" the elbow found his ribs at that point, but he pressed on "— but at no time did we ever consider cheating Volodya Andrichev out of a single dinar, zloty, ruble, or any other coin. We are leaving tonight with nothing but what is in my purse at this moment, and supported by nothing but my medical talents, such as they are, and Frau Andrichev's vocal gifts. By these we will survive, and discover our happiness."

Yes, yes, I know — he was not only an adulterer and a betrayer, but a very bad orator as well. And all the same, I could not help admiring him, at least at the time. Even bad orators can be sincere, and I could not avoid the troubling sense that this man meant what he was saying. It did not seem to trouble Sigerson, who responded coolly, "I will not contradict you, Dr. Nastase. I will merely ask you to open the small traveling case next to Lyudmilla Plaschka's valise — that one there, yes. If you will? Thank you."

I may or may not be a forbidding personality; he could certainly, when he chose, be a far more commanding one than I had ever imagined. I would have opened any kit of mine to his inspection at that point. Dr. Nastase hesitated only a moment before he silently requested the key from

Lyudmilla Plaschka and turned it in the dainty silver lock of the traveling case. I remember that he stepped back then, to allow her to open the lid herself. Love grants some men manners, and I still choose to believe that Dr. Nastase loved Volodya Andrichev's wife, rightly or wrongly.

There was no money in the traveling case. I looked, I was there. Nothing except a vast array of creams, lotions, salves, ointments, unguents, decoctions...all the sort of things, my doddering brain finally deduced, that an anxious Juliet, some years the senior of her Romeo, might bring along on an elopement to retain the illicit magic of the relationship. I had only to glance at Lyudmilla Plaschka's shamed face for the truth of that.

To do Sigerson justice, his resolve never abated for an instant. He simply said, "By your leave," and began going through Dr. Nastase and Lyudmilla Plaschka's belongings just as though he had a legal right to do so. They stood silently watching him, somehow become bedraggled and forlorn, clinging together without touching or looking at each other. And I watched them all, as detached as the coachman: half-hoping that Sigerson would find the evidence that Volodya Andrichev had been viciously swindled by the person he loved most; with the rest of myself hoping...I don't know. I don't know what I finally hoped.

He found the money. A slab of notes the size of a brick; a small but tightly packed bag of coins; both tucked snugly into the false lid of a shabby steamer trunk, as were the tickets he had discovered earlier. The faithless wife and the devious doctor gaped in such theatrically incredulous shock that it seemed to make their culpability more transparent. They offered no resistance when Sigerson took them by the arm, gently enough, and ordered the coachman to take us back to town.

At the police station they made formal protest of their innocence; but they seemed so dazed with disbelief that I could see it registering as guilt and shame with the constables on duty. They were placed in a cell — together, yes, how many cells do you think we have in St. Radomir? — and remanded for trial pending the arrival of the traveling magistrate, who was due any day now. The doctor, ankles manacled, hobbled off with his warder without a backward glance; but Lyudmilla Plaschka — herself unchained — turned to cast Sigerson and me a look at once proud and pitiful. She said aloud, "*You* know what we have done, and what we did not do. You cannot evade your knowledge." And she walked away from us, following Dr. Nastase.

Sigerson and I went home. When we parted in front of my house, I said, "A wretched, sorry business. I grieve for everyone involved. Including ourselves." Sigerson nodded without replying. I stood looking after him as he started on toward the Widow Ridnak's. His hands were clasped behind him, his high, lean shoulders stooped, and he was staring intently at the ground.

Our tour began the next day — we did well in Gradja, very well in Plint, decently in Srikeldt, Djindji, Gavric and Bachacni, and dreadfully in Boskvila, as always. I cannot tell you why I still insist on scheduling us to perform in Boskvila every year, knowing so much better, but it should tell you at least something about me.

But even in foul Boskvila, Volodya Andrichev played better than I had ever heard him. I detest people who are forever prattling about art in terms of human emotions, but there was certainly a new — not power, not exactly warmth, but a kind of deep, majestic heartbeat, if you will — to his music, and so to all of ours as well. He said nothing to anyone about his wife's arrest with her lover, nor did anyone — including Sigerson and his friend Progorny — ask him any questions, nor speak to him at all, except in praise. We did not see St. Radomir again for a week and a half, and the moment we arrived Andrichev tried to commit suicide.

No, no, not the precise moment, of course not, nor did it occur just as the wagons rolled past the town limits. Nor did anyone recognize his action for what it was, except Sigerson. As though he had been waiting for exactly this to happen, he leaned swiftly forward almost before Andrichev toppled over the side in a fall that would have landed him directly under our team's hooves and our wagon's iron-bound wheels. A one-armed scoop, a single grunt, and Andrichev was sprawling at our feet before the rest of the company had drawn breath to cry out. Sigerson looked down at him and remarked placidly, "Come now, Herr Andrichev, we did not play *that* poorly in Boskvila." The incipient screams were overtaken by laughter, quickly dissolving any suggestion of anything more sinister than an accident. At the livery stable, before shambling away, Andrichev thanked Sigerson gruffly, apologizing several times for his clumsiness. It was early in the evening, and I remember that a few snowflakes were beginning to fall, a very few, twinkling for an instant in his mustache.

This night, for some unspoken reason, I passed up my own house and walked on silently with Sigerson, all the way to the Ridnak farm. The Widow and her sons were already asleep. Sigerson invited me into the back kitchen, poured us each a glass of the Widow's homebrewed *kvass*, and we toasted each other at the kitchen table, all without speaking. Sigerson finally said, "A sorry business indeed, Herr Takesti. I could wish us well out of it."

"But surely we are," I answered him, "out and finished, and at least some kind of justice done. The magistrate has already passed sentence — three years in prison for the woman, five for the man, as the natural instigator of the plot — and the money will be restored to Volodya Andrichev within a few days. A miserable matter, beyond doubt — but not without a righteous conclusion, surely."

Sigerson shook his head, oddly reluctantly, it seemed to me. "Nothing would please me better than to agree with you, concertmaster. Yet something about this affair still disturbs me, and I cannot bring it forward from the back of my mind, into the light. The evidence is almost absurdly incontrovertible — the culprits are patently guilty — everything is properly tied-up...and still, and still, *something*..." He fell silent again, and we drank our *kvass* and I watched him as he sat with his eyes closed and his fingertips pressed tightly against each other. For the first time in some while — for there is nothing to which one cannot become accustomed — I remembered to be irritated by that habit of his, and all the solitary self-importance that it implied. And even so, I understood also that this strange man had not been placed on earth solely to puzzle and provoke me; that he had a soul and a struggle like the rest of us. That may not seem to you like a revelation, but it was one to me, and it continues so.

How long we might have remained in that farm kitchen, motionless, unspeaking, sharing nothing but that vile bathtub brandy, it is impossible to say. The spell was broken when Sigerson, with no warning, was suddenly on his feet and to one side, in the same motion, flattening his back against the near wall. I opened my mouth, but Sigerson hushed me with a single fierce gesture. Moving as slowly as a lizard stalking a moth, he eased himself soundlessly along the wall, until he was close enough to the back door to whip it open with one hand, and with the other seize the bulky figure on the threshold by the collar and drag it inside, protesting, but not really resisting. Sigerson snatched off the man's battered cap and stepped back, for all the world like an artist unveiling his latest portrait. It was Volodya Andrichev.

"Yes," Sigerson said. "I thought perhaps it might be you." For a moment Andrichev stood there, breathing harshly, his blue eyes gone almost black in his pale, desperate face. Then with dramatic abruptness he thrust his hands towards Sigerson, crossing them at the wrists and whispering, "Arrest me. You *must* arrest me now."

"Alas, all my manacles are old and rusted shut," Sigerson replied mildly. "However, there is some drink here which should certainly serve the same purpose. Sit down with us, Herr Andrichev."

A commanding person, as I have said, but one who did not seem to command. Andrichev fell into a kitchen chair as limply as he had rolled out of the wagon, only an hour or two before. He was sweating in great, thick drops, and he looked like a madman, but his eyes were clear. He said, "They should not be in prison. I am the one. You must arrest me. I have done a terrible, terrible thing."

I said firmly, "Andrichev, calm yourself this instant. I have known you for a long time. I do not believe you capable of any evil. Drunkenness, yes, and occasional vulgarity of attack when we play Schubert. Spite, vindictiveness, cruelty — never."

"No, no one ever believes that of me," he cried out distractedly. "I know how I am seen: good old Volodya — a bit brusque, perhaps, a bit rough, but a fine fellow when you really get to know him. A heart of gold, and a devil of a cellist, but all he ever thinks of is music, music and vodka. The man couldn't plan a picnic — let alone a revenge."

Sigerson had the presence of mind to press a drink into his hand, while I sat just as slack-jawed as Lyudmilla Plaschka and Dr. Nastase themselves at the sight of the money they were accused of swindling from Lyudmilla's besotted husband. Andrichev peered around the glass at us in an odd, coy way, his eyes now glinting with a sly pride that I had never seen there before.

"Yes, revenge," he said again, clearly savoring the taste and smell and texture of the word. "Revenge, not for all the men, all the deceptions, all the silly little ruses, the childish lies — they are simply what she is. As well condemn a butterfly to live on yogurt as her to share the same bed forever. Her doctor will learn that soon enough." And he smiled, tasting the thought.

The words, the reasoning, the *sound* — they were all so vastly removed from the Volodya Andrichev I was sure I knew that I still could not close my mouth. Sigerson appeared much cooler, nodding eagerly as Andrichev spoke, as though he were receiving confirmation of the success of some great gamble, instead of receiving proof positive that he and I had been thoroughly hoodwinked. He said, "The doctor made it different."

Andrichev's face changed strikingly then, all the strong features seeming to crowd closer together, even the forehead drawing down. He repeated the word *different* as he had the word *revenge*, but the taste puckered his mouth. "That fool, that wicked fool! For that one, she would have left me, gone away forever. I *had* to stop her." But he sounded now as though he were reassuring himself that he had had no choice.

"The money," Sigerson prompted him gently. "That was indeed your money that I found in the steamer trunk?"

The furtively smug look returned to Andrichev's face, and he took a swig of his drink. "Oh, yes, every bit of it. Everything I could raise, no matter what I had to sell, or pawn, or beg, no matter how I had to live. The cello — that was hard for me, but not as hard as all of you thought. One can get another cello, but another Lyudmilla..." He fell silent for a moment, looking at the floor, then raised his eyes to us defiantly. "Not in this life. Not in my life. It had to be done."

Nor will we find another such cellist, I thought bitterly and selfishly. Sigerson said, "It was you alone who spread the story of Frau Andrichev's chronic mortal illness. She and Dr. Nastase knew nothing."

"Progorny was a great help there," Andrichev said proudly. "It was easy to circulate the tale, but difficult to keep it from reaching Lyudmilla's ears. Progorny is a real friend —" he looked directly at me for the first time "— though he will never be a real cellist. But I am happy that he has the Fabregas."

I realized that I had been constantly shaking my head since he began speaking, unable truly to *see* this new Volodya Andrichev; trying to bring my mind into focus, if you will. I asked, lamely and foolishly, "Progorny put the money into the trunk lid, then?"

Andrichev snorted derisively. "No — when would he have the opportunity for that? The tickets under the woodpile, that was Progorny, but all the rest was my idea. The police were prepared to stop them on the road —" here his voice hesitated, and his mouth suddenly rumpled, as though he were about to cry "— just when they were thinking themselves safe and...and free." He took another deep swallow. "But you two made that unnecessary. I had not counted on your interference, but it was the last touch to my plan. Having two such reputable, distinguished witnesses to their crime and their flight — even having one of them find the money — *that* closed the door behind them. That closed and locked the door."

"Yes," Sigerson said softly. "And then, with your plan successful, your revenge accomplished, your faithless wife and her lover in prison, you attempted to kill yourself." There was no question in his voice, and no accusation. He might have been reading a newspaper aloud.

"Oh," Andrichev said. "That." He said nothing more for some while, nor did Sigerson. The kitchen remained so quiet that I could hear the tiny rasping sound of a mouse chewing on the pantry door. Andrichev finally stood up, swaying cautiously, like someone trying to decide whether or not he is actually drunk. He was no longer sweating so dreadfully, but his face was as white and taut as a sail trying to contain a storm. He said, "I do not want to live without her. I can, but I do not want to. The *revenge*... it was not on her, but on myself. For loving her so. For loving her more than the music. That was the revenge." Once again he held his hands out to Sigerson for invisible manacles. "Get her out of that place," he said. "*Him*, too. Get them out, and put me in. Now. Now."

Lyudmilla Plaschka and Dr. Nastase were released from prison as soon as the magistrate who sentenced them could be located. This is a remarkable story in itself...but I can see that you wouldn't be interested. Lyudmilla Plaschka threatened to sue her husband, the court, the town, and the Duchy of Bornitz for a truly fascinating sum of money. Dr. Nastase must have prevailed, however, for she hired no lawyer, filed no claims, and shortly afterward disappeared with him in the general direction of New South Wales. I believe that a cousin of hers in Gradja received a postal card.

Volodya Andrichev was formally charged with any amount of undeniable transgressions and violations, none of which our two St. Radomir lawyers knew how to prosecute — or defend, either, if it came to that

— so there was a good deal of general relief when he likewise vanished from sight, leaving neither a forwarding address nor any instructions as to what to do with his worldly goods. One of the lawyers attempted to take possession of his house, in payment for unpaid legal fees; but since no one could even guess what these might have been, the house eventually became the property of the Greater Bornitz Municipal Orchestra. It is specifically intended to accommodate visiting artists, but so far, to be quite candid...no, you aren't interested in that, either, are you? You only want information about Herr Sigerson.

Well, I grieve to disappoint you, but he too is gone. Oh, some while now — perhaps two months after Volodya Andrichev's disappearance. As it happens, I walked with him to catch the mail coach on which he had arrived in St. Radomir. I even carried his violin case, as I recall. Never friends, colleagues by circumstance, we had little to say to one another, but little need as well. What we understood of each other, we understood; the rest would remain as much a mystery as on that very first evening, and we were content to leave it so.

We were silent during most of the wait for his train, until he said abruptly, "I would like you to know, Herr Takesti, that I will remember my time here with both affection and amusement — but also with a certain embarrassment." When I expressed my perplexity, he went on, "Because of the Andrichev matter. Because I was deceived."

"So was I," I replied. "So was the entire orchestra — so was everyone with any knowledge of the business." But Sigerson shook his head, saying, "No, concertmaster, it is different for me. It is just different."

"And that is exactly why I recognized you in your beggar's disguise," I responded with some little heat. "It is always somehow different for you, and that so-called *difference* will always show in your eyes, and in everything you do. How could you possibly have guessed the secret of Volodya Andrichev's revenge on his wife and her lover? What is it that you expect of yourself, Herr Oscar Sigerson? What — *who* — are you supposed to be in this world?"

We heard the train whistle, so distant yet that we could not see the smoke rising on the curve beyond the Ridnak farm. He said, "You know a little of my thought, Herr Takesti. I have always believed that when one eliminates the impossible, what remains, no matter how improbable, must be the truth, the one solution of the problem. In this case, however, it turned out the other way around. I will be considering the Andrichev matter for a long time to come."

The train pulled in, and we bowed to each other, and Sigerson swung aboard, and that is the last I ever saw of him. The mail coach runs to and from Bucharest; beyond that, I have no idea where he was bound. I am not sure that I would tell you if I did know. You ask a few too many questions, and there is something wrong with your accent. Sigerson noticed such things.

A Dance for Emilia

For Nancy, Peter and Jessa,
And for Joe

First published as a small stand-alone gift book several years ago, I am pleased to see "A Dance for Emilia" in wider circulation at last. This is the story within these pages that means the most to me. It's fiction, certainly, and very much a fantasy in its nature; but it's also as autobiographical as anything I've ever written, and it was born out of mourning for my closest friend, who died in 1994. His name was Joe Mazo, and we did meet in a high-school drama class, as Jake, the narrator, and his friend Sam do. But Joe was a frustrated actor, not a dancer (just as I'm a writer who, like most writers, would love to be a performer), and who became in fact a well-known dance critic and the author of three highly respected and influential books on modern dance. Jake and Sam's daily lives are as different from Joe's and mine as they were meant to be; but the relationship between them is as close to the way things were as I could write it. As for the original of Emilia, I couldn't really do justice to her, and her love for Joe, but I tried my best.

THE CAT. *The cat is doing what?*

Believe me, it's no good to tell you. You have to see.

Emilia, she's old. Old cats get really weird sometimes.

Not like this. You have to see, that's all.

You're serious. You're going to put Millamant in a box, a case, and bring her all the way to California, just for me to...When are you coming?

I thought Tuesday. I'm due ten days' sick leave....

No. This isn't how you do it. This isn't how you talk about Sam and Emilia and yourself. And Millamant. You've got hold of the wrong end, same as usual. Start from the beginning. For your own sake, tell it, just write it down the way it was, as far as you'll ever know. Start with the answering machine. That much you're sure about, anyway....

The machine was twinkling at me when I came home from the Pacific Rep's last-but-one performance of *The Iceman Cometh*. I ignored it. You can live with things like computers, answering gadgets, fax machines, even email, but they have to know their place. I hung up my coat, checked

193

the mail, made myself a drink, took it and the newspaper over to the one comfortable chair I've got, sank down in it, drank my usual toast to our lead — who is undoubtedly off playing Hickey in Alaska today, feeding wrong cues to a cast of polar bears — and finally hit the PLAY button.

"Jacob, it's Marianne. In New York." I only hear from Marianne Hooper at Christmas these days, but we've known each other a long time, in the odd, offhand way of theater people, and there's no mistaking that husky, incredibly world-weary sound — she's been making a fortune doing voiceovers for the last twenty years. There was a pause. Marianne could always get more mileage out of a well-timed pause than Jack Benny. I raised my glass to the answering machine.

"Jacob, I'm so sorry, I hate to be the one to tell you. Sam was found dead in his apartment last night. I'm so sorry."

It didn't mean anything. It bounced off me — *it didn't mean anything*. Marianne went on. "People at the magazine got worried when he didn't come in to work, didn't answer the phone for two days. They finally broke into the apartment." The famous anonymous voice was trembling now. "Jacob, I'm so terribly...Jacob, I can't do this anymore, on a machine. Please call me." She left her number and hung up.

I sat there. I put my drink down, but otherwise I didn't move. I sat very still where I was, and I thought, There's been a mistake. It's his turn to call me on Saturday, I called last week. Marianne's made a mistake. I thought, Oh, Christ, the cat, Millamant — who's feeding Millamant? Those two, back and forth, over and over.

I don't know how late it was when I finally got up and phoned Marianne, but I know I woke her. She said, "I called you last. I called his parents before I could make myself call you."

"He was just here," I said. "In July, for God's sake. He was fine." I had to heave the words up one at a time, like prying stones out of a wall. "We went for walks."

"It was his heart." Marianne's voice was so toneless and uninflected that she sounded like someone else. "He was in the bathroom — he must have just come home from Lincoln Center —"

"The Schönberg. He was going to review that concert *Moses and Aron* —"

"He was still wearing his gangster suit, the one he always wore to openings —"

I was with him when he bought that stupid, enviable suit. I said, "The Italian silk thing. I remember."

Marianne said, "As far as they — the police — as far as anyone can figure, he came home, fed the cat, kicked off his shoes, went into the bathroom and — and died." She was crying now, in a hiccupy, totally unprofessional way. "Jacob, they think it was instant. I mean, they don't think he suffered at all."

I heard myself say, "I never knew he had a heart condition. Secretive little fink, he never told me."

Marianne managed a kind of laugh. "I don't think he ever told anyone. Even his mother and father didn't know."

"The cigarettes," I said. "The goddamn cigarettes. He was here last summer, trying to cut down — he said his doctor had scared the hell out of him. I just thought, lung cancer, he's afraid of getting cancer. I never thought about his heart, I'm such an idiot. Oh, God, I have to call them, Mike and Sarah."

"Not tonight, don't call them tonight." She'd been getting the voice back under control, but now it went again. "They're in shock; I did it to them, don't you. Wait till morning. Call them in the morning."

My mouth and throat were so dry they hurt, but I couldn't pick up my drink again. I said, "What's being done? You have to notify people, the police. I don't even know if he had a will. Where's the — where is he now?"

"The police have the body, and the apartment's closed. Sealed — it's what they do when somebody dies without a witness. I don't know what happens next. Jacob, can you please come?"

"Thursday," I said. "Day after tomorrow. I'll catch the redeye right after the last performance."

"Come to my place. I've moved, there's a guest room." She managed to give me an East Eighties address before the tears came again. "I'm sorry, I'm sorry, I've been fine all day. I guess it's just caught up with me now."

"I'm not quite sure why," I said. I heard Marianne draw in her breath, and I went on, "Marianne, *I'm* sorry, I know how cold that sounds, but you and Sam haven't been an item for — what? — twelve years? Fifteen? I mean, this is me, Marianne. You can't be the grieving widow, it's just not your role."

I've always said things to Marianne that I'd never say to anyone else —

it's the only way to get her full attention. Besides, it made her indignant, which beat the hell out of maudlin. She said, "We always stayed friends, you know that. We'd go out for dinner, he took me to plays — he must have told you. We were *always* friends, Jacob."

Sam cried over her. It was the only time that I ever saw Sam cry. "Thursday morning, then. It'll be good to see you." Words, thanks, sniffles. We hung up.

I couldn't stay sitting. I got up and walked around the room. "Oh, you little bastard," I said aloud. "Kagan, you miserable, miserable *twit*, who said you could just leave? We had *plans*, we were going to be old together, you forgot about that?" I was shouting, bumping into things. "We were going to be these terrible, totally irresponsible old men, so elegant and mannerly nobody would ever believe we just peed in the potted palm. We were going to learn karate, enter the Poker World Series, moon our fiftieth high school reunion, sit in the sun at spring-training baseball camps — we had stuff to *do!* What the hell were you *thinking* of, walking out in the middle of the movie? You think I'm about to do all that crap alone?"

I don't know how long I kept it up, but I know I was still yelling while I packed. I didn't have another show lined up after *Iceman* until the Rep's *Christmas Carol* went into rehearsal in two months, with Bob Cratchit paying my rent one more time. No pets to feed, no babies crying, no excuses to make to anyone...there's something to be said for being fifty-six, twice divorced and increasingly set in my ways. I'm a good actor, with a fairly wide range for someone who looks quite a bit like Mister Ed, but I've got no more ambition than I have star quality. Which may be a large part of the reason why Sam Kagan and I were so close for so long.

We met in high school, in a drama class. I already knew that I was going to be an actor — though of course it was Olivier back then, not Mister Ed. The teacher was choosing students at random to read various scenes, and we, sitting at neighboring desks, got picked for a dialogue from *Major Barbara*. I was Adolphus Cusins, Barbara's Salvation Army fiancé; Sam played Undershaft, the arms manufacturer. He wasn't familiar with the play, but I was, and with Rex Harrison, who'd played Cusins in the movie, and whose every vocal mannerism I had down cold. Yet when we faced off over Barbara's ultimate allegiance and Sam proclaimed, in an outrageously fragrant British accent, Undershaft's gospel of "money and gunpowder — freedom and power — command of life and command of death," there wasn't an eye in that classroom resting anywhere but on him. I may have known the play better than he, but he knew that it was a play. It was the first real acting lesson I ever had.

I told him so in the hall after class. He looked honestly surprised. "Oh, good *night*, Undershaft's easy, he's all one thing — in that scene, anyway." The astonishing accent was even riper than before. "Now Cusins is bloody tricky, Cusins is much harder to play." He grinned at me — God, were the cigarettes already starting to stain his teeth then? — and added, "You do a great early Harrison, though. Did you ever see *St. Martin's Lane*? They're running it at the Thalia all next week."

He was the first person I had ever met in my life who talked like me. What I mean by that is that both of us much preferred theatrical dialogue to ordinary Brooklyn conversation, theatrical structure and action to life as it had been laid out for us. It makes for an awkward childhood — I'm sure that's one reason I got into acting so young — and people like us learn about protective coloration earlier than most. And we tend to recognize each other.

Sam. He was short — notably shorter than I, and I'm not tall — with dark eyes and dark, wavy hair, the transparent skin and soft mouth of a child, and a perpetual look of being just about to laugh. Yet even that early on, he kept his deep places apart: when he did laugh or smile, it was always quick and mischievous and gone. The eyes were warm, but that child's mouth held fast — to what, I don't think I ever knew.

He was a much better student than I — if it hadn't been for his help in half my subjects, I'd still be in high school. Like me, he was completely uninterested in anything beyond literature and drama; quite unlike me, he accepted the existence of geometry, chemistry, and push-ups, where I never believed in their reality for a minute. "Think of it as a role," he used to tell me. "Right now you're playing a student, you're learning the periodic table like dialogue. Some day, good *night*, you might have to play a math teacher, a coach, a mad scientist. Everything has to come in useful to an actor, sooner or later."

He called me Jake, as only one other person ever has. He was a gracious loser at card and board games, but a terrible winner, who could gloat for two days over a gin rummy triumph. He was the only soul I ever told about my stillborn older brother, whose name was Elias. I knew where he was buried — though I had not been told — and I took Sam there once. He was outraged when he learned that we never spoke of Elias at home, and made me promise that I'd celebrate Elias's birthday every year. Because of Sam, I've been giving my brother a private birthday party for more than forty years. I've only missed twice.

Sam had surprisingly large hands, but his feet were so tiny that I used to tease him, referring to them as "ankles with toes." It was a sure way to rile him, as nothing else would do. Those small feet mattered terribly to Sam.

He was a dance student, most often going directly from last-period math to classes downtown. Wanting to dance wasn't something boys admitted to easily then — certainly not in our Brooklyn high school, where being interested in *anything* besides football, fighting, and very large breasts could get you called a faggot. I was the one person who knew about those classes; and we were seniors, with a lot of operas, Dodgers games, and old Universal horror movies behind us, before I actually saw him dance.

There was a program at the shabby East Village studio where he was taking classes three times a week by then. Two pianos, folding chairs, and a sequence of presentations by students doing solo bits or *pas de deux* from the classic ballets. Sam's parents were there, sitting quietly in the very last row. I knew them, of course, as well as any kid who comes over to visit a friend for an afternoon ever knows the grown-ups floating around in the background. Mike was a lawyer, fragile-looking Sarah an elementary school teacher; beyond that, all I could have said about them — or can say now — was that they so plainly thought their only child was the entire purpose of evolution that it touched even my hard adolescent heart. I can still see them on those splintery, rickety chairs: holding hands, except when they tolerantly applauded the fragments of *Swan Lake* and *Giselle*, waiting patiently for Sam to come onstage.

He was next to last on the program — the traditional starring slot in vaudeville — performing his own choreography to the music of Borodin's *In the Steppes of Central Asia*. And what his dance was like I cannot tell you now, and I couldn't have told you then, dumbly enthralled as I was by the sight of my lunchroom friend hurling himself about the stage with an explosive ferocity that I'd never seen or imagined in him. Some dancers cut their shapes in the air; some burn them; but Sam tore and clawed his, and seemed literally to leave the air bleeding behind him. I can't even say whether he was *good* or not, as the word is used — though he was unquestionably the best: in that school, and more people than his parents were on their feet when he finished. What I did somehow understand, bright and blind as I was, was that he was dancing for his life.

When I went backstage, he was sitting alone on a bench in his sweat-blackened leotard, head bowed into his hands. He didn't look up until I said, "Boy, that was something else. You are something else." The phrase was fairly new then, in our circles at least.

He looked old when he raised his head. I don't mean older; I mean old. The glass-clear skin was gray, pebbled with beard stubble — I hadn't thought he shaved — and the dark eyes appeared too heavy for his face to bear. He said slowly, "Sometimes I'm good, Jake. Sometimes I really think I might make it."

I said something I hadn't at all thought to say. "You have to make it. I don't think there's a damn thing else you're fit for."

Sam laughed. Really laughed, so that some color came back into his face and his eyes became his age again. "Good *night*, let's just hope I never have to find out." He got dressed and we went out front to meet Mike and Sarah.

He didn't have to find out for some time. We graduated, and I went off to Carnegie Tech in Pittsburgh on a genuine theater scholarship, while Sam stayed home, attending CCNY to please his parents, and literally spending all the rest of his time at Garrett-Klieman, a dance school whose top prospects seemed to be funneled directly into the New York City Ballet. I'd see him on holidays and over the summer, and we'd do everything we'd always done together: going to plays and baseball games, hitting the secondhand bookstores on Fourth Avenue, drinking beer and debating whether the internal rhymes in the songs we were always trying to write were as clever and crackling as Noël Coward's. On Friday nights, we usually played poker with a mixed bag of other would-be actors and dancers. As far as either of us was willing to acknowledge, nothing at all had changed.

But while I talked about plays I'd been in, about Artaud, Brecht, the Living Theatre, the Method, improv workshops and sense memories, Sam avoided almost all mention of his own career. If he danced in any of the Garrett-Klieman showcases, he never told me — it was all I could do to persuade him to let me sit in on a couple of his choreography classes. As before, I couldn't look away from him for a moment; but I was already beginning to learn that some dancers, actors, musicians simply have that. It doesn't have a thing to do with talent or craft — it just *is*, like blue eyes or being able to touch your nose with your tongue. I don't have it.

We were eating lunch at the Automat on Forty-second and Sixth the day he told me abruptly, "They haven't recommended me. Not to City Ballet, not to anybody. It's over."

I gaped at him over my crusty brown cup of baked beans. I said, "What *over?* This is crazy. You're the best dancer I ever knew."

"You don't know any dancers," Sam said. Which was perfectly true — I still don't know many; I'm not in a lot of musicals — but irritating under the circumstances. Sam went on, "They didn't tell me it was over. I knew. I'm not good enough."

I was properly outraged, not only at Garrett-Klieman, but also at him, for acceding so docilely to their decision. I said, "Well, the hell with them. What the hell do *they* know?"

Sam shook his head. "Jake, I'm not good enough. It's that simple."

"Nothing's that simple. You've been dancing all your life, you've been the best everywhere you've gone —"

"I was *never* the best!" The Noël Coward accent had dropped away for the first time in my memory, and Sam's voice was all aching Brooklyn. "You remember that story you told me about Queen Elizabeth — the real one — that thing she said when she was old. 'No, I was never beautiful, but I had the name for it.' It was like that with me. I can be dazzling — I worked on it, I about killed myself learning to be dazzling — but there isn't a move in me that I didn't copy from d'Amboise or Bruhn or Eddie Villella or someone. And these people aren't fools, Jake. They know the difference between dazzling and dancing. So do I."

I didn't know how to answer him; not because of what he had said, but because of the utter nakedness of his voice. He stared at me in silence for a long time, and then suddenly he looked away, the break so sharp that it felt physical, painful. He said, "Anyway, I'm too short."

I laughed. I remember that. "What are you talking about? Even I know ballet dancers can't be tall — Villella's practically a midget, for God's sake —"

"No, he's not. And he's strong as a horse; he can lift his partners all day and not break a sweat. I can't do that." All these years, and I can still see the absolute, unarguable shame in his face. "My upper body's never going to be strong enough to do what it has to do. And I look wrong onstage, Jake. My legs are stubby, they spoil the line. It is that bloody simple, and I'm very glad someone finally laid it out for me. Now all I have to do is figure out what exactly to do with the rest of my life."

He stood up and walked out of the Automat, and by the time I got outside, he was gone. We didn't see each other for the rest of the summer, although we talked on the phone a couple of times. By then, thanks to sending out ninety-four sets of résumés, I actually had a job waiting for me after graduation, building sets and doing walk-ons for a rep company in Seattle. Over the next five years I worked my way down to the Bay Area, by way of theaters in Eugene and Portland and stock jobs all over Northern California. I've been here in Avicenna ever since.

But we did stay in contact, Sam and I. I broke the ice, sending light postcards from the summer tours, and then a real letter from my first real address — South Parnell Street, that was. Two rooms and a ficus plant.

He didn't answer for some while, long enough that I began to believe he never would. But when it did come, the letter began with typical abruptness, asking whether I remembered *The Body Snatcher*, an old Val Lewton movie we'd loved and seen half a dozen times.

> *Remember that splendid, chilling moment when Karloff says through his teeth, "And I have done some things that I did not want to do..."? Me these last several years. I'll tell you the worst straight off, and leave the rest to your imagination. No, not the year spent teaching folk-dancing in Junior High School 80 — much worse than that. I am become an Arts Cricket! Pray for me....*

We'd been using Gully Jimson's term for a critic ever since reading *The Horse's Mouth* in high school. Sam's letter went on to say that he was writing regularly for a brand-new Manhattan arts magazine, now and then for a couple of upstate papers, and lately even filing occasional dispatches to Japan:

> *I mostly review music, sometimes theater, sometimes movies, if the first-stringer's off at Sundance or Cannes. No, Jake, I don't*

*ever cover dance. I don't dare write about dance, because I couldn't
possibly be fair to people who are up there doing what I want to do
more than I want anything in the world. Music, yes. I can manage
music....*

We wrote, and sometimes called, for another three years before we met
again. I hope my letters weren't as full of myself as I'm sure they were:
entirely concerned with what plays I'd auditioned for, what roles I should
have gotten, what actors I scorned or admired; what celebrated director had seemed very impressed but never called back. Sam, on the other
hand, recounted the astonishing success of *Ceilidh*, the new magazine,
described every editor and photographer he worked with; detailed, with
solemn hilarity, the kind of performance he was most often sent to cover.
"Most of them are so far *avant* that they lap the field and become the
derrière-garde. Try to imagine the Three Stooges on downers."

But of his own feelings and dreams, of his world beyond work, of how
he lived without dancing — nothing, not ever. And there we left it until
I came to New York for a smallish part in a goodish play that survived
barely a month. It was to be my Broadway break, that one — to be in it
I turned down a TV movie, which later spun off into a syndicated series
that's probably still running somewhere. I have an infallible gift for pick-
ing the losing side.

I never regretted the gamble, though, for I stayed with Sam during our
brief run. He had found a studio apartment in the West Seventies, half
a block off Columbus: one huge, high room, a vestigial kitchen nook,
a bathroom, a deep and sinister coat closet that Sam called "The Dark
Continent," a solid wall of books, the two biggest stereo speakers I'd ever
seen, and a mattress in a far corner. I slept on the floor by the stereo
that month, in a tangle of quilts from his Brooklyn bedroom. It was the
first time we'd ever spent together as adults, with jobs to go to instead of
classes. We kept completely different hours, what with me being at the
theater six nights and two afternoons a week, while Sam put in five full
days at the magazine, and was likely to be off covering a performance in
the evenings. Yet we bumbled along so comfortably that I can't recall a
cross word between us — only an evening when something changed.

At the time I was skidding into my first marriage, a head-on collision,
born of mutual misunderstandings, with the woman who was lighting

the play. On the windy, rainy evening that the closing notice was posted, she and I had a fight about nothing, and I sulked my way back to Sam's place to find him practicing a Bach sarabande on his classical guitar. He wasn't very good, and he wouldn't ever be good, no matter how dutifully he worked at it, and to my shame I said so that night. "Give it up, Sam. You haven't made a dent in that poor Bach in all the time I've been here. Guitar's just not your instrument — it's like me and directing. I can't even get three people lined up properly for a photograph. It's not the end of the world."

Sam didn't pay the least bit of attention to me. When the sarabande finally lurched to a close, he said, "Jake, I don't have any illusions about the way I play. But I don't think anyone should write about music who doesn't have at least some idea of what it takes to make your fingers pull one clear note out of an instrument. Out of yourself."

"The guitar you keep hacking at. The thing you could *do*, you quit. Right." I can still hear the pure damn meanness in my voice.

Sam put the guitar away and began rummaging in the refrigerator for a couple of beers. His back was to me when he said, "Yes, well, I did have some illusions about my dancing." He hadn't used the word all during my visit. "But that's what they were, Jake, illusions, and I'm glad I understood that when I did. I haven't lost any sleep over them in...what? Years."

"You were good," I said. "You were terrific." Sam didn't turn or answer. Completely out of character, out of control, I kept pushing. "Ever wish you hadn't quit?"

"I still dance." For the first time since that long-ago lunch in the Automat, the voice was raw Brooklyn again, but much lower, a harsh mumble. "I take classes, I keep in shape." He did turn to face me then, and now there was anger in his eyes. "And no, Jake, I don't wish a damn thing. I'm just grateful that I had the sense to know what to stop wishing for. I didn't quit, I let go. There's a difference."

"Is there?"

What possessed me? What made me bait him, invade him so? The failure of the play, premonitions about my Lady of the Follow Spots? I have no more idea now than I did then. I said, "I've envied you half my life, you know that? You were born to be a dancer — *born* — and I've had to work my butt off just to be the journeyman I am." The words chewed their way out of me. "Sam, see, by now I know I'm never going to be anything more than pretty good. Professional, I'll settle for that. But you... you walked away from it, from your gift. I was so furious at you for doing that. I guess I still am. I really still am."

"That's your business," Sam said. His voice had gotten very quiet. "My loss is my loss, you don't get to deal yourself in. Sorry." He said it carefully, word by word, each one a branding iron. "I have enough trouble with my own dreams without living yours."

"What dreams?" I asked. He should have hit me then — not for the two words, but for the way I said them. I can still hear myself today, now, as I write this, and I am still ashamed.

But Sam smiled at me. Whatever else I manage to forget about my behavior that night, I'll always remember that he smiled. He said, "Anyway, you're a bloody good actor. You're much better than a journeyman." And he handed me a bottle of beer, and suddenly we were talking about my career, about me again. We weren't to have another moment that intense, that intimate, for a very long time.

Over the years I came east more often than he came west, unless he had a Seattle Opera *Ring* to cover, or a Los Angeles symphony conductor to interview. He published three books: one on a year spent with the musicians of the Lincoln Center orchestra, one on Lou Harrison, and one — my favorite — about Verdi's last four operas. They got fine reviews and neither sold nor stayed in print. But the studio apartment was rent-controlled, and *Ceilidh* flourished, to its own considerable surprise. Occasionally they were even able to send Sam abroad, to cover music festivals in England or Italy. He visited his parents — long retired in Fort Lauderdale — four times a year, had another floor-to-ceiling bookcase installed, and got a cat.

About the cat. It was an Abyssinian female, almost maroon in color, and even as a kitten she had the slouchy preen of a high-fashion model. Sam named her Millamant, after Congreve's wicked heroine. Because both of the women I married had been cat-lovers, Sam appointed me his feline expert, and called me almost every day during the first weeks of Millamant's residency. "She just sits in her litter box and stares — is that normal?" "She keeps catching moths in The Dark Continent — should I make her stop?" "Jake, I took her for her shots, and now she's mad at me. How long do cats stay mad?" "Is it all right for her to eat pizza?" Millamant grew up to look like a miniature mountain lion, the reigning *grande horizontale* of the studio, and whenever I slept on the floor, she honored me with her favors. Usually at three in the morning.

As for myself, I peaked early. Right or wrong about Sam's talent, I was bang on the money about my own. I've never worked in New York again, unless you count summer stock in Utica, and there have been stretches when a voiceover, a TV cameo, or residuals from a soap-opera guest shot were all that kept a roof over my head. It's mostly theater, especially the Pacific Rep, that pays the bills; but the only long-running stage gig I have ever had was as a villain in a camp 1890s melodrama, which inexplicably ran for five years at a tiny San Francisco theater. It coincided almost exactly with my second marriage; they closed in the same week. That one's a director, and she's good. I think she's off doing *Sweet Bird of Youth* in China right now.

All the same, for good or ill, I'm still doing what I'm fit for and living as I always wanted to live — just not quite as well as I'd imagined — and Sam wasn't. That was a wider gap by far than the continent that separated us, but we never again talked about it. Everything else, yes, on weekends, when the rates were down — everything else from politics, literature, and the general nature of the universe to shortstops and whether Oscar Alemán could really have been as good a guitarist as Django. We went along like that until Marianne.

No, we went along like that until *after* Marianne. After she'd moved in with him, and after she'd left him two months and five days later for a playwright who'd written a one-woman show about Duse for her. I borrowed plane fare to New York because of the way he sounded on the phone. He was fine all the way through the nice dinner at the deli, and fine through the usual amble along Columbus, twenty blocks or so down, twenty blocks back. It wasn't until we were in the apartment, until I'd found a hairbrush of Marianne's and casually asked him where I should put it, that he came apart. I held him awkwardly while he cried, and Millamant came down from the bookshelf where she generally lived to sniff at his tears and butt her hard round head against his chin. It was a very long night, and I don't know whether I did or said anything right or anything wrong for him. I was just with him, that's all.

He came to Avicenna more often after that, always spending at least a weekend, sleeping on a futon, content with my books and record albums if I was in rehearsal; ready for a walk on balmy evenings — he never quite lost the unmistakable near-waddle of the ballet dancer — equally easy with silences long grown as comfortable as the lazily circular arguments that might go on until one of us dozed off. I recall asking one midnight, during his last visit, "Do you remember what your dad used to say, every time he heard us discussing something or other?"

Sam laughed in the darkness. "'Those two, they're a couple of *alte kockers* already! Old men sitting in the park, squabbling about Tennessee Williams and Mickey Mantle.' Fifteen, sixteen, and he had us pegged."

I remember everything about that visit, when he holed up in my house for a full week, trying so determinedly to quit smoking. The walks got longer, to keep his mind off cigarettes; he managed quite well during the daytime, but the nights were hard, as I could tell from the smell in the bathroom most mornings. Even so, he cut down steadily until, a couple of days before he left, he got by on two half-smoked cigarettes, and we went out to my favorite Caribbean restaurant to celebrate. He had the jerk chicken and I had the *ropa vieja*.

There's an unmarked alley not far from my house that leads to a freeway overpass, and from there into a children's park as dainty and miniature as a scene in one of those gilded Victorian eggs. We walked there after dinner, talking obliquely of Marianne, for the first time in a long while, and of my ex-wives. It was when we stopped to drink at a child-size fountain that Sam said, "You know, when you think about it, you and I have been involved with a remarkable number of highly improbable women. I mean, for just two people."

"We could start a museum," I suggested. "The Museum of Truly Weird Relationships." That set us off. We walked round and round for hours, opening up the one aspect of our lives kept almost entirely private for all the years of our friendship. The public defender, the bookstore owner, the poet, the set designer, the truck mechanic — it doesn't matter which of us was embrangled with whom; only that the romances almost invariably ended as comedies of errors, leaving us to lick our wounds and shrug, and present our debacles to each other like wry trophies. We laughed and snorted, and said, "*What?*" and "Oh, you're *kidding*" and "You never said a word about *that* — that's a whole wing of the museum just by itself," until the children and their parents were all gone home, and we were the only two voices in the little park. It was just then that Sam told me about Emilia.

"She's too young," he said. "She is twenty-six-and-a-half years younger than I am, and she's from Metuchen, New Jersey, and she's not Jewish, and if you say either *bimbo* or *bunnyrabbit*, Jake, I will punch you right in the eye. I shouldn't have mentioned her, anyway. I don't think this one belongs in the Museum at all."

"Hoo-*ha*," I said. He looked at me, and I said, "Sorry, sorry, hoo-ha withdrawn — it's just I've never heard you sound like that. So. Would you maybe marry this one?"

"You're the chap who marries people. If I were the sort who gets married, I'd *be* married by now." He fell silent, and we walked on until we came to the swings and the sliding pond and the monkey bars. We sat down on the swings, pushing ourselves idly in small circles, letting our shoes scrape the ground. Sam said, "Emilia covers New York for a paper in Bergen County — that's how I met her, about a year ago. She takes the bus in on weekends."

"A journalist, yet. Not a cricket?"

"Good *night*, no, a real writer. If there were any real newspapers left, she'd have a real career ahead of her. I keep telling her to get into TV, but she hates it — she won't even watch the *News Hour*." He pushed off harder, gripping the chains of the swing and leaning back. "The whole thing's crazy, Jake, but it's not weird. It's just crazy." He looked over his shoulder at me and grinned suddenly. "But Millamant likes her."

"I'm jealous," I said, and I actually was, a little. Millamant doesn't like a lot of people. "She stays the weekend? And it works out?"

He was a heavy sleeper, and you had to be really careful about waking him, because he always came up fighting. I never knew why that was. Sam laughed then. "On top of everything, she's an insomniac. Only person I ever gave full permission to wake me up at any time. It works out."

"Hoo-*ha*. So she'll be moving in?"

Sam didn't answer for a long time. We swung together in the darkness, with no sound but the slow creak of the chains. Finally he said, "I don't think so. I think maybe I lost my nerve with Marianne." I started to say something, and then I didn't. Chains, owls, a few fireflies, the distant mumbling of the freeway. Sam said, "I couldn't go through that again. And it will happen again, Jake. Not for the same reasons, but it will."

"You don't know that," I said. "It works out sometimes, living with somebody. Not for me — I mean, both my marriages were absolute train wrecks — but there were good times even so, and they really might have worked. If I'd been different, or Elly had, or Suzette had. Anyway, it was worth it, pretty much. I wouldn't have missed it, I don't think."

"That," Sam said, pausing as precisely as our old hero Noël Coward would have done, "is the most inspirational tribute to the married state I've ever heard. You ought to crochet it into a sampler." He dropped lightly off the swing, and we went on walking, angling back the way we had come. Neither of us spoke again until we were on the overpass, looking down at the lights plunging toward the East Bay hills. Sam said, "She's not moving in. Millamant doesn't like her *that* much. But I want you to meet her, next time you come to New York. This one I want you to meet." I said I'd love to, and we walked on home.

At the airport, two nights later, we hugged each other, and I said, "Catch you next time, Jake." I don't remember when we started doing that at goodbyes, trading names.

"Next time, Sam. I'll call when I get home." He picked up his garment bag and started for the gate; then turned to flash me that fleeting grin out of childhood once more. "Keep a pedestal vacant in the Museum. You never know." And he was gone.

Marianne had Millamant, as it turned out when I made my way from JFK to her East Side town house. The Abyssinian met me at the door and immediately sprang to my shoulder, as she had always done whenever I arrived. Arthritis had set its teeth in her right hind leg since we last met, and it took her three tries, equally painful for us both. I tried to remove her, but Millamant wasn't having any. She dug her claws in even deeper, making a curious shrill sound I'd never heard from her before, and constantly pushing her head against my face. Her eyes were wide and mad.

"He's not with me," I said. "I'm sorry, cat. I don't know where he's gone."

Marianne — still all flying red hair and opening night, down to her gilded toenails — informed me that Sam hadn't left a will, which surprised me. He was always far neater than I, not merely about the apartment or his dress, but about his life in general. Letters were answered as they came in; his filing cabinet held actual alphabetized files; he always knew where his book and magazine contracts were; and he had a regular doctor and a real lawyer as well, who doubled as his literary agent. But there was no will in the filing cabinet, no will to be found anywhere.

"We'd been talking about it," the lawyer said defensively. "He was going to come in. Anyway, I've spoken to the parents, and they want you to act as executor."

I called Mike and Sarah from the lawyer's office. They were frail insect voices, clouded by age and distance and despair, static from deep space. Yes, they did wish me to be Sam's executor — yes, they would be grateful if I could clean out the apartment, sort his business affairs, and get the police to release his body, as soon as the coroner's report came in. Sarah asked after my mother and father.

The report said things like *myocardial infarction* and *ventricular fibrillation; death almost certainly instant.* We buried Sam in an Astroturf cemetery in Queens, within earshot of the Van Wyck Expressway. Mike and Sarah had managed to handle the funeral arrangements from Fort Lauderdale, which proved they remembered me well enough to know that I'd likely have wound up stashing their son in a Dumpster or a recycling tin. A limousine from the mortuary brought them to the funeral: they stepped out blinking against the sharp autumn sunlight, looking pale and small, for all the years in Florida. I went over to embrace them, and we had a moment to murmur incoherently together before two men in dark suits took them away to the grave site. I followed with Marianne, because there was no one else I knew.

It didn't surprise me. I'd learned long since that Sam preferred to keep the several worlds in which he moved — music, theater, journalism, ballet classes — utterly separate from each other. I'd known the names of some of his friends and colleagues for years, without ever meeting one. By the same token, I knew myself to be the entire mysterious, vaguely glamorous West Coast world into which he vanished once in a great while. Until now, it had all suited and amused me.

An old Friday-night poker acquaintance drifted up on my left as I stood at the coffin behind Mike and Sarah and the dark suits. We shook hands, and he whispered, "Yes, I know, I got fat," while I was still trying to remember his name. I never did.

The rabbi looked like a basketball player, and he hadn't known Sam. It was a generic eulogy, no worse for the most part than many I've sat through, until he fixed his shiny blue gaze on Mike and Sarah and started in about the tragedy of living to bury an only son. I turned away, eyeing the exits. Damn, Sam, if you hadn't stuck us with these damn ringside seats, we could slide out of here right now, and be on the second beer before anyone noticed. But he had to stay, so I did too.

That was when I saw the small dark woman standing alone. Not that she was physically isolated — you couldn't be in that crowd, and still see grave and rabbi — but her solitude, her apartness, was as plain as if she had been a homeless lunatic, trundling a Safeway cart, all by herself with God. She was looking at the rabbi, but not seeing or hearing him. I patted Marianne's arm and eased away. It's okay, Sam. I see her.

Close to, she was thin, and looked paler because of her dark hair and eyes. She looked older, too — I'm bad at ages, and I'd been braced for a schoolgirl in a leather miniskirt, but this woman had to be twenty-eight or twenty-nine, surely. I said quietly, "You're Emilia. He never told me your last name."

When she turned to face me, I saw that her nose must have been broken once, and not set quite right. The effect was oddly attractive, the bumpy bridge lending strength and age to a face whose adult bone structure had not yet finished its work. Only her eyes were a full-grown woman's eyes, an old woman's eyes just now. An intelligent, ordinary face that grief had turned shockingly beautiful.

"It's Rossi," she said. "Emily Rossi." Her voice was low, with the muffled evenness that comes with fighting not to cry. "Please, is there any chance at all that you could be Jacob Holtz?"

"Sam called me Jake," I answered. "We can go now."

As we started to move away, she paused and looked back at the rabbi, who was still telling Mike and Sarah what they felt about their loss. We could smell the raw earth from where we stood. She said softly, "I imagined going up to them, talking with them, letting them know that I loved him, too, that he didn't die alone. But he did, he did, and I'd never have the courage anyway." The back of her neck seemed as vulnerable as a small child's. She said, "He always called me Emilia."

Being an executor means, finally, cleaning the place up. In a legal sense, there wasn't that much for me to do, once the police had finally unsealed the apartment and released Sam's body for burial. Bills paid off, bank account closed out, credit cards canceled, Mike and Sarah's names replacing his on God knows how many computers — how little it takes, after all, to delete us from the Great Database. A heavenly keystroke, no more.

But somebody has to clean up, and the landlord was anxious to have Sam's apartment empty, ready to be rented again for quadruple what Sam had been paying. I spent all day every day for more than three weeks at the apartment, sorting my friend's possessions into ever more meaningless heaps, then starting over with a new system for determining what went or stayed. With electricity and telephone long since cut off, the place remained cold even when the sun was shining in the windows, and tumultuous Columbus Avenue outside looked so remote, so unattainable, that I felt like an astronaut marooned on the moon.

Emily Rossi — Sam's Emilia — came all the way from New Jersey almost every day, inventing assignments for herself as a partial cover. She usually arrived at the apartment around noon; though sometimes she would bring a sleeping bag and a cassette player — and Millamant, whom Marianne was happy to relinquish — stay the night, and be at work before I got there. I was uneasy about that, but Emilia liked it. "I was always happy here," she said. "This was my safe place, with Sam. I want to be here as long as I can."

I was grateful for her presence, in part because she was far less sentimental than I about most of Sam's belongings. Not all of them: once she had been folding and setting aside clothes for donation (gangster suit apart, his wardrobe could have been worn by the average British prime minister), when I returned from one more trek through the uncharted depths of The Dark Continent to find her rocking back and forth, dry-eyed, holding a gray silk shirt tightly against her cheek.

"The first time he ever held me," she whispered. "Look," and she turned the shirt so that I could see the scattering of faded brown stains on one sleeve. "My blood," Emilia said. "It got all over him, but he never even noticed."

I stared at her. She said, "There was a man. I stopped seeing him before I ever met Sam. He followed me. He caught me on the street one day — downtown, near Port Authority." She touched her nose quickly, and then the area around her left eye. "I don't know how I got away from him. I knew somebody at *Ceilidh*, but I don't remember going there. The only thing I'm clear on, even today, is that somebody was holding me, washing my face, talking to me, so gently. It turned out to be Sam."

She kept turning the shirt in her hands, revealing other bloodstains.

"He called the police, he called an ambulance, he went with me to the hospital. And when they wouldn't keep me, even overnight, he took me home with him and fed me, and gave me his bed. I stayed three days."

"It's the feeding part that awes me," I said. "I could see everything else, but Sam didn't cook for anybody. Sam didn't even make coffee."

"Chinese takeout. Mexican takeout. For a special treat, sushi." She smiled then, sniffling only slightly. "He took care of me, Jake. I wasn't used to it, it made me really nervous for a while." She turned sharply away from me, looking toward the corner where the bed had stood. "I was getting used to it, though. Tell me some more about how he was in high school."

So I told her more, day by day, as we worked, and the apartment grew emptier and even colder, and somehow smaller. I told her about writing songs, doing homework together, playing silly board games late at night, and about trying to sneak into jazz clubs when we were too young to be admitted legally. I told her everything I could about what it was like to see him dance at seventeen. In return, Emilia told me about Adventures.

"The phone would ring late at night, and I'd hear this hissing, sinister, Bulgarian secret-service voice telling me to be at Penn Station or Grand Central with a rose in my teeth at nine the next morning, and to look for a man in dark glasses carrying an umbrella, a rubber duck, and a rolled-up copy of *Der Spiegel*. And we'd each skulk around the station, with people staring at us, until we met, and wind up taking Amtrak to anywhere — to Tarrytown or Rhinecliff or Annandale — still being spies on the Orient Express the whole way. We'd spend the night, go out on a river tour, visit the old estates and museums, buy really dumb souvenirs, and never once break character until we walked out of the station again — back in the city, back in real life. And that was an Adventure."

Her eyes never filled when she talked to me about their outings, but they stopped seeing me, stopped seeing Millamant roaming her old home step by crouching step, stalking ghosts. Emilia's eyes were doing just the same. "We took turns — one time I rented a car and took him to the caverns in Schoharie County, up near Cobleskill. We were agents who didn't speak each other's language, so we had to make up other ways to communicate." Millamant climbed into her lap, batted at her chin, bit it lightly, and put her paws on Emilia's shoulders. Emilia put her aside, but she kept coming back, meowing fiercely.

It lasted almost a year and a half, counting two separate weeks of vacation: one spent being international spies in Saratoga Springs, and one being contract assassins trailing a famously vicious theater critic who lived in Kingston. "We were always aliens, one way or another, always foreigners, outsiders, Martians. That was the whole thing about Adventures — just having each other, and our secret mission."

On the last day, with everything of Sam's packed up, sold, given away, donated or dumped, and the apartment echoing, even with our breath, we made one last pass through the shrunken Dark Continent in search of Sam's guitar. We never found it. I still worry over that, at very odd hours, wondering whether he might have given it up because of what I said to him on that bad night long ago. I swept the floor while Emilia picked up our own debris and shoehorned an unusually recalcitrant Millamant into her traveling case. Then we hugged each other goodbye, and stood back, awkward and unhappy, in that cold, empty place.

"Write," she, said. "Please." I nodded, and Emily said, "There's only you for me to talk to about him now."

I hugged her again. Inside the case Millamant was making a sound like a jammed garbage disposal, and Emilia laughed, bending to admonish her through the wire mesh. Her dark hair was gray with dust, but she looked very young in that moment, even her eyes.

For the next year — almost two — we wrote more letters than I've ever exchanged with anyone except Sam, and that includes anybody I ever married. How Emilia managed to balance her output against her newspaper work, I can't guess; it was tricky enough for me — especially once *Christmas Carol* rehearsals started — to drag myself out of Bob Cratchit's intolerably benign consciousness back into my own sullen grief. And after wretched Cratchit came Canon Chasuble, Mr. Peachum, Grandpa Vanderhof, St. Joan's Earl of Warwick...actually that wasn't a bad run of roles, thinking about it. Though I should have at least read for Macheath.

But I still wrote to Emilia two and three times a week, unearthing for her sake, and my own, moments as long forgotten as Sam's youthful terror of FBI agents coming back to interrogate his father once more about Mike's ten-minute membership in the Communist Party. I rooted through tattered, filthy cardboard boxes to find fragments of the songs we'd written together. I even woke her up one night, calling with a remembrance of our one attempt at fishing, out on Sheepshead Bay, that couldn't wait until morning. Irrational, surely, but I was suddenly afraid of forgetting for another forty years.

Emilia wrote to me about living without Adventures. She wrote about answering the phone at work or at home, knowing that she might hear any voice on the planet except the whisper of the mad Bulgarian spy, enticing her away to ridiculous escapades in the dark wilds of the Catskills.

> *But I don't believe it, any of it, either way. I don't believe that it'll*
> *be him on the phone, but at the same time I still can't believe that*
> *I won't ever hear him again. Nothing makes sense. I do my work,*
> *and I go home, and I cook my meals and eat them, and I pick up the*
> *phone when it rings, but I'm really always waiting for the call after*
> *this one....*

Once she wrote, "Thank you for always calling me Emilia. I liked her so much — she was so passionate and adventurous, so different from Emily. I was sure Emilia died with Sam, but now I don't know. Maybe not."

For my part, writing usually at night, often when rehearsals had run late and I was weary enough that memory and language both tangled with dream, the stories I told of Sam and myself were as true as phoenixes, as imaginary as computers. Things we had done flowed together with things we had always meant to do, things that I think I felt we *would* have done, once Emilia believed them. I recalled for her the time that Sam had withered a school bully with a retort so eviscerating that it would have gotten us both killed had it ever actually been spoken. I even dredged up a certain Adventure of our own, in which we tracked a celebrated Russian poet (recognized crossing Ninth Avenue by Sam, of course) back to his hotel, and then — at Sam's insistence — returned early the next morning to haunt the elevator until he came down to breakfast, which we wound up sharing with him. "He defected a few days later, and got a university gig in San Diego. Sam always felt it was the Froot Loops that did it." Well, Sam did spot the poet on the street, and we did follow him until we lost him in Macy's. And Russian poets did defect, and maybe it all practically happened just that way. Why shouldn't it have?

What Emilia was after in my memories of Sam, what she needed to live on, was no different from what I needed still: not facts, but the accuracy under and around and beyond facts. Not a recital of events — not even honesty — but truth. Résumés have their place, but there's no nourishment in them.

Emilia arrived weary at the Oakland Airport, looking as small and windblown as she had at Sam's funeral. But her eyes were bright, and when she smiled to recognize me I saw her meeting my friend, her lover, in Penn Station to embark on one more Adventure. It wasn't entirely meant for me, that smile.

Millamant herself had apparently been quite docile on the flight from New York — even banging around on the luggage conveyor belt didn't seem to have fazed her. Uncaged in my house, she didn't exhibit any of the usual edginess of a cat in strange surroundings: she stretched here, strolled there, leisurely investigated this and that, as though getting reacquainted, and finally curled herself in the one good chair, plainly waiting for the floor show to begin. I looked at Emilia, who shrugged and said, "Like the washing machine when the repairman arrives. Wait. You'll see."

"See what? What the Baptist hell are we waiting for?"

"Dinner," Emilia said firmly. "Take me out to that Caribbean place — I don't know the name. The one where you took Sam."

I hadn't been back since the time we celebrated his being down to two cigarettes a day. I ordered the *ropa vieja* again. I don't remember what Emilia had. We talked about Sam, and about her work for the Bergen County newspaper — she'd recently won a state journalism award for a series on day-care facilities — and I went into serious detail regarding the technical and social inadequacies of the Pacific Rep's new artistic director. We didn't discuss Millamant at all.

The evening was warm, and there was one of those glossy, perfect half-moons that seem too brilliant for their size. We walked home the long way, so that I could show Emilia the little park where Sam had told me about her. We sat on the swings, as I'd done with Sam, and she told me then, "He lied about his age, you know. I didn't realize it until you told me you were two months younger. He'd been taking seven years off, all the time I knew him. As though it would have mattered to me."

I'd had a second margarita with dinner. I said, "He was two months and eleven days older than I am. We were both born just after three in the morning, did he ever tell you that? I was about an ounce and a half heavier." And *whoosh*, I was crying. I didn't *start* to cry — I *was* crying, and I was always going to be crying. Emilia held me without a word, as I'd once held Sam when he wept just as hopelessly, just as endlessly. I have no idea how long it went on. When it stopped, we walked the rest of the way in silence, but Emilia tucked her arm through mine.

Back home, we settled in the kitchen (which is bigger and more comfortable than my living room) with a couple of cappuccinos. The director ex-wife took the piano, but I hung on to the espresso machine. Emilia said, "I was thinking on the flight — you and I have already known each other longer than I knew Sam. We had such a short time."

"You learned things about him I never bothered to find out in forty years. I thought we had forever."

Emilia was silent for a while, sipping her coffee. Then she said, very softly, not looking at me, "You see, I never thought that. Some way, I always understood that there wasn't going to be a happy ending for us. I never said it to myself, but I *knew*." She did look straight at me then, her eyes clear and unmisted, but her mouth too straight, too determinedly under control. "I think he did, too."

I couldn't think of an answer to that. We chatted a little while longer, and then Emilia went to bed. I stayed up late, reading *Heartbreak House* one more time — no one's ever likely to ask me to play Captain Shotover, but the readiness is all — had one last futile look-around for Millamant, and turned in myself. I slept deeply and contentedly for what seemed like a good fifteen minutes before Emilia shook me out of one of the rare dreams where I know my lines, whispering frantically, "Jake — Jake come and see, hurry, you have to see! Jake, hurry, it's her!"

The half-moon was shining so brightly on the kitchen table that I could see the little sticky rings where our coffee cups had been. I remember that, just as I remember the shuddery hum of the refrigerator and the *bloop* of the leaky faucet, and a faint scratching sound that I couldn't place right away. Just as I remember Millamant dancing.

It's a large table, older than I am, and it lurches if you lean on it, let alone dance. I don't know how Millamant even climbed up, arthritic back leg and all, but there she floated, there she spun, tumbling this way, sailing that, one minute a kitten, the next a kite; moving so lightly, and with such precision, that the table never rocked once, but seemed to be the one moving impossibly fast, while Millamant drifted over it as slowly as she chose, hanging in the air for exactly as long as she chose. She was so old that her back claws no longer retracted entirely — that was the scratching noise — but she danced the way human beings have always dreamed of dancing, and never have, not the best of them. No one has ever danced like Millamant.

Neither of us could look away, but Emilia leaned close and whispered, "I've seen her three times. I couldn't talk about it on the phone." Her face was absolutely without color.

Millamant stopped so suddenly that both Emilia and I leaned toward her, as though it had been the planet that halted. Millamant dropped down onto all fours, paced to the edge of the table and stood looking at us out of once-golden eyes gone almost tea-brown with age. She was breathing rapidly, and trembling all over. She said, "Emilia. Jake."

How can I say what it was like? To hear a cat speak — to hear a cat speak our names — to hear a cat speak them in a voice that was unmistakably Sam's voice, and yet not Sam's, not a voice at all. Her mouth remained slightly open, but her jaws did not move: the words were coming through her, not out of her, without inflection, without any sort of cadence, without any trace of a homemade English accent. Millamant said, "Jake. Clean your glasses."

I wear glasses, except onstage, and the lenses are always messier than I ever notice. It used to drive Sam crazy. I took them off. Millamant — or what was using Millamant — said, "I love you, Emilia."

Beside me, Emilia's breath simply stopped. I didn't dare look at her. I had all I could do to babble idiotically, "Sam? Sam? Where have you been? Sam, are you really in there?"

At that Millamant actually seemed to raise an eyebrow, which was unlikely, since cats don't have eyebrows. She — Sam — *it* said quite clearly, "You want I should wave?" And she did raise a front paw to gesture in my direction. Her ears were flicking and crumpling strangely, as though someone who didn't know how a cat's ears work were trying to lay them back. "As to where I've been —" the toneless march of syllables faltered a little "— it comes and goes. Talk to me."

Emilia's face was still so pale that the color on her cheekbones stood out like tribal scars. I don't know what I looked like, but I couldn't make a sound. Emilia took a step forward, her hands out, but Millamant immediately backed away. "Talk to me. Please, talk to me. Tell me why we're all here, tell me anything. Please."

So we sat in the kitchen, Emilia and I, talking to an old cat as we would have talked to our dear lost friend, solemnly telling her our commonplace news of work and family, of small travels and travails, of his parents in Fort Lauderdale, of how it had been for us in the last two years. Our voices stumbled over each other, often crumbling into tears of still-untrusted joy, then immediately skidding off into broken giggles to hear ourselves earnestly assuring Millamant, "It's been a miserable couple of theater seasons — absolutely nothing you'd have liked." Millamant looked from one to the other of us, her eyes fiercely attentive, sometimes nodding like a marionette. Emilia clutched my hand painfully tightly, but she was smiling. I have never seen a smile like that one of Emilia's ever again.

She was saying, "And Jake and I have been writing and writing to each other, talking on the phone, telling each other everything we remember — things we didn't know we remembered. Things *you* maybe wouldn't remember. Sam, we missed you so. I missed you." When she reached out again, Millamant avoided her touch for a moment; then suddenly yielded and let herself rest between Emilia's hands. The arid, rasping voice said, "Behind the ears. Finally, a body I can dance in, but I can't figure out about scratching."

Nobody said anything for a while. Emilia was totally involved in caressing Millamant, and I was feeling more and more like the most flagrant *voyeur*. I didn't have to look at Emilia's face, or listen to Millamant's purring; merely to watch those yearning hands at work in the thin, patchy fur was to spy on an altogether private matter. I make jokes when I'm edgy. I said to Emilia, "Be careful — he could be a *dybbuk*. It'd be just like him."

Emilia, not knowing the Yiddish word, looked puzzled; but Millamant let out a brief, contemptuous yowl, a feline equivalent of Sam's old *Oh, good night!* snort of disdain. "Of course, I'm not a bloody *dybbuk*! Don't you read Singer? A *dybbuk*'s a wandering soul, demons chasing it all around the universe — it needs a body, a place to hide. Not me — nobody's chasing me." The voice hesitated slightly for a second time. "Except maybe you two."

I looked at Emilia, expecting her to say something. When she didn't, I finally mumbled — just as lamely as it reads — "We needed to talk about you. We didn't have anyone else to talk to."

"If not for Jake," Emilia said. "Sam, if it weren't for Jake, if he hadn't known me at your funeral —" she caught her breath only momentarily on the word "— Sam, I would have disappeared. I'd have gone right on, like always, like everybody else, but I would have disappeared."

Millamant hardly seemed to be listening. She said thoughtfully, "I'll be damned. I'm hungry."

"I'll make you a *quesadilla*," I said, eager to be doing something practical. "Cheese and scallions and Ortega diced chilies — I've still got a can from the last time you were here. Take me ten minutes."

The look both Millamant and Emilia gave me was pure cat. I said, "Oh. Right. Wet or dry?"

Nothing in life — nothing even in Shakespeare — adequately prepares you for the experience of opening a can of Whiskas with Bits O' Beef for your closest friend, who's been dead for two years. Millamant ambled over to the battered stoneware dish that Emilia had brought with her from New York, sniffed once, then dug in with a voracity I'd never seen in either Sam or her. She went through that red-brown glop like a snowplow, and looked around for more.

Scraping the rest into her dish, I couldn't help asking, "How can you be hungry, anyway? Are you the one actually tasting this stuff, or is it all Millamant?"

"Interesting point." The Abyssinian had Whiskas on her nose. "It's Millamant who needs to eat — it's Millamant getting the nourishment — but I think I'm beginning to see why she likes it. Very odd. Sort of the phantom of a memory of taste. A touch of nutmeg would help."

She dived back into her dinner, obliviously, leaving Emilia and me staring at each other in confusion so identical that there was no need to speak, possibly ever again. Emilia finally managed to ask, "What do we do now?" and I answered, "Like a divorce. We work out who gets custody, and who gets visiting rights."

Emilia said, "She doesn't belong to us. She was Sam's cat, and he's... returned."

"To take possession, as you might say. Right. We can't even be certain that she's exactly a cat anymore, what with Sam in residence." I realized that I was just this side of hysterical, and closing fast. "Emilia, you'd better take him — her — them — home with you. I'm an actor, I pretend for a living, and this is altogether too much reality for me. You take Millamant home — what I'll do, I'll just call on the weekends, the way we used to do. Sam and I."

I don't know what Emilia would have said — her eyes were definitely voting for scooping up Millamant that very moment and heading for the airport — but the cat herself looked up from an empty dish at that moment to remark, in the mechanical tone I was already coming to accept as Sam, "Calm down, Jake. You're overplaying again."

It happens to be one of my strengths as an actor that I *never* overplay. The man saw me act exactly three times after high school, and that makes him an expert on my style. I was still spluttering as Millamant sat down in the kitchen doorway, curling her tail around her hind legs.

"Well," the voice said. "I'm back. Where I'm back *from* —" and it faltered momentarily, while Millamant's old eyes seemed to lose all definition between iris and pupil "— where I'm back from doesn't go into words. I don't know what it really is, or where — or when. I don't know whether I'm a ghost, or a zombie, or just some kind of seriously perturbed spirit. If I were a *dybbuk*, at least I'd know I was a *dybbuk*, that would be something." Millamant licked the bit of Whiskas off her nose. "But here I am anyway, ready or not. I can talk, I can dance — my God, I can *dance* — and I'm reunited with the only two people in the world who could have summoned me. Or whatever it was you did."

Abruptly she began washing her face, making such a deliberate job of it that I was about to say something pointed about extended dramatic pauses, when Sam spoke again. "But for how long? I could be gone any minute, or I could last as long as Millamant lasts — and *she* could go any minute herself. What happens then? Do I go off to kitty heaven with her — or do I find myself in Jake's blender? One of Emilia's angelfish? What happens then?"

Nobody answered. Millamant sat up higher on her haunches, until she looked like the classic Egyptian statue of Bastet, the cat goddess. Out of her mouth Sam said very quietly, "We don't know. We have no idea. I certainly wish somebody had read the instruction manual."

"There wasn't any manual," I said. "We didn't know we were summoning you — we didn't know we were doing anything except missing you, and trying to comfort ourselves the best we could." I was calming down, and paradoxically irritable with it. "Not everybody has people wishing for him so hard that they snatch him right back from death. I'm sorry if we woke you."

"Oh, I was awake." The cold voice was still soft and faraway. "Or maybe not truly awake, but you can't quite get to sleep, either. Jake... Emilia...I can't tell you what it's like. I'm not even sure whether it's death — or maybe that's it, that's just it, that's really the way death is. I can't tell you."

"Don't," Emilia whispered. She picked Millamant up again and held her close against her breast, not petting her.

Sam said, "It's like the snow on a TV set, when the cable's out. People just sit watching the screen, expecting the picture to come back — they'll sit there for an hour, more, waiting for all those whirling, crackling white particles to shape themselves back into a face, a car, a box of cereal — *something*. Try to think how it might feel to be one of those particles." He said nothing more for a moment, and then added, "It's not like that but try to imagine it anyway."

Whereupon Millamant fell asleep in Emilia's arms, and was carried off to bed in the guest room. She sauntered out the next morning, looking demurely pleased with herself, shared Emilia's yogurt, topped that off with an entire can of Chunky Chicken, went back to sleep on a fragrant pile of new-dried laundry, woke presently, and came to find me in the living room, settle briskly onto my lap and issue instructions. Fondling your best friend's tummy and scratching his vibrating throat for a solid hour at a time may possibly be weirder than responding to his demand for more kibble. I'm still not sure.

Presently he remarked, in that voice that wasn't him and wasn't human, and was yet somehow Sam, "In case I haven't said it, I'm very happy to see you, Jake."

"I'm happy to see you, too." I stopped petting him once we were talking: it felt wrong. "I just wish I could...*see* you."

Sam didn't laugh — I don't think he could — but a sort of odd grumbly ripple ran through Millamant's body. "You surprise me. You didn't actually plan to have me come back with fleas and hair balls?"

"Just like old times," I said, and Millamant did the ripple thing again.

"Truth is, I think it's easier to accept you like this than it would be if you'd showed up in some other person's body. You always had a lot in common with Millamant."

"Did, didn't I?" For a moment the words were almost lost in Millamant's deep purr. "We both love peach yogurt, and having things on our own terms. But I couldn't dance like Millamant the best day I ever saw. Jake, you don't *know* — when she was a kitten, pouncing and skittering around the apartment, I used to watch her for hours, wondering if it wasn't too late, if I could still make my body learn something from her that it never could learn from anyone else. Even now, old as she is, you can't imagine how it feels...." He was silent for so long that I thought Millamant must have fallen asleep once more; but then he said suddenly, "Jake. Maybe you should send me back."

Emilia was in the guest bedroom, talking on the phone to her editor in New Jersey, so there was just me to be flabbergasted. When I had words again, I said, "Send you? We don't even know how you got here in the first place, and you don't know where *back* is. We couldn't send you anywhere the BMT doesn't run." No furry ripple out of Millamant. "Why would you want to? To leave us again?"

"I don't ever want to leave." Millamant's dull claws dug harder into my leg than they should have been able to. "If I were in a rat's body, a cockroach's body, I'd want to stay here with you, with Emilia. But it feels strange here. Not wrong, but not — not *proper*. I don't mean me inhabiting a cat — I mean me still being me, Sam Kagan still aware that I'm Sam Kagan. However you look at it, this is a damn afterlife, Jake, and I don't believe in an afterlife. Dead or alive, I don't."

"And being part of the snow on a television screen, that's an improvement? That's proper?"

Sam didn't answer for a time. Millamant purred drowsily between my hands, and my Betty Boop clock ticked (at certain times of day, you can almost pretend she's dancing the Charleston), and in the guest bedroom Emilia laughed at something. Finally Sam said, "You see, I don't think I was always going to be TV snow. There was more to it. I can't tell you how I knew that. I just did."

I unhooked a rear claw from my thigh. "Purgatory as a function of the cable system. Makes sense, in a really dumb way."

Sam said, "There was more. I don't know that I missed anything much, but there was more coming. And if it's an afterlife, then the word means something they never told us about. I don't think there is a word for it — what I was waiting for. But it wasn't this."

Emilia hung up and came out to us then, and Millamant stopped talking. Instead, she leaped down from my lap, landing with the precise abandon of a cat ten years younger, and began to dance. Last night it had been for herself — at least, until we showed up — this time the dance was entirely for us, Sam showing off joyously, taking the whole room as his stage, as Millamant swam in the air from chair to bookcase and flashed like a dragonfly between bookcase and stereo, setting a rack of tape cassettes vibrating like castanets. Partnering my furniture, she swung around my three-foot-high Yoruba fetish, mimicking Gene Kelly in *Singin' in the Rain*; then whirled across the room by spinning bounds, only to slow to a liquidly sensuous cat — waltz in and out of the striped shadows of my window blinds. I couldn't remember ever seeing Sam dance like that: so much in authority that he could afford to release his body on its own recognizance. Millamant finished with a sudden astonishing flare of pirouettes from a standing start, and jetéed her way into Emilia's lap, where she purred and panted and said nothing. Emilia petted her and looked at me, and we didn't say anything either.

Neither of us said anything after that about Emilia's taking Sam home with her. She spent all ten days of her leave like an inheritance at my house. Sly smiles, grotesquely rolled eyes and hasty thumbs-up signs from my neighbors made their opinion of my new little fling eminently clear. I really can't blame them: we almost never went out, except for a meal or a brief walk, and we must have seemed completely absorbed in one another when they saw us at all. But what they'd have thought of the hours we passed, day and night, watching an old Abyssinian cat dance all over my house, let alone arguing with the cat about afterlives and the last World Series...no, it would have broken their hearts if I'd told them. Mine is a very dull neighborhood.

There was never a chance of anything happening between us, Emilia and me. We had grown far too close to be lovers: we were almost brother and sister in Sam, if that makes any sense at all. Once, midway through her visit, she was ironing her clothes in the kitchen when I came in to fill the cat dish and the water bowl. She watched in silence until I was done, and then she said with a sudden half-strangled violence, "I hate this! I can't bear to see you doing that, putting food down for him. It's not —" and she seemed to be fighting her own throat for a word "— it's not honest!"

We stared at each other across the ironing board. I said slowly, "Honest? How did honesty get into this?"

"Did I say that?" She scrubbed absently at her forehead with the back of her hand. "I don't know, I don't know what I meant. If he's Sam, then he shouldn't be eating on the floor, and if he's Millamant, then he shouldn't be making her dance all the time. She's old, Jake, and she's got arthritis, and Sam's dancing her like a child making his toys fly and fight. And it's so beautiful, and he's so *happy* — and I never saw him dance, the way you did, and I can't believe how beautiful..."

She didn't start to cry. Emilia doesn't cry. What happens is that she loses speech — when Sam died, she couldn't speak for three days — and the few sounds she does make are not your business or mine. I went to her then, and she buried her face in the ruinous gray cardigan I wear around the house, and we just stood together without speaking. And yes, all right, there was an instant when she held me hard, tilting her head back so we could look at each other. I felt very cold, and my lips started to tingle most painfully. But neither of us moved. We stood there, very deliberately letting the moment pass, feeling it pass, more united in that wordless choice than we could have been in any other way. Emilia went back to folding her ironing, and I took the garbage out and paid some bills.

Then I spent some time studying Millamant. The cat didn't seem to be suffering, nor to object to being sported and soared and exalted all around my house, day and night. But the bad back leg was plainly lamer than ever; her eyes were streaked and her claws ragged and broken, and for all the serious eating she was doing, she was thinner than she had arrived, if you looked. Playing host to Sam — playing barre and floor, costume, makeup, mirror to Sam, more accurately — was literally consuming her. I couldn't know whether she understood that or not. It didn't matter to me. That was the terrible thing, and all I can say is that at least I knew it was terrible.

The next evening was a warm one, pleasantly poignant with the smell of my next-door neighbor's jasmine, and of distant rain. Sam/Millamant hadn't danced at all that day, but had spent it necking and nuzzling with Emilia, taking naps with her and exchanging murmured *do-you-remembers*. We sat together on my front steps: a perfectly ordinary couple with a drowsy old cat in the long California twilight. I made small talk, fixed small snacks, felt my throat getting smaller and smaller, and finally blurted, "You were right. I can't say if it's honest or not, but it's no good. What do we do about it?"

Emilia petted Millamant and didn't meet my eyes. Three high school boys ambled past, slamming a basketball into one another's chests by turns, their talk as incomprehensible as Czech or Tamil, and strangely more foreign. I said again, "Sam, it's no good. I don't mean for Millamant — I mean for you, for your *ka* or your karma, or whatever I'm talking to right now. This can't be what you're supposed to be...doing, I guess. Emilia made me see."

In a very small voice, still not looking at me, Emilia said, "I changed my mind." I remember to this day how sad she sounded, and how neither Sam nor I paid any attention to her. An errant Irish setter, outrunning his jogger mistress, wandered up to say hello to everybody's crotch, but Millamant spat viciously and scratched his nose as Sam said, "I told you you ought to send me back. I did tell you, Jake."

I started to answer him, but Emilia interrupted. "No," she said, much louder now. "No, I don't care, I *can't*, never mind what I said. I don't care about Millamant, I don't care about anybody except Sam. I just want Sam back, any way I can have him. *Any* way. It's disgraceful, I know it's disgraceful, and I don't care."

She bent over Millamant, who slipped away from her as a yellow-haired young man in a Grateful Dead T-shirt and Bermuda shorts strode by, pumping his arms like a power-walker, totally absorbed in laughing, comradely conversation with his Walkman. I still see him, most days — it's been years now. Sometimes he's quite angry with the Walkman, but mostly he laughs.

Very gently for a voice out of a P.A. system in bad repair, Sam said, "He's right, Emilia. And you were right the first time. I have to go."

"Go where?" she cried. "You don't even know, you said so yourself. You could end up someplace worse than your damn TV screen — you could lose yourself for good, no Sam anymore, in the whole universe, not the least bit of Sam, not ever, not ever." She stopped herself with a jolt that was actually audible — you could hear it in her chest. Newspaper reporters probably aren't allowed hysterics. With actors it's part of the Equity contract.

"Maybe that's the idea." Millamant sat down and scratched — very professionally, I noticed. "Maybe that's it — maybe you're not supposed to come back as the least bit of yourself, but to be completely scattered, diffused, starting over as someone utterly different. I almost like that." And the mechanical voice sounded in that moment more like *my* Sam — thoughtful, amused, truly savoring doubt — than it ever had.

Emilia was hugging herself, rocking herself slightly. She said, "I couldn't bear to lose you twice. I'm telling you now, I have no shame, I don't care. I don't care if you show up as a — an electric can opener. Don't leave me again, Sam."

Only a few of the cars going by had turned their headlights on, but all the porch lights were lit now, and the lawn sprinklers hissing to life, and I could smell Vietnamese cooking two houses down, and Indian cooking clear across the street. Two young women in identical jogging suits walked past, each carrying a pizza box and a six-pack. Millamant walked slowly to Emilia, climbed into her lap and stood up — surprisingly firm on the bad back leg — to put her paws on each side of Emilia's neck.

"Matter can neither be created nor destroyed," Sam said. "Didn't they teach you that in high school, out in frontier Metuchen? *Listen!*" for she had turned her head away and would not even touch Millamant. "*Listen* — when I was a speck, a dot, nothing but a flicker of TV snow, I knew you. Do you understand me? By the time you and Jake got me back here, I had already forgotten my own name, I'd forgotten that there was ever such an idea as Sam Kagan. But I was a speck that remembered Emilia Rossi's birthday, remembered that Emilia Rossi loves cantaloupe and roast potatoes and bittersweet chocolate, and absolutely cannot abide football, her cousin Teddy, or Wagner. There's no way in this universe that I could be reduced to something so microscopic, so anonymous that it wouldn't know *Emilia Rossi*. If they give my atoms a fast shuffle and shake most of them out on some other planet, there'll still be one or two atoms madly determined to evolve into something that can carve Emilia Rossi on a tree. Or whatever they've got on the damn planet. I promise you, that's the truth. Are you listening to me, Emilia?"

"I'm listening," she said dully. She still would not look at Millamant.

"You'll never forget me, wherever you are — or *whatever*. Wonderful. But you're leaving."

Millamant bumped her head hard against Emilia's chin, forcing her to turn her head. Sam said, "I don't belong here. You knew it before Jake did — probably before I knew myself. It's all I want in any world, but it's not right. Let me go, Emilia."

"Let you go?" Emilia was so outraged that she stood up, dumping Millamant off her lap. "What hold did I ever have on you, living or dead? What about Jake? Why don't you ask Jake if he'd be so kind as to...." And her voice went. Completely. I told you it happens with Emilia.

I put my arms around her. An old couple passing by nodded benignly at us through the dusk. I looked at my friend in the ancient eyes of a cat, and I said, "She's not going to understand. If you're going, go."

"You'll explain to her?" The robot voice couldn't possibly sound desperate, any more than it could convey anger or love, but I felt Sam's grief in my body, even so. "You'll make her see?"

"I won't make her do anything." I ached for Sam, but I was holding Emilia. "I'll do the best I can. Go already."

Millamant didn't approach Emilia again, so she never saw the last look that Sam gave her. But I did, and I told her about it afterward. Then Millamant scampered up the steps, lightly as a kitten, and began to dance.

My front porch could be better described as a catwalk with a railing. You can't even rock on it in comfort — your feet keep hitting things — and it's the last place you'd imagine as a dance floor, even for a small domestic animal. But Sam used to tell me, when we were young and I'd been awed by the flamboyance of some performer's style, "Good *night*, Jake, anybody can throw himself around Lincoln Center — all that takes is space and a little energy. The real ones can dance in a broom closet; they can stand on line at a checkout counter and be dancing right there. The real ones." And Millamant was a real dancer, that one last time on my checkout line of a porch.

I can't be sure of what I saw through the gathering dark then and the gathering years now. Millamant seemed to me to be moving almost on point, if you can imagine that in a cat, but moving with a kind of ardent restraint in which every stillness implied a leap at the throat, and violence trembled in the shadow of rigor. At moments she appeared to be standing completely motionless, letting the twilight dance around her, courting her like a proper partner. There should have been a moon, but there wasn't: only my rust-colored bug light to catch the glitter of her eyes and the ripple of her fur: So the one thing I am certain about, even at this dim distance, is that that dance was entirely for Emilia. Not for me, not for Emilia and me together, like that first time. Emilia.

She wouldn't look at first. She turned her head completely away, staring blindly back at the street, one hand clenching white on a fold of my sweater. So something else I can't say is just when the dance took hold of her, drawing her gently home to what Sam and Millamant, Millamant, too — were telling her forever. All I know is that she was crouched beside me, paying such attention, *paying*, as I never paid to my wives, my directors, or to Sam himself, at the moment when someone's headlights played briefly over us and it was only Millamant there, limping down the steps to clamber heavily into Emilia's lap and lie there, not purring. Only old Abyssinian Millamant, tired and lame, and uninhabited.

I also don't remember when it was that I said, "He made us let him go. He danced us away from thinking about him, holding him. Just for that little, but it was all he needed." Emilia didn't answer. The lighted kitchens along my street were long dark when I finally got her into the house and put her to bed.

That was long ago. Emilia went back to New Jersey with Millamant and married a nice special-education teacher named Philip, some years later. She didn't write to me for some time after her return, but she telephoned when Millamant died. Gradually we took up our correspondence again, though Sam was as notably absent from it as he had once been its prime mover. I sent a gift when the boy was born: a complete Shakespeare and a *Baseball Encyclopedia*. If those don't cover a growing child's major emotional needs, he's on his own.

Me, I haven't yet been summoned to play Captain Shotover — or Lear, either — but the Falstaffs have started coming lately, and the James Tyrones, and I did do a bloody good Uncle Vanya in Ashland one summer. And I got to New York for the first time in decades, for a get-killed-early role in a big-budget thing where they blew up the Holland Tunnel at the climax. I rather liked that one.

I stayed with Emilia and Philip over a weekend after my part of the shooting was over. They live in an old two-family house in a working-class neighborhood of Secaucus. Secaucus still has one of those, a working class. The place could use a new roof, and there's a draft in the kitchen that Philip hasn't been able to trace down yet. It's a good house, with a black kitten named Rita, for Rita Hayworth. Philip loves old movies and early music.

On the day I left, Emilia and I sat in the kitchen while she gave Alex his lunch. Alex was ten-and-a-half months old then, with a rapturous smile and the table manners of a Hell's Angel. But today he was in one of his dreamy, contemplative moods, and made no difficulties over the brown stuff, which he normally despised, or the green stuff, which he preferred to play with. I sat in a patch of sunlight, watching the two of them. Emilia's gained a little weight, but on her it looks good, and there's a warmth under her pale skin. Marriage suits her. Secaucus suits her.

I think I was actually half-asleep when she turned suddenly to me and said, "You think I don't think about him."

"Actually, I hope you don't," I said, rather feebly. "I try not to, myself."

"There isn't a day," Emilia said. "Not one." She wiped Alex's mouth and took advantage of his meditations to slip some of the yellow stuff into him. "Philip always knows, but he doesn't mind. He's a good man."

"Does he know the whole story? What can happen when you think too much about someone?"

She shook her head without answering. When Alex had reached capacity and was looking remarkably like Sydney Greenstreet in the noonday sun of Casablanca, she took him to his crib, singing "This Time the Dream's on Me" softly as she set him down, already asleep. It was one of Sam's favorite old songs, and she knew I knew. I looked down at Alex and said, "Nice legs. You think there might be a dancer at the other end of them?"

Emilia shook her head quickly. "No, absolutely. He's very much Philip's child. He'll probably play football and grow up to be an ACLU lawyer, and a good thing, too. I'm not going to make him into my dreams of Sam." We tiptoed out of the room, and she gave me one of the heavy black beers for which Philip and I — and Sam, too, for that matter — shared a taste. She said clearly and firmly, "Alex is real. Philip is real. Sam is dead. My dreams are my own business. I can live with them."

"And you never wonder —"

She cut me off immediately, her eyes steady on mine, but her mouth going tight. "I don't wonder, Jake. I can't afford it."

She seemed about to say something more, but the doorbell interrupted her. When she answered it, there stood a small brown girl, no older than five or six, on the step, asking eagerly before the door was fully open, "Miz Larsen, can I play with Alex now?" She looked Filipina, and she was dressed, not in the T-shirt and jeans which children are born wearing these days, but in a white blouse and a dark woolen skirt, as though she were going to church or to visit grandparents. But her accent was unadulterated New Jersey, born and bred.

Emilia smiled at her. "He's having his nap, Luz. Come back in an hour or so. Do you know how long an hour is?"

"My brother knows hours," Luz said proudly. "Okay. 'Bye." She turned away, and Emilia closed the door, still smiling.

"Luz lives a block down from us," she said softly. "She's been crazy about Alex from the day he was born, and he adores her. She's over here almost every day, after school, talking to him, carrying him, inventing games to make him laugh. I'm sure the first real word he says will be *Luz*."

She was talking fast, almost chattering, which is not something Emilia does. We looked at each other in a way that we hadn't since I'd been there. Emilia turned away, and then stood quite still, staring through a front window. Without turning, she beckoned, and I joined her.

On the sidewalk in front of the house, little Luz was dancing.

Not ballet, of course; not the self-consciousness that suggested lessons of any sort. Her movements were just this side of the jump-and-whirl of hopscotch, and there were moments when she might have been skipping double-Dutch without the ropes. But it was dancing, pure and private, and there was music to it — you had only to look at the intense brown face for that. Luz was hearing music, and to watch her for even a little time was to hear it too.

"Every day," Emilia said. "Her parents don't know — I asked them. She waits for Alex to wake up, and while she waits she dances. Nowhere else, just here. I hoped you'd see."

Luz never looked up toward the house, toward us.

I said, "She doesn't dance like Millamant." Emilia didn't bother to answer anything that dumb. We watched a while longer before I said, "He told you, whatever became of him — his soul, his spirit, his molecules — he'd always know you. But he didn't say whether you'd know him."

"It doesn't matter," Emilia said. She took my arm, hugging it tightly, and her face was as bright and young as the child's. "Jake, Jake, it doesn't matter whether I know him or not. It doesn't *matter*."

Luz was still dancing on the sidewalk when the taxi came to take me to the train station. I said goodbye as I walked past her, trying not to stare. But she danced me escort to the cab door, and I looked into her eyes as I got in, and as we drove away. And what I think I know, I think I know, and it doesn't matter at all.

For news and information about Peter S. Beagle and his works, go to
www.peterbeagle.com.